SIX WAYS OF DYING

Angelo's peculiar involvement with an old man, two brothers, their hired gunmen and a treasure map starts well, but in less time than it takes to cock a Colt, the deal goes bad. Double-crossed, Angelo sets out to track down the men responsible. But then, saddled with a cavalry officer, some raw recruits — and a beautiful girl — he meets Ulzana, the Apache renegade, and they find themselves outnumbered and exhausted. Angelo, however, is undaunted and will go down fighting . . .

CODY WELLS

SIX WAYS OF DYING

Complete and Unabridged

LINFORD
Leicester

First published in Great Britain in 2011 by
Robert Hale Limited
London

First Linford Edition
published 2013
by arrangement with
Robert Hale Limited
London

A catalogue record for this book is available
from the British Library.

ISBN 978–1–4448–1637–2

Published by
F. A. Thorpe (Publishing)
Anstey, Leicestershire

Set by Words & Graphics Ltd.
Anstey, Leicestershire
Printed and bound in Great Britain by
T. J. International Ltd., Padstow, Cornwall

This book is printed on acid-free paper

For Sherry Negrete
She's my inspiration

1

For Angelo it had been a long, slow ride from the small town of Gatlin to the West Texas military outpost of Fort Conchos, but he was in no great hurry. As he made camp, a gentle breeze blew dust across the prairie. It was almost sundown and the sky cast a serene crimson glow across the land.

He took a mouthful of coffee. He'd been watching the rider heading towards him for the past half-hour. As the newcomer drew closer Angelo could see that he was astride a large mule that seemed to be giving him trouble. It came to an abrupt halt, and shook its head. The rider threw his arms in the air and appeared to be cursing the animal.

'Can you believe that?' muttered Angelo, rubbing the nape of the dog lying by his side. 'Folk would say *our* relationship was strange.'

The dog was an odd-looking thing; mostly Canaan but with a little something else thrown in. He had wolflike features, but his cream-white coat was much smoother, his snout shorter. Low-set ears and a bushy tail completed the picture.

Angelo gave the beans cooking over the small fire a vigorous stir. After cussing the animal some more, the newcomer finally slid from the saddle and tried desperately to get the mule to move.

'Yer selfish and stubborn. If'n I didn't need ye so bad, I'd make jerky out of yer hide.'

The animal kicked its hind legs in the air, then took off across the prairie. The man took off his hat, threw it on the ground and stamped on it.

'Come back here, ye sumbitch . . . Damn mule!'

When the man was about twenty yards from Angelo's camp he called, 'Mind if I join ye, young 'un?'

He was in his mid-sixties and about

five and a half feet tall. His hair was as white as snow, and matched his beard. He wore an old gray cavalry slouch hat, the brim pinned up at the front with a brass crossed-saber insignia. The red bib-shirt was worn with the top and two side buttons undone, and his black wool pants were held up by white canvas suspenders.

'Come on in, old-timer,' Angelo called back. 'Take some warmth from the fire.'

The old man smiled, revealing toothless gums. 'Thanks son. I just needs to rest me a while, then I'll be on my way.'

As he came in he studied his host more closely. The man by the fire was a dark-skinned half-blood who'd seen maybe thirty-five summers. He stood a lean six feet two, with high cheekbones, a strong jaw and raven-black hair that tumbled to his shoulders. He wore a wine-colored cotton shirt and buff canvas pants that were faded with age, and his low-crowned Stetson was pulled down slightly at the front to shadow his blue, hawk-sharp eyes. He packed a short-barreled but fancily engraved Colt Peacemaker .45 in a brown Mexican single-looped holster on his right hip.

'Looks like that mule of yours just won the argument,' Angelo noted.

'He's one ornery son-of-a-gun. I swear, the night he wus born he wus blessed by the devil himself. Yeah . . . he's kinda off his mental reservation.'

The old man was just about to sit next to the dog when it stood up and growled. Angelo said, 'This here's Mr Jinx. I wouldn't get too close if I were you. He don't take kindly to strangers.'

The old man took a red bandanna from his pants' pocket and used it to pick up the hot coffee pot from the fire. 'Mind if I pour myself a cup?'

'Go ahead,' Angelo said as he pulled another cup from his sack of supplies and handed it to the old man.

'You gotta name, son?'

'Angelo. You?'

'Jebediah Tumbleweed O'Malley. Most folks jus' call me Tumbleweed.'

'Tumbleweed! What kind of a name is that?'

The old man raised his eyebrows. 'When I wus born, my pa said a baby around the farm wus as much use as tumbleweed. So the name sorta stuck. Guess it must have bin his Irish sense of humor.'

'What you gonna do about that mule of yours?' Angelo asked.

'Ah, he'll turn up in the mornin'. He always does. My place is about eight miles down the trail there. It's not much, but I call it home.'

Angelo threw the old man a spare blanket. 'Well, why don't you get your head down here for tonight? Then we can double up on my horse in the mornin' and I'll take you home.'

'Well that's mighty kind of ye, son. Happen I'll take ye up on that.'

★ ★ ★

O'Malley's place, when they reached it the following morning, wasn't much to speak of, just a small shack set well back from the main trail, with a corral and a lean-to at the far end. Twenty feet from the shack stood an outhouse with a sign nailed to the door that read TRESPASSERS WILL BE SHOT! A vegetable patch lay to the right of the corral, where the mule was making a meal out of whatever had been planted.

Tumbleweed slid from Angelo's horse and ran towards the beast, waving his hands in the air. 'Ye sumbitch, git the hell outta thur, ye dumb mule!'

The spooked animal ran off into the corral with Tumbleweed close behind. The mule walked up to the lean-to and took a long drink from the water trough. The old man secured the gate.

'I swear, one of these doggone days, I'm gonna blow what little brains he's got all over this darn prairie.'

Angelo climbed down from the saddle and tied his horse to the hitching rail in front of the shack. The front door was ajar. The old man sauntered in and gave out a loud yell.

Joining him in the doorway, Angelo peered over the old-timer's shoulder and saw that the whole room was in disarray. The few bits of furniture had been damaged, the shelves cleared of the pots, pans and cooking supplies, which were now scattered all over the floor. Tumbleweed's personal belongings and clothes were covered in cooking oil and flour.

'Looks like that mule of yours really has it in for you,' Angelo commented wryly.

'Mule, my ass . . . I've bin robbed!' He scurried up to the stove. It had been shifted to reveal a small hole in the floor, just big enough to fit a small box. 'Sumbitch!'

'What's up, old man?'

'Some varmint's stole my darn map! That's wut's up!'

'Map?'

'Wus a treasure map,' the old man said, adding quickly, 'An' don't gimme that look. My map wus the real thing. I just knows it wus.'

Just then Mr Jinx tugged at Angelo's shirt-cuff and barked to get his attention. Turning, he saw that six mounted men were riding in at a slow, steady pace. Six dangerous-looking men.

'We've got company, old man.'

Tumbleweed came to join him. 'Darn it, if it ain't Tom and Quincy Randall.'

'Friends of yours?'

'Pains in the ass, more like.'

'You got any guns around this place?'

'Got myself a Colt coach gun lyin' around some-whurs, if I kin find it amongst this here mess.'

'Fetch it.'

As the old man went in search of his gun Angelo went outside and slid his Winchester from its scabbard, all the while keeping a steady gaze on the approaching men, with Mr Jinx sitting by his side. As the riders brought their horses to a halt in front of the shack Tumbleweed came running through the doorway.

'Got it! Wut now?'

Angelo gave the strangers a cold stare. 'See that burly fella in the white shirt?'

'Yeah, I see him. That thur's Quincy.'

'Well, old man, if Quincy so much as blinks an eyelid, blast him out of his saddle.'

'That's no way to greet friends!' Quincy bellowed. He was a robust specimen in his early forties, with a round face and small piggy eyes. His auburn hair was short and he wore a bushy mustache and long sideburns. He wasn't a tall man, five and a half feet, but what he lacked in height, he made up for in muscle. His attire was nothing out of the ordinary: blue denim pants, white cotton shirt and a brown suede vest. He wore a gunbelt with the holster tied down on his left thigh.

'You're no friend of mine,' Angelo said. 'So state your business or move on out.'

'No need to take that attitude, mister. We've known Tumbleweed since we were knee-high to a grasshopper. We're all friends here. Ain't that right, old-timer?'

'Go to hell!' Tumbleweed snarled.

It was true, however, that Tumbleweed had known the brothers for years. Quincy and Tom, who was his junior by barely ten months, made a dubious living by hanging around the cattle auctions in town and preying on unsuspecting businessmen who didn't know one end of a cow from the other. They made the deals and took a fat percentage from the businessmen for their questionable 'guidance'.

'Get to it,' said Angelo.

Quincy leaned forward. 'Well, it's like this. We were passing here late yesterday, when we noticed that you had visitors. Well, me and the boys here chased 'em off, but not before they could make a mess an' all. When we checked around I came across what looked like a map lying on the floor.'

Tumbleweed pulled back both hammers on the shotgun. 'Yer a no-good thievin' sumbitch, Quincy, an' a liar to boot! I oughta blow yer brains out.'

'Take it easy, old man. Just listen to what I've got to say,' Quincy said. 'Mind if we climb down awhile?'

'Yup.'

'OK, have it your way. Now, we both know there's gold buried somewhere around these parts. You know the place, and I know how many paces and in which direction. Put 'em both together . . . and what do we have? A partnership.'

Angelo glanced at Tumbleweed and muttered, 'Will someone please tell me what the Sam Hill's going on here?'

'Nuthin', that's wut,' said the old man. He stamped over to Quincy. 'Supposin' I just sit tight and say nuthin'?' he countered. 'Ye'll never git yer hands on it. How's 'bout that?'

'Then neither will you, old man,' Quincy snarled.

'Well, I guess there's nothin' left to talk about,' said Angelo.

Quincy threw him a withering stare.

Then: 'I'll be back, you old coot, you can count on it.' Quincy turned his horse and spurred it into a gallop. The others followed suit.

The two men watched until the riders were just specks in the distance. Then Angelo placed his hand on the old man's shoulder. 'You gonna be all right, old-timer?'

'Ah, don't ye worry 'bout me, son. Them thur brothers are full of cow dung. They ain't gonna do nuthin'. I'll be fine.'

Angelo slid the rifle into the boot and climbed into the saddle. He leaned down and extended his hand. 'Well, I guess I'll be on my way. You take care of yourself, and don't let that mule get the better of you.'

Tumbleweed shook Angelo by the hand. 'If yer ever in the area, drop in and we'll share a jug of Honest John.'

Angelo laughed. 'Sure, old man, we'll do that. So long!'

2

Around midday Angelo decided to spell himself and his horse along the banks of the Concho River. There was an oak tree near to the water's edge and he slid from the saddle and allowed his horse to drink. After tending to its needs, he took shelter under the shade of the tree with Mr Jinx lying beside him, panting heavily to cool off, but he couldn't shake the feeling that had been nagging at him ever since he and Tumbleweed had parted their ways.

'You know, boy, I can't get that old man out of my head. I've the darndest feelin' that he's headin' for a heap of trouble.' The dog gave a short woof. 'You think so too, huh?'

The dog stood up and wagged his tail.

'OK, OK. We'll go back and see what he's up to. I just hope I don't live to regret it!'

He felt a shiver run down his spine as he rode up to Tumbleweed's shack. There were six horses tethered out front, and raised voices coming from inside. He climbed from the saddle and took out his rifle. Holding the Winchester close to his chest, he put his back to the wall next to the front window and listened carefully to what was being said inside.

Quincy's voice was urgent. 'It don't make sense, all that gold just sittin' there and no one makin' a move to claim it. Why're you being so stubborn, you old fool? Just tell us where the location is so we can use the map.'

'Do ye think I wus born yesterday? If'n I tell ye whure it is, wut use would I be to ye after that?' Tumbleweed countered.

'You think we'd do you harm, old man?' Quincy chuckled. 'You have us all wrong! We want to share the gold with you. Like I said earlier . . . partners.'

'Yeah, partners until my back's turned, thun I'd be pushin' up daisies.'

Quincy grabbed the old man by the front of his shirt. 'Listen, you old coot, you'd better start talkin' or I'm gonna lose my temper!'

Angelo had heard enough and he kicked open the door. Startled, Quincy's brother Tom went for his gun but Angelo brought the Winchester's butt up and around, crushing his nose like it was a peach. As Tom squealed and dropped his gun, Angelo leveled the rifle on Quincy. Beside him, Mr Jinx bared his teeth.

'Never thought I'd see ye again, son,' Tumbleweed said with obvious relief, scurrying to Angelo's side.

Quincy meanwhile went to his brother's aid. 'You sonofabitch, just look what you've done! There was no need for that!'

Angelo ignored him. He knew the old man wouldn't get any peace until this business was settled once and for all. 'OK, Tumbleweed, let's hear all about this gold. Might be best all round if we do.'

Tumbleweed looked towards Quincy, then scratched his head. 'I'll tell ye, but I'll be darned if I tell ye the exact location whur the gold is hidden. How'll that be?'

'That'll be just fine, old man.'

Tumbleweed went over to the fireplace and rummaged around his bits and pieces and picked up a clay pipe. 'It were two years after the war, and I wus a scout at Fort Chadbourne. There wus a young half-breed by the name of Charlie Two-Shoes. I kinda liked the young 'un. He would often talk to me 'bout the days when he used to go huntin' with his pa, and helped his ma with the daily chores. But Charlie used to have these nightmares 'bout the time whun his life wus turned upside down. See, one day a bunch of drunken cowpokes stopped by their cabin. They called his ma a dirty Comanche whore an' then raped and butchered her, and made the young 'un watch as they tortured his pa and killed him.'

Tumbleweed drew in smoke.

'Anyways, me and the young 'breed got on well together. The Comanche scouts saw him as a white man and didn't trust him. The soldiers saw him as a son of a Comanche whore and wouldn't talk to him, less'n it wus fer scoutin' information. Me, though, I always saw him as a friend.

'Fort Chadbourne wus comin' to an end, and they wanted to build a new fort along the Concho River. They sent a team of surveyors out to the proposed site, along with a detail of soldiers. They also sent out a couple of scouts. Charlie wus one of 'em.

'When they got to the site and the surveyors began their work, young Charlie was ordered to clean up the area where a couple of old wagons had been abandoned years before. The wheels were broken and the wood was rotten, so he decided to smash the wood up and burn it. But whun he comes to the second wagon, he found a secret compartment in the floor. They was four ammunition boxes with CSA

17

markin's. At fust Charlie thought nuthin' of it, just dragged the boxes from the wagon and opened one of 'em. There, starin' him in the face was twenty small unmarked gold bars!'

'So all four boxes had twenty bars of gold in 'em?' Quincy asked excitedly.

'Yep.'

'What did he do next?' Angelo asked.

'Well, seein' as it was Confederate gold, it would be classed as treasure . . . finders' keepers. Charlie'd seen wut gold could do to a man, and so's not to cause a gold fever amongst the troops, he buried it. No-one took any notice as to wut he was doin'. The soldiers took shelter in their tents and played cards or slept, while the surveyors did their work.'

'How come you ended up with the map?' Angelo asked. 'And how do you know that Charlie didn't make the whole thing up?'

Tumbleweed wandered over to the pantry and dragged out a sack of flour. He dug deep into the contents and pulled out a heavy parcel wrapped in brown paper. Looking Quincy right in the eye he said, 'Somethin' ye fellas missed whun ye was here the first time.' He undid the package to reveal two small gold bars. 'Now do ye believe me?'

Angelo took one of the bars and checked it over. There was no doubt about it, they were the genuine article, and must have been worth a small fortune.

Tom Randall forgot all about his busted nose and took a close look at the gold. 'We could never spend all that gold in a lifetime, even if we did split it six ways!'

'I think yer all forgettin' somethin',' growled Tumbleweed. 'That thur buried gold is techne — technal — technic . . . it's darn well mine. And it stays thur unless we can make a fair deal.'

'What do you call fair?' asked Quincy.

'We'll split it fifty-fifty. I'll share mine with my friend here,' the old man said.

19

'Ye can split yer share whichever way ye please.'

'Why can't we just split it eight ways?'

'I'm not gonna argue 'bout it, Randall. Take it or leave it.'

'All right, you sonofabitch, have it your way . . . fifty-fifty. Now let's get some shovels and go dig it up.'

Tumbleweed scratched his beard. 'It ain't gonna' be that easy, fellas.' He walked over to Quincy and held out his hand. 'Give me the map an' I'll show ye wut the problem is.'

Quincy hesitated. 'You better not be trying to double-cross me, old man.'

'I'm not.'

Reluctantly he handed the map over. Tumbleweed unfolded it and pointed to the symbols that Charlie had drawn. There were a tree, four drawings of the sun and lots of crosses.

'See this here tree?' he said. 'Wull, the cross-marks go left four paces, right ten paces, right three paces and left five paces and so on! Charlie made it so ye would need the map, as no one would ever remember all the steps an' directions.'

Tom could hardly contain himself. 'All right,' he said nasally. 'So where's the tree?'

'Thur lies the problem. It's slap bang in the middle of Fort Concho!'

Quincy frowned. 'You mean to say the gold is in the *fort*? Are you serious?'

'Darn right I'm serious. Three weeks after Charlie Two-Shoes buried it, they began to build the new fort in the exact same location as the gold. Lucky for us they left the tree intact.'

Angelo laughed. 'Well, I guess that's the end of that!'

Quincy rubbed his chin vigorously. 'Let's not be too hasty. There has to be a way around this.'

'That gold's buried on Federal land. If we get caught with it, we're each lookin' at a minimum of twenty years' hard labor,' Angelo said grimly.

'Yeah — *if* we get caught! I say let's go for it. If your friend here don't want in, Tumbleweed, that's his loss.'

'I'll talk him round,' said Tumbleweed.

He led Angelo out into the sunshine
and over toward the corral, where they
wouldn't be overheard. Before he could
speak, however, Angelo said, 'I'm no
saint, Tumbleweed, but everythin' I've
done up till now has been honest. I
don't intend crossin' that line, old-
timer.'

'Ye don't have to, ye darn fool!'

'What do you mean?'

'Ever heard of a finder's fee? Reward
fer finding treasure?'

Understanding finally dawned and
Angelo gave a low, admiring whistle.
'Well, you sneaky old goat! You intend
get the gold and turn it in for a reward?'

' 'Course that's wut I mean. But
don't ye go tellin' them bastards inside.
Let that be a surprise fer 'em.'

'My lips,' said Angelo, 'are sealed.'

3

Before they could do anything else they had to get inside the fort without arousing suspicion. Stagecoaches and settlers often stopped there before traveling further south to Santa Angela. But Angelo and his companions needed a reason to stick around for a while, and to do some digging.

'I think I've got it,' Angelo said after a few minutes. 'Supposin' one of us was to pretend to be some kind of government official, say he'd been sent to check for sinkholes or somethin'?'

Tumbleweed's eyes lit up. 'Ye might just have somethin' thur, big 'un. But I reckon we can do better'n that sinkhole crap. I know fer a fact the colonel's bin askin' fer a hospital an' school fer the kids. So far his requests have always been denied.'

'So our government man'll be an

architect, then, there to draw up plans for exactly what the colonel wants,' Quincy decided.

'It'll sure get him on our side,' Tom agreed. 'If he thinks it'll get him what he wants, he'll bend over backwards to accommodate us.'

'Who plays the official?' asked Angelo, not caring much for the idea of building the soldier's hopes up only to dash them again.

'You do,' said Quincy. Catching Angelo's look he explained, 'You're the only one who isn't known in these parts.'

'Well, fer once I'll have to agree with Quincy here,' muttered Tumbleweed. 'Yer the only one of us that looks halfway honest. An' ye could say that ye hired us as yer laborers.'

Angelo's lips thinned down. But if Quincy was right, he *was* their best bet. After giving the matter some thought he said, 'All right, I'll give it a whirl. But I can't ride in like this. If I'm gonna play the part, then I've got to *look* the part.'

'Ye'll need a suit,' said Tumbleweed.

'And a haircut,' gloated Tom.

Angelo threw him a withering glance. But again, he knew it made sense. Much as he preferred to wear his hair long, it was going to have to come off, leastways for a while.

'We'll wait for you here,' said Quincy. 'Then we'll all ride to the fort together.'

'*You* can wait,' said Angelo. 'But I'll take Tom along with me.'

'Why?'

'Because I don't trust you, Quincy. I don't trust any of you. I keep you brothers apart, I keep you from cookin' up any schemes against me and the old man. Besides, we'll need a wagon and team: tools, too. Tom can buy everythin' while I'm gettin' scalped.'

Tumbleweed put the gold back into the flour sack. 'I'll tag along wuth ye, if that's OK?'

'You gonna trust us to sit here with that gold lyin' around?' Quincy said wryly.

Tumbleweed laughed. 'I know ye

25

only too well. Why steal two bars of gold whun thur's another seventy-eight waitin' to be dug up?'

As they headed for town, Angelo again found himself wondering just what he was letting himself in for. He'd never been a greedy man. Like 'most everyone else, he'd only ever craved a dollar more than he could spend. And here was a chance to make good money, legally. But still something sat uneasily with him. He didn't care much for the subterfuge involved, of promising this here colonel a school and hospital that would never materialize.

Like just about every army town, Santa Angela had more than its share of brothels, saloons and gambling houses. The town bustled with activity as the three men rode down Main Street. Boisterous voices and loud music poured from the saloons. Angelo reined his gelding and brought it to a halt in front of the Golden Horseshoe.

'This'll do fine,' he announced as he slipped from the saddle and tied his horse to the hitching rail.

'We're goin' in here?' Tom asked.

'This is where we're leavin' our mounts,' corrected Angelo. 'You got chores that don't involve whiskey, Tom. Just go buy us a halfway decent rig an' team, an' tools for diggin'. An' Tumbleweed?'

'Yup?'

'Make sure he don't pay any more than he has to.'

'Wull, ye just take ye time, son. We'll be fine,' Tumbleweed said as he checked to see how much cash he had on him.

'An' remember,' Angelo added sternly, 'we don't want to attract any unnecessary attention. Got that?' He fixed them with a hard look, then added, 'Take Mr Jinx with you.'

Tom watched Angelo cross the road and head for the bank. Then he turned and headed for the saloon. Tumbleweed grabbed him by the arm and said, 'Hey, thur! Ye heard wut Angelo said!'

'The day I take orders from that sonofabitch is the day you can bury me in the stone-cold ground,' Tom replied, and shoved through the batwings.

Tumbleweed sighed, then glanced down at the dog and followed him inside.

The place reeked of stale tobacco and kerosene. The barroom was smaller than most, just enough room to fit six sets of tables and chairs, all of which were occupied. Five soldiers stood around a piano player who was whipping out an awkward version of 'Oh Susannah'. They were all so well-oiled that it was a struggle for them to sing in tune.

There was a small bar in the far corner of the room next to the stairwell. A scrawny, bald-headed man stood behind it, polishing glasses with a dirty towel. He cracked a professional smile as they bellied up. 'Name your disturbance, fellers.'

'Gimme a bottle of whiskey,' said Tom. 'The good stuff.'

'Tell ye what,' said the barkeep. 'I got a new batch in yesterday. Real Scotch whiskey, brewed in Kentucky.'

'I don't care what it is, as long as it don't steal my sight,' Tom said.

Tumbleweed prodded Tom on the arm. 'The big fella said to keep a low profile.'

'So, what's your point?'

'Wull, it's a known fact that ye and yer brother can't hold yer liquor to save yer lives.'

'Ah, quit your gripin', old man.'

The barman put the bottle of whiskey on the counter, took payment and went back to rearranging the smears on his dirty glasses.

At the bank, meanwhile, Angelo withdrew enough money to shop with. He had saved a sizeable amount over the last three years, almost $10,000, and he'd earned every penny of it. At one of the small outfitters he managed to find himself a decent suit which was an almost perfect fit. He also treated himself to a new shirt and tie, along with a derby hat that went perfectly with the newly acquired garments. He had his old clothes wrapped in brown paper and took them with him when he left.

All that remained was the ticklish matter of his haircut. For a man of his free-and-easy sensibilities, that was going to hurt. He found a tonsorial parlor and took his place in the barber's chair. The barber, a fat man with black curly hair around an otherwise hairless crown, asked him what he wanted. Angelo shrugged uncomfortably. 'I don't know. What's all the rage these days?'

'I should say the pompadour,' came the reply. 'Swept back from the forehead, worn quite tall, perhaps with muttonchops?'

Angelo grimaced. 'Just cut it short, oil it and give me a centre part.'

Afterwards, as he made his way to the Golden Horseshoe, he stopped outside a baker's shop and used the window as a mirror to admire his new look. It would take some getting used to, but he reckoned he'd manage it in time. He put the parcel down on the sidewalk and adjusted his hat, then stood back, tilting his head from left to right.

'My, my. Did you know that vanity is one of the cardinal sins?'

He turned quickly to see a young lady smiling at him as she prepared to mount her horse. She was in her mid-twenties, and in bare feet would stand about five and a half feet tall. Her large brown eyes looked the tall man up and down, which made him feel a little uneasy. She wore a white cotton blouse, and tight-fitting pants which left little to the imagination. Her auburn hair, cascading down over her left shoulder, was pushed forward by the fullness of her breast under her tight-fitting blouse.

'Ma'am?' Angelo managed in a strangled voice.

The young lady gave no reply, just climbed into the saddle and spurred the sorrel into a lope.

As he bent to pick up his package he heard a sudden flurry of cries and curses coming from the Golden Horseshoe. A burly soldier came running through the swing doors, holding the shredded crotch of his pants and yelling for a doctor.

Another soldier crashed through the front window and landed on the sidewalk, his face covered in glass-cuts. Just as Angelo came level with the doorway, the batwings were almost taken from their hinges as a third soldier ran out into the street, the backside of his pants torn to ribbons, with Mr Jinx giving chase.

Tumbleweed waved his arms to get the tall man's attention. 'Duck!'

A wiry middle-aged man threw a punch and hit Angelo clean on the jaw. He retaliated with a blow to the man's gut and followed through with a punch to his nose which made a sickly crunching sound. The man stumbled backwards, tripped over a chair and plunged to the floor.

'What the hell's been goin' on here?' Angelo demanded. 'I thought I told you to go buy a wagon — *and* keep a low profile!'

The place was in disarray. Injured bodies were lying all around the room. Smashed tables and chairs were scattered on the floor along with broken bottles. Tom was propped up on the foot rail, holding his bloody nose.

Tumbleweed removed his hat and scratched his head. 'It wus 'em darn soldiers from the fort started it all. That big 'un tried to kick Mr Jinx, and he wus havin' none of it! Tried warnin' the big fool, but he took no heed. One of his friends hit Tom here on the nose, and thun all hell broke loose. Everyone seemed to want to fight. 'Nother one of them thur soldiers wus as crazy as a sheepherder! No tellin' wut he would have done if'n Mr Jinx hadn't stepped in, and chased him clean outta the bar.'

'I hope your friends are goin' to pay for the damage, seeing it was them that started it!' the barkeep said in loud voice.

Angelo frowned. 'The way I see it, I think you'd better take that up with the fort commander. I'm sure those soldiers did their fair share.' He took a fresh twenty-dollar bill from his shirt pocket and placed it on the counter. 'That'll help cover your loss.'

Tom got to his feet and checked himself in the mirror behind the bar. He wiped the fresh blood from his face with his sleeve. 'I swear, if anyone else hits me in the nose, I'm gonna explode!'

'Then I suggest that from here on out you keep it real clean,' growled Angelo.

★　★　★

Evening was drawing in as the three men headed back toward Tumbleweed's shack. Angelo rode alongside Tom, who was driving the newly acquired wagon with a two-horse team. The old man dawdled behind, constantly urging the mule to quicken its pace.

'Hey, big fella, we've trouble a-comin'!' the old man yelled.

Angelo looked over his shoulder. There were a dozen cavalrymen riding at full gallop towards them. 'Let me do the talkin',' he replied quickly, turning to face them.

The troopers reined their mounts to

a halt in an uneven line in front of the three men. The forty-year-old captain in charge sat tall in the saddle as he held Angelo's steady gaze with his dark eyes.

'Evening, gentlemen!'

'Anythin' we can help you soldier-boys with?' asked Angelo.

'One of my troopers reckons you had a little set-to back in town with some of my men.'

'What of it?' growled Tom, belligerent as ever.

'I have three men out of action because of it.' He pointed to a trooper to his left. 'This man was lucky; he only received minor injuries to his buttocks. The others were too badly injured to move, so we had to leave them in town.' The officer directed his attention to the animal. 'And there, unless I'm much mistaken, is the culprit. Is he yours, old man?'

'Mr Jinx don't belong to anyone,' said Angelo.

'Then no one will mind me putting

him out of his misery,' said the captain, starting to draw his Colt from leather.

Almost faster than the eye could follow, Angelo drew his own six-shooter. 'Let's get one thing clear, Captain, I don't make friends easy, but that dog's the closest thing I've got to one. You pull a gun on him, and it's like you're pullin' it on me. And I don't take too kindly to that. Get the picture?'

The officer moved his hand away from his pistol and turned to Angelo. 'I don't know who you are, mister, but pull a gun on an army officer in these parts and you're in a heap of trouble.'

'Well, we sure don't want any trouble, do we?' Angelo said wryly. 'So if you wouldn't mind clearin' the way, I'd be obliged.'

The captain heeled his horse forward. 'You haven't heard the last of this, mister! There might not be any law as such around these parts, but I'll find a way to see that you all pay for what happened back there.'

The officer and his men headed north for the fort while Angelo, the old man and Tom carried along the eastern trail towards Tumbleweed's shack.

4

As soon as they got back Quincy cleared everything off the small wooden table with a sweep of his arm. 'All right, gather round,' he snapped. 'We all have jobs to do, so listen up.'

The old man grabbed a chair. 'And who put ye in charge?'

'Listen to me, you stupid old goat. I know that fort like the back of my hand and most of the folk who work alongside the military. If we need somethin', I can get it. If we run into trouble, I know who will be able to get us out of it.'

'As long as everyone does as they're told, there shouldn't be any problems,' Angelo pointed out, throwing a meaningful glance at Tom.

Quincy said, 'Angelo, in the mornin' you ride alone to the fort and make yourself known to the CO, Colonel

Joshua Winthorpe. We'll give you a head start. By the time we get there, you should've cleared everythin' with him.'

'What's this colonel like?'

'He's easy-goin'. You've nothin' to worry about with him,' Quincy replied. 'But the same can't be said for his adjutant, Captain John Burke. He likes everythin' done strictly by the book. If anythin' looks out of place, he'll be on to it.'

As the night went on Angelo chose to separate himself from the rest of the men. He sat quietly smoking a cigarette on the porch with Mr Jinx lying at his feet. Listening to the sounds of the nightlife and gazing at the moon, he gave a little smile as he remembered the young lady he'd seen in town. The way her eyes sparkled as she spoke to him, the way her full lips had smiled at his embarrassment. Then he went across to the barn and made himself comfortable in an empty stall. He had an early start tomorrow.

Angelo crossed the prairie at an easy pace, and dawn was an hour into the past by the time Fort Concho came into view. It would take another hour to reach the fort gates, which would give him plenty of time to get his story straight. He'd left Mr Jinx behind with the old man, as he wanted nothing to jeopardize his initial meeting with the colonel.

Although he hadn't said much while he was in their company, he had made a careful study of each of his companions. Apart from Quincy, they all looked as if they couldn't tell skunks from house cats. There was Ryan, a young kid of nineteen. He was of average height and build, with long greasy hair, small grey eyes and buck teeth. Brad Matlock was in his mid-twenties. The first thing that was noticeable about him was his tight red curly hair. It matched his fiery temper, for he was loud-mouthed and aggressive with it. Baby-faced Frank McCall, on the other hand, was the quiet one, but always to be found gently caressing the butt of his six-gun. Finally there was young Jimmy Brown, twenty-one years of age. His wiry frame stood four inches short of six feet. His face was pear-shaped, with beady eyes that were drawn close together.

Fort Concho covered an area of forty acres and consisted of forty buildings which were built from sandstone and pecan wood. There were two sets of gates on the south wall. Angelo took the east gate, which gave access to the offic- ers' and commanding officer's quarters. He was soon challenged by a heavily built sergeant and a trooper carrying a carbine.

'State your name and business!' the sergeant said in husky voice.

'The name's, uh, Grubb,' Angelo said. 'Edward Grubb.' No sooner had the words left his mouth than he wished he could take them back. *Grubb!* . . . *Who the hell has a name like Grubb?* 'I'm here on government business and need to talk to Colonel Winthorpe.'

'He's at headquarters, far side of the fort.' The sergeant turned to the trooper. 'Take him to the colonel.'

So far so good, Angelo thought. He looked around. There seemed to be plenty going on. Hopefully that meant they could get on with digging for the gold without arousing too much unwanted interest.

Angelo's escort left him outside headquarters, which was situated on the northeastern side of the fort. The tall man dismounted and tied his horse to the hitching post. He dusted himself down and straightened his tie before entering the reception. It was a small, rather plain room containing a two-seater leather couch and a small table and chair by an open fireplace. There was a portrait of George Armstrong Custer hanging from the chimneybreast along with the regimental colors. To the right, a corridor ran the full length of the building, leading to the administration offices, and to the left was the CO's office. A corporal was sifting through paperwork at the desk directly opposite the main door.

The corporal looked up. 'Yes, can I help you?'

'I'm here to see the colonel.'

'Is he expecting you?'

'No, but I'm here on government business and it's important that he knows I'm here.'

The corporal gave Angelo the once over, then said, 'Your name?'

Inwardly Angelo cringed again. 'Edward Grubb.'

'Wait here.'

He went and knocked on the CO's door, then walked in and closed it behind him. A moment later he came back out with the colonel in tow.

Colonel Winthorpe beckoned Angelo with his hand. 'Good day, Mr Grubb. I understand you've come to see me on government business? Please, step inside.'

Angelo entered the CO's office and at the colonel's bidding sat in the chair on the visitor's side of the desk.

Colonel Winthorpe was in his late

forties. He was of average build and height, with light-brown hair that was just showing signs of graying at the temples. His bronzed face and hooded eyes told a story of a man who for many years had been used to being exposed to the elements.

'I'm here to do a survey for a new hospital and school,' said Angelo, surprised at just how uncomfortable he was with lying.

Winthorpe's eyes lit up, which only made Angelo feel worse. 'This is amazing news! We've been asking for a new hospital for months now, and as usual we thought that no one had taken any notice.'

'Well, nothin' is set in stone just yet, Colonel — if you'll, uh, pardon the pun. It all depends on the land hereabouts. When we raise buildings, we like to make sure they *stay* raised.'

'Ah, I see. You need to check the land first, make sure you have a stable foundation to build upon.'

'Exactly, sir. There's a lot of underground streams, caves and possibly even sinkholes in these parts, and we don't want the new buildings subsidin', now do we?'

Before the colonel could respond, the door behind Angelo opened wide. The colonel pushed his chair back and stood up. 'Abigail! You'll never guess what, my dear! We're to have a new hospital and school!'

'Oh, that's wonderful news, Father!'

Recognizing the voice, Angelo swung around in his chair and came face to face with the girl he'd encountered, albeit briefly, in Santa Angela. He almost leapt to his feet in order to bow his head in her direction.

'Ma'am.'

'Let me introduce my daughter, Abigail,' said the colonel. 'Abigail, this is Mr Edward Grubb.'

Angelo winced.

'It's a pleasure to meet you, Mr — '

'Please, ma'am. Call me . . . Edward.'

She was dressed much as she had been the day before, which did nothing to dampen his excitement.

'Are you planning on staying long?' she asked.

'Well, at least until I've, uh, drawn out the plans for the new buildings. A few days, is my guess.'

'Well, I'll make arrangements for you to have a pleasant stay while you are here,' said the colonel. 'I'm sure you'll find the officers' quarters to your liking.'

'I don't want to put you to any trouble, Colonel.'

'Ha! Think nothing of it. You are a godsend, my friend; it's the least I can do.'

'And you have come just at the right time!' piped up Abigail. 'We are having a dance at the officers' club tonight.' She gave Angelo a smile. 'Do say you'll come?'

'Well, I'm not quite sure, ma'am. I may have to work late tonight.'

'Fiddlesticks! I'm sure there is nothing that can't wait until tomorrow. Let's say seven o'clock. We'll be expecting you.'

5

Angelo watched as the men unloaded the digging tools. Tumbleweed unhitched the horses and led them to the stables to get feed and water.

Quincy, meanwhile, opened up the map and began to follow the directions. He suddenly stopped about three yards from the colonel's living quarters. 'This is it!' he hissed, then handed a pick and shovel to Brad and Frank. 'You can start diggin' while the rest of us can keep a lookout.'

'How come we get to do the diggin'?' Frank whined.

'Keep it quiet,' said Angelo. 'We got company!'

A trooper came up to the two men, took off his slouch hat and wiped the sweat from his brow with his forearm. 'Which one of you is Grubb?' he asked.

Again Angelo winced. 'That'll be me,'

he confessed reluctantly.

'Captain Burke's compliments, sir. He wonders if you'd like to join him in the officers' mess for lunch.'

Angelo gave the trooper a curt nod. 'Tell the captain I'll be along shortly.'

The soldier turned and headed back towards the mess hall.

Quincy scowled. 'Remember what I told you about that man. If he smells that somethin's wrong, he'll be on to us. So you better go and keep him from snoopin' around. Oh, and what in tarnation possessed you to pick a name like Grubb?'

Hacked off by the question, Angelo shook his head, then made his way to the officers' mess. He was greeted by a young lieutenant, who escorted him the final distance to Captain Burke's table.

'Excuse me, Captain. This is Mr Grubb.'

Captain Burke turned around, smiled up at his visitor — and froze. 'You!' he husked.

Burke's surprise was mutual, for

Angelo had come face to face with none other than the officer who'd threatened to shoot Mr Jinx the night before.

'So *you*'re the man that the colonel wants to keep sweet.' Burke sneered.

'And you're the man he's chosen to nursemaid me,' Angelo replied.

As he took a seat across from the officer, Burke hissed, 'Listen, mister, if I had my way, you'd all be locked up for what you did to my men. Especially those villains you have working for you. I've seen them around town, and here in the fort. I wouldn't trust them an inch. So be very careful, because I'll be keeping a close eye on you all.'

'Hey, big fella! I need to talk to ye.'

The voice came from the far side of the room, where Tumbleweed stood with his hat in hand.

Burke grimaced. 'It looks like one of your men needs you more than I do. Maybe we should just skip lunch.'

Angelo shrugged. 'I kinda lost my appetite anyways.'

He hurried over to the old man. 'What is it? You're supposed to be keepin' an eye on things.'

The old man fidgeted with his hat. 'We got a problem,' he said.

'What kind of problem?'

'The gold,' said Tumbleweed. 'It's not there!'

* * *

Mr Jinx started barking excitedly when Angelo approached. Quincy said, 'You can see to him later. I need you to take a look at this first.'

Ryan and Jimmy were standing in the hole, which was around five feet deep. Ryan pointed downward. 'Do you see it?'

Angelo peered inside. 'See what?'

'Nothin', that's what! No boxes, no gold, nothing save more dirt!'

Tom shook his head. 'I might've known it! That map's a fake!'

'The hell it is!' blustered Tumble-weed. 'Those two bars I got stowed

50

away in my cabin're real enough!'

'Quit it!' snapped Angelo. 'Let's think about this a moment.' He did just that, then said, 'Give me the map.'

Quincy unfolded it and handed it to him. He knelt and laid it out on the dirt. After studying it for a while, he took out the makings and rolled himself a smoke.

'Well?' barked Quincy.

'Charlie Two-Shoes was a clever man,' Angelo replied. 'And he drew up a well-detailed map. It's just a pity we missed it the first time around. It would have saved us from diggin' in the wrong place.'

Quincy and Tom studied the piece of paper. Tumbleweed joined the brothers and gave the map the once-over.

'Missed wut?' the old man grumbled. 'I don't see nuthin' different.'

'There are four symbols of the sun. No one thought to ask why he'd drawn these on the map. Also, there's the figure nine beside the tree.'

Quincy growled impatiently, 'Can we

please get to the point?'

'OK, listen up. The first symbol of the sun is directly above the tree. I reckon that would mean midday. The others more'n likely represent hourly intervals. So I figure at three in the afternoon the tree will cast a shadow, and that's where we start. The nine would have been the height of the tree all those years ago . . . nine feet. So all we do is put a marker on the tree nine feet from the base and when we see the shadow of the marker on the ground, we start from there.'

'Sounds easy enough, young 'un,' Tumbleweed said.

'You'd better be right, big man,' grouched Quincy. ' 'It's already a little after two.'

'OK, so we have a little time to kill.'

'Uh-huh. And we'll all pass it together, while my boys fill in this here hole.'

Angelo gave Mr Jinx a bowl of water and some beef jerky from the wagon, then lay with his back to the tree, which gave him shade from the harsh sunlight. The dog lay quietly next to him, chewing on the jerky.

At three, Angelo showed a thin-lipped smile and said, 'All right, on your feet. It's time!' He took their tape measure and moseyed over to Quincy. 'Give me your knife and squat against the tree. I'll climb up on your shoulders to mark the height.'

From the base of the trunk, Tumble-weed held one end of the measure and handed the other to Angelo, who without warning stood on Quincy's head to get the extra height needed to mark off the nine feet.

'Sonofabitch! You almost took my eye out,' yelled Quincy.

'Stop your whinin', Quince,' Angelo said, then thrust the steel blade into the tree. As it cast its shadow over the ground, the knife marker could clearly be seen.

Quincy handed the old man the map. 'You do it . . . you follow the directions.'

Tumbleweed stood directly above the shadow and began to mumble. 'Left five paces . . . one, two . . . '

Everyone watched with anticipation as the old man moved in the directions that were marked on the map. He then froze as if his feet had suddenly grown roots.

'Is that it? Is that the place?' Quincy asked.

The old man didn't answer.

'What's wrong, you old fool? Is that the place or not?'

'Wull, not quite.'

'What do you mean?' Tom asked. 'Is it or isn't it?'

'The last turn is ten paces.'

'So walk ten paces, you stupid old goat.'

'I can't!'

Quincy threw down his hat. 'Dagnabit, Tumbleweed. What the hell's wrong?'

'I got ten paces still to walk. To do that I'd need to be able to walk through walls . . . an' thun I'd end up smack inside the colonel's livin' quarters!'

He was right. The directions led directly to a spot inside Colonel Winthorpe's bedroom. Angelo peered through the window and corrected himself. 'Unless the colonel's taken to wearin' women's clothin', my guess is that it's his daughter's bedroom.'

'So where does that leave us?' demanded Quincy.

'I figure an hour ought to do it.'

'Do what?' Quincy barked.

'You'll need at least an hour to get in, dig up the gold and get out again. We'll have to make sure the colonel and his daughter are kept busy.'

'And how the hell do we do that?' asked Tom.

'There's a ball tonight at the officers' mess, and I've been invited. I'll make sure the colonel and his daughter don't get any ideas about leavin' until I know you have the gold safely loaded on the wagon.'

'How will ye know?' Tumbleweed asked.

'Because Quincy here will send word to the officers' mess, saying that my presence is required elsewhere.'

'And ye can trust the sumbitch to do that?'

'Oh, yes. Because I'll be takin' Tom here with me as insurance.'

'What?' Tom bellowed.

'Quincy might be a lot of things,' said Angelo, 'but I doubt that he's low enough to double-cross his own brother.'

Well, that was the plan, anyway.

6

As Angelo and Tom entered the mess hall, they were greeted by a corporal in dress uniform. Angelo recognized the man as being the one he'd met on the front desk at headquarters. A look of disapproval shadowed the man's face as he looked the two grubby men up and down.

'The colonel is expecting you, sir, if you'd like to follow me.'

Angelo glanced at Tom and said, 'You stay right here. When Tumbleweed shows up, point him in my direction.'

There were at least two dozen couples on the floor, dancing to the music of the regimental band. A large group of officers looked on, hoping to catch the eye of one of the young ladies. Some of the older couples were sitting in a group. To their right stood a gingham-covered table filled with punch bowls and hors d'oeuvres. There, another group of officers were smoking cigars and drinking whiskey. It was to this table that the corporal led Angelo.

'Glad you could make it, Edward,' said the colonel, immediately filling a glass from the nearest punch-bowl and handing it to him. He put his glass down and pulled out a cigar case. 'Finest Cubans that money can buy, young man,' he said. 'Help yourself.'

Angelo took one from the case, rolled it between his thumb and forefinger, then put it to his nose to take in the aroma. 'Mm, it's been a long time since I've had the pleasure, Colonel.'

As the colonel struck a match and held it towards him, Angelo spotted Abigail entering the room. He froze. She was on the arm of Captain Burke, who appeared only as a faint blur to him. She was elegantly dressed in a flowing midnight-blue velvet evening gown that clung to her curves. A matching ribbon held her brushed-back hair in place, and a cameo brooch choker adorned her slender neck.

Angelo blew out the match and placed the Cuban in his top pocket. Abigail greeted him with a smile and held out one small hand. He bowed slightly and gently kissed it.

Captain Burke raised his eyebrows. 'I must say, I'm taken aback, Grubb. You do have some gentlemanly attributes after all! Maybe there's more to you than meets the eye.'

'You'd be surprised,' Angelo replied briefly.

'Well said, Edward.' Abigail smiled, adding, 'I take it that you have already met our Captain Burke?'

'You could say that I've had the pleasure. Twice, actually.'

Burke frowned. 'Why don't you get the lady a cup of punch while we take this dance?'

Before Angelo could answer, Burke took hold of Abigail's arm and led her on to the dance floor.

The colonel poured himself another cup of punch. 'Well, if you'll excuse me,

I think I'll leave you young people alone. I must be seen to mingle, you know.'

'Don't mind me, Colonel. I'll have to be leaving shortly myself. We have an early start tomorrow.'

He glanced toward the main door, where Tom was sitting drinking a cup of punch. He hated deceiving these folks, especially Abigail. But the way he saw it, with the reward money he stood to gain by the recovery of the gold, he could still give them the school and hospital they so desperately needed anyway.

He watched enviously as Captain Burke held Abigail and danced to a slow waltz. After a moment he stepped on to the dance floor, weaved between the other dancers until he reached Abigail and Burke. He tapped the officer on the shoulder and as he turned to see who it was, Angelo cut in, took Abigail in his arms and waltzed away with her.

Abigail looked softly into Angelo's

eyes. 'I think Captain Burke is a little angry at you, and quite frankly I can't blame him!'

'Well, ma'am, I thought this was an 'excuse me', so it's not entirely my fault.'

'You intrigue me, Edward!'

'Ma'am?'

'Well, if you'll forgive me for saying, you look more like a saddle tramp than a government official. Some of your noticeable traits could be that of a hired gun. But yet when the need arises, you step up to the mark. And may I also say that you dance rather well.'

Angelo looked over at Tom. The man was gesturing to him. Regretfully he released Abigail and stepped back from her. 'I'm sorry, Miss Abigail, but it seems that I'm wanted elsewhere.'

He was gratified by the look of disappointment that came into her eyes.

Burke wasted little time in seizing his opportunity. He shoved Angelo aside and swept Abigail back into the swirl of dancers. Angelo turned and hurried across to Tom. 'What is it?'

'You'd better come quick,' he said. 'There's been trouble.'

'What kind of trouble?'

Tom turned and hurried out into the night. 'All I know is that it's all gone wrong.'

They crossed the parade ground at a trot, and were quickly swallowed up by the shadows. 'It's all gone wrong,' Tom muttered again as they turned a corner and Angelo saw at once that the wagon was gone — and so were Quincy, Tumbleweed and the others. Only Mr Jinx was still there — and one of them had tied him to the tree before they lit out.

'Wha — ?'

Without warning Tom turned on his heel so that Angelo ran straight into him, then he punched Angelo hard in the stomach. 'For you, that is!'

He crowded Angelo fast, giving him no chance to recover, and all the spite he'd been saving up for the man came boiling to the surface in a flurry of punches against which Angelo could do nothing but go down.

He lost count of the number of punches, and when Tom started throwing vicious kicks into the mix, the world he'd known to this point became a world full of hurt. He had no idea when it ended. He was unconscious long before Tom finally stopped.

⋆ ⋆ ⋆

'You have a lot of explaining to do, mister.'

Angelo awoke with a start. He had been taken into the headquarters block and thrown roughly on to the two-seater sofa. Captain Burke was towering over him, and in the background Colonel Winthorpe and Abigail were frowning at him. Angelo squeezed his eyes shut against a thumping headache. He felt stiff, achy, thirsty, and nauseous.

'I don't know what the hell you're up to, but I'm going to get to the bottom of it!' Burke continued.

The colonel cut him short. 'Captain Burke!'

Burke stepped aside so that Winthorpe could take center stage. The colonel said, 'What's this all about, Edward? My men find you beaten half to death, your workmen and their wagon have disappeared and my daughter's room has been ransacked and dug up! Just what have you and your friends been up to?'

It was, Angelo thought, a very good question. If only his head would stop pounding long enough for him to form an answer. For just a moment he thought about denying any knowledge, but he knew that wouldn't wash. Besides, he had an honest man's instinctive dislike of subterfuge.

'Gold,' he said softly, and looked away from Abigail before he could see the hurt in her face.

'What?' asked the colonel.

'I'm not a surveyor. I don't work for the government. My name is Angelo, not Edward Grubb. I — we — came here to dig up a cache of Confederate gold that was buried here years ago. Our plan — that is, the old man and me — was to retrieve the gold and then turn it in for the reward. Our so-called 'partners' had other ideas.'

'Captain, arrest this man, whoever he is!'

'Hold hard, there, Captain. I know things don't look too good from where you're standing, but believe me when I say that my intentions were honorable.'

'Honorable! You don't know the meaning of the word,' Burke growled.

Angelo got up, swayed a little, and when the room stopped tilting, went over to the corporal's desk. He took a slip of paper from his jacket pocket, helped himself to a pen and then wrote briefly on the reverse side. 'I want you to have this, Colonel,' he said when he was finished.

'What is it?'

'I'd already made up my mind that you were gonna get the school and hospital you want. This is a receipt for ten thousand dollars I just deposited in the Bank of Santa Angela. I've written a note on the back and signed it over to you. If I'm not back within ten days, do what you want with it.'

The colonel looked surprised. 'I don't understand!'

'Look, it's like I said. The old man and me, we were going to hand the gold over to you for the reward. Now they've doubled-crossed me and taken the old man with them, and I'd bet my life he didn't go willingly. Take your men and track down these thieves, sure — but let me go along. My concern is for him. They'll either kill him or leave him out in the middle of the desert to rot.'

'I swear, if this is some sort of trickery . . . .'

'It's not. And with respect, Colonel, time's a-wastin'.'

Winthorpe took the point. 'Captain, prepare C troop to move out at first light. Take enough supplies to last the week. I want those thieves caught and that gold returned, do you understand?'

'Sir!'

As Burke left the room, Angelo looked sheepishly at Abigail. Her expression was almost impossible to read. 'My apologies, Miss Abigail,' he said quietly. 'My part in this isn't anywhere near as bad as it seems.'

The girl turned away and made no reply, and her silence was worse than a slap in the face.

7

Angelo finished tightening his saddle girth. He'd recovered his gunbelt from his gunny sack and was tying the strap to his leg when Captain Burke rode up to him.

'Just remember, Angelo. This is a military operation, and I'm in command of it. You're just a civilian — and a suspect one, at that. So keep out of my way and do as you're told.'

'Anything you say, Cap'n,' Angelo replied softly.

'Take your place at the back of the column with the wagons.'

The twenty-four troopers rode in single file with two wagons at the rear. Captain Burke and a shavetail lieutenant took point at the head of the column. Ignoring Burke's order, Angelo rode out ahead to scout the trail, with Mr Jinx racing alongside him.

The gold-heavy Randall wagon had left a trail that headed south along the banks of the River Conchos. They followed it right through the day, and though men and horses both were showing signs of fatigue by late afternoon, Burke wouldn't let up the pace.

Angelo finally dropped back to ride alongside the captain. 'I suggest you camp in yonder gorge,' he said. 'It's got good cover.'

Burke frowned. 'I'll decide where and when to rest, mister.'

'Then you'll know it's best to find your campsite before full dark hits. Besides which, if you don't rest these animals soon, you'll end up walkin' the rest of the way.'

Captain Burke raised his hand. 'Ho! Lieutenant, I think we'll camp over there among those rocks for the night.'

Angelo raised his eyebrows.

'Why the surprised look?' Burke asked. 'I was just about to give the order to camp for the night anyway, before you cut in.'

* * *

Angelo found himself a spot with good cover away from the soldiers. He sat with his back against the rockface with Mr Jinx at his feet keeping watch. After rolling a smoke, he lit it from the small fire that he'd made to keep out the night chill. The young lieutenant strolled over carrying two plates of food.

'Thought you and your dog might like some grub.' He handed a plate to Angelo and put the other next to Mr Jinx. 'It's not much . . . what passes for beef stew out here. But it's wholesome.'

'Thanks.'

'My name is Robert Feathersham. I believe everyone already knows who you are.'

Angelo glanced down at Mr Jinx and then smiled. 'Funny, that,' he said.

'What is?'

'I do believe you're the first person besides me that he hasn't growled at.'

The lieutenant crouched and gave Mr Jinx a rub behind the ears. 'I love dogs. I guess he can sense that I mean him no harm. Tell me something, though, Angelo. These men we're chasing. Are they as dangerous as they say?'

'The Randalls are nothin' more than opportunists and petty thieves. But gold can change a man. An' there ain't much that's more dangerous than a desperate man with gold fever. How old are you, kid?'

'Twenty, sir.'

'Fresh out of the Point, no doubt.'

'Yes, sir.'

'Been out here long?'

'Two weeks.'

'Seen any action?'

'Nope.'

'Well,' Angelo assured him, 'be patient, Lieutenant. You will. And soon!'

* * *

The night passed without incident and at first light C Troop was ready to push on. Captain Burke and Lieutenant

71

Feathersham were busy studying a map as Angelo crossed over to them.

'They're heading for the Mexican border, I'm sure of it,' Burke was saying to Feathersham. 'We'll keep heading south.'

'You're wrong, Cap'n,' said Angelo. 'My guess is that they'll turn and head back along the Goodnight-Lovin' trail. They're probably goin' to cross the border into New Mexico. If that's so, then they have two choices — keep on the cattle trail or go into El Paso. But I figure they'll follow the cattle trail, as the canyon will give more cover from the elements and anythin' else they might run into.'

Burke took off his hat and wiped the sweat from his forehead with his sleeve. 'I don't remember asking for your opinion, mister.'

'Well, you've got it anyway. And it's not just an opinion, Cap'n. My gut tells me it's a cast-iron certainty.'

'He might be right, sir,' said Feathersham.

'No, we'll keep on going south. Lieutenant, prepare the men to move out.'

* * *

Disgruntled muttering could be heard from some of the troopers as Burke led them further south into the badlands of Texas towards Del Rio and the Rio Grande. They were out in the open, and away from cover of the gorge that ran along the Conchos River. It was way past noon, it had been a long, hot and demanding ride, and once again Burke showed no indication of calling a halt any time soon.

The rugged terrain slowed progress still further. On the high ground up ahead there were any number of rock formations which would be an ideal place to take a few hours' rest.

Suddenly Lieutenant Feathersham reined his horse to a halt. 'We've got company! There, up on the ridge to the left . . . smoke. See it?'

'I see it,' murmured Angelo.

'What do you reckon?' Feathersham asked.

'Well, I'd rule out a welcomin' committee.'

Captain Burke took a pair of binoculars from his saddle-bags and focused on the top of the ridge. 'I can't see a damn thing. Except for the smoke, everything looks fine.'

'Well, I suggest we proceed with caution,' suggested Angelo.

'We can do better than that. Lieutenant, send one of the men to check it out.'

'Not a wise move, Cap'n.'

Burke glared at Angelo. 'I'll decide what's wise and what isn't.'

Lieutenant Feathersham cut one of the troopers from the column and sent him to investigate the trail of smoke that climbed into the clear blue sky. Angelo watched as the trooper rode out of sight. A few moments later, a single gunshot filled the air.

Burke gently spurred his horse into a

walk. 'Bring six men, Lieutenant, and follow me.'

Angelo pulled his Winchester from its boot and followed the troopers as they moved off. They made their way up the slope to the top of the ridge. The sight that greeted them made the young lieutenant turn his head and shudder.

Angelo surveyed the immediate area for signs of danger. 'You satisfied now, Cap'n?' he asked as he slid the rifle back into its boot.

There were telltale signs of dry shrubbery around the small fire which had been used to produce the white smoke that first got their attention. The trooper who had been sent to scout ahead lay face down with three arrows in his back. His horse was missing, along with the cartridge belt, carbine and sidearm. Close by lay the naked body of one of the outlaws. He was spread-eagled face up and secured with rawhide thongs staked to the ground by narrow wooden poles. His eyes had been gouged out and were lying in the dirt next to his tongue and ears.

Deep knife cuts covered the torso and face where scores of fire ants feasted on the honey that had been poured into them. The ruthless sun had blistered his whole body. Hot coals from the fire had been placed between his legs.

'Dear God, who could have done this? Comancheros?'

'No . . . Apaches, and not your every day Apache, neither. These are Chiricahua,' said Angelo. 'The best of the best.'

'How the hell do you figure that one out, mister? There are no hostiles in this area.'

'Well, there are now. They've left their callin' card!' Angelo pointed to an arrow stuck in the ground with a colored sash tied to it. 'See that? Every Chiricahua carries a sacred arrow and a sash. He uses it to show that he'll stand his ground and fight to the death. This is a message for you, Cap'n. I figure they want our horses and guns.'

'Ha! I don't think a few Apaches are

going to be much of a problem, if they are Apaches!'

'You carry on along this trail, fella, and you're gonna to find out and lead everyone to their deaths in the process. Now, you can do what the hell you like, but I'm headin' west to catch up with what-ever's left of the Randalls.'

Burke dismounted and looked closely at the mutilated body of the man staked to the ground, then he turned to face Angelo. 'Who was he?'

'If it wasn't for that mop of red hair, his own mother wouldn't recognize him. That was Brad Matlock.'

Mr Jinx ran up the slope, barking excitedly. Angelo asked, 'What's up, fella?'

A trooper yelled, 'Rider coming in fast, sir!'

Up on the high ridge heading towards them at full gallop was a rider low in the saddle. He was being pursued by four Apache warriors on horseback.

Angelo swung his horse around. 'Cover me!' he yelled as he heeled the gelding hard in the flanks, and the animal took off at full speed with Mr Jinx at its side.

As he drew closer to the Indians Angelo drew his Colt and fired it at the lead Apache. The bullet missed the rider but tore through the horse's shoulder. Its forelegs buckled and it went down head first, throwing its rider into the dirt. The Apache quickly recovered from the fall and returned fire with a Spencer carbine, using the dead horse for cover.

The lone rider was almost level with Angelo when suddenly his horse stumbled, incapable of maintaining the speed the rider demanded. The animal came to an abrupt halt and he was thrown over the horse's head. A cloud of dust exploded as he thudded to the ground.

Angelo yelled out as he passed him, 'Keep down, don't move!' The rider did as he was told.

Mr Jinx leapt over the dead horse just as the Apache struggled to reload the carbine. The dog locked on to his arm, tearing through muscle and bone.

Angelo, meanwhile, emptied his Colt at the remaining warriors. The Apache to his far left yelled out his death cry as a bullet tunneled through his throat and exited in a rush of blood at the back of his neck.

As the last two rode parallel, one of them took aim with a bow while the other raised his lance in the air. There was only forty feet between them; Angelo sensed the danger of being caught in the middle and quickly reined his gelding to a halt. He tore his Winchester from its boot, levered and squeezed the trigger, but not before the Apache released his bowstring.

The bullet drilled through the Apache's temple. The arrow skimmed the surface of Angelo's thigh, leaving a shallow groove. The gelding reared up on its hind legs, its belly facing the oncoming Apache. As it came back down on all fours, Angelo fired the rifle a second time. The bullet penetrated the top of the horse's head, throwing bone and tissue into its rider's face. The lance fell from his grip and he toppled back over the horse's croup and into the dirt.

Saliva dripping from his bared fangs, Mr Jinx was quick to follow through, attacking the warrior. It didn't take the dog long to finish him.

Angelo reined the gelding to a halt, took his canteen and poured water on the wound, then used his kerchief as a makeshift bandage. Mr Jinx wandered over to him, his snout and paws covered in blood.

'OK, feller,' Angelo said, dry-mouthed from the recent action. 'Let's go see to this greenhorn, then we can get cleaned up.'

Now that the danger was over the rider had recovered his horse and was adjusting the girth. From the back, his build looked more like that of a young skinny kid. He was dressed in a fancy buckskin jacket and tight-fitting pants to match, and wore a large-brimmed, low-crowned hat.

'You all right, friend?' Angelo called as he closed the last few yards.

The rider took off the hat, allowing the long hair that had been tucked inside to flow freely on to her shoulders, as she turned and gazed into Angelo's eyes.

'You!' he breathed in disbelief. 'What in tarnation are *you* doing here?'

'I thought you'd be pleased to see me,' said Abigail.

Then she fainted.

8

Angelo dismounted, scooped Abigail into his arms and carried her back down to the waiting column. He stretched her out in wagon-shade and then spilled some water between her lips. She coughed and came back to consciousness.

'Good grief, girl!' blustered Burke. 'Have you lost your mind? What on earth are you doing out here?'

She fixed Angelo with a look, then turned her attention to Burke. 'I needed to find out something,' she said. 'This man Angelo . . . I made the mistake of taking him at face value, and I was hurt — deeply hurt, Angelo — when he proved to be a complete fraud. However, I have a Christian nature. I'd give anyone the benefit of the doubt.'

'So you came out here to see for yourself whether or not I was still here or had left to join up with my 'partners-in-crime',' Angelo finished.

She nodded.

'Well,' he said, 'as you can see, I'm still here. And a good thing for you that I am. Now, I think we'd better get the heck out of here, Cap'n.'

Burke frowned. 'You think they'll be back?'

'You'd better believe it. 'Fact, I'd say they're watchin' us right now, plannin' their next move.'

The column turned west and headed for the cattle trail. Because it was too risky to send her back to the fort, Abigail rode in the chuck wagon along-side the driver, with Mr Jinx resting in back. They were traveling over open ground, which made them vulnerable to any prying Apache eyes. Angelo knew it would take at least another day to reach the Pecos, which meant spending one night on the prairie.

It was almost sundown when Captain Burke ordered the troop to dismount and take up defensive positions, while the appointed cook prepared a meal and fresh coffee. At Abigail's insistence, Angelo hopped up on to the tailgate and allowed her to clean and bind his leg wound.

Mr Jinx got up and wagged his tail as Lieutenant Feathersham approached. He crouched and gave the dog a rub behind the ears. 'How's the leg?' he asked Angelo.

'Couple of days from now it'll be as good as new.'

After supper, Burke drew up a roster for guard duty. He placed six men in a small perimeter close to the wagons. Angelo had cleared a place for Abigail's bed on the floor of the chuck wagon, while he bedded down underneath. He took out the makings and rolled himself a cigarette. After lighting it, he lay with his head resting on his saddle and smiled at the thought of her sleeping so close to him.

The clatter of pots and pans being thrown into the storage drawers of the chuck wagon woke Angelo from his sleep. The camp was in disarray, with men yelling and shouting as they ran in all directions with horse tack and their bedding. Abigail climbed down from the wagon.

'What's going on?' she asked Angelo.

He shook his head, stood and put on his gun-belt, then grabbed his hat and headed for the supply wagon, where Lieutenant Feathersham was fastening the back curtain. 'Somethin' I should know?'

The lieutenant looked over his shoulder. 'Two of the men had their throats cut while they slept. No one saw or heard a thing. Captain Burke is furious.'

Just then a middle-aged sergeant hurried over to them. 'Compliments of Captain Burke, sir. He says to move out and he'll catch up.'

'Where is the captain, anyway?' Feathersham asked.

'He took a handful of troopers out to see if he could find the Apaches that got into camp last night.'

'Thank you, Sergeant. Have the men ready to move out in ten minutes.' He looked anxiously at Angelo. 'It's going from bad to worse, isn't it?'

'Look on the bright side, Lieutenant. There's always the chance that Burke might get lost.'

★ ★ ★

As the wheels of the supply wagon rolled over the hard dry trail, the driver fastened his kerchief over his nose and mouth to eliminate the foul stench coming from the corpses he was hauling.

Once more they came to a halt. Angelo heeled his horse and rode to the head of the column. 'What's up, Lieutenant?'

'I'm not sure, but it looks like a wagon about a mile up ahead.'

Angelo narrowed his eyes and searched the terrain. 'Yeah, I see it. I'll go take a closer look.'

Mr Jinx jumped around excitedly. 'Stay boy. No need for us both to go, I'll be back before you know it.'

86

He heeled the gelding into a lope and pulled the Winchester from its boot. It didn't take him long to reach the covered wagon. There was no sign of anyone or the team of horses. He slowly circled around it, reined the gelding and slid from the saddle.

Suddenly he heard snoring coming from inside. He cautiously pulled back the curtain to reveal a familiar face. He climbed over the tailgate and prodded the old man with the barrel of his rifle.

'Get up! This is no time to be sleepin'.'

Tumbleweed sat up. 'Huh? Sumbitch . . . you! Whure the hell have ye bin, young 'un? I'd almost given up on ye.'

'Well it sure is good to see you, too, old man.'

'Are ye alone?'

'No, old-timer, I've got some soldier-boys with me.'

'Darn soldiers. Ye knows how much I detest 'em.'

'You might be glad of 'em before this is over.'

'As long as that sumbitch we met on the road to my place ain't one of 'em.'

Angelo bit his bottom lip. 'Well — '

'Doggone it, Angelo. I thought things wur lookin' up. That piece of horse dung's so mean, he'd steal a fly from a blind spider.'

'Maybe he would. But right now we got bigger things to worry about.'

'Such as?'

'Apaches.'

The sound of approaching horses prompted Angelo to pull back the curtain just enough to catch a glimpse of Captain Burke and six troopers reining their mounts to a halt.

Angelo turned to the old man. 'Damn!'

'Wut's up?'

'Nothin' for you to worry about, old man. You stay here until I tell you to come out. Got it?'

'Sure! Get a wiggle on, my throat's parched. Feels like the backside of a 'coon's butt.'

'I'll be as quick as I can.'

Six carbines were trained on him as

he climbed from the wagon.

'Whoa there, boys. A man can get the wrong idea when you're pointin' guns at him. Could save us all a whole lot of trouble if you put 'em up.'

Burke leaned forward. 'I assume this is the wagon the outlaws used to carry off the gold?'

'Yup.'

'I heard voices coming from inside. Who else is in there?'

'Just the old man.'

Burke turned to his men. 'If he comes out carrying a weapon, blast him.'

'Come on out, Tumbleweed, and keep your hands where everyone can see 'em.'

The old man slowly climbed down and strolled over to Angelo's horse. Moving his gaze toward Burke, he said, 'Ye don't mind if'n I get myself a swig of water, do ye?'

'Make it quick. Angelo, relieve the prisoner of his gun. He can double up with you till we join the rest of the troop.'

'Now just wait a doggone minute, Cap'n. I ain't no outlaw!'

'You made off with gold that didn't belong to you. In my eyes, that makes you as guilty as the rest of those rogues.'

The old man took off his hat and slapped his thigh with it. 'Is that a bluff, or do ye mean it for real play?'

'He was taken against his will, Burke, and well you know it,' snapped Angelo. 'Besides, you might just have need of his gun if we run into those Apaches again.'

Burke made an angry sound in his throat. 'Just get him back to the column! Right now we're sitting targets out here!'

9

Abigail and Lieutenant Feathersham were waiting by the chuck wagon as the captain and the others approached.

Tumbleweed tapped Angelo on the shoulder. 'Wut in tarnation is she doin' way out here?'

'She wants to make sure I really am one of the good guys.'

Angelo brought the gelding to a halt and the old man slid from the horse and stretched. The lieutenant looked Tumbleweed up and down with a puzzled frown.

'Wut ye gawkin' at?' the old man asked.

Before the lieutenant could answer, an excited bark came from under the wagon as Mr Jinx ran out to greet Angelo.

'Wull, cut off my legs an call me Shorty, if it ain't Mr Jinx,' Tumbleweed said with a gleam in his eye. The dog greeted the old man, yapping excitedly and wagging his tail. Tumbleweed crouched and rubbed the dog's ears. 'Ye still lookin' after the big fella?'

Mr Jinx responded with a loud bark.

They reached the banks of the River Pecos early afternoon. The trail ran northwards on a slight down-slope with a sheer rock escarpment rising to about forty feet or so, which broadened into an open hillside littered with large rocks. It was perfect ambush country. The troop headed along the gorge, which gave them ample cover from the sun. Tumbleweed and Mr Jinx were riding in the chuck wagon while Abigail rode her mare alongside Angelo at the rear of the column.

After a while Lieutenant Feathersham joined them. 'Has the old man had a chance to tell you yet why he and the wagon were abandoned by the Randall brothers?'

'Not yet, Lieutenant. I'm sure he'll tell us when he's good and ready.'

Feathersham looked concerned. 'I

think the captain is expecting a full account when we — '

'*Up ahead!*' a trooper yelled.

About 1,000 yards in front there seemed to be what looked like a dead horse with several buzzards feasting on its carcass. A corporal took off to investigate. The birds were so intent on eating their fill that they hardly noticed the soldier as he hastily brought the mount to a halt.

'Git out the way, you sonsofbitches!' he hollered.

The large birds flapped their wings but made no attempt to abandon their meal. The corporal undid the flap on his holster and removed his pistol, pointed it skyward and fired two shots. They were finally persuaded to take flight.

Angelo turned to the lieutenant. 'The damn fool! If the Apaches didn't know we were here before, they do now!'

The corporal stood in the stirrups. 'Looks like one of ours, Capt — '

His voice cut off as a bullet drilled

him through the neck.

'*Take cover!*' yelled Burke.

Angelo pulled the Winchester from its boot and leapt from the saddle. He steadied Abigail's skittish mare while she quickly dismounted and grabbed hold of his hand. Then they ran for cover behind the chuck wagon, where Tumbleweed was grousing.

'Wut in tarnation's goin' on now? Can't a man get any sleep around here?'

'Shut up, old man, and stay low. We have ourselves a sharpshooter.'

The designated horse-handlers had gathered the mounts and dragged them towards the cover of some rocks while their riders found defensive positions. The driver of the chuck wagon sat aboard his high seat, uncertain whether to leave the vehicle or stay where he was in case he needed to make a run for it.

'See anything?' Burke asked in a low voice.

No one answered, and then the sound of a second shot echoed through the air.

With a scream, one of the troopers taking cover by the water's edge pitched over.

'He's way up on that ledge to the left of us, sir!' someone shouted.

'Do you think it's Apaches?' asked Abigail.

'Could be . . . or the Randalls. Either way, they've got the edge on us.'

Captain Burke ordered the men to fire on the ledge.

'You damn fool!' Angelo yelled. 'You're wasting ammunition, and that's just what they want!'

Burke broke cover and ran towards the chuck wagon. Another shot rang out from the top of the ridge, the bullet dug deep into the dirt just a few inches in front of him. He threw himself behind the wagon, landing at Angelo's feet.

'Damn your eyes, Angelo! You question everything I say! But can you do any better?'

'Well, if it was me wearin' those shoulder-bars, I'd sit this one out. We

95

can't go forward an' we can't go back. An' right now we ain't got anythin' to shoot at. But after dark . . . '

'Yes?' said Burke, despite himself.

'After dark he won't have anything left to shoot at, either.'

Burke considered that for a moment, then said, 'My own reasoning exactly.'

'I thought it might be.'

Burke turned away and yelled, 'Cease firing! Has anyone been hit apart from Murphy over there?'

'Don't think so, sir,' yelled the non-com.

'Then make the men comfortable. We're sitting tight until dark.'

★   ★   ★

There were disgruntled mutterings from behind a mound where several troopers, and Feathersham, had taken cover. They had been sitting quietly for over two hours now and the tension among them was becoming apparent.

'Keep the noise down over there,

Lieutenant,' Burke hissed.

Angelo decided to chance moving out into the open to get a better view of the sharpshooter's position. He picked up his Winchester and ran to Murphy's dead body, then propped him into a sitting position, using him as a shield. He shaded his eyes from the sun's glare, and scoured the skyline for movement. There was nothing. The area looked quiet.

'I think it's safe to come out now. Looks like whoever was up there has gone.'

'You sure?' Burke asked.

'Yeah, I'm sure.'

The men remounted and the body of Murphy was thrown in the back of the supply wagon. They moved off at a steady pace with two troopers scouting a mile ahead of the column. Tumbleweed complained about riding with a wagon full of corpses. The driver adjusted his neckerchief covering his nose and mouth. 'Tell you what, old man,' he snarled. 'I don't know which is worse, the smell from these here dead men, or the stink comin' from you!'

A full moon dominated the cloudless night sky as the troop stopped to rest beside the thin ribbon of a stream. Angelo took hold of his gelding's reins and led him towards the water's edge to drink. Abigail followed suit.

'You all right?' he asked.

'Sure,' she replied.

He looked at her in the moonlight and smiled. She caught the flash of his teeth and said, 'What?'

'Nothin'.'

'So you just grin like a village idiot for no good reason, is that it?'

'Well, if you must know, I was just . . . admiring you. Your grit. I mean, here you are, out in the middle of nowhere, Apaches breathin' down our necks, and do you complain about it? Not one bit.'

'Why, thank you, kind sir. But maybe you're overlooking the one reason I'm not complaining.'

'Which is . . . ?'

'Because I'm here with you,' she said softly.

Hearing that, he grabbed her tiny waist and pulled her towards him. Her eyes softened as she gazed into his, and closed when his lips gently touched hers.

The softest scuff of boot-leather distracted him.

'Sorry to bother you, Angelo,' the lieutenant interrupted. 'But . . . '

Angelo pulled away from what was almost but not quite a kiss. 'What is it?' he asked as Abigail concentrated on watering her horse.

The lieutenant blushed to the ears. 'I'm sorry, I didn't mean to, uh . . . I mean, I had no — '

'Forget it,' sighed Angelo. 'What do you want?'

'The captain has decided to make camp for the night. Just thought you ought to know, so that you can see to your horse and find yourself a good spot to bed down.'

10

Angelo carried his saddle towards the chuck wagon, where the cook was preparing a meal. Mr Jinx was gnawing on a bone next to Tumbleweed, who was sitting by the fire he'd prepared, stirring what looked like a thick stew in a large skillet borrowed from the cook's supplies. He took a wooden ladle, scooped up some of the liquid, and took a sip.

Angelo drew in the aroma. 'It sure smells good.'

'Sit ye down, it'll be ready in a few minutes.'

Angelo felt the old man watching him covertly. At length Tumbleweed said, 'Yer moonin' after that gal, ain't ye? I can tell. Wull, it ain't healthy.'

'Quit your gripin', old man, and tell me somethin' I don't know!'

After the meal, Angelo lay back and

rested his head on his saddle. He took out the makings, rolled a cigarette and lit it with a glowing twig from the fire.

He gazed at the stars in the clear night sky. As he exhaled the smoke, he got to thinking that if it hadn't been for the old man, he would have been well on his way to Tombstone by now. But just like Mr Jinx, Tumbleweed seemed to be in need of a friend. And if the truth be told, he'd become quite attached to the pair of them.

At first light, Angelo kicked Tumbleweed awake.

'Eh? Wut in tarnation are ye up so early fer?'

'I'm going to ride with one of the scouts for a day or two.'

He swung aboard the gelding and allowed the animal to pick its way through camp, until Captain Burke suddenly appeared in his path. 'I hear you are going to do a little scouting,' he said.

'What of it?'

'Nothing. It's probably a wise decision under the circumstances.'

'Oh?'

'Yes. Last night I couldn't help but notice you with Miss Abigail down by the river. You would be well advised to remember that she is a lady, and not one of the dollar whores you're probably used to. Just remember your place, and keep well away. She doesn't need some low-down saddle tramp taking advantage of her. Do I make myself clear?'

Angelo spat off to one side. 'I've got six ways of dyin' sittin' low on my hip, and you've given me cause to use every one of 'em, Burke. But I ain't gonna let you rile me, fella. Leastways not today.'

Burke's top lip twitched nervously as he stalked off to join the burial detail.

'I wouldn't pay too much attention to him, Angelo.'

Angelo hipped around just as Feathersham came out of the slowly retreating shadows. 'It's just his way.'

'He should have stayed at the fort, pushin' his pen. He's not cut out for leadin' men.'

The lieutenant pointed at two mounted men a hundred yards or so upriver. 'Those two will be scouting today. You decide who you want to go with.'

Angelo gave a short, sharp whistle and Mr Jinx came trotting over to him, wagging his tail. 'Ridin in the wagon has put a few pounds on you, boy. Runnin' around with me for a couple of days will soon get rid of it.' He looked toward the top of the gorge. 'Which one will be ridin' up there?'

'That'll be Sergeant Hogan. Trooper Scott will be taking point.'

'OK, I'll ride with Hogan,' Angelo said, heeling the horse into a walk. He gave a curt nod as he neared the soldier. 'You ready?'

'Ready as I'll ever be.'

Hogan was a big man, three inches taller than Angelo, and he weighed close to 200 pounds, mostly muscle. They ascended the hill at a slow, cautious walk, their eyes everywhere at once. It was slow going, and the gelding stumbled once and almost took a tumble. 'Easy

103

there, big fella, we're almost there,' said Angelo, gently stroking the neck of the skittish horse.

At last they reached the summit. The ground was covered in shrubs and clusters of broom-weed. They had a good all-round view of the area, which showed no signs of danger. Hogan dismounted and crouched to better inspect the ground.

'What is it?' asked Angelo.

'Hoof prints . . . unshod ponies, 'bout six of 'em.'

'Which way are they headed?'

Climbing back into the saddle, Hogan said, 'Looks like they're headin' for the hills to the east of us. Probably miles away, by now.'

Angelo moved to the edge of the gorge, and could see that C Troop was on the move again.

They kept at a slow pace, always keeping a couple of miles between them and the column. At noon, the column stopped to rest.

Hogan reined his horse to a halt and

turned to Angelo. 'Looks like the cap'n's takin' a break. We might as well make the most of it. If you can collect some wood from that thicket over there, I'll prepare us a pot of the best coffee you've ever tasted.'

Angelo made a small fire next to a clump of rocks which gave them ample protection from the midday sun.

While the coffee was brewing, Hogan added a generous amount of Scotch whisky. 'Give it another minute, and it'll be perfect. Lessen you're Temperance, that is?'

Angelo sat two tin cups by the fire. 'The way I feel right now, fella, I could drink the full pot all by myself.'

'That's what I like to hear,' Hogan said as he wrapped his kerchief around his hand, lifted the coffee from the fire and poured. 'There's sweetenin' in my sack if you want it.'

'No, it's fine the way it — '

Angelo was cut short by the sound of a rifle being levered. Mr Jinx jumped up and growled.

A young Apache came from behind the rocks carrying a Henry rifle braced against his hip. Angelo figured that, with the warrior's finger clearly on the trigger, it would be foolish to make a move on him.

The Apache's small frame wavered slightly as he turned the rifle on the dog. Angelo quickly grabbed Mr Jinx around the neck. 'Easy, boy. It's OK.'

The warrior looked to be in his late teens. His dark eyes showed no emotion as he turned the rifle back towards the two men and mumbled something in his native tongue.

Hogan turned to Angelo. 'You speak Chiricahua?'

'Nope. But I think it's obvious he wants us to lose our hardware.'

Without saying another word, both men loosened their gunbelts and let them slip to the dirt.

Angelo looked at the buck and wondered where he'd come from and what he was doing way out here all by himself. It was then that Mr Jinx started growling, and Hogan suddenly stiffened. 'He's brought company!'

Angelo followed the line of his companion's gaze and cussed. They were being watched by fifteen mounted Chiricahua Apache warriors who had appeared as if out of nowhere.

It was hard to remain calm, but Angelo knew better than to show the gut-tightening fear he was feeling. The Apaches would take it as a sign of weakness and punish it accordingly.

A warrior at the center of the line moved his pony forward. It was then that Angelo noticed that the Apache was doubled up with a dark-haired woman. When the Apache was level with Angelo and Hogan, he brought his pony to a halt and the woman slipped from the mount. She was about thirty or so, her dark skin and facial features suggesting Mexican heritage. She glared at the two white men.

'I'm Camila, Ulzana's woman. I also translate for him.'

Hogan spat grimly. 'Ulzana. Yeah,

I've heard of that sonofabitch. He's nothin'
more than a jumped-up renegade Injun,
with a handful of followers.'

Camila forced a smile. 'I'd watch my
tongue if I was you, soldier blue. It
would be easy for my man to pluck it
from your mouth.'

Before Hogan could reply, Angelo cut
in, 'She's right. That kinda talk could
get us both killed, soldier, so button it!'

'What do ya mean . . . *could* get us
killed?'

'If he wanted us dead, he would have
done it already.'

'Enough!' Camila yelled and then began
conversing with the young Apache in
Chiricahua. She returned her gaze to
Angelo and said, 'Ulzana respects you.
He saw you and your wolf kill four of
his warriors while the soldier blue cow-
ards stood by and did nothing.'

'Wolf?'

'Your dog look like wolf, and a
white wolf is strong medicine to the
Chiricahua.'

'What else?'

Camila conversed once more with the Apache leader. His tone seemed to suggest that he was getting a little irritated. 'Ulzana say he has the four gringos and the gold you seek. He say he will trade them for the new rifles and ammunition you are carrying in the wagons.'

Angelo was taken aback. 'Rifles? What rifles?'

Camila frowned. 'Don' play games, señor. The rifles that the gringo Quincy told us about.'

'Tell Ulzana there are no rifles. The man called Quincy lied to him.'

His answer didn't seem to go down well with Ulzana. He dismounted and walked up to Angelo. His nut-brown skin was smooth and flawless. His long black hair was partially covered by a red bandanna. He was a head shorter than Angelo and the only clothing he wore was a loincloth and high-top moccasin boots.

He began talking again, but this time in broken English. 'The white eyes,

Randall, told me that the bluecoats have many new rifles. So why you say different?'

'The Randall brothers would've told you anythin' to avoid a fight.'

Ulzana appeared to be deep in thought for a moment. Then he said, 'We will get the truth from the bluecoat chief. If your words are twisted like a snake, I will know soon enough.'

'You want to talk with Burke? What do you think you can you achieve by that?'

'I will make deal with him. You can lead us safely into the bluecoat camp.'

Angelo thought fast. He assumed that Ulzana had many more warriors hidden. He looked at the array of weapons they were carrying, and noticed that several had rifles that were old and ill-kept. The only decent weapons on display was the Henry repeater that the young Apache had used when the two men were taken by surprise, and the one in Ulzana's hands, and they were probably short on ammunition for these.

'We will ride under a white flag and talk to this man, Burke.'

'Not a good idea, chief. There will be no deal. Burke isn't the kind of man you can talk to. He won't listen.'

Ulzana smiled. 'You are wrong. When he sees the gold and the white-eyes that he is hunting, then he will trade.'

The young Apache leader made a hand gesture to one of his mounted braves. 'Now *you* will see.' The warrior turned his mount and rode back down the trail, then out of sight. He returned moments later with one of the prisoners. Angelo immediately recognized him, it was Quincy Randall. He was tied at the wrists and stagger-stumbling along behind the Apache leading him towards the others.

He spat as he caught sight of Angelo, then cussed, 'Sonofabitch!'

The warrior yanked on the rope forcing Quincy to his knees. He clenched his teeth and glared at his captor, then back to Angelo. 'I swear, if he . . . does that one more time, I'm gonna . . . wrap this rope around his scrawny . . . red neck and choke the life out of him.'

Angelo walked a little closer, and then looked down at Quincy with contempt. 'Where're the others?' he asked.

'If you . . . mean Tom and the . . . boys . . . they're b-back there a-ways. Except for Brad, that . . . is.'

Angelo grimaced. 'Yeah, we saw what they did to Brad.'

'Well then, you could . . . say we have us a . . . situation, big fella. It'll be interestin' to see what happens next,' husked Quincy.

Angelo turned his attention back to Ulzana. 'OK, we'll try this your way. But let me tell you somethin', chief. The cap'n's the kind of man who'll shoot first and ask questions later, if he bothers to ask 'em at all — even if you are carrying a white flag.'

He and Hogan remounted and turned toward C Troop. 'Get the rest of captives ready to move out along with the gold, and follow me. Stay well back,' Angelo told Ulzana. 'But close enough so that the cap'n can see at first glance, you've got what he wants.'

11

When C Troop came into view Angelo saw that they had already taken up defensive positions with their backs against a large rock formation. The wagons were being used as barricades with the horses and men safely behind them.

Ulzana brought his group to a halt. 'You go now. Talk with white chief. *Dále'é Sháa.*'

Angelo glanced at Camila for a translation. '*Dále é Sháa* mean you have until the sun rises in the sky again. At first light, Ulzana wants an answer.'

The young chief drew up alongside Angelo and held out an arrow. 'Take this as sign that my words are straight. Hand it to bluecoat chief and tell him, give us what we want, and we can go our ways without bloodshed.'

Angelo took the arrow and nodded as

he heeled the horse forward, Hogan riding right alongside him.

He was grim-faced as he rode the grey gelding to within a couple of hundred yards of the barricade; not because of the thought of having to deal with Captain Burke, but because Abigail was caught up in this dangerous mess and there would be no way to guarantee her safety.

Burke, Feathersham, Tumbleweed and Abigail hurried forward to greet them. When he was level, he reined to a halt and dismounted.

'What's happening?' Burke demanded. 'Those are Apaches out there!'

'Yup,' said Angelo. 'And they've got the men and gold we've been after. We can have 'em, too — for a price.'

'I don't cut deals with Indians.'

'I've already told 'em that. But if we don't give 'em what they want, we can kiss the gold goodbye.'

'What are their terms?'

'Simple enough. They want rifles and ammunition.'

Burke laughed. 'Are they crazy? Do they really expect me to hand over our guns to them?'

'Yes, they really do.' He produced the arrow that was tucked inside his rifle boot and handed it to Burke. 'He gives you this as a sign that his words are straight and true. If you give him what he wants, he'll let us to go home in peace.'

Burke took the arrow and gazed at it for a moment, then threw it to the ground. 'And we're supposed to trust his word?'

'It looks to me as if we don't have much choice, Captain,' said Feathersham.

Burke flicked him a contemptuous glare. 'I'm not going to give in to some jumped-up Apache buck. You got that, Lieutenant?'

'That jumped-up Apache buck, as you call him, can wipe us out at the blink of an eye,' said Angelo. 'He's got enough men to do it, too. I counted fifty, at least. You've got till daybreak to come up with somethin'.'

He brushed past the captain and Abigail followed him. 'Why are you ignoring me?' she asked. 'Have I done something to offend you?'

'Best if you keep your distance, ma'am. That way it will keep my feelin's from — '

'From what?'

'I got to be honest, Abigail. Every time I get really close to you, I feel like I-I — '

'Go on.'

Angelo looked around for kindling to start a fire. 'Look, if you don't mind, I'd rather be on my own right now. I have a lot of thinkin' to do.' Mr Jinx sat and extended his paw. 'Yeah, you can stay, boy. You're not the one that's confusin' me.'

★   ★   ★

By first light the encampment was alive with activity.

Captain Burke was talking to the lieutenant over by the chuck wagon as the men went about their duties. Tumbleweed and Abigail were resting against the rockface eating a hasty breakfast while they still had the chance.

'Ye want some chow?' the old man asked when Angelo finally showed his face.

'No thanks.'

About a mile from the camp, lined up on a hilltop, were a small group of Ulzana's warriors. On spotting them Angelo hustled over to the captain and lieutenant. 'Have you made your decision, Cap'n?'

'Oh yes,' said Burke. 'I know exactly what I'm going to do!'

'Good.' Angelo picked up the arrow that Burke had thrown to the ground the previous evening. 'Lift this in the air. They'll see it as a signal to come forward.'

Burke took hold of the arrow. Using both hands, he raised it above his head. 'Like this, mister?'

'Yes, that'll do it.'

Then, to everyone's amazement, Burke snapped the arrow in two.

Angelo snatched the pieces from Burke's hand. 'You sonofabitch, you're gonna get us all killed!' He held the pieces as if they were one and waved them in the air. The small group of Apaches turned their mounts and rode off. They never saw Angelo's signal.

'I must say, Captain,' Feathersham said stiffly, 'Your actions today will not go unnoticed. I'll be making a full report. If any of us get out of this alive, it will be no thanks to you.'

'Do as you will, Lieutenant. Just remember one thing. The colonel would have us both court-martialed if we'd handed over guns to the Apache.'

'Better to give 'em a few of our guns than to have us all butchered,' Angelo scowled. 'Leastways we'd get what we came for, the outlaws and the gold. Or had you forgotten about that?'

Burke took hold of his binoculars and followed the progress of the departing Indians. 'I'll think of some other way of getting the gold and the scum that took it, without giving up anything to those savages.'

'There's no talkin' to you, Burke. You're stubborn as a mule, and just about as smart.'

He stalked over to his horse and picked up his saddle.

'Leave it,' Abigail said as she handed him the reins to her horse. 'You can take mine, she's ready to go.'

'You best keep your head down and stay out of sight,' he advised. 'I'm goin' to try and talk to Ulzana, and see if I can salvage somethin' from this mess. If I'm not back within the hour, you'll know I've failed.' He climbed into the saddle. 'Tumbleweed, you look after Mr Jinx for me. He's a good dog when treated right.'

'Don't ye worry none 'bout the dug. Ye'll be back before ye knows it.'

Angelo swung the horse around and heeled the mare into a lope. He headed up the hill to where the Apaches were last seen. Even before he reached the summit, an arrow whipped past his head, and as he drew rein and hipped around, he spotted an Apache already stringing a second arrow to his bow.

He dismounted quickly and threw himself behind a rock, dragging his Colt from leather as he went. An arrow dug into the dirt next to his left thigh. He rolled over and saw that it was Ulzana himself who'd fired the shot.

Camila appeared beside the Apache leader. 'It would be wise to put away your gun.' She beckoned him to follow as she moved toward the large group of warriors. He holstered the pistol and cautiously tagged along behind her.

Ulzana kept a watchful eye as Angelo closed in on the warriors. The five captives were lined up close together, kneeling on the ground with their hands bound behind their backs with rope.

'Angelo, you have to help us, you're the only one that can get us out of this mess!' Quincy pleaded.

Ignoring him, Camila said, 'Ulzana

says you are either very brave or a fool to have come back after insulting him.'

Angelo directed his speech at Ulzana. 'It wasn't me that broke the arrow; it was that damn ass of a cap'n.'

'It does not matter. Ulzana has taken the actions of the soldier blue chief as an insult. Now he is after blood.'

Two warriors closed in on the five captives and dragged Jimmy to his feet. 'What are you goin' to do to him, you red sonsofbitches?' Tom bellowed.

One of the warriors struck Tom on the back of the neck with the shaft of his lance. Tom cried out and keeled over into the dust.

There was nothing any of them could do save watch helplessly as the two Apaches tied Jimmy spread-eagled to four stakes in the ground.

'You don't have to do this,' Angelo told Camila.

'An example must be made,' she replied. 'Now, go. And tell the bluecoat captain that his stupidity has just cost the life of this young one — and that his death will not be the last.'

Angelo climbed into the saddle as the small group of Apaches encircled young Jimmy and pulled out their knives. He took in the grisly scene, then swung around the corner of the rocks and made his way down the narrow trail, trying hard to block out the screams that followed him every yard of the way.

12

Abigail and Tumbleweed rushed to greet him as he stepped down from the saddle. 'Are you all right?' asked Abigail.

'Not as you'd notice,' he replied, handing the reins to the old man. 'Where's Burke? He's got a lot to answer for!'

Tumbleweed pointed to the lean-to he'd set up a little ways from the main camp. 'Burke can wait. You look like you need to be alone awhile. Thure's some coffee brewin', too.'

Knowing the old man was right, Angelo wandered over to the fire, took the weight off and then rolled himself a cigarette. Sensing his somber mood, Mr Jinx lay quietly beside him with his head resting on his lap. But try as he might, there was nothing Angelo could do to wipe out the sound of Jimmy's screams. He flicked the half smoked cigarette on to the fire.

Lost in thought, he failed to see Abigail watching him until he finally heard the jingle of her spurs as she turned to walk away. Then he broke his long, moody silence. 'No, wait! Abigail ... stay a while. I reckon I could do with a little company right now.'

'Are you sure? Tumbleweed said not to — '

'I'm sure,' he cut in, and then he added in a low, choked voice, 'Tumbleweed didn't see what I saw out there.'

Mr Jinx lifted his head and watched as Abigail sat beside Angelo.

'Do you want to talk about it?'

'I reckon not.'

'Are you sure? It might help.'

'I watched a young man die out there and there wasn't a single damn' thing I could do to help him. Right now I don't feel too proud of myself.'

'You're a good man, Angelo,' she said. 'You'd have helped him if you could.'

'I know. But somehow that doesn't help.'

'It will . . . in time. Right now you're too upset to think straight.'

'Let's just talk about something else,' he growled.

She nodded. 'All right. Such as . . . ?'

He took his eyes off the flames and allowed them to settle on her. He thought, *Damn it, girl. If you only knew how I felt about you.*

Without warning she asked, 'Do you ever wonder what it would be like to soar up amongst the stars?'

The question did what she'd been hoping it would do — it distracted him from his miseries. 'There's lots of things I wonder about,' he replied, and then added hesitantly, 'For a start, I often wonder about you.'

'Me?' she asked. 'What do you wonder?'

'I wonder what you'd do if I kissed you again,' he said softly.

All at once she grew very, very serious, and when at last she broke the sudden silence, her voice came out softer even than his. 'Why don't we find out?'

Well, there it was. An open invitation. For a brief moment he was lost for words. He thought, *Well, what are you waiting for? Kiss her, you idiot. You might never get another chance like this.* But then her expression changed subtly, and he knew that she'd seen something in his eyes that he didn't even realize was there himself.

'No,' she said gently. 'Let's wait. This is neither the time nor the place, and when it *does* happen between us, I want both to be right. Besides . . . '

'What?'

'Your mind's still out there, isn't it? With that poor man they killed.'

He put his eyes back on the fire. 'Yeah.'

'That will pass,' she assured him, and something about the way she said it made him believe it completely. 'This dreadful *situation* will pass. And then it will be *our* time.'

'That,' he said earnestly, 'is something I look forward to.'

★ ★ ★

At the crack of dawn Angelo rekindled the fire and was busy preparing coffee when Burke strode over, looking distinctly ill at ease.

'A word, Angelo?' he said tersely.

Angelo met his gaze. 'I've got a couple of good ones for you, Cap'n. Massacre. Slaughter. Defeat.'

Burke's jaw muscles worked furiously, but he held his temper. 'We need to talk,' he said. He turned and walked off a few paces so that he could stare out across the prairie. Angelo, curious, went after him.

'The Apaches are watching us from the hilltop on our right flank,' said Burke. 'They could attack at any moment.'

Angelo nodded.

'Then I think it's about time we set our differences aside, don't you?'

He turned to face Angelo and offered his hand.

Angelo hesitated just a moment, then

took it. 'Agreed.' He put his eyes on the distant slope. 'I've done a lot of thinkin' this mornin', Cap'n, and for what it's worth, I think you made the right decision. Givin' Ulzana the guns *would* be a big mistake.'

'Which leaves only one option,' said Burke. 'Let him try and take them — and make him pay heavily for the privilege.'

'Either that, or we could take the fight to *them*.'

'Attack Ulzana, you mean?'

'Well, it's that or make a run for it.'

Burke winced. 'Either way would be suicide.'

'That's why I think we'll go with one final choice instead.'

'Well, don't keep me in suspense, man. What is it?'

'You'll know soon enough,' Angelo replied mysteriously. 'Are there any boxes in the supply wagon that's big enough to fit the size of a rifle?'

'Yes, I should think so, why?'

'I'll need two of 'em.'

'What do you plan to do?'

Ignoring the question, Angelo continued, 'Move the supply wagon about a hundred yards out with the two boxes inside, along with a box of shells. Make sure you take the cover off the bows, so Ulzana can see what he's getting.'

'Are you proposing to trade with them?'

'I'm gonna *trick* 'em,' Angelo corrected. 'Rope ten of the horses together and have 'em tethered to the wagon. I'll do the rest. Oh, and before I forget, have a loaded rifle inside a marked box so I know which one to open.'

'You do know there'll be hell to pay if this goes wrong.'

'Cap'n, there'll be hell to pay if we don't at least try it.'

Burke thought for a moment, then turned and gestured Feathersham over and passed along Angelo's instructions. Feathersham gave Angelo a long look, then nodded and said, 'I'll see it to immediately.'

'What are *you* going to do?' asked Burke.

Angelo said, 'I'm gonna get me a cup of coffee, then make contact with Ulzana. And after that, I'll be hoping to hell that he takes the bait.'

13

Tumbleweed watched as his friend moved off toward the Apaches on the hilltop. 'He'll be back befer ye knows it,' he said, patting Mr Jinx's head.

Ulzana's men let Angelo get within fifty yards of the crest of the hill, just close enough to let him see the promise of death in the way they held themselves. There were a dozen of them, but no sign of Ulzana. Briefly he considered the wisdom of the course upon which he'd set himself. If it all went wrong, he could very well end up paying for it with his life.

He eased the gelding to a halt and yelled, 'Ulzana, I cannot see you, but I know you can see me. Look over toward the soldier blues, there is a wagon. Inside that wagon are guns and ammunition! There are also horses for you! Bring the yellow metal and the captives and we will trade! Now I will go and wait.'

He was slowly turning the horse back down the trail when a gunshot tore through the early-morning air. The gelding reared up, almost throwing Angelo into the dirt. 'Easy fella,' he said as he swung back to see Ulzana's silhouette rising from the jagged skyline, holding a rifle.

'I hear your words, Liga Ba'cho,' called Ulzana. 'Go. Soon we will follow.'

Rattled by the shot and knowing how easily it could have punched him out of this life and into the next Angelo started the gelding moving again, at the same slow pace as before. Up ahead, he noted, everything was in position.

Burke along with Feathersham, Sergeant Hogan and six troopers, were waiting by the wagon as Angelo reined in his horse and slid from the saddle. 'Lieutenant, when the Injuns turn up with the prisoners and gold, you take charge and get 'em behind the barricade as quick as you can.'

'Yo! Anything else?'

'Yeah, make sure your men don't do any shootin'. I don't want to be caught in crossfire.'

The wagon driver looked over his shoulder. 'What do you want me to do?'

'When I give the word, head for the barricade as if the Grim Reaper was on your tail.'

The driver nodded. 'Don't worry. Once I crack the whip, you'd better hang on for dear life.'

Angelo eyed Burke, sitting on the tailgate, and joined him. 'I thought you'd be behind the barricade by now, ready to take charge of the gold and prisoners.'

'What, and miss out on you getting one over on that no-good renegade? No, I'll stick around here if it's all the same.'

'Be my guest.' Angelo sat patiently watching for the Apaches as he took a swig of water from his canteen. He noticed Burke was in rather a strange mood. Maybe their new alliance had something to do with it. Whatever it was, he was only too pleased that Burke was going along with the plan.

Tumbleweed moseyed over to the wagon and screwed his eyes at Angelo. 'Whut in tarnation's goin' on? That sumbitch corporal down thur's grinnin' like a jackass eatin' cactus and nobody's tellin' me nuthin'. It's like I wasn't even here.'

'What the hell are you doin'? Get back with the others.'

Tumbleweed lowered his head and began to saunter back toward the rest of the men, muttering darkly as he went. 'I might be old, but not too old to know whun I'm not wanted.'

'And keep Mr Jinx in check,' Angelo called after him. 'I don't want to have to worry about him neither.'

'Here they come!' someone shouted.

Ulzana and ten of his warriors came down the trail at a trot. In tow were the eight packhorses carrying gold, and the prisoners on foot with their hands bound behind their backs. Camila rode alongside the young Apache leader, who carried a lance with a white rag tied at the head.

'Remember, Lieutenant, get the gold and the prisoners over to the barricade as soon as I give the word,' Angelo said as he stood and followed Burke beside the two boxes.

The Apaches stopped a few yards from the wagon and dismounted. 'I see Liga Ba'cho has brought horses. Has he also brought the rifles?' Ulzana asked.

Angelo was at a complete loss as to why the Apache kept calling him by such a strange name. He looked to Camila for an answer. 'Liga Ba'cho?'

'You are named for your dog, white-eyes. Liga Ba'cho means White Wolf.'

Angelo rubbed the growth around his chin and smiled. He liked the idea of the Apaches giving him an Indian name. But after this day it wouldn't be a name they'd remember with any fondness. 'Yes, Ulzana, I have your guns.'

The young leader signaled one of his warriors to go take a look.

Angelo hadn't anticipated anyone else checking the boxes. 'Whoa there!'

The Apaches froze, watching him suspiciously.

'The glory of holding the first rifle should go to you, Ulzana.'

Before the warrior could get close enough to inspect the rifles, Ulzana shouted something in his native tongue and the warrior stopped and rejoined his group. The young leader moved cautiously toward the wagon, shifting his gaze from left to right.

Angelo opened the box the lieutenant had scratch-marked with a piece of rock and pulled out the rifle. Raising it high above his head he yelled, 'Look, Ulzana. Fine rifles for you to take back to your people.'

Ulzana smiled. He jumped on to the back of the wagon and took hold of the rifle.

'OK, Lieutenant,' Angelo said evenly. 'You know what to do.'

The lieutenant and his men quickly moved off with the prisoners and packhorses.

Ulzana crouched and rested the rifle on the side of the wagon, then began rummaging through the box, obviously looking for more.

Angelo quickly came up behind the Apache and grabbed him by the hair. He yanked his head back, then to the side and followed through with a head-lock. Ulzana tried elbowing his attacker, but couldn't make contact as the grip around his neck tightened.

Angelo then skinned his six-shooter and thrust the barrel at the back of Ulzana's head. 'Hogan, get someone to take the horses back behind the barricade. And hurry!'

The warriors looked helplessly on, not daring to retaliate for fear of hitting their leader by mistake. Camila, however, rushed forward. 'What are you doing? You're no different from the rest of the bluecoat pigs!'

Even though Angelo felt badly for the

138

young woman, he could show no remorse for his actions. 'I'm sorry, *señorita*, but we can't allow your man to run loose with army issue carbines. Now, you're welcome to come with us, or you can stay right here. Either way, it's all the same to me.'

Ulzana growled, 'You think you can just take me, white-eyes?'

'I just did. But don't worry, I don't mean you any harm. As soon as we're well on our way to the fort, I'll let you go. These are my words of truth.'

Ulzana gave a little laugh. 'My braves will kill you all long before then, white-eyes, and these are *my* words of truth!'

Their exchange was cut short when Burke intervened. 'OK, mister, step aside! I'll take it from here. I'm going to show this renegade the error of his ways!'

As Burke undid the flap on his holster and pulled out his pistol, Angelo's blood went cold. 'Damn it, Burke!'

'Let him go!' said Burke. 'One wrong

move and I'll *shoot* the heathen sonofa-bitch!'

'Captain, I suggest that whatever crazy idea you've got floating around inside that head of yours, you'd be wise to forget it.'

Ignoring him, Burke grabbed hold of Ulzana's throat and looking him in the eye said, 'You should have known better than to pit your wits against us, you red devil! You're mine now, and I'm going to make sure you hang high for your crimes!'

Angelo swore. 'I might have known you wouldn't miss the opportunity of taking a renegade like Ulzana back to the fort as your prisoner! Hunting glory, Burke?'

'Think whatever you like. One thing's certain. This savage's raiding days are over.'

Ulzana's warriors began moving closer to the wagon. Angelo knew it would only take one stupid mistake for the small band of renegades to get the upper hand.

Making a snap decision Angelo moved quickly, shoving Burke away from his prisoner and slamming him hard in the gut. Burke groaned and fell to his knees.

In the same moment an arrow skimmed the side of the captain's head. A shallow furrow appeared as he fell sideways off the wagon and into the dirt.

The sudden attack on Burke distracted Angelo and Ulzana took full advantage of it. The Apache threw a punch that caught Angelo clean on the jaw and sent him reeling over the boxes and sprawling on to the wagon bed.

Ulzana was on him like the devil on sin. He dragged Angelo back up, kneed him once, twice, a third time, hard in the stomach. The air left Angelo in a rush and at least one rib popped. Suddenly he was powerless to defend himself and with sudden, unholy relish, Ulzana knew it. The Apache grabbed him by the ears, held him steady, rammed his knee up into Angelo's face.

There was a jet of blood that stained the Indian's leggings, and then Angelo's eyes rolled up into his head.

The driver panicked when he saw what was happening, and with a swift snap of the reins brought the team into a frenzied dash.

The unexpected jolt unbalanced Ulzana and he fell to the side of Angelo, who was half-dazed but still trying desperately to get to his feet. The two exchanged blows as they were thrown around by the unsteady motion of the wagon, which was now heading away from the barricade. In the heat of the struggle, Angelo desperately tried to take control, but found it difficult to get the better of this young Apache who was proving to be an even match for him.

The wagon slammed over a fold in the trail and Ulzana fell sideways, coming up hard against the wagon's sideboard. Angelo, clinging to consciousness for all he was worth, rolled over, pushed to all fours and then, hugging his busted rib with one arm, threw himself at the other man. The wagon rattled and shook as he landed on Ulzana, empty boxes slipping and sliding this way and that, and he punched him in the head.

The Apache snarled, shook his head as if he were trying to rid himself of a pesky fly, and made a clumsy grab for him. Each sought a hold on the other, but with the see-saw motion of the wagon it was like trying to fight on the deck of a storm-tossed whaler.

The wagon veered to the right, leaving the beaten track, and hit a steep incline which threw both men into the air. Angelo bounced heavily off the tailgate and on to the bed, knocking the wind out of him and finally knocking himself unconscious. Ulzana landed awkwardly and tumbled over the side, narrowly escaping the churning rear wheels.

Leading the Apache's pony to where he'd fallen, Camila reined her mount and jumped down to help her man to his feet. He grabbed the mane of his pony and heaved himself up on to its back, then headed toward his warriors.

Realizing the Apaches weren't giving chase and were, for the time being at least, no longer a threat, the wagon driver slammed on the brake and pulled hard on the reins until the horses came to a gradual halt.

Sergeant Hogan quickly made his way to the wagon and peered over the side at the unconscious Angelo.

Still shaking from the almost uncontrollable wild flight, the driver wiped the beads of sweat from his face with his kerchief. 'Looks like he's all done in, Sergeant.'

Angelo began to stir. He raised his hand to block the sun from his eyes and cringed as the sharp pain of a broken rib ricocheted through his body. 'What . . . what happened to Ulzana?'

'He decided he didn't want to stick around.'

'He's gone?'

'Yeah, he's gone all right,' Hogan said

as he helped Angelo to his feet.

Angelo looked toward the horizon to see if he could catch a glimpse of the renegades, but saw nothing. He tried to take in what had happened. Only a few moments ago they'd had the upper hand. But once again Captain Burke's ability to disrupt well-laid plans without even trying was more than he could grasp.

'Ulzana won't let this insult slide,' he croaked.

They watched the lieutenant riding toward them on the captain's horse. Burke was lying unconscious over the pommel. 'Is he dead?' Hogan asked.

'No, but he's lost a lot of blood. Give me a hand to get him down from here. We need to stop the bleeding as quickly as possible.'

Hogan reached for the driver's canteen and poured a little water over his bandanna. After he'd cleaned the dirt from around the wound the captain began to stir.

'You're gonna be OK, Cap'n,' he said

as he dabbed the moist bandanna over Burke's dry lips.

Feathersham tied the reins of Burke's mount to the rear of the wagon and climbed up and sat beside the driver. 'Try and keep him still, Sergeant. OK, let's move out.'

The driver released the brake lever, flicked the reins and the wagon moved off at a steady pace, heading for the barricade.

14

After carefully inspecting his wound Captain Burke glared at Angelo. 'I'll not forget what you did back there, mister,' he snarled. 'You almost got me killed!'

'Your damn' fool attempt to play the hero nearly got us *all* killed!' Angelo returned hotly. 'Christ Almighty, Burke, did you *really* think Ulzana's men would have given us safe passage out of here, knowing what you had planned for him when we reached the end of the trail? First chance they got — full dark tonight, like as not — they'd have hit us just as hard as they could. And why? Because they had no reason *not* to! They'd have wiped us out, all save one or two, whom they'd allow to survive only so they could take the story of what had happened back to the fort. The rest would be just about as dead as a man — or a woman, comes to that — can get!

Wincing with pain he propped himself against the side of the wagon. Knowing it was useless to reason with such a pompous ass, he decided the best thing for him to do would be to keep quiet and concentrate on regaining his strength for the conflict that lay ahead.

As Angelo limped off to join Abigail and Tumbleweed, Burke grabbed the front of Hogan's shirt and drew him close. 'I want that saddle tramp in irons, and put with the rest of the prisoners. No one's to talk to him, and that goes for Miss Abigail too. You got that, Sergeant?'

'He's got no such thing, Captain,' said Feathersham. 'That man is absolutely right on the money, sir. You jeopardized this entire company by what you did out there, and since you're clearly in no fit state to maintain command, I am taking over until further notice.'

Burke's eyes went wide. 'What? What was that?'

'You heard me, Captain.'

'Damn you, Feathersham, I'm wounded, not dead! I can still carry out my duties as good as any man around here.'

'Really, sir? It seems to me that that blow has severely impaired your judgement.'

'Why, you — '

'For once just do the decent thing and shut up, Johnny!' said Abigail, storming over.

'Who are you to take that tone with me?' Burke demanded.

'I may not have come from West Point, but I know the evidence of my own eyes. I know we are in the devil of a situation here and I know also that your actions have made it considerably worse! Turning Angelo into a scapegoat won't make it any better, and I will see that my father hears the truth of this as soon as we get back to the fort!'

Burke bridled. 'I resent the implication of your words — '

'That is because the truth has a habit of *hurting*!' she replied forcefully.

Lieutenant Feathersham gave her a sympathetic smile, then turned to Burke and said, 'She's right, sir. You made a mistake. A wise man would own up to it and make sure it doesn't happen again.'

Burke looked angrily at him. 'Let's get one thing clear, mister. Just because you pulled me out of harm's way back there doesn't give you the right to dictate to me what I should or shouldn't do.'

'Perhaps not. But may I respectfully suggest that you look to your responsibilities toward the men under your command, sir. They in turn are looking to you for leadership. With the right leadership they may survive this nightmare. Without it they may decide to follow someone who inspires greater confidence.'

Burke's eyes bugged. 'Good grief, man, you're talking mutiny!'

'I am merely pointing out what could happen, sir, if you don't get down off your high horse and start thinking about others instead of yourself.'

Burke's mouth opened and closed a few times. 'I'll see you court-martialed for that remark!'

'Please do, sir. I shall be more than happy for this entire story to come out in the open.'

'Enough!' Burke yelled.

'Yes,' said Feathersham. 'More than enough. Now, get some rest. As of this minute I am assuming command. If you don't like that, sir, I suggest we put it to the vote. Then you'll see just how popular your leadership has made you!' He turned and fixed Hogan with a glare. 'Sergeant, detail a couple of men to guard the captain. I want him watched at all times, and I'll hold you personally responsible if he gets in my way.'

★   ★   ★

As night approached the camp was in a state of vigilance. Lieutenant Feathersham secured the perimeter while everyone else cautiously went about their duties. Several of the troopers led the horses down by the river to drink, and those who were stood down played cards or grabbed some well-earned sleep.

A young trooper who was guarding the prisoners sat with his back against a water barrel, playing his mouth organ.

After tending Angelo's wounds and strapping up his ribs, Abigail snuggled up to him and listened to the tune the young soldier was playing. 'What a pretty tune,' she remarked.

The trooper nodded. 'Yeah, my father taught it me. The tune and this here mouth organ is the only memory I have of him since he passed on.'

Abigail looked at the young soldier with empathy. 'I'm sorry to hear that.'

'Oh, it's OK; it was way back in 'sixty three. He was killed at Chattanooga, crossing the Tennessee River under the command of General Thomas. Ma said he was a hero. But I guess there were a lot of heroes that day.'

'Yeah, I guess so.' Angelo dug into his shirt pocket for the makings and rolled a cigarette. 'You got a light?'

The trooper pulled a match from his pocket and struck it against the stock of his carbine. Angelo leaned forward and lit his cigarette. 'Thanks. That tune, what's it called?'

' 'Going Home'. I can play it again if' n you like?'

Angelo gave a curt nod and the young trooper put the instrument to his mouth and began playing. Some of the troopers gathered around to listen. Taking into account all that had happened over the past few days, it was hard to believe how serene the atmosphere was around the camp.

Abigail stood and began to sing along to the music.

There's a place in my mind, that I'm hoping to see.
It's far, far away, made for you and for me.
I know in my heart, if we get

through this fray.
The struggle will be over, at the
break of the day.

'Thanks, miss,' the trooper said, clearing his throat with emotion. 'My ma used to sing it to me, just like that, when I was a kid.'

Abigail smiled and gently patted him on the shoulder. 'You're welcome.'

'Oh, so damn touchin'. It makes me wanna puke,' Tom Randall said, spitting to the side.

Quincy laughed. 'Yeah, and before you know it, the big fella here'll be playin' house.'

Angelo locked his gaze on him. 'Why don't you save your jokes for Ulzana, Quincy? He might find 'em a lot funnier than I do.'

Tom looked over Quincy's shoulder. 'Ulzana! Ha, we've seen the last of him. I mean . . . I heard someone say he'd run off with his tail between his legs.'

'You can believe what you want,' Angelo said. 'But I figure Ulzana is

154

plannin' his next move even as we speak.'

'All the more reason why you should think about our original plan!' Quincy offered.

'Meanin'?'

'Hobble your tongue, Quince,' Tom snarled. 'We don't need him.'

Not shifting his gaze, Angelo said, 'Oh, I get it, you're still plannin' on makin' off with the gold, huh?'

Quincy winked. 'Why not, big fella? The renegades are pissed at the soldier boys, not us.'

'Yeah, let's put our differences behind us, and get the hell out of here,' Frank said, holding out his bound wrists. 'C'mon Angelo, what do you say?'

'You're not going to listen to them, are you?' asked Abigail.

'You of all people should know that I wouldn't go back on my word. I made a promise to your father and I intend keepin' it.'

'Then to hell with you, mister,'

Quincy barked. 'You can rot, as far as I'm concerned.'

Just then Tumbleweed came over with Mr Jinx by his side. The dog lay at Angelo's feet while the old man crouched, then pulled out his pipe and tobacco. 'It's such a darn peaceful night, tonight.'

Angelo nodded. 'Yeah, it's a pity, there's a storm a-brewin'.'

'Storm? I don't see nuthin',' Tumbleweed said, looking upward. 'It's so darn clear.'

'I wasn't talkin' about the weather, old man. Those renegades are out there. I just know it. I can feel 'em watchin' us.'

The old man edged closer to Angelo. 'I wish ye wouldn't talk like that, young 'un, yer givin' me the willies.'

'Yeah, well with that in mind, it'll be best if'n you keep your wits about you and your gun close by your side.'

★　★　★

In the early hours no one saw the dozen Apache warriors crouching in the shadows north of the camp. Ulzana's eyes narrowed as he picked out a target in the moonlight and then released the bowstring, which sent an arrow hurtling toward his unsuspecting victim.

Ryan, the bucktoothed kid, gasped in horror as he stared at the shaft protruding from his gut. The metal arrowhead dripped with blood as he keeled over.

The remainder of the prisoners panicked, and huddled up behind the wheel for cover.

'Jeez, Quincy, we're sittin' ducks here!' Frank shrieked as an arrow skimmed overhead.

Tom pulled frantically at the chains. 'For crissakes, somebody, get us out of here!'

The lieutenant, with his pistol drawn ran toward them. He called to a trooper who'd taken cover behind a rock, 'Help me get them loose!' The lieutenant managed to get one of Frank's wrists free when Sergeant Hogan came barging over.

'What the hell are you doin', sir? The cap'n gave strict orders they were to remain in chains, no matter what.'

'It may have slipped your memory, Sergeant, but I'm in command now, not the captain. Now get out of my way and let me get on with it.'

'I can't let you do that, sir.'

The moment the trooper freed Tom from his shackles an arrow hit him in the chest. He cried out as he slumped forward and died. Tom reached down for the key then quickly began to free Quincy.

The lieutenant glared at Hogan. 'Sergeant, I don't have time to argue about this!'

The lieutenant went to open the remaining metal cuff on Frank's wrist, when Hogan grabbed hold of him by the shoulder and punched him square on the jaw, knocking him off his feet.

Abigail gasped as she watched the lieutenant's head bounce off a rock where he landed. 'Have you taken leave of your senses, man? You've just struck an officer,' she yelled, as she rushed to the lieutenant's aid.

Hogan pushed past her, but was taken aback when Angelo came at him swinging wildly with his fists, one of which caught him hard in the gut. He let out a deep groan, then, catching his breath, retaliated by grabbing Angelo by the throat and looking cruelly into his eyes. 'That's gonna cost you, mister!' he grated.

Angelo felt a sharp bolt of agony when Hogan prodded at his busted rib.

He dropped hard on to one knee, and there was nothing he could do to stop the irate sergeant from rushing off toward the horses.

Tumbleweed and Abigail dragged the unconscious lieutenant out of harm's way over by a clump of rocks, while the prisoners collected weapons from the dead and took up defensive positions. Quincy crouched in front of Angelo, blazing away with a six-shooter at anything that moved among the shadows.

'You don't look too good there, big

feller. By the time this little skirmish is over you might be beggin' us to include you in our little plan.'

'Go to hell!' Angelo yelled above the gunfire.

'Have it your way.' Quincy laughed. 'I won't be askin' again.'

'Glad to hear it.'

'Do ye wants me to put a bead on that no-good sumbitch sergeant? I can plug him from here. Just say the word.'

Angelo thought for a moment, then decided that a quick death from a Sharps carbine would be an injustice. No, Angelo wanted to see this bully squirm a little before he walked through the gates of hell. 'Leave him to me, old man. You just concentrate on looking after Miss Abigail and the lieutenant.'

'Ye got it, young 'un.'

Hogan saddled up one of the mounts and shiftily looked around before securing the bulky saddlebags.

Angelo watched with curiosity. Hogan might have been many things, but Angelo hadn't pegged him for a coward, so why was he attempting to ride out under the cover of darkness while the whole camp was in disarray?

The noise of gunfire and the war cries from the Apaches spooked the horses. They pulled back, trying to free themselves from the rope to which they were tethered. Hogan's horse reared up, almost throwing him from the saddle when a trooper stepped in and grabbed the bridle with both hands.

'Easy there, boy. It's OK, Sarge, I've got him.'

Hogan lashed out with the reins. 'Get out of my way, you damn fool,' he yelled, then spurred the gelding forward.

He didn't get far.

Ulzana released an arrow from the darkness that whacked the sergeant in one beefy shoulder. As he cried out his horse stumbled and he fell from the saddle. 'Sonofabitch!' he yelled.

Before making their way back into the night shadows, Ulzana signaled to one of his men to finish off the helpless sergeant.

The renegade was only too happy to be given the chance to snuff out the life of this vulnerable blue-coat. He ran forward with his knife unsheathed until Hogan could almost smell his sour breath. He struggled to open the flap of his holster, but his attempts were in vain as the steel of the long blade cut deep into his flesh, slicing him from ear to ear.

The renegade threw up his arms and gave a triumphant yell. Two rounds in the chest from Angelo's pistol made sure his celebration was short-lived.

15

Half a dozen soldiers lined up behind the barricade and waited grimly for the second assault. The guard, who'd been on duty at the front of the wagons, lay dead with several arrows in his back. No longer under guard, Captain Burke ran up and down the line, yelling orders.

'Can ye believe that sumbitch?' asked Tumble-weed disgustedly. 'He's about as crazy as a lizard on a hot stove.'

'Yeah, maybe that head wound hit him harder than we thought,' Angelo said as he reloaded his pistol. 'How's the lieutenant doin'?'

'He's got a lump on his head the size of a turnip. He's conscious, but I figure it'll be a while before he's thinkin' straight again.'

'Damn!'

With the lieutenant out of action,

Angelo knew Burke would try to retake command, and in his present state of mind could prove to be their downfall.

'Would you believe it?' Quincy growled, looking at the gold bars that had spilled from Hogan's saddle-bags. 'The darn fool was tryin' to run off with some of our gold.'

That explained everything to Angelo. The sergeant had seen a chance to make off with the gold and had taken it — or tried to. 'Well, it did him about as much good as it'll do you, happen you stick to your plan. No good'll come of it.'

Quincy glared at Angelo. 'Well, we all know where you stand, big fella. Just remember when the time comes, keep out of our way . . . or you'll — '

'Enough!' Burke yelled, drawing his saber from its scabbard and raising it high. 'All right, you men, get ready to move out and be quick about it.'

The soldiers glanced at each other uncertainly. One of them said to Angelo, 'What do we do? I mean, I thought the lieutenant was in charge!'

Before Angelo could reply, Burke snapped, 'Well, you thought wrong! Now get those mounts saddled or you'll answer to me! Got that?'

'Stay where you are!' snapped Angelo. 'And that goes double for you and your boys, Quincy! In the first place, no one's about to let you ride out of here with that gold, and in the second, you'll be lucky to get all of a yard before Ulzana cuts you down!'

The trooper who'd been playing the mouth organ gestured with a trembling hand to the ridge south side of the camp. An instant later an axe split the back of his skull. A look of disbelief shadowed the young soldier's face as he slumped at Burke's feet.

Burke gulped. 'Take up defensive positions, we're under attack!'

'Ye don't say.' Tumbleweed said, reaching for his carbine.

Once again Ulzana and his men came out of the shadows, using whatever means they had to pick off their enemy.

One of the renegades charged forward with his knife raised high, ready to strike at Burke, who was unaware of the danger. The Apache let out a loud war whoop, and then lunged at the captain, who spun around and fell sideways into the dust. The Apache crouched, bringing the knife down in a murderous thrust.

Burke grabbed his attacker's wrist but the Indian fought back with everything he had. Seconds passed, and then Burke felt the tip of the blade prick his throat. Warm blood spilled and he immediately started to panic. Then, from out of nowhere, Mr Jinx leapt at the Apache, locked on to his forearm and drove him backwards into the dust.

Burke scrambled to his feet, retrieved his pistol, took careful aim and shot the warrior three times in the chest.

As the Apache twitched, Mr Jinx gave a short bark and ran off.

A renegade carrying a short lance managed to get inside the camp perimeter unnoticed by climbing down from a ledge, but was then taken by surprise when he came face to face with one of the soldiers.

They looked each other up and down. Then the Apache glanced at the soldier's carbine, which wasn't cocked, and made his move. He raised his lance and hurled it with such a force that it almost knocked the trooper off his feet as it sliced through his chest.

Kneeling behind the cook's supply boxes, Angelo discharged his six-shooter until he heard the dull sound of the hammer striking a spent cartridge. He felt around his gunbelt to replenish his pistol, but to his dismay realized he was out of ammunition. His timing couldn't have been worse. Ulzana and two of his warriors were advancing on him.

The renegade leader stopped in his tracks and fired his carbine, missing his target by inches. Angelo quickly rolled over to escape the arrow which another had released from his bow. It whizzed overhead and stuck firmly into the chuck wagon's water barrel. The third renegade was about to throw his knife when Ulzana grabbed him by the arm and spoke in his native tongue. The warrior looked fiercely at Angelo, then took off into the night.

Angelo couldn't understand what had just taken place. Ulzana had spared his life, that much was for certain. But why?

Mayhem around the camp grew more intense as the death toll mounted. Ulzana lowered his weapon. 'Liga ba'cho, I did not know it was you in my path. Earlier, you had my life in your hands, and you could have killed me but chose not to. Now I have spared your life, so we are even.'

Angelo gave a slight nod, knowing when and if they met again, things wouldn't be so friendly. He watched Ulzana and his companion dash toward the rocks and out of sight.

Another one of the renegades struggled to release the pistol from a dead soldier's clutches. He froze when he heard the sound of a loud snarl. His head whipped around, and looking over his shoulder he saw Mr Jinx running toward him. Before the warrior could get to his feet, the dog pounced, tearing fiercely at his flesh. The Indian shrieked and then tried for his knife, but it never cleared leather. A bullet from Tumbleweed's carbine drilled through his skull.

Even though Ulzana was nowhere to be seen, more Apaches joined the skirmish. Abigail snatched up a discarded pistol, checked to make sure it was fully loaded. She took aim and fired at the hostiles. Slow and deliberate, she kept on pulling back the hammer and squeezing the trigger. 'I think I got one!' she yelled.

The old man scratched his beard. 'Wull if'n ye didn't, yer sure givin' 'em somethin' to think about.'

The attack ended as quickly as it had begun when Ulzana and his warriors dispersed among the rocks.

'Cease fire!' Burke yelled. He dusted himself down and adjusted his coat and saber belt. 'Lieutenant, get the men ready to move out.' When there was no answer he narrowed his eyes. 'Where the hell is Feathersham? He should be here!'

A shout came from one of the troops, 'Sir, don't you remember? The lieutenant was injured!'

Burke gave a blank look. 'Ah yes, er ... get the wagons loaded, we're moving out.'

'Liga ba'cho!' Ulzana yelled from a safe distance high up amongst the rocks. 'Liga ba'cho, I know you can hear my words! Tell the white-eyes chief to give us what we want ... horses, guns and bullets! We have tested your strength! You are no match for us! Give us what we want, Liga ba'cho, or when the sun is next high in the sky, we will show no mercy!'

For some moments an eerie silence fell upon the encampment as Ulzana's words unsettled the men.

'Did you hear that, Cap'n?' a trooper yelled. 'We're dead meat, that's for sure.

What we gonna do?'

'I'll tell you what we're *not* gonna do,' Angelo told Burke softly. 'We're not pullin' out. If Ulzana wants our hides so bad, let him come an' get 'em.'

'Angelo's right, Johnny,' Abigail said.

Burke studied for a moment. 'I can go along with that . . . for now!'

Angelo glanced at the silhouette of the hills. 'If Ulzana is true to his word, we've got until midday. That should give us enough time to come up with somethin'.'

Just then a heavily built corporal walked up to Burke and saluted. 'Sir, things ain't too good. We've taken heavy losses.'

'How many?'

'Seven dead, including Sergeant Hogan.'

Burke frowned. 'Hogan?'

'Yeah, the sumbitch wus tryin' to sneak off wuth some of the gold,' Tumbleweed drawled.

Looking at the Randall brothers, Burke sighed. 'It would seem we can trust no one where the gold is

171

concerned. Did I overhear you saying something about leaving?'

'First damn' chance I get,' Quincy replied grimly.

'Very well. Corporal — get the prisoners secured for the night!'

Tumbleweed, with Mr Jinx by his side, went over to Angelo. 'That feller is two cents short of a dime. Whur the hell does he think they're goin' to run to? Ain't nothin' out thur but them savages. And I knows fer a fact, the Randall brothers ain't gonna chance runnin' into *them* again.'

16

The sound of activity around the camp stirred Angelo from a shallow sleep. The pain from his injuries seemed worse than ever. He opened his eyes and watched the soldiers go about their business.

With a smile, Abigail knelt and handed him a mug of lukewarm coffee. 'How are you feeling?'

He reached for the mug with both hands and took a sip. 'I'm getting' there,' he replied. 'What's goin' on?'

'Johnny is preparing to move out. He's had everyone up since the crack of dawn, packing everything away. Gramps has made space in the supply wagon for you and Lieutenant Feathersham.'

'What?'

'You can't ride. Not in your condition.'

'The hell I can't!'

Angelo heard footsteps behind him and turned as Tumbleweed came up. 'I see yer awake, young 'un. I've fed Mr Jinx and I've made yer a bed in the wag — '

'I know what you've done, old man.' Angelo cut in, tossing his blanket to one side and getting unsteadily to his feet. 'And I ain't gonna be caught lyin' in no bed when we're attacked.'

Abigail breathed an impatient sigh. 'And how do you expect to heal, may I ask, if you are being jolted around on the back of a horse?'

'She's got a point, young 'un,' Tumbleweed said. 'You got a busted rib there. Somethin' happens to bust it up some more an' — '

'Don't *you* start. My mind's made up. Now, I'd be obliged to you both if you stop fussin' and saddle my horse . . . seein' how I can't do it for myself.'

'He's as stubborn as a mule, Gramps. There's just no getting through to him.'

'Reckon yer right, missy. It'll be best if'n I saddle his horse.'

Abigail wagged her finger. 'Don't blame me if you end up with a fever or worse.'

Angelo couldn't help but smile. He gently grabbed her hand. 'I'll be fine, and I promise if I feel giddy I'll ride in the wagon. How'll that be?'

'Promise?'

'I promise.'

Meanwhile, on the other side of the camp, Burke kicked at Quincy's feet. 'OK, get up. Going against my better judgement, I'm going to let you ride without restraints. But as a precaution you won't be carrying any weapons.'

'Well, that's mighty decent of you, Cap'n,' Quincy hissed. 'Why don't you cut our throats and be done with it?'

'Don't push your luck, mister or I'll have you back in chains before you know it!'

Tom nudged his brother. 'Touchy, ain't he?'

Quincy frowned. 'Yeah, well it ain't funny, Tom. That sonofabitch is gonna get us all killed if we're not careful.'

Captain Burke opened the water barrel beside the chuck wagon, took a ladleful of water and poured it over his head.

Close by, a group of troopers were discussing their predicament. 'We've lost over half the troop since we started out on this patrol, and with only ten men left, it might be best if we use the prisoners to help us. I say give 'em guns, and to hell with Burke.'

Burke took a towel from the chuck table and dabbed his face, then walked over to the group. 'You, trooper! Any more talk like that and I'll clap you in irons, too! In the first place, no one here gives a hoot about what you think. In the second, we've got enough to worry about with Ulzana breathing down our necks, without having to worry about the Randalls back-shooting us as well!' He then yelled over to the burly corporal who was tending to the horses. 'Corporal, organize a burial detail, and be quick about it; we'll be moving out as soon as you're through.'

He looked Angelo's way. 'What's the news on the lieutenant?'

'Why don't you check for yourself? He's in the supply wagon.'

As C Troop prepared to move out, Abigail took a canteen of water and some beef jerky and laid it on the wagon bed next to the lieutenant. She gave him a little smile as he began to stir.

'Where am I?' he asked, trying to sit.

'You took a nasty knock to the head.'

Rubbing his eyes, the lieutenant looked confused. 'I don't remember a thing.'

'Give it time, Robert; it will all come back to you. We'll be moving shortly, so try and get some rest. I won't be very far away if you need me.'

Burke peered over the tailgate. 'How is he?'

Abigail brushed his arm to one side and stepped from the wagon. 'I'm surprised you even care.'

'Why do you say that?'

'Don't pretend to be concerned,

Johnny. I know you too well. The lieutenant's condition has given you the opportunity to seek the glory you crave for . . . and at what price, I wonder.'

Burke moved away from the wagon, and called out, 'Angelo, a word if you please.'

Angelo pushed back his hat. 'What is it?'

'If we move out now we'll have a good few hours' start on Ulzana,' said Burke. He pulled a map out of his saddle-bags and hunkered down to unfold it. 'See, we can't go back the way we came, it would be too dangerous. We need to cross the river to get back on track. It's too wide here, so we need to find a spot where it narrows and we can cross it quickly.' He pointed to an area on the map. 'Heartbreak Pass is about two miles north of here. Seems like the perfect place; it's only about fifty feet wide.'

Angelo studied the map for a moment, then looked towards the hills. He knew Ulzana would be watching and wouldn't let them get away so easily. No matter where they crossed the river, they would be vulnerable.

Tumbleweed crouched beside the two men. 'Heartbreak Pass, are ye crazy?' he demanded.

Burke glared at the old man. 'Now what?'

'I've heard stories 'bout that place, and none of 'em good. The river's deep and thur's strong undercurrents. Only a fool would chance crossin' thur, specially wuth wagons.'

Burke's impassive gaze switched from the map to the old man. 'Good. Then there's less chance of the Apaches following. Besides, if we cross the river there, it'll save us almost a day's ride.'

'I just don't believe ye! Is thur anythin' 'tween those ears of yers besides fresh air?'

Burke folded the map and pushed it into his saddle-bags, then mounted his horse. 'No one's asking you to come with us, old man. You're welcome to stay here if you want.'

'Sumbitch!'

Sliding the freshly loaded pistol from its holster and waving it at the prisoners, Burke raised his voice, 'You will all be riding point, with you, Quincy, leading the spare horses. That way I can keep an eye on you.'

Quincy spat. 'Well, that's very thoughtful of you, Cap'n. I'm overwhelmed by your generosity.'

Everything was packed away, and there were still two hours before Ulzana's deadline. The men were tired and morale was low. The ragtag company, which was now only a remnant of what it had once been, sat astride their mounts waiting for the order to move out.

Angelo's face showed deep concern as he led the bay mare over to Abigail. 'I don't want you ridin' in the wagon, so I've had one of the men saddle your horse. Be ready to ride like the wind if need be.' Placing his hands on her shoulders, he looked deep into her eyes. 'As soon as we begin to move, Ulzana will realize there's no deal, and attack.

Stay close to me.' Giving Tumbleweed a curt nod, he said, 'You too, old man . . . stay close.'

Mr Jinx jumped up at him excitedly.

'Yeah and that goes for you too, fella. Don't you go wandering off, I might need you.'

The dog gave off a thunderous woof.

17

Burke stood in the stirrups and raised his hand. 'C Troop, get ready to move . . . move out!'

They started off in single file with Quincy, Tom and Frank in the lead, followed by Burke, then his troopers with the wagons at the rear. Angelo, Tumbleweed and Abigail rode side by side, flanking the troopers to the left.

When Heartbreak Pass came into view, the driver of the chuck wagon let out a yell. Angelo looked back to see him falling into the dust with an arrow in his chest. Ulzana and thirty of his warriors were close on their heels, riding at full gallop.

'Burke, you'd be wise to dismount the men and take cover.'

The captain ignored the advice and shouted, 'Follow me, men!'

'Darn fool,' Angelo snarled. Not

letting Abigail out of his sight, he heeled the gelding into a gallop.

The clattering of hoofs and the churning of wagon wheels were drowned out by the high-pitched war cries from the renegades as they gained ground.

Burke was the first to reach the point of crossing, but his horse was reluctant to move off from the riverbank. It reared up, lashing out with its forelegs. The captain dug his heels hard into its flanks. It neighed in protest, tossing its head from side to side. Burke tried desperately to gain control. Thrashing the beast's hindquarters with the reins, he finally managed to urge the horse into the water.

'Sir, the renegades have taken the chuck wagon!' someone yelled.

'Forget it! Keep moving!' Burke called back as he went a little further into the river. He'd gone only a few yards when an arrow pierced his side.

Terror leapt into his eyes as he stared at the blood trickling on to his holster and down his thigh.

Angelo grabbed the reins of the captain's horse, turned and headed toward a mass of mesquite and large rocks with Tumbleweed and Abigail following. When they reached cover, Burke tugged at the arrow. His eyes rolled, his limp body slipped from his horse.

Angelo jumped from the saddle. 'Abigail! You take the horses. Tumbleweed, give me a hand with Burke.' They dragged the captain over to a large boulder and propped him up.

A horse galloped into the enclosure, almost crashing into the rock face with two troopers on its back, one with an arrow buried in his shoulder. The rider climbed out of the saddle and helped his comrade dismount. They both scrambled for cover beside Captain Burke. 'I don't want to die!' the wounded man cried out.

'Shut up . . . no one's gonna die, you hear me?' his friend barked.

Frank rode low in the saddle trailing the supply wagon. At Angelo's insistence, the canvas cover had been removed in case of burning arrow attacks. As Frank got closer, he called out to the lieutenant, 'Throw me a gun, for Chris'sakes!'

Feathersham quickly glanced around the floor, but all he could see was the boxes of gold, sacks of flour and an array of assorted tools. 'I've only got my pistol!' he called back. 'Head for the rocks, I'll cover you!'

Frank never got the chance. A bullet tore through his knee and sent him reeling from the saddle and into the dirt.

The lieutenant crouched behind the sideboards, loosing off pistol fire at the Apaches. One of them fell over the back of his pony, blood gushing from a fatal head wound. Feathersham held on to one of the wagon bows and waited until the unmanned pony was close enough to reach. Then he swung around and jumped, landing awkwardly on its back. Seizing the mane with both hands, he turned the distraught animal and headed back to help young Frank.

The pony's hoofs threw up a cloud of

dust as it was brought to a sudden halt. Lieutenant Feathersham leant forward. 'Give me your hand!'

The outlaw rolled around screaming as the blood flowed from his shattered kneecap. 'I can't!' he called out, struggling to get to his feet.

Feathersham leaped from the pony. 'Come on, we need to get out of here!' Using all his strength, he lifted Frank up on his shoulder and carried him to the clump of rocks where the others had taken cover.

When Burke came to he looked down at the arrow shaft jutting from his side. 'It's bad, isn't it?'

'It's not good.'

'Can it be removed?' Abigail asked worriedly.

Angelo shook his head in frustration. 'If I try, I might as easily kill him as save him.' He ran over to his gelding and pulled the rifle from its scabbard, then dove into the prone position, rapidly firing at the renegades.

The wounded trooper glared at

Burke. 'You got us into this mess, you sonofabitch. I hope you're satisfied!'

Burke's irate expression was clear. 'Watch your tongue, trooper. Or by God, I'll have you court-martialed.'

The trooper snorted. 'You really think I give a damn? Take a look around you, Cap'n. This is all what's left of your precious C Troop. None of us are gonna make it outta here alive.'

Ulzana and his warriors charged after the stragglers who were out in the open. The driver of the supply wagon turned the team and headed for the river.

'No!' a trooper called out. 'You'll never make it, the current's too strong!'

The driver didn't hear him above the rattle and rush of wagon wheels.

Shouting over his shoulder to his brother, Quincy edged alongside the wagon, 'C'mon, Tom, here's our chance. The gold's ours for the takin'.'

Tom reined his horse to a slow trot and looked around. It seemed as if he were torn between following his brother or heading for cover with the others.

The renegades closed in, throwing an array of missiles his way. The spinning blade of a tomahawk buried itself between his shoulder blades. He tumbled from his horse, kicking, screaming and trying frantically to reach the wooden handle. A warrior gave a loud whoop as he jumped from his pony and drew a knife that claimed the scalp of the dying outlaw.

The wagon team, meanwhile, struggled to pull the heavy load through the hazardous water. When Quincy came level with the driver he reached for the handrail and heaved himself up on to the seat, leaving his horse free to head back to the riverbank.

The driver gave the outlaw a quick glance, then focused on the task of controlling the skittish horses across the river.

Quincy looked over his shoulder and caught sight of the boxes of gold lying on the floor. His eyes lit up when he saw the loose bars that Sergeant Hogan had tried to make off with. He climbed over the seat, and picked one up and kissed it.

'What the hell are you doin'?' the driver asked. 'Get up here and give me a hand with the horses!'

Quincy reached down, picked up a shovel and slammed it against the driver's head. The soldier slumped forward, falling from the seat and landing between the charging horses. The shock pushed them further into deep water.

Quincy started picking up the loose bars and placing them in a canvas sack when suddenly water started flowing over the sideboards. He sprang to his feet, dropped the gold and lunged for the driver's seat. He looked in horror as he watched the horses thrashing about trying to keep their heads above water.

Without warning the strong currents dragged the wagon under, taking everything with it. All that was left of Quincy and the gold was a few ripples on the surface.

Partway along the trail Ulzana stood

beside Camila, watching a handful of his warriors rummage through the contents of the chuck wagon. Several others rounded up the horses and collected the weapons from the dead.

Feathersham reloaded his pistol. 'We must look a pretty sorry sight about now.'

Angelo was inclined to agree but instead said: 'We can still give 'em hell.'

'What are they waiting for?' asked the wounded trooper.

This time Angelo didn't reply. Ulzana knew they were beaten. Now he planned to take his time finishing them off. 'How many rounds you got left, old man?'

' 'Bout a half-dozen.'

'I got about the same for my Winchester.'

'I still have my rifle,' said Abigail. 'And there's a full box of cartridges in my saddle-bags.'

Angelo hustled cautiously over to Abigail's horse. Mr Jinx followed him. As Angelo grabbed the carbine and shells he felt the dog's eyes on him.

When he could stand it no more he looked down into Mr Jinx's face. 'You're a good friend,' he muttered thickly. 'You've pulled me out of a good few scrapes, and I'm grateful. But when Ulzana gets here, you better high-tail it.'

The dog lowered his head and offered his paw. Angelo took hold of it, glanced away, cleared his throat. 'Now don't think I'm goin' all soft on you,' he said. 'It's just a little dust in my eye is all.'

Mr Jinx wagged his tail, as if to say he knew better.

Watching the exchange, Tumbleweed sniffed and wiped his eyes with his shirtsleeve. 'I guess you have some dust in your eyes too, Gramps,' Abigail said softly.

'Shucks, missy. This is all my doin'.'

'How so?'

'Wull, if it hadn't bin for me and my big mouth 'bout the gold, we wouldn't be in this fix.'

'It's no good blaming yourself. We all had choices,' Abigail replied.

Tumbleweed shook his head. 'It's all bin fer nuthin'.'

Angelo squatted beside the old man and began loading the Winchester with fresh cartridges. 'I wouldn't say it was for nothin'.'

'How do ye figure?'

'For one thing, I found myself a good friend in you. You might be a pain in the butt sometimes, but that counts for somethin'.' Angelo caught Abigail's eye and winked at her. 'And I've also found someone very special. So you see, old man, the way I see it . . . it hasn't been for nothin'.'

'Wull, all I can say is yer one crazy sumbitch.'

'Liga ba'cho, Liga ba'cho, do you hear me?' Ulzana hollered.

Angelo glanced at Mr Jinx, Tumbleweed and then Abigail. 'Well, I guess this is it. Wait here, this is my call.' He stood, then walked out into the open. 'I hear you.'

Ulzana held a lance as he sat tall astride his pony. His cold eyes studied

Angelo from head to toe.

'What're we waitin' for?' Angelo asked impatiently. 'Let's finish it!'

Ulzana hurled his lance. It stuck firmly in the ground several feet in front of Angelo. Angelo forced himself to stand tall and steady. 'Is that the best you've got?' he demanded. 'We've enough guns and ammunition to hold out for days, Ulzana. Many more of your warriors will die. Is that what you want?'

Ulzana grinned. 'The Apache could wait for days, until you are weak from hunger and you have no bullets for your guns. But we have taken what we came for. You are defeated, and in that I take great pleasure.'

Angelo frowned. 'So that's it? You're saying it's *over*?'

'It is over.'

'I thought the Apache way was to kill your enemy?'

'You thought wrong. There is nothing to gain by staying here.'

Angelo could see Ulzana's warriors moving down the hill toward them.

Camila rode a horse taken from one of the dead soldiers. She stopped alongside her man, then looked over at Angelo and smiled.

Angelo touched the brim of his hat. '*Señorita.*'

Then he heard a sound behind him and glanced over his shoulder, his gut tightening unpleasantly when he saw Burke standing a few feet away. 'You want somethin', Cap'n?' he asked, narrowing his eyes, his tone ice-cold.

Burke didn't respond. He dropped to his knees and pointed a finger at Ulzana. 'I'm dying,' he managed, 'and you were my undoing.'

Angelo grimaced. 'Get back with the others. You're not helpin' any.'

Burke's eyes widened as he undid the flap on his holster and pulled out his Army Colt. 'What's up, Angelo? You taking sides with the savage?'

'Damn it, man, it's over!'

Burke held the pistol in a two-handed grip, thrust out in front of him to the full length of his arms. Beads of sweat formed on his forehead as he leveled it at Ulzana. He pulled back the hammer and put his finger on the trigger.

Angelo rushed at him, trying to ignore the pain in his ribs. 'Are you crazy?' he bellowed, knocking Burke off balance. The gun went off, but the bullet fell short of its target, spraying dust just inches from Ulzana's feet.

A look of hate shadowed Ulzana's face. He quickly dismounted and signaled to his warriors not to intervene as he walked toward Burke, plucking the lance from the ground as he did so.

Again Burke squeezed the trigger and to his dismay, heard the distinct sound of a hammer striking an empty cartridge. Not taking his eyes off Ulzana, he cocked the gun and squeezed the trigger again.

Nothing but a faint click could be heard.

Burke let the pistol slip from his hand. He looked around with pleading eyes, but no one made a move to help.

Ulzana passed Angelo and stopped

only when his shadow draped Burke like a shroud. He prodded the captain with the tip of his lance. 'I cannot kill you, white man,' he said softly, and Burke gave a sigh of relief, hearing that. But then Ulzana looked meaningfully at the arrow in the captain's side and said flatly, 'You are already dead. You just don' know it yet.'

Knowing what Ulzana said was true, Burke's eyes widened, he managed a single croak of sound and then keeled over, dead.

Ulzana stood proud, clutching the lance as he looked at Angelo. 'Now, it is over, Liga ba'cho. I will return to my people and you are free to return to yours. I will not forget you, white-eyes. Maybe we'll meet again someday.'

Angelo nodded. 'Maybe.'

The Apache leader remounted his pony and led his band of men towards the hills, heading west.

Abigail rushed to Angelo's side, breaking step briefly as she passed Burke. 'Are you all right?' she asked.

His eyes met hers. 'I am now,' he said softly.

Tumbleweed and Mr Jinx walked over to them. The dog sniffed at the captain's face and gave a little bark. The old man spat. 'Ye gonna bury the sumbitch, or whut?'

Angelo eyed the old man. 'I guess.'

Tumbleweed pushed back his hat and scratched his head. 'Good, the quicker we get him underground the better.'

Abigail's brow creased into a frown at the old man's remark.

'Whut?' Tumbleweed asked with a puzzled look. 'Wull, we don't want to be givin' those darn buzzards gut rot, now do we?' An hour later shock began to set in. Angelo knew only too well that the long journey home would prove too much for some of them. The wounded needed medical attention, and without it the chances of infection were high. They were low on supplies, low on ammunition, and the outlook was bleak, the mood one of defeat and melancholy.

And then Mr Jinx pricked up his ears.

Angelo looked around. 'What is it, boy?'

The dog gave him a brief glance, then ran off toward the hills.

'Whut's gotten into him?' Tumbleweed said.

'Beats the hell outta me,' Angelo replied. 'At times he's a mind of his own.'

He sighed and went down to the river's edge, splashed water on his sweat-run face. It was hard to believe that only a few days ago he had been sitting by a campfire with Mr Jinx at his side, and neither of them had a care in the world as they'd watched an old man arguing with his mule.

'Mind if I join ye, young 'un?' Tumbleweed asked, following him down.

Angelo looked at him. 'If I remember correctly, those were the first words you uttered the night we met.'

'Whut?'

'Nothin'. Just reminiscin' is all.'

'Wull, ye can hark back to anytime ye want, but the fact still remains. Because of me, all yer hard-earned cash in the bank will be turned over to the colonel for his school and hospital. Yep, losin' the gold really stinks.'

'Stop your complainin' and follow me,' said Angelo. He made his way over to the abandoned chuck wagon, climbed over the side, took out his knife and prised open one of the floorboards to reveal the gold bars.

The old man's eyes lit up. 'Huh? I don't understand!'

'Late last night I took the liberty of moving the gold. After Hogan tried to run off with some of it, I figured if anyone else tried the same thing, they'd be in for a surprise.'

'So ye hid it in here, eh?'

'Well, with the help of Feathersham and Abigail. I couldn't have done it all on my own, not with a busted rib and all.'

'Wull, ye sneaky young pup. Who would've thought it? Is it all there?'

'Except for the few loose ones taken from Hogan, yeah.'

Abigail looked sheepish as she walked over and took hold of Angelo's hand. 'Happy now, Gramps?' she asked.

'Only one thing'd make me happier,' he replied. And sobering, he said quietly, 'Standin' up as best man at your weddin'.'

Angelo glanced at Abigail. 'I got a feelin' the colonel might have something to say about that.'

'I'm not so sure,' said Abigail. 'You kept your word, Angelo. He'll have to take that into consideration.'

'Well, let's eat this pie one bite at a time,' said Angelo. 'We've got to get back to the fort yet, and that's not gonna be easy.'

Suddenly they heard barking in the distance. Angelo shaded his eyes and looked over to the northern ridge; there, to his amazement, he saw Mr Jinx running ahead of two columns of soldiers, led by an officer on a dapple-grey mount. Lieutenant Feathersham joined the young couple to find out what was going on.

Angelo gave Abigail a tight squeeze. 'Will you take a look at that? I don't believe it!'

'It's my father!' Abigail yelled tearfully. 'I'd know his horse anywhere! He's found us, Angelo! We're going home! We're going home!'

THE END

We do hope that you have enjoyed reading this large print book.

Did you know that all of our titles are available for purchase?

We publish a wide range of high quality large print books including:
**Romances, Mysteries, Classics
General Fiction
Non Fiction and Westerns**

Special interest titles available in large print are:
**The Little Oxford Dictionary
Music Book, Song Book
Hymn Book, Service Book**

Also available from us courtesy of Oxford University Press:
**Young Readers' Dictionary
(large print edition)
Young Readers' Thesaurus
(large print edition)**

For further information or a free brochure, please contact us at:
**Ulverscroft Large Print Books Ltd.,
The Green, Bradgate Road, Anstey,
Leicester, LE7 7FU, England.
Tel:** (00 44) **0116 236 4325
Fax:** (00 44) **0116 234 0205**

Cassidy Yates had been stripped of his Sheriff's star by the townsfolk of Monotony. Leland Matlock's son had died, due to his error of judgement. Then Leland, ready to reveal information that could have shed new light on the sheriff's downfall, was shot. Cassidy believed that Leland's shooting was connected to the death of his son. So, rising to the challenge to uncover the link, Cassidy endeavoured to get that star pinned back on his chest where it belonged.

THE DEVIL'S PAYROLL

Paul Green

When bounty hunter John Harrison captures fugitive outlaw Clay Barton, he's persuaded by Maggie Sloane to allow the captive to lead them to the loot robbed from an army payroll. But Barton double-crosses them and the mysterious Leo Gabriel kidnaps Maggie. With a veteran Buffalo Soldier, Sergeant Eli Johnson, at his side, Harrison battles ruthless vaqueros and a Comanche war party to recover the money, re-capture Barton and rescue Maggie . . . but a surprise awaits him when he finally catches up with his enemies . . .

HELL ON HOOFS

Lance Howard

Arriving in Lancerville, John Laramie hoped to escape his old life as a man-hunter and settle down. But there he finds he's torn between the demons of his past and hope for a brighter future when a young woman seeks his help in getting rid of a vicious outlaw. Then the Cross Gang attacks him and the young woman's life is put in danger. But will it cost Laramie more to win than to lose in a deadly showdown?

TROUBLE AT MESQUITE FLATS

Will Keen

Arriving in Mesquite Flats, ex-New York businessman Bodene Rich is committed to Yuma Penitentiary for a vicious assault. He's released, in light of new evidence, and pardoned by Warden Bradley Shaw. On the day of Rich's release, Shaw resigns, but an unknown gunman then shoots him dead on the trail. Rich once again is in trouble. And, in a showdown, he's embroiled in a bloody gun battle, where the outcome hangs in the balance until the final shot . . .

HELL STAGE TO LONE PINE

Jack Dakota

At Lone Pine Ranch, young Ben Brewer wants to prove himself to the owner, Morgan Hethridge and his beautiful daughter Josie. But Hethridge's rival is scheming to take over Lone Pine ranch. To protect the land, Brewer faces the feared gunhawk Calvin Choate. A desperate situation, until old timer Whipcrack Riley steps in. Will his wily ways and his skills driving a stagecoach be enough to help Brewer once the situation gets really rough and the bullets are flying?

SHERIFF OF VENGEANCE

Rob Hill

With a failing farm, and with night-mare memories of the war, Clay Butterfield and his wife Rose Alice abandon life in the East. They join a wagon train bound for California. However, when their departure is de-layed, Clay finds out that a gunman is in town, intent on killing him. Instinct tells him to run, but to pro-tect Rose Alice, and make his new life secure, he rides into town to confront the stranger who wants him dead.

KU-783-857

Collins Lions

A Solitary Blue

As they turned the boat to head towards the dock, Jeff saw a blue heron standing on a little muddy point of land across the creek. The blue raised its head to look at them, its feet in the water and its feathers slightly ruffled, as if by a recent annoyance. He waited for it to take off, but it merely turned its back on them, looking out across the marsh, unconcerned, solitary, ignoring them with great determination.

Jeff looked back at Dicey. "You know who that bird reminds of? You."

Her expression changed, and he didn't know what he'd said wrong. Then he saw she was trying not to laugh. "I was thinking how much it was like you."

A Solitary Blue is the companion to *Homecoming* and *Dicey's Song*. Cynthia Voigt won the Newbery Medal for *Dicey's Song*.

Cynthia Voigt

A Solitary Blue

Collins Lions
An Imprint of HarperCollins*Publishers*

To Gail Paris
Editor ludorum,
editor egregia et fidelis

First published in the USA 1983
by Atheneum Publishers, New York
First published in Great Britain in 1985
by William Collins Sons & Co. Ltd
First published in Lions 1986
Seventh impression April 1991

Collins Lions is an imprint of
the Children's Division, part of
HarperCollins Publishers Ltd,
77–85 Fulham Palace Road,
Hammersmith, London W6 8JB

Printed and bound in Great Britain by
HarperCollins Book Manufacturing, Glasgow

feeling lay all over his body like a wet blanket, and he started to cry. He wrapped his arms around himself and cried.

Jeff knew he shouldn't cry, he knew he had to stop. The Professor, his father, didn't like crying, because he wanted things regular and even. He wanted a boiled egg every day for breakfast and his usual times in his study when nobody disturbed him. He had all of his classes in the afternoons so he could stay home and study in the mornings. After supper, he went back into his study to do more. Melody had explained that and Jeff knew how to keep the kind of quiet house his father wanted, the kind Melody always kept.

When Jeff was too young to go to school, his father took him to a day care centre, every morning. Melody picked him up in the afternoon, when she was free. Usually, that was on her way home to get supper. Sometimes, if the weather was nice, she would be free early and they would go to the zoo or to a museum or shopping together. If the day care centre was closed, she would take Jeff with her to her work, and he would colour at the table where she was talking. Once he started school, he could spend all day there. He even went to both kindergarten classes, the morning one and the afternoon one.

Melody wasn't free most of the time because she worked to make the world better. As he got older, she explained to Jeff how people were making the world worse. Industries dumped their rubbish into the water, into the rivers and into the Chesapeake Bay. Because of the rubbish, the water got too dirty to swim in, and the fish couldn't live there, and the animals who ate the fish died. People put dirty smoke into the air. Politicians and countries fought wars and murdered people with bombs and fire and even, if they wanted to, poisons. Not everybody was as lucky as Jeff, not everybody had a mummy and a daddy, not everybody had enough to eat, not everybody had their own rooms or got to go to Ocean City for a week every summer – but Melody could help those unlucky people. It was her job to help make things better because if she didn't, things might get worse.

That was sad and scary. It was that picture of the world getting worse that came to haunt Jeff when he woke up in the middle of the night and tried not to think about it. Sometimes, at night, Jeff wanted to go into Melody's room, just to hear her breathing, just to see her. But she had explained to him that the Professor didn't like to have his sleep disturbed, so he couldn't.

Melody didn't talk to the Profesor the way she talked to Jeff; she didn't talk to him very much at all. When she tried to, he asked her questions that she answered unhappily until he finally said, "It's not as simple as that."

Jeff, still crying, thought about his father now. He wasn't sure what his father liked. He knew what Melody liked, she liked lots of people at her

meetings, she liked Jeff to know about what was
going on in the world, she liked to hold his hand
outside the lion's cage and tell him about how the
lion's life used to be. She didn't mind if he was
sad or cried, because she would hug him. She
liked new people and new ideas, and sometimes
she worried about Jeff because he was too much
like the Professor, no matter how hard he tried.

All Jeff knew about the Professor was that he
liked things regular and even. He didn't like
feelings, and crying. Melody said he wasn't much
of a father, and now – Jeff cried quietly, alone –
he was all Jeff had. Jeff would have to stop this
crying.

He had stopped before the Professor got home at
five. He had stopped with a glass of milk, looking
out of the window over the sink through a cold,
sleety rain to the row of houses behind the row of
houses they lived in, looking out to the taller
buildings behind them, sticking up into the grey
sky like irregular teeth. The rain spattered on the
tin roof of the back porch.

When the Professor entered the kitchen and
put his worn briefcase down on the table, Jeff
turned round, holding the empty cold glass in his
cold hand. He watched his father open the envelope she had addressed to him and read the short
note once. He watched him throw the note and
envelope away, crumpled up, into the yellow

11

plastic wastebasket. His father didn't look surprised, his father didn't look unhappy, his father didn't look worried. His father didn't look anything.

"Did she leave you a note, too?" the Professor said to Jeff.

Jeff nodded. "Do you want to read it?"

The Professor shook his head quickly. "Is there anything for dinner?"

Jeff nodded.

"Can we eat at six-thirty?"

The Professor left the kitchen, but he forgot his briefcase. He didn't come back for it. Jeff heard him go into his study, which used to be a living room, back through the hall at the front of the house. What used to be the dining room was the living room. They ate all their meals at the Formica table in the kitchen. Jeff did his homework at that table too, because there was no room for a desk in his tiny bedroom tucked under the eaves at the back of the house.

That evening, after his father had left him alone, Jeff did homework. He did a page of mixed addition and subtraction problems; he copied out sentences into his French notebook, being as neat as he could. He boxed in all the verbs in the ten English sentences and then went back to find the subjects and label them with an S. He wrote a paragraph about lizards for science. He filled in the names of the original thirteen colonies on the social studies map, then memorized it. He worked carefully, because teachers liked neat, careful work. When he was finished, he gathered his books up into a pile and set them on the counter by the refrigerator, for the morning. He looked at the clock: six.

Jeff knew how to lay the table and how to get a hot dog dinner for himself and his father, because Melody often could not get home for dinner, when she had a meeting, or when she had a lot of work to do with a committee, or a demonstration to plan. Jeff and the Professor were pretty used to getting themselves a hot dog dinner. Jeff set the table, then cut up lettuce and tomatoes for a salad. He split the hot dogs and piled the slices of bread up beside the toaster. He put the bottle of salad dressing out on the table and the mustard, ketchup, and relish. He kept himself busy except for just a couple of minutes when he had nothing to do but wait; for these minutes he stood at the sink and looked out of the window into the darkening rain. Across their little square of cement yard, blocks of yellow light shone from the kitchens of the row of houses a street up. The tall shape of the humanities building of the university was all dark, and in the rain its edges merged fuzzily into the clouds. "But what will I do?" Jeff asked himself, inside his head.

He knew that if he stayed there, looking out, with room for questions to rise up in his head, he might cry again; so he took a warm sponge and washed down the draining board by the sink,

13

scrubbing it with Comet. He had lost his mother, he didn't want to run any risk of losing his father too.

When supper was on the table, Jeff went down the hall to knock on his father's door and say that everything was ready. Then he went back to sit down. The Professor always came right away and poured himself a glass of wine from the carafe in the fridge before he sat down to eat. After the Professor had tasted the wine, he lifted his fork and took a bite of salad. That was Jeff's signal to begin. When Melody was there, it had been her fork he waited for.

They ate without talking. After he had finished, the Professor put on some water to boil and took out the small Chemex pot. Melody had tried to get him not to drink coffee, she had told him all about caffeine and cancer in it, she had even made him taste some of the herb teas she drank; but he wouldn't change. "Coffee's addictive," she had warned him.

"Anything in excess tends to be addictive," the Professor answered. "The point is to avoid excess. Isn't it?"

"I can't talk to you," Melody said. "You already know all the answers." Her voice sounded as if she didn't think what she said was true.

"I never said that," the Professor said.

Melody didn't answer, just sat staring at her cup of tea; but Jeff saw tears come up in her eyes, so he went round to hug her.

★　★　★

14

But this night she was gone. Jeff cleared the table, then sat down again, watching his father drink his mug of coffee. The bright white light bulb in the kitchen shone on the straight white hair that lay across the top of the Professor's head and reflected off his big, square glasses. Jeff's father looked like a professor, Jeff thought, even though he knew every professor looked different. Jeff's father was tall and broad-shouldered, and he never put on weight no matter how much he ate. He had pale blue eyes and thin lips. His white eyebrows were almost straight, his nose hooked out where it joined his face. He looked, in his calm face, in his quiet way of sitting or slow way of moving, as if nothing could upset him. Jeff knew that his father would want to say something about Melody, so he waited.

"She's not coming back," the Professor said at last.

"I know."

"We'll rub along all right," the Professor said. "Although there will be a couple of changes."

Jeff felt alarmed. His father didn't like changes, his father couldn't change; Melody said that. "What changes?"

"We'll have to get someone to live in, a student, room and board in exchange for housekeeping and babysitting. We can't afford a maid and there has to be someone while you're so young. I'll move my books upstairs, to the bedroom, that'll give us a room for him." The Professor sipped at

15

his coffee. "I suspect we'll find it doesn't make much difference at all. Most things don't. I'll see if we can't find a boy, they're more reliable."

Jeff relaxed. The Professor always said things didn't make much difference, wouldn't make much difference. He said that when Melody talked about women's rights and signing anti-war petitions or endangered species. "Don't you *care?*" Melody would ask him, her voice ringing, her big grey eyes filled with feeling. She was fifteen years younger than her husband and had long, thick dark hair that she let hang loose down her back, all the way below her waist. "What about nuclear war?"

"That would make a difference," the Professor agreed, without any change of voice or expression. His mild blue eyes looked at his wife.

"Oh my *God*," she would say, turning away impatiently. Her dark hair rippled down her back. Her patchwork skirt whirled around her slender legs. When she was unhappy like this, Jeff didn't know how to comfort her.

Jeff went to the University School, where children of professors could attend without paying, but the children from other families had to be rich. There were sixteen children in his second-grade class, six boys and ten girls. One of the girls had a mother who taught maths at the university. Two of the other boys, Sean and Jason, had fathers there. Sean's father and mother both taught, physics and English. Jason's father

16

taught history too, only Jason's father taught American History and the Professor taught European. The boys weren't friends, because the parents weren't friends. Jason's father wanted to be chairman of the department, but the Professor had that job because he was older. Jason's father wrote articles that got published in history magazines, and he wrote reviews of history books for the Baltimore paper and sometimes the *Washington Post* too: Jason brought them into school for show-and-tell. Jason's father said the department was a shambles and that was why they didn't attract good students. Jason's father said the curriculum hadn't been changed since 1958, and it was out of date. Any man who didn't publish in his field, Jason's father said, could offer no leadership to his department. Melody agreed with Jason's father, but the Professor didn't pay any attention. "It wouldn't make any difference," he said and went back to the work he was doing.

That Melody had gone away didn't make any difference to Jeff at school. His father walked him over in the mornings anyway, and he went home by himself in the afternoons. He wasn't friends with the university children. The town kids never played with the university kids, because the children of professors weren't rich enough to have good toys, and besides, they were the geniuses of the class. Except Jeff, who didn't ask many questions, who did his homework neatly and handed it in on time, who sat quietly at his desk.

17

Jeff was never a favourite with the teacher, nor with the student assistants from the Education Department, but the town kids didn't like him even so, because he was a university kid. Jeff sat quiet and did his best to do exactly what the teacher said she wanted them to do. His papers were always perfect.

Sometimes Jeff wondered how everybody knew, right away, what kind of child you were. They all dressed in uniforms, grey flannel trousers, white shirts, and blue jackets for the boys, with a red and blue striped tie. The girls wore grey pleated skirts and white blouses and blue sweaters. Everybody looked alike, but just the same, everybody knew the difference.

That spring, after Melody left, the Professor found a student to live with them, a young man named Jackson. Jackson moved into the Professor's old study. For a month he did the shopping, vacuumed the house, saw to the laundry and meals. Jackson was thin, with long hair he tied at the back of his neck like George Washington and terrible pimples on his face that he tried to hide with a wispy blond beard. He almost never went out except to classes. He studied all the time, because he wanted to graduate *summa cum laude* and go right to graduate school without being drafted. At the beginning of May, he told Jeff he had exams and long papers coming up, so Jeff did the vacuuming and shopping and put fewer clothes into the laundry. Jeff wasn't tall enough

sandwiches, and I will be very sad and missing you.
But you are old enough now, and there are people
everywhere who need me, little boys like you who
don't get enough to eat and are hungry every night
when they go to bed. Imagine that, Jeffie. You
know how I feel about that. Or children with no
parents at all to take care of them and grown-ups
who can't help themselves and little animals hunted
down and wiped out and air and water made dirty.
I have to help the people who need me. I have to try
to make things better, for you and for all the little
children. You are big enough to understand. It is
such a big job that I will not be able to come back to
see you, so I have to say goodbye. Goodbye, little
boy, my own sweet Jeffie, from your sad

M.

M was for Mummy and for her own name,
Melody. Jeff read the note twice. He did understand about all the work she did, because she had
explained to him about how people had made the
whole world sick, all of nature, and it was the last
chance to make it better, or little children like
Jeff wouldn't have any world when they grew up.
He knew how sad it made her to think about
rivers or the lion in his cage at the zoo or the dirty
pavements and streets. He knew she couldn't be
happy unless she was doing something to make
things better – she said so.

But he didn't know why she had to go away to
do that. And not come back. A cold, frightened

8

1

When Jeff Greene was in second grade, seven and a half years old, he got home from school one Tuesday afternoon in early March, and found a note from his mother, saying that she had gone away and would not be coming back. He could read the note all by himself:

Dear Jeffie,

You know I love you best, better than anything. I love to come into your room when you are in bed, and read The Lorax *to you, and then kiss you on each big grey eye before you go to sleep. I am going away, but I'm not really going away from you. I will hold you in my heart, and you will hold me in your heart, and we can't ever be very far from each other then, can we?*

There are some hot dogs in the refrigerator. If you don't remember how to cook them for bread sandwiches, you will have to ask the Professor for money when he gets home and go and get some rolls. But you shouldn't bother him for unimportant things, so try hard to remember. You're my helper, my best assistant, you remember everything. You won't need to ask, will you?

I will think about you tonight, eating hotdog

7

Part One

to run the machines at the laundromat so Jackson still had to do that, and the cooking. Jackson cooked huge pots of stew that they could eat for two or three days in a row or spaghetti sauce or pot roasts you could warm up. The Professor didn't seem to mind, so neither did Jeff. But after Jackson had gone, the Professor told Jeff they'd have a better selection of possibilities in the autumn.

"You could get a girl," Jeff suggested quietly. Girls could cook, probably, at least as well as Melody. He thought a girl would clean the house to brightness.

"They tend to be unreliable," the Professor answered.

During the summer, the Professor concentrated on his research and Jeff amused himself. "Thank God you can amuse yourself," the Professor had often said. Jeff thought probably they wouldn't go to the beach for a week, the way they used to, because Melody wasn't there any more, but they did. They drove over to Ocean City on a Saturday morning and stayed in a one-bedroom apartment a block away from the water. Jeff played on the beach, digging, building castles, watching the people. The waves towered and crashed beyond him. In the mornings, the Professor took him across the road to the beach and left him there while he went for a walk. "Stay out of the water until I come back," the Professor told Jeff. "I will," Jeff promised. He watched his father walk away down the beach to think, walking at the water's edge where there were fewer legs to step over. His father wore long khaki trousers, even on the beach, and a cotton shirt; but he rolled up the sleeves of his shirt in the heat, and he took off his shoes and socks to go barefoot.

When the Professor walked back, Jeff could tell him from far off, because nobody else wore long trousers or walked so slowly along the packed sand down by the water. Jeff always watched for the first glimpse of the Professor, because he always knew he might not return. "He doesn't know anything about being a father," Melody had told him, "so you can't expect very much from him, Jeffie."

They ate sandwiches Jeff had made, then he could play in the water until it was mid-afternoon and they returned to the apartment to cool off. There, the Professor wrote notes.

They ate dinners in restaurants, crab cakes and crab imperial and steamed crabs, and once, steamed lobsters. They both got sunburned, but not badly. One night, they went down to the boardwalk, and Jeff rode the roller coaster and the rocket – but it wasn't fun any more, so they came straight back to the apartment. It was different when Melody was sitting beside him, being scared and excited, laughing out loud when the car rolled down an incline, holding him within her arm. Every night Jeff indulged in the pleasures of watching television, because there was a television set that came with the apartment. At the end of the week, they packed up and went back to Baltimore. "It'll be good to get back to work, won't it?" the Professor asked Jeff. Jeff said yes.

The year Jeff was in third grade, the housekeeper was named Tony and he was a sociology major who liked to have noise around him. He liked to tell the Professor what was wrong with the university when they sat at meals, he liked to listen to his radio while he did housework. And he liked to cook. He taught Jeff to help him and also taught him good recipes. Jeff did his homework after supper that year, because, as Tony said, since they didn't have a TV, there was nothing else for him to do. The Professor worked before dinner and after, as usual.

"I never thought they worked so much," Tony said to Jeff. "I always figured professors had kind of an easy life. Not your old man. But he doesn't publish, does he? I dunno, there must be more to life than this. Where is your mother, anyway?"

"I don't know," Jeff said.

"I saw her a couple of times, my sophomore year. At rallies, across a crowded room. She was a good looker. She seemed sincere. Taste that spaghetti sauce and tell me what it needs, will you, kid?"

It was Tony who, by forgetting to take Jeff down to the barber to keep his crewcut short, changed Jeff's way of wearing his hair. Before then, it was cut off short and straight, like a mown field, and it would grow out slowly until it stuck out over his head like a puffball until the Professor would say, "Isn't it about time to cut his hair?" But Tony didn't get round to it, and Jeff's hair grew until it lay long and flat on his head, like the Professor's. But Jeff's hair was dark, almost black, like Melody's.

When Jeff was in fourth grade, a boy named Andrew kept house for them because he had to or he couldn't afford to go to the university. Andrew really wanted to live in a fraternity, he wanted to go to friends' parties, he went to all the football games and basketball games and baseball games. What he did around the house he did angrily, his face angry above the vacuum cleaner, his hands angry in the dishwater. That year, the Professor started going out every Thursday evening, to have dinner and then play whist afterwards. If Andrew had something he wanted to do on a Thursday night, Jeff was old enough to be left alone. Andrew didn't tell the Professor this, but he told Jeff. Jeff didn't tell the Professor either, because he didn't want to upset the Professor's routine. When he was alone at night in the house, he just went up to his room with a book and sat on his bed reading until he heard someone come in. Then he turned off the light and fell asleep.

★ ★ ★

The year Jeff was in fifth grade, they had a graduate student from the Physics Department, Ian, who had a thick beard and spent long hours in the lab, working on his thesis. At the beginning of each week, Ian put up a list of when he would be in the house. He took Friday and Saturday nights off and went to see his girlfriend. He was going to be married in June, "Although why anybody gets married these days I don't know. Given the statistics on divorce. What about your old man?" he asked Jeff. He sat with Jeff at the table, doing labs or problems, while Jeff did his homework. Jeff looked up at Ian. If he was teasing, Jeff was ready to show that he got the joke. He didn't seem to be teasing, so Jeff looked serious. "Your father, for example; he's easy to live with. Maybe he was just too old for her. What do you think?"

"I don't know," Jeff said, although he thought he did know, maybe. He knew Melody's complaints, anyway. He didn't know about his father; his father never said anything, one way or the other.

"Don't you wonder?" Ian asked.

Jeff shook his head. As long as the Professor's life suited him, he would probably stay. "He's afraid of changes," Melody used to tell Jeff. "He's a creature of routine. And he doesn't know how hard it is on other people." It wasn't hard on Jeff, however; not nearly as hard as it would be if the Professor decided to leave too. So Jeff didn't wonder, he just made sure that the Professor's life was what the Professor wanted.

The summer before sixth grade, sitting behind his father as they drove back from their week at Ocean City, Jeff asked who was going to house-keep for them that year. "Nobody," the Professor said. "You're old enough now, aren't you?"

Jeff could hear that his father wanted him to be old enough. "Yes," he agreed. He looked at his father. The back of the Professor's neck was sunburnt, and so were his hands on the steering wheel. They got caught in two traffic jams, where the road narrowed to bridges to cross rivers.

But the Professor didn't mind. He turned round to Jeff. "It doesn't make any difference what time we get there, does it?"

"No," Jeff agreed.

That autumn, one of the Professor's whist players became a friend. This friend came to their house to visit and do Greek with the Professor, so Jeff met him. He was a man in his forties, younger than the Professor, who taught theology at the university. He was a Catholic Brother, Brother Thomas. "Doubting Thomas", he introduced himself to Jeff, the first night he came to their house. Jeff wondered, without asking, what he meant. The brown eyes studied his face. "It was a joke," Brother Thomas said, so Jeff smiled. "I had no idea you had a son, Horace. Well, I guess gossip said you did, but I'd forgotten."

Jeff shook his hand and looked at the man. He was round and short, his round head was bald except for a fringe of pale hair that ran round the base of his skull. Like the Professor, he wore big, square glasses. He wore a black suit, with the round white collar showing above his black shirt front. "You're old for such a young son, aren't you, Horace?"

"I married late," the Professor answered.

"Ah," Brother Thomas said. He had brought a bottle of wine with him. He insisted that the Professor let Jeff taste it. Jeff sat quiet at the table, working out how they wanted him to behave. He watched their eyes and listened carefully to their conversation. Brother Thomas's eyes often rested on Jeff, but the man didn't ask him questions so he didn't volunteer anything. The Professor paid close attention to what Brother Thomas said, so Jeff deduced that he thought the man was interesting and wanted him to enjoy himself. Jeff took special care over the dinner, so that the brother would like the food, even if it was only hamburgers on rolls. He toasted the rolls and buttered them. He turned the hamburgers frequently, so that they would be cooked but not too thickly crusted. He chopped onions and sliced celery to add to the salad.

"A man with your taste should have a decent set of wine glasses," Brother Thomas said, holding up his glass. They were all sitting round the kitchen table after dinner. The Professor had moved his study back downstairs, and after three years the living room was filled with boxes of books and boxes of papers and boxes of old clothes. There was no other place in the house to sit.

"I can't afford to indulge my tastes," the Professor said.

"You could strike for a raise," Brother Thomas suggested. "Carry placards, deliberately teach untruths. Or how about a sitdown strike?" Jeff had never heard of anyone talk to his father in the easy, off-hand way Brother Thomas did. It looked like the Professor didn't mind.

It was from Brother Thomas that Jeff learned that some people thought the Professor did a good job at the university. "What do you think of your father, putting together the best history department in Baltimore, maybe even Maryland?" Brother Thomas said.

"I think that's good," Jeff said. Brother Thomas winked at him.

The Professor, however, denied it. "It's nothing like first rate."

"Academic reputations take a while to spread; there's a five- to ten-year lag, you know that – or you should; you're a historian." Brother Thomas sounded very sure. "You watch, Horace, your reputation is catching up with you. The students you've dreamed of are lurking on your horizon."

The Professor opened his mouth as if to say something, but just shook his head. Jeff sipped at the wine. It didn't taste fruity to him, but thick, so that it left a coating across his tongue, and slightly bitter. He kept his face expressionless.

"Look at the sign-ups for your courses," Brother Thomas insisted. "Horace, you can add two and two. Honestly, Jeff, your father," he said, but he said it fondly, as if the Professor amused him.

Jeff looked at his father. He wondered if this was the way the Professor liked to be talked to, but he knew he himself couldn't talk that way.

"Time will tell," was all the Professor said.

"Time is telling," Brother Thomas corrected him. "The other members of your department have even stopped trying to get you fired."

"Have they? That's a blessing," the Professor said.

Brother Thomas chuckled. "I must admit I wondered if you handled their attempts at rebellion the way you did on purpose."

"I didn't handle them at all. I knew it didn't make any difference what they said."

The Professor sounded pleased, though. Jeff could hear that, and he offered Brother Thomas another hamburger.

Jeff waited a couple of weeks before asking his father about Brother Thomas. "Who is he?"

"A monk. A Christian Brother, that's a teaching order," the Professor said. "From the Catholic University; he teaches a Bible course for us."

"That's not in your department. How did you meet him?"

"He played whist with us – then I wanted to study Greek and he wanted to freshen his up."

Jeff sat in surprised silence, wondering why his father needed to learn Greek, wondering how long this friendship had been going on. While he wondered, his father got up from the table and returned to his study. Jeff didn't mind. As long as the Professor was doing what he wanted he would be content with Jeff. The hard thing was trying to figure out what he wanted, because he seldom asked for anything. Jeff washed the dishes, rinsed them, and placed them in a rack to dry. He took out the broom and swept the floor. The Professor liked things neat. All their extra belongings they packed away into the unused living room, and the rest of the house they kept neat. After four years, Jeff was pretty good at figuring out what the Professor might want, reading his reactions. It was pretty easy, after all, because mostly the Professor didn't think things made any difference. He often said that. And in the same way, so he could give the teachers what they wanted to get, Jeff worked at school, listening carefully not only to instructions, but also to the teachers' reactions.

Occasionally that autumn, Brother Thomas would come over to their house for supper. He always brought a bottle of wine with him. Early on, he brought four wine glasses, tall, stemmed

28

crystal glasses, formed from what he called flashed glass, a layer of coloured glass on top of a layer of clear. An intricate design had been cut through the outer coloured layer, so the glasses shone like jewels. One was red, one blue, one yellow, one green, and the men would say what colour they wanted as Jeff set the table. Brother Thomas liked to eat, so Jeff cooked some recipes Tony had left for him, like a chicken roasted with two pierced lemons tucked into the cavity so that the meat tasted slightly of lemon, and the juices made a sauce for rice. "The boy has a real hand for it," Brother Thomas said to the Professor. "How did you get so lucky? He certainly didn't get it from you – was his mother a good cook?"

Jeff kept his eyes on his plate and his face still as he listened to what his father would answer.

"No, she hated housework of any kind."

Nobody said anything else. Jeff turned the red glass around in his fingers.

"Let's take our coffee in and get to work," the Professor suggested.

"With pleasure. After I toast the cook." Brother Thomas raised his glass to Jeff and the Professor did the same. Jeff tried to smile at Brother Thomas, but he saw how the man's brown eyes studied him, and he did not know what the man was thinking. He did know, however, that Brother Thomas wouldn't say anything. That much he had figured out, that although Brother Thomas had a lot of ideas, he kept them to himself. Jeff would have liked to hear some of them, but he didn't ask.

In the winter a flu ran through the University School, and Jeff caught it. He spent two days in bed, unable to eat, listening to the sound of his father's typewriter in the silent house. *Tickety-tick. Tickety-tick.* Outside, a grey Baltimore snow fell steadily. Jeff studied the ceiling of his room and kept alert for the first signs of nausea or diarrhoea, so that he could be sure to make it to the bathroom. At meal times, his father came to the door and asked if he wanted anything. "No, thank you," Jeff said, trying to sound better than he felt, so that the Professor wouldn't be disturbed. He hadn't been really ill for such a long time that he had forgotten how terrible it felt.

On the third day, a Friday, he went back to school, but when he got home in the afternoon and tried to climb the stairs to get to bed, he felt so dizzy he couldn't make his legs move. He rested on the stairs for a while, until he could get to the kitchen and sit in a chair. He was terribly thirsty so he poured himself a glass of ice water, which he guzzled down. For a couple of seconds he felt wonderful. Then he started to cough, deep racking coughs of the kind he had suppressed most of the day. Between the coughing and the dizziness, he threw up in the sink, the water he'd just drunk as well as the little lunch he had eaten. Then he felt better, so he cleaned out the sink.

Jeff made soup for supper and toasted cheese sandwiches, and he was careful not to eat much so that he would be able to wash the dishes and get up to his bedroom without his father noticing. He kept his coughing down as much as he could. His ears rang and his body alternated between being too hot and being over-run with chills. He wondered, as he lifted his soup spoon, if his hands were shaking, because it felt as if they were; but, when he looked to check, he could see that they weren't. In bed, he fell asleep without even taking off his clothes.

The next morning he couldn't get out of bed. His teeth chattered and his chest ached and his hair lay cold and wet across his forehead, at his neck, all round his head. He woke himself up, coughing, then drifted off again. Late in the morning, the Professor looked into his room. When he opened the door he awoke Jeff from a shallow sleep. Jeff tried to sit up, but he didn't want to raise his head from the pillow, because then he would feel dizzy, and when he felt dizzy he felt sick.

"I'm going to see Brother Thomas," the Professor said. "I don't know how long we'll be on this passage, the syntax is strange. We're almost out of milk and coffee," he said. Then, about to leave, he asked, "Jeff? You look pale, or is that the light? Is there something wrong?"

Jeff had to say yes.

The Professor came in then and stood looking

down at Jeff. He hesitated, then rested a hand on Jeff's forehead. His hand felt cool and dry. "What's your temperature?" the Professor asked. "I thought you were over that flu."

"I'm sorry," Jeff said.

"Where's the thermometer?"

"We don't have one. I'm sorry."

The Professor left the room. The door was open, so Jeff heard him going down the stairs before he slipped back into uneasy sleep.

The next thing he heard was Brother Thomas asking him to wake up. Obediently, he opened his eyes. Brother Thomas put a thermometer into his mouth. The Professor stood tall behind him in a blue cardigan. "Who's his doctor?" Brother Thomas asked. The Professor shook his head helplessly. Jeff had to take the thermometer out of his mouth to cough, but he put it right back in when he had finished. The two men listened to him. "What do you mean you don't know?" Brother Thomas asked the Professor. He sounded cross; Jeff hoped he wasn't going to get Brother Thomas angry at the Professor. "Jeff, do you know your doctor's name?" Jeff shook his head.

"When's the last time you saw him?" Jeff shrugged; it was too long ago, he was too tired. "It'll be on the school records," Brother Thomas said. His worried brown eyes were fixed on Jeff.

"Today's Saturday," the Professor said. "The school's closed."

"Who would remember the doctor?"

"His mother might. I suppose."

"Can you get in touch with her?"

"I haven't heard from her in four years," the Professor pointed out.

"It's all right," Jeff said. He coughed again, then added, "I had flu this week. Just a relapse. I'm sorry."

Brother Thomas read the thermometer. "One hundred and four. And this is still morning, Horace. Have you got any aspirin?"

The Professor looked at Jeff. "In the bathroom," Jeff told him.

"He needs a doctor," Brother Thomas said. "We can give him a couple of aspirin to bring down the fever, but he needs a doctor. His own doctor might make a house call – I don't want to take him outside in this weather."

"I could try calling her family, to see if they know where she is."

"I think you'd better do that," Brother Thomas said. His round face looked sternly at the Professor, and then he hurried out to get the aspirin for Jeff. The Professor put his hand on Jeff's forehead again, before going downstairs. When they had both gone, Jeff rubbed his hands over his chest, because coughing made it hurt. Brother Thomas gave him two aspirins with a glass of water, and he sank back into sleep.

There was a third man in the room when he woke up again, a youngish man. "Do you remember me?" Jeff shook his head. "Well, I wouldn't recognize you either. You've grown." He opened his bag and put a thermometer into Jeff's mouth. He took out a torch and looked into Jeff's eyes and ears. He read the thermometer and said, "Hmmmm." He listened to Jeff's chest, front and back, with a stethoscope. He looked down Jeff's throat.

"We gave him two aspirins an hour ago," Brother Thomas said.

The doctor nodded. He took out a pad and wrote something on it, then ripped off the page. He wrote something on the second page and ripped that off too. He handed them both to the Professor. Jeff watched.

"My name's Baker," the doctor said to Jeff. He sat down on the bed, beside Jeff. "You're pretty ill, bronchial pneumonia, and you'll need to stay in this bed for at least three days. No school for a week. Is that going to break your heart?" He smiled at Jeff. Jeff nodded to show he understood. "I want to see you in my surgery next Friday afternoon. Believe it or not, you're going to feel much better by then. You've got some jabs to catch up on, young man."

Jeff nodded. The three men left the room. Dr Baker started to talk while they were on the stairs, quick and questioning, but Jeff couldn't distinguish the words.

He slept most of the day. Either the Professor or Brother Thomas came into Jeff's room to give him spoonfuls of medicine, every two hours, and ask him if he wanted a cup of tea or some Coke. By Sunday afternoon, he did feel better. In the evening, when the sky beyond Jeff's window was black, Brother Thomas came in with a tray, which he put down on the table beside Jeff. He told Jeff to sit up and then rearranged the pillows behind him. He put the tray across Jeff's thighs and sat down in a chair pulled up beside the bed. It was a chair from the living room, a rocking chair, that the Professor had brought up earlier.

There was clear chicken soup on the tray and a slice of unbuttered toast and a glass of Coke. Jeff tried the soup. He wasn't hungry, but he felt empty.

"It's been a shock for your father, your being ill," Brother Thomas said. His brown eyes watched Jeff. Jeff swallowed quickly so that he could apologize. "It's good for him," Brother Thomas said, "but it is a shock. I never even thought to ask whether he was sending you for check-ups. And I'll bet you haven't been to a dentist either."

"I didn't need to," Jeff said. He started to cough again, and Brother Thomas lifted the tray up until he had finished.

Brother Thomas *ttched* as he put the tray back down. "Well, you're a pair of blessed innocents. And you never asked about your mother, did you?"

Jeff shook his head.

"Do you know anything about her? I don't."

"Her name's Melody," Jeff said. "She has long black hair and she's beautiful. She has grey eyes."

"She's living with her family, in South Carolina. I know that much more. Your father wasn't pleased to talk to her." Jeff kept his face empty. "Are they divorced?"

"I don't know," Jeff said.

"You ought to get him to tell you about her," Brother Thomas advised. "It would be good for him; anyone can see that."

But Jeff knew better than that, although he didn't argue.

Jeff stayed in bed for four days, and the Professor or Brother Thomas came to read *Ivanhoe* to him. They brought him books from the library and, when he could go downstairs, Brother Thomas gave him three paperbacks in a set, *The Lord of the Rings*. "This will keep you busy while you have to stay inside," Brother Thomas said. The long solitary hours did go by quickly as Jeff read the story of unlikely heroes in another world, of magic and love, of battles against unremitting evil, the long, arduous journey, of friendship and betrayal.

On Friday, Dr Baker gave Jeff a complete check-up, two jabs, and asked if his father was with him.

"No sir, he has a class," Jeff answered. The doctor looked up from the file he was writing in and said, "Well, then, I'll expect you in here for a check-up around your next birthday. That'll be September. You'll be twelve."

"Yes, sir."

"Do you have any questions you want to ask? Anything that's worrying you?"

"No, sir."

"Well, if you think of any. How do you do in school?"

"OK," Jeff told him. He did not want to say that his grades had been drifting down, that his teachers said he was "lazy" or "dreamy".

The doctor nodded and closed the file. "Don't disappear on me again, all right?" Jeff nodded. "You look like a normal enough kid to me; you're doing fine. No problems. I'll see you next September, unless you need me in between."

"Thank you," Jeff said, leaving.

When he got home, his father was waiting. "Everything OK?" the Professor asked.

Jeff nodded.

"I'm really sorry, Jeff," the Professor said then, his mild eyes apologetic behind their glasses. "I don't know what I was doing, letting that happen."

"It's OK, really. It doesn't make any difference, really. And I liked the books," Jeff told him. If his father started worrying about him that would be a change, and you couldn't tell what would happen when things changed.

"I just didn't know about the check-ups," the Professor said. He sounded discouraged. Jeff felt alarmed. He remembered that his father didn't like to apologize, didn't like to feel sorry; he remembered the way the Professor got all shrivelled up when he had made Melody unhappy or angry.

"I'm sorry," he had said, "I'm sorry."

"No you're not, you don't even understand what I'm talking about, you don't have any feelings at all," she answered, her eyes spilling over with tears.

"I'm sorry," the Professor had said, again.

Jeff tried to reassure his father: "It doesn't make any difference." He hoped that was true. "The doctor says I'm a normal enough kid. That's exactly what he said."

A month later, the whole thing was forgotten. Jeff had caught up the schoolwork, his cough had disappeared, and everything was back to normal, except that Brother Thomas came round more frequently than before, often bringing the ingredients for a dinner which he and Jeff would cook together, as well as the inevitable bottle of wine. As the brief Baltimore spring deepened into the heat of premature summer, the Professor spent an unusual amount of time typing in his study, but that was the only other difference, and like the first, it was no real difference. Jeff relaxed, gradually convinced that his being ill hadn't ruined anything.

But in May his father told him, over their

dinner of pork chops and rice, that Melody wanted him to spend the summer with her.

Jeff took a long time answering. "Where?"

"In Charleston, South Carolina," the Professor told him, neatly cutting the meat from the bone of his third pork chop. "Her family is down there," he said.

Jeff tried to think of what he was supposed to say.

"Is that all right with you?" his father asked, salting his rice.

Jeff looked at the Professor's expressionless face. He hoped he was answering the right thing when he said, without expression, "Yes."

Jeff got off the plane at Charleston as the sun was going down. The crowd of people from the plane hurried, and he let himself be carried along by them. It was hot, so hot he was not surprised to see palm trees along the cyclone fencing that bordered the runways, hotter because he wore his school uniform to travel in, the grey flannel trousers and blue blazer, the white shirt and the striped tie. He moved along with the crowd towards a pink one-storey building with a glass tower on top of it, the airport. The sky over this flat countryside was soaked with the colours of the setting sun, and Jeff stepped out of the line of traffic to look at it for a minute.

A hot, reddish gold shone at the horizon and faded out to orange pink about a third of the way up the arc of the sky. The flowerlike heads of the taller palm trees turned into black silhouettes to the west. Wispy stray clouds drifted across the western sky.

Jeff found the baggage claim area without trouble, by following the general drift of traffic. Unlike the Baltimore airport an hour and a half to the north of him, this airport would be hard to get lost in. "Melody will meet you," the Professor had told him as they'd waited for Jeff's plane to be announced. "Just let me know when you're returning and I'll pick you up," he had said. Jeff had the return portion of his ticket – paid for, but the flight unspecified – in the inside pocket of his blazer. He had shaken the Professor's hand and he had not looked back as he walked along the passage to his plane. He didn't even look back to see if the Professor had waited for him to look back; and once you were on your plane it was impossible to see into the plate glass windows of the observation area if there was someone watching for you or not.

At the luggage claim Jeff picked out his father's battered leather suitcase and went to the waiting area. This was a big room, with two long walls of windows and two short walls of ticket counters. He sat on a plastic chair, his suitcase at his feet.

Outside the window to the runway, the sun went down and the sky turned dark. Outside the opposite window, cars pulled up, their twin headlights unnecessary on the brightly lit unloading area. People moved through the big air-conditioned room, some arriving, some leaving, meeting and parting. A voice overhead announced planes. Jeff waited. He had thirty dollars in his pocket, twenty from his father and ten from Brother Thomas to bring back a bottle of local wine. Jeff kept an eye on his suitcase and on the clock. He wasn't hungry, he wasn't tired. He waited.

And he waited. The room was less crowded now, and the twin headlights drove up less frequently. The air grew quiet, except for an occasional low-toned conversation. Jeff sat motionless, his legs side by side, his hands in his lap, his mind empty; and waited.

A rush of sweet air washed around him, enveloped him; a voice murmured half laughing, half sad. "Oh Jeffie, Jeffie." He closed his eyes as his cheek came to rest on her shoulder and her flowery scent flowed around him. Her arms wrapped round him and he could feel her hands on his back. He tried to grab at all the sensations at once, the sound of her voice, honey sweet with its lazy vowels ("I'm so sorry to be so late, I was – it doesn't matter, I was just afraid you'd give up on me and go back, and then there was a traffic jam and – Oh, my little boy"), her arms round him holding him close, the perfumed air she carried with her. He remembered.

"But let me look at you. Aren't you going to kiss me? Haven't you missed me? Aren't you going to hug me? Jeffie? Are you angry? Don't be angry with me."

He lifted his head and opened his eyes.

"You're all grown up," she said. One hand stayed on his shoulder; the other touched his cheek, brushed his hair back from his forehead. It was like – the sunshine on the first day of real spring.

"Look at you, grown up. But you look pale.

Oh Jeffie, have you been terribly unhappy?" Her eyes filled with tears, which flowed down her cheeks in a thin line. "I'm so happy to see you," she said, touching his cheek again.

Jeff's heart hurt him, it was so full with the warmth and sweetness. The warmth seemed to run along his bloodstream. He felt his eyes fill with tears. She smiled. "Not so grown up after all, are you? I'm glad." She smiled right into his eyes. Jeff felt his mouth quiver. "But aren't you going to say anything? Haven't you got anything to say?" Her lips brushed his cheek, the palm of her soft hand held his other cheek, and his heart thudded so painfully in his chest that he knew if he had to stand his legs would be too weak to support him. "Say something," she insisted.

Every painful beat of Jeff's heart was saying something – *Mummy* – but he couldn't speak.

"Then at least sit back and let me look at you." She held both of his hands in both of hers and sat staring at him. He stared back. "Well, what do you think of me?" she finally asked.

"Beautiful," Jeff said. His voice croaked a little, so he cleared his throat and said it again, "You're so beautiful." He felt like a man must who has been kept in a dungeon for years and years, and he steps out into the sunlight for the first time. He couldn't possibly have said what he felt. And she was beautiful, too; so beautiful she took his breath away. Her long black hair curved smoothly down along the sides of her face, until it was gathered back to form a gleaming circle at the top of her head. Her eyes – he had forgotten how dark the outer circle of grey in her eyes was and how the lighter grey shone within that circle. Her black eyelashes framed her eyes, and her curved black eyebrows made another circle. Her oval face, her small straight nose, her smiling mouth, the high cheekbones and the tanned skin – "I'd forgotten how beautiful you are," he said softly.

She laughed, a sound like honey, and stood up, still holding on to both of his hands. He stood in front of her, noticing vaguely that she wore a dress and noticing clearly how small her waist was, how long and slender her tanned arms and legs. "Oh, Mummy," he said, and he reached out to hug her, wrapping his arms round her neck, just as he now remembered he had done when he was little, before she went away.

She held him close against her. The top of his head came to her ears. "You're tall," she said.

Jeff shook his head. "I think you're short," he corrected her.

At that she laughed again and stepped back while the sound still sang in his ears. "Get your suitcase, the car's outside and parked where it's illegal. Didn't you have any pictures of me?" Jeff held his suitcase at the end of one arm. She tucked her hand in under his other arm and kept looking at him. "But your father must have a couple, didn't you ask him?"

Jeff shook his head.

"You goose." She smiled at him, like sunlight, again. He had been afraid she would be angry. "You silly, silly goose. We'll have to give you some. And take some of you, for me. I almost didn't recognize you. I had to study you for a minute, you're so different. Then I saw the suitcase. I thought you'd be looking for me," she said.

"I'm sorry," Jeff said. "I was just waiting."

He had hurt her feelings, so he added quickly, "It doesn't matter; I don't care."

"And everything's all right now," she said. "I'm here, and you're here, and we're back together again. I'm so happy," she said, her voice singing the words as they stepped out into the night air.

She made Jeff sit in the back seat of the car, an old four-door saloon. "Children should always sit in the back," she said to him. "And strap yourself in. Children are so light, if there's an accident they fly around inside the car. The back is the safest place." He did what she asked, gladly. He sat in the right hand corner, where he could look across to her as she drove. "I have to make a stop," she said, pulling out on to the road. "Do you mind?"

"No." Jeff wouldn't mind anything.

"How do you like Charleston?"

"I don't know, I haven't seen any of it."

She laughed again, as if he had said something

funny. He thought he ought to ask her a question, so he did. "Is this your car?"

"No, heavens, I don't have enough money to buy a car. A friend of mine lets me use it when he's out of town. I couldn't afford to insure a car, I can barely afford to buy petrol, but I don't mind. Detroit doesn't have any of my money, and neither do the fat-cat oil companies – most of the time. And that keeps my personal pollution contribution down."

Jeff was remembering more about her with every minute. He watched her hands on the steering wheel and wondered about the rings she wore; the lights overhead and from passing trucks flashed over her hands, lighting them purple and yellow. She turned off the road after a few minutes and negotiated a number of turns before stopping in front of a small one-storey house, one of a row of similar houses, each with a chain link fence round it. She turned round in her seat to ask, "Do you want to wait in the car or come in?"

"I'll wait," Jeff decided.

"You'd better come in, we may be a while," she told him. She opened the low gate for them and then took his arm again as they went up the walk to the small porch. A yellow light, covered with the bodies of bugs, shone over the door.

Inside, two women sat at a kitchen table, folding letters into a pile of envelopes. Most of the house was taken up by this kitchen, which had a sofa at the wall furthest away from the stove and sink, with a small TV set on the coffee table. "Mel," the women said, "we were wondering where you were."

"I was meeting someone," Jeff's mother said. "The man in my life; let me introduce him, Jefferson Greene. This is Phoebe."

"Hello," Jeff said, to a young woman whose short, curly dark hair framed her face. Phoebe nodded at him.

"And Willa." Jeff said hello to Willa whose brown hair curled like Phoebe's into fussy curls.

"Sit down, Jeffie, my goodness," his mother told him. He sat obediently in one of the two empty chairs at the table. She took the other. "My son," she announced.

Jeff stared at her. She had sounded so proud and glad as she said that. Her big eyes moved from one to the other of the people at the table. A smile teased at her mouth.

"For heaven's sake," Phoebe said. "You never said a word." Both of the women stared at Jeff.

"From the marriage?" Willa said.

"Oh, yes," Melody said. "I had to pick him up at the airport, and I was late and so worried – I can't tell you." She pressed her hand over her heart. "Talk about anxiety."

Melody did not wear a wedding ring, Jeff noticed, but she wore two silver rings with pieces of turquoise set in them, on one hand. On the other hand she wore a big ring with a dark red stone in it and a plain pearl ring. Her fingers were delicate.

"We'd better get going on this, if we want to do a mailing tomorrow. Jeffie will help, won't you? It's women's lib material," she teased.

"Sure," Jeff said. "It doesn't make any difference to me."

Melody's laugh floated over the table. "But it will, Jeffie, it will. You just wait."

They folded the letters into envelopes. This was the second of five mailings, "and we've got all the facts and figures," Melody said, her hands working.

"For all the good it does," Phoebe said. "I don't know, sometimes I think women just don't care."

"What do you expect?" Melody asked, "when we've all been brought up to get married and let a man support us."

"Well, it serves them right," Willa said. "Sometimes I think I'll do just that, it would certainly be easier than – earning the money and keeping the house too. Especially when I think of the men who earn more than I do and don't work as hard. Or as well. It's just what they deserve, some woman hanging like a leech off them. Then they complain about women."

"The trouble with that," Melody said, her voice serious and sad, "is that it's bad for you. Bad for women to do that, bad for themselves, because it just perpetuates things. We have to fight for our self-respect, don't we?"

The other two women nodded in agreement.

"And if we don't do something," Melody went on, "if people like us don't try to do something to change it – then we're contributing to it. If you think about it, we are. Why, I wouldn't take a job working for a man for – all the tea in China."

"Yes, but you've got family to live with," Willa told her.

"And an ex-husband," Phoebe said.

"My goodness, you don't think I'd take a penny from *him*," Jeff's mother said, angry. "I'm insulted. Yes, insulted that you'd think that and then work with me on this campaign. Why, I have more self-respect than that. And so should you."

They apologized, and after a few minutes Melody's voice resumed its ordinary tones, lazy, full of subdued laughter. Jeff relaxed.

It was late when they left, the streets deserted, most of the little houses dark. They got back on to the motorway and drove for several miles. Melody yawned and asked Jeff how he had liked the two women. He said he had liked them all right. "They're so young," she said, "barely over twenty, both of them. It's good for the young women to learn from the beginning the fight they'll have to make if they're not going to be taken advantage of. It's worse here in the South," she said, "it's much worse."

49

"I guess so," Jeff agreed.

Sleep hung on his eyelids and pulled at his shoulders. He barely noticed when his mother parked the car in front of a tall house, he noticed only that he stumbled on uneven bricks as they walked to the front door. Inside, she led him up a broad staircase and opened a door for him, with her finger on her lips. "We don't want to wake them up, they sleep lightly," she said. "Oh Jeffie, I'm so happy to have you here with me. Sleep well. Until the morning," she said softly, and kissed him on the forehead.

Jeff peeled off his clothes and stripped back the spread from the bed before lying down on it in just his underpants. He was too tired to look for his pyjamas, too tired to see where he should put his clothes away. He turned off the bedside light and lay dazzled and bemused in the darkness before slipping into sleep.

He woke early, but without any sense of strangeness. His room – he sat up in the bed and looked around him – was large and square, airy. All four windows were open, and the gauzy curtains hung still in the motionless air. He heard, beyond the silence of the house around him, an occasional engine, an occasional bird, no human voices. He had to go to the bathroom – badly – but he didn't know where it was. He sat up and curled his legs underneath him.

His bed had four tall posts: four fluted, slender

poles, each with an acorn carved at its tip. The walls of the room were white, faded to a kind of pearly colour, the high ceiling had cracks running along it, the floor was boards of wood. A dresser stood next to one bare wall, with a mirror set on it and a large, dark wood wardrobe beside it. Under the windows on one wall stood a little writing table, with a chair pulled up to it. Jeff's bed was placed between two windows. He saw only one door. He *really* had to go to the bathroom; he hadn't been since he was on the plane.

Jeff got out of bed and unpacked his bag, hanging his trousers and dress shirts up carefully in the wardrobe. He refolded his underpants and T-shirts into the drawers of the dresser and made neat piles of his jeans and shorts. He placed his brush and comb on the dresser top, putting his toothpaste and toothbrush down beside them. He selected the drawer he would use for soiled clothing, dropped yesterday's clothes into it, and dressed in flannels and a shirt. He wondered how early it was and where the bathroom was.

He went to a window and looked out, over little patches of bright flower gardens and bright green lawns to the backs of three other sleeping houses. The air hung moist and cool around him; it came sweet and warm into his lungs. Very early, he guessed. Two of the houses were brick, all of them had a second storey veranda, and he wondered if he might push back the screen and pee

51

out of the window. Of course he couldn't do that, and he wouldn't, but the idea made him smile.

He forced himself to open the door of his room. His bare feet made no noise on the wooden floor of the half-lit hall. On one long wall, tall lace-curtained windows and two lace-curtained french doors opened on to a veranda. His room was at the far end. The broad staircase they had ascended the night before was at the centre, where it turned to mount up another flight. There were two doors on his half of the hall and two on the far half.

One of them had to be a bathroom. Jeff stood, trying to decide which it might be. He thought the second door on his side of the stairs was closer to the staircase than the second door on the far side, which made him guess that was the bathroom. The closeness might mean a smaller room. If he was wrong, if, for instance, it was his mother's bedroom, how would she feel if he opened the door and woke her up? Or, worse, her family's bedroom door, some total stranger. Jeff silently argued with himself that perhaps he didn't have to go to the bathroom after all, but he did, and badly. He opened the door next to his, gently turning the white porcelain handle, gently pushing the heavy door inwards. It was – he saw with a rush of relief that brought tears to his eyes and was immediately dominated by intense pressure on his bladder – a bathroom.

While he was there he washed his face in a

quiet trickle of water. He would have liked to take a bath in the long tub, but decided he ought not to. He rubbed cold water over his teeth with a forefinger, until they squeaked, because he had forgotten to bring his toothbrush and toothpaste. Then he returned to his own room.

There he put on socks and shoes, brushed his hair, made the bed and sat down on it. Except for the items on the top of the dresser, nobody would know he was there. He hadn't disturbed anything. The light in the room grew brighter as the sun moved up the sky, the sounds outside the window grew louder and more frequent. An odour of bacon rose into his room from somewhere below. He heard footsteps on the stairs. The temperature in his room mounted. He sat with his hands in his lap.

After a while the door of his room burst open. "What are you doing?" Melody asked him. "We've all eaten, why don't you come down?"

Jeff looked at her. She wore her hair in one thick braid down her back, she wore sandals on her feet and a pink sundress. Her eyes looked cross, and her pink mouth was not smiling. "*Just* like your father, come on *down*, Jeffie. Gambo wants to meet you, we've all been waiting. Honestly. You goose." She smiled at him then and held out her hand. Jeff hurried to take it and hold it. "Nobody will eat you." She smiled into his eyes. Her perfume was fresher than the early morning air had been, sweeter.

They descended the broad staircase, and she led him into a dining room where a white-haired woman with liquid brown eyes and loops of pearls over the bodice of her lacy blouse stared at him down the length of the table. On either side of her sat two aged women, who also stared at him. They all had breakfast plates in front of them stained with egg yolk.

Melody pulled Jeff down the length of the table. "Gambo? He was awake and dressed. He didn't know what to do, I suppose. This is my little boy, Jefferson Greene. Jeffie, this is Gambo, my grandmother. It's about time you two met," she said, stepping back.

Jeff smiled politely. "Hello," he said. "It's very nice of you to let me come and visit."

She looked up at him, and he was alarmed to see all the sentiment in her eyes. "You may kiss me," she said, and he bent to kiss her cheek. "Sit there" – she waved him to the seat opposite her – "since you're the man of the house. You must be hungry."

Jeff sat. Melody left the room to get him some breakfast. The table was covered with a white linen cloth. A china bowl in which pink camellias floated decorated the centre. A long-stemmed glass of iced water was set at Jeff's place and heavy silver utensils. Melody came back in with a plate for him and a glass of orange juice and a miniature rack where two slices of toast seemed to stand at attention. She sat at a fifth chair, beside one of the two aged women, a place where there was no silver or napkin set out. "Gambo is my mother's mother," she told Jeff. "Go ahead and eat, before the eggs get cold. And this" – she indicated the woman beside her, who twittered words Jeff couldn't hear but seemed to be smiling at him – "is Aunt Booty and that" – the woman on the opposite side, who ducked her head in a nervous gesture – "is Aunt Dodo, and that is all the family."

Jeff smiled and nodded and started to eat. Gambo, then, would be his great-grandmother. She didn't look old enough to be a great-grand-mother. Her hair was thick and healthy looking, her skin wrinkled but not with the same creepy look that the aunts' faces had, her eyes seemed lively and interested as she stared at him. The other two wore sweaters, even in the warmth of the room, and peered at him through glasses as if even then they couldn't really see him.

He ate two fried eggs, six slices of bacon, and fried potatoes. Melody reached out and took a piece of toast, buttered it, and put it on his plate for him. A white-haired black woman came into the room to pour coffee into three cups. His mother got up and followed her out of the room, to return with her own cup of coffee. Jeff guessed Melody had eaten breakfast in the kitchen.

When he put his fork down on the empty plate, his mother asked him, "Had enough?" She had watched him eat, as if she too were enjoying every mouthful.

"And what are you two children going to do today?" Gambo asked.

"I'd like to show Jeffie Charleston," Melody answered. "And get to know him again."

"That's all right," Gambo said. "We'll talk later, then, Jefferson. After all, I have some rights in you too, you're the last of my line, and I expect you know very little of your family. Tell me, is that correct?"

Her voice was soft, low, and slow. Jeff nodded his head.

"I'm very glad to see you here in my house, at last," Gambo said. "Except for – I don't like to say critical things but – and at the breakfast table too, but – a gentleman" – she looked at him seriously down the length of the table – "always lowers the lavatory seat. After," she added, coughing gently into her napkin, rising from the table before Jeff had time to answer.

"I'm awfully sorry," he said as she approached him.

"We all make mistakes." She smiled down at him and reached out one hand to touch the top of his head. She wore a thin wedding band and a big diamond on that hand. Her hand was gentle as a bird's wing on Jeff's hair. "I suspect nobody ever taught you any better." She slid her hand under Jeff's chin and lifted his face to study it. "He's a handsome boy, Melody; he has the Boudrault look to him."

"Yes," Jeff's mother said, pride in her voice. The two women looked at each other over the top of Jeff's head. He knew he had done something right, and he was glad for Melody's sake.

"Ready to go outside?" Melody asked him. "Don't you want to see my old home town?"

Jeff jumped up from his seat, said a general farewell, and followed his mother to the front door, where she awaited him, a broad-brimmed hat on her head. The streamers, like the flowers on her sundress, were pink. She took his arm as they stepped outside.

The air was moist and warm, filled with sunlight. Melody led him down a narrow brick path, bounded by Gambo's house on one side and a tall whitewashed wall on the other, and into the street. They turned towards the sun and walked. The street was quiet, the houses – many of them, like Gambo's set sideways to the street – tall; their lawns were hidden behind walls. But the gates were left open and Jeff caught glimpses of tall trees with broad shiny leaves, hedges of azaleas, beds of rosebushes, and white wrought-iron furniture. His stride matched his mother's, and they moved slowly down the shady pavement. The street – with those courtyard-like lawns and narrow alleys leading off unexpectedly, with the houses opulent even when they had fallen into disrepair, with the sun-drenched air – the street seemed foreign to Jeff, ancient and mysterious. He looked up at the shuttered first-floor windows and wondered about the people who lived in those houses.

They walked down to a broad park at the end of a tip of land. This park was ringed with trees, crossed by pavements, circled by a four-lane road. They passed a monument to the Civil War dead. "This is Battery Park," Melody told him, "and you'll get more than enough history from Gambo." She laughed and her smile poured into Jeff's eyes. They walked along one end of the park, ran across the road, and climbed a set of cement steps to an elevated walkway that ran along the harbour. "That's the Ashley River coming in," Melody said, "and over there" – she walked in that direction – "is the Cooper. You can see Fort Sumter." She stood still and pointed. Jeff looked obediently to where he could see a brief, dark line on the horizon. They continued walking at a lazy pace, Melody's hand tucked under his forearm. At the end of the walkway they leaned against the railing and looked out over the water. Here, a breeze stirred, blowing down from the land across the river's mouth. "What do you think?" Melody asked Jeff.

He looked at her profile and couldn't find words.

"You must think something," she insisted. Her mouth curved up into a smile.

"Beautiful," Jeff said. He was about to say more when she interrupted him.

"That's Aunt Booty's name, or rather Belle is, but when my mother was little she called her Booty, from *Beauty and the Beast*, and it stuck. It's crazy, isn't it? There is something crazy about the South, you know that, don't you?"

"No," Jeff said.

"The land of lost causes," his mother said. "But what I really wanted was for you to look at the river here."

Jeff looked down and across to where what seemed to be an aircraft carrier was moored, up river. "Is that an aircraft carrier?" he asked.

"Boys." Melody sighed. "Yes, there's a big naval base, carriers and nuclear subs go out of Charleston. I hope you don't want me to take you over the boats; I hope you don't expect that."

"No," Jeff said. He didn't expect anything.

"What I wanted you to see was the water – see how green it is? You know what that means. There are factories, refineries, too, up river, and they've killed the river. Killed it," she repeated. "It used to be you could fish in this river, and it ran brown with mud, and turtles stuck their heads up, so many that they looked like grass. Herons lived in the marshes, crabs and clams. Not any more," she said. "I don't know whether to get angry or just weep. And I'll tell you something else; the Chesapeake Bay is worse." She turned to face him. "Do you know what Captain John

Smith said about the Chesapeake Bay? He said it teemed with fish, so all a man had to do was step into its water with his sword out, and fish would leap on to it and he could feast. You've seen it, what do you think?"

Jeff thought about the harbour at Baltimore, where tankers lined up at piers edged by high brick warehouses, and he remembered Sparrow Point, where the air was thick with industrial pollution. "It smells much worse than this," he said.

"Only because the air's right today," Melody told him. "When the wind comes down from the refineries and plants, it stinks – no, it really stinks. But you're right, things are better down here, and you know why? Because it's a poor country, the South. Poverty may save it – that's ironic, don't you think? The only thing that saves what's left of the ecology down here is because we're too poor to develop. I think, if I didn't know about the victims of that poverty, I'd be grateful for it. But I don't think – in the long run – anything will save us." Her hair hung long and black in the braid down her back, gleaming in sunlight. "Let's sit down in the shade," Melody said.

She led him back down the steps and across the street and across the park to a bench facing the row of houses that faced out over the harbour. These were mansions, with verandas on all three floors, with curved staircases leading up to their broad front doors. They were the kinds of houses that might welcome women in hoop skirts and gentlemen in tall boots. The ancient trees around them were twisted, broad-branched, and hung with Spanish moss.

"We can really *talk*," Melody said. "Are you still at the University School?" She sat close enough beside him to hold on to his hand.

"Yes. I'm going into seventh grade."

"That's the year I was going to take you out, because no girls can enroll – is that still true? No girls after sixth grade?"

Jeff sensed that she wanted him to talk about school, but he was bemused by sensations and couldn't chatter. He felt as if he had been cold, frozen down to his bones and into the marrow, and suddenly now he lay under the warmth of the sun. He could feel himself growing easy, relaxed, under the warmth; he couldn't distract himself from the enjoyment of that. It had something to do with the way his mother held his hand, held to his arm when they walked, touched him with her glance. His sensations were half remembered, memory growing stronger with every minute he was with her.

"How do you do at school?"

"All right. I get some Bs, mostly Cs."

"Bs without working or Bs with working?" she asked.

"With working," he said. The silver and turquoise rings looked wrong on her hand, too big and clumsy for her fingers.

"Oh, dear, you must have got my brains, not your father's," she said. "Poor Jeffie, is that hard on you?"

"No," he said, "I don't mind."

She laughed. "I never did myself. His brains don't do him much good, do they? I remember when you left for school for your first day, do you remember?" He shook his head. "You were quiet, but you weren't frightened. After all, you'd been in day care for years. I even remember the first time ever I saw you. In the hospital – oh Jeffie, I'd never even suspected what it would be like. Having a baby. They tell you, but you never take it in. I thought I'd died and gone to hell, the *pain* and the horrible bright lights and sterile boxwalls with machines on them, and the nurses who didn't care about what you were going through. I dream about it sometimes."

"I'm sorry," Jeff said.

"Then, when they brought you to me – after I came out of the anaesthetic – this little baby, so little and helpless. Your eyes were open but you couldn't see anything really, I knew that. Your fingers were all curled up, and then when I nursed you – " She looked up at him. "Does that embarrass you?"

"No," Jeff lied.

"Then I knew that none of the pain mattered a whit, as long as you were the result of it. It was like ten Christmases all at once. I couldn't breathe properly." Her voice caressed the memory. "I didn't mind that or the bleeding. None of it could make even a dent in my happiness. Sometimes I think that was the happiest time of my life. And we were always together, for as long as I could, we'd go everywhere together. You'd look at me with your big eyes, you'd only look at me, always – your eyes have changed," she observed.

Jeff didn't know what to say.

"I'm so glad to see you again," Melody declared. "You don't know how I've missed you. Have you missed me? Was it very terrible for you? Is it still? No, I don't think I really want to hear about that, it'll just make me feel more guilty. And besides, it's all behind us now, isn't it?"

"Yes," was all Jeff could say.

"Come on, why are we sitting here? I want to show you my city. You can walk for hours and never see it all. Come on, Jeffie."

They ambled up streets and down alleys, through a church graveyard, and along a business street where they peered into the windows of antique shops. She showed him the oldest part of the city, where houses built in Revolutionary times were being renovated. At last they stopped at a small restaurant for something to drink.

Melody wanted to sit outside. The glass-topped tables were small, the chairs set on uneven bricks, the area roofed over by a rough wooden trellis over which grapevines had been trained. They sat in dappled sunlight. Their table had a little vase of fresh daisies on it, the napkins were linen, brick walls enclosed the garden. Melody studied the handwritten menu, Jeff studied her. She looked at him mischievously over the top and asked if he wasn't hungry, because she was. They ordered sandwiches and iced tea, which Melody said was very good here. "Do you like it?" Melody asked him, as he ate his sandwich.

"It's good."

"No, you silly goose, the restaurant. It's my absolute favourite for lunch; I'd eat here every day if I could afford it. Do you?"

"Very much."

"Why?" she asked him. Her grey eyes were teasing. "Well, Jeffie, you don't say very much and I really do want to hear what you have to say. I don't want to pry into your secret thoughts, so I thought – if he'll talk to me about the scenery, then I can hear what he has to say."

Jeff, who felt by this time as if all the hard frozen places within him had melted away, smiled happily back at her. "I like it – the way I like Gambo's house, and everything we've seen today – because . . . it looks as if somebody has taken the trouble to make it pretty. And it's lasted such a long time. It makes my eyes feel good, because – it's the same way you look."

"A compliment? Then you're not disappointed in me?"

Jeff just shook his head.

"But don't you have any questions? There

should be so many questions you want to ask me and you haven't asked me any. Not one."

As if she summoned them up, Jeff realized that he did have questions, answers he badly wanted to hear. "Yes," he said.

"Then ask them, for heaven's sake – what do you think I'm here for?"

"How old are you?" he asked.

"Oh dear, the worst first." She smiled across the table at him. "I'm thirty-two. What do you think of that?"

"Then you were twenty when I was born. Isn't that young?"

She leaned her chin on her hands and nodded her head. He had the feeling she wanted to laugh at him, but if she did, her laughter would be friendly.

"How tall are you?"

"Five-six and a half."

"Where did you go?"

"Home. Here. I came right here, and I've been here ever since. I grew up here, Gambo raised me, well, from the time I was nine. This is my real home."

"What about your parents?"

"My father was killed in the Second World War, and after a few years my mother remarried. He was a nice enough man, I suppose, but – they moved up to Minnesota, we all did, and he didn't have any luck. One summer, when I was eight, I visited Gambo – and I was so happy. There wasn't all the worry about money and keeping jobs and to make it worse my mother had had a couple of children in the meantime – I don't know. It was what you said, as if somebody had taken so much trouble to make things look nice. So I asked Gambo if I could live with her. It didn't matter how much it cost because she's rich. And we got along so well, she sort of adopted me. I'm the only young person in her family, so it'll all come to me some day anyway."

"I thought you said your mother was her daughter."

"She is. Otherwise how could Gambo be my grandmother?"

"But didn't you say there were other children? So you have brothers and sisters or something," Jeff said.

Melody shrugged. "Maybe, I don't know; they don't keep in touch – and they're not the same kind of people at all. Gambo's never even seen them.

"My mother never brought them here. Well, she couldn't afford the journey, not on what he makes, so as far as Gambo's concerned I'm the only one. More questions?"

"How old were you when you married the Professor?"

"Nineteen – I dropped out of school. He was my teacher in the World History survey course. That takes me back, it really takes me back."

"Why did you go away?" Jeff finally asked.

"Oh, Jeffie." She reached across to put the palm of her hand against his cheek. "There were so many reasons. What does the Professor tell you?"

Jeff couldn't answer. That irritated her, so he said quickly, "I never asked him. We never talk about you."

At that she laughed again and clapped her hands together. "Isn't that like him? Just like him, just exactly like him. I thought I could save him, I thought I could wake him up, but I never could. Nobody ever could, that's what I think now. Look," she suggested, "you just got here, and you don't know me, you ought to get to know me and then see what you think. Whether I could have been happy with him. OK?"

"OK."

"Is that all the questions? After all this time?"

"Well – what are those rings?"

She held her right hand out. "These" – she touched the turquoises with a fingertip – "were given to me by a man I'm dating. You'll like him. I hope you'll like him. It's his car. And this one" – the old-fashioned looking ring, with the reddish stone – "I found in an antique shop. I thought it might be worth something, if the stone was a ruby, and the dealer didn't have any idea of what she had – she was just some old lady who didn't know anything; she had no business being in business, I felt so sorry for her – so I bought it, on speculation. But when I had it valued . . ."

She threw her hands up, empty. "But it's a hundred dollar ring I got for three hundred dollars."

"And that one?"

She spread her hands out on the tabletop. "The pearl Gambo gave me for my sixteenth birthday. It was one of hers."

Jeff looked at her hands, the fingernails glistening with clear polish, the nails shaped, the delicate bones at her wrist. He reached across and put his own hand over hers, surprised at himself for doing it. "You have beautiful hands," he said to her.

She understood what he was feeling, what he really wanted to say to her. "I love you too," she answered him.

Melody had left her purse behind, so Jeff paid for the lunch out of the twenty dollars of his own money. The bill came to twelve dollars, to which Melody insisted that he add a three dollar tip. "Do you know what waitresses get paid in places like this? A dollar fifty an hour, and the owners get away with it because it's not a big enough business to require minimum wage. So they depend on tips."

Jeff took the change he had just been given out of his wallet. "Were you a waitress?"

"No, but I know some people who were. And part of it is because they're women, they get away with paying women less and the poor women just

. . . take it. I don't want you to be like that, Jeffie."

Jeff nodded his agreement. He would try. He felt guilty that he had never thought of it before.

Back at Gambo's house, Melody took him into the kitchen and introduced him to the black woman who was working out there, Miss Opal. The kitchen, back behind the house and attached to it by a short hall, was a low-ceilinged, dark room, its temperature even higher than that outside because of the heat from the big range. Miss Opal had set out two trays, for the old ladies, she said. They wanted afternoon tea in their rooms, so they would be rested for the celebration dinner in young Jefferson's honour. Miss Melody, she said, had had several phone calls, the messages were written down. Melody told Jeff that her friends didn't believe she had a son, they didn't believe she was taking some days off just to be with him, she guessed she wouldn't bother returning those calls too quickly because she had told them and told them she wouldn't be available to help out. She told him to wait there, she would go up and get her guitar then they would sit outdoors. "I'll serenade you."

. When they were settled outdoors, Jeff said. "I didn't know you played the guitar," as he watched her tune the strings.

"I've just started," she told him. She sat cross-legged, her feet tucked up under her bright skirt, her hat set beside her on the grass. Jeff lay on his stomach, resting his chin on his folded arms so he could look at her. She watched her own hands as she played and sang. "What kind of songs do you like?" she asked him.

Jeff couldn't tell her any. She forgave him that and simply played what she wanted. Her songs were mostly sad. "Where have all the flowers gone?" one asked, then, "Where have all the young men gone?" They had all gone to war and been destroyed so the song asked, "When will they ever learn?" She sang a song about a calf being taken to market, a song with a refrain in the voice of the uncaring winds: "Calves are easily bound and slaughtered, never knowing the reason why," she sang; "But whoever treasures freedom, like the swallow must learn to fly." She sang a song he rather liked, about a mine caving in, in Nova Scotia. She played the same thin strum on the guitar for that one that she had played for the others, but Jeff could hear in the song itself how the guitar might sound behind the melody line, how it should sound, strong and rhythmic: "For all their lives they dug a grave, two miles of earth for a marking stone, two miles of earth for a marking stone."

The guitar didn't sound so good, but Melody's voice – low and sweet, holding on to the notes – poured over him. She sang as if she believed each and every word. Her eyes shone with sincerity and she curved over the instrument like a flower bending in the wind.

70

Jeff watched and listened, basking in his own feelings: of being with his own mother, who wrapped her love around him; of being – strange as it seemed – home, where he was welcome; of waking up to a world where his help was needed to right what was wrong; of lying on soft grass under trees hundreds of years old beside walls that his ancestors had built; of being heavy with the perfumed heat of the day.

Melody had to go out to a party that night. She piled her hair on top of her head, put on a lacy blouse and a long patchwork skirt, and kissed Jeff goodnight. "I have to go," she said. He didn't mind and said so. "See you in the morning," she said, her hand lingering on the top of his head just as his eyes lingered on the place where she had been standing, long after she had gone out of the door.

He sat with Gambo and the two aunts in a living room dominated by a big colour television set. Gambo held the remote control box in her hand, and she turned the sound down so that she could talk with Jeff, who sat beside her on a satin-covered love seat. The two aunts had straight-backed chairs drawn up close to the television screen.

"You're a Boudrault and you don't even know what that means," Gambo said. "There's so much to tell you." Jeff looked alert and concentrated on not being distracted by the moving figures on the screen at the corner of his vision. Gambo folded

71

her hands on her lap. The large diamond ring she wore on her left hand glittered. On her right hand, a ring of small diamonds surrounded a flat green stone. Her eyes followed Jeff's glance.

"An heirloom." She held out her right hand for Jeff to look more closely at the ring. "My great-grandmother's engagement ring, made to order here in Charleston. She loved jade. Her collection of jade figurines is in the bank now – the cost of insuring it is prohibitive, over sixty pieces, each exquisite. The goldsmith worked her initial into the setting, but you can only see that under a magnifying glass, the letter D. They say the goldsmith was in love with her. Of course, everybody was: she was a great beauty in her day. We had a portrait, but like so much else it has been lost to us. I never saw her. She died young, in childbirth, but this ring my grandmother left to my mother, my mother to me. Dolores, her name was Dolores. This other" – she held up her left hand – "was my engagement ring and I always wear it. But the jade is dearer to me as the years go on. He was killed, you know, in the First War, and I was left with my memories and the one child. Just as Melody's poor father was killed in the Second War. The Boudrault women have married young. They have not been fortunate in their marriages, not fortunate at all." Her voice was dry, cracked like fine china after years of wear. She went on and on, until Jeff had a sense of family spreading out around them endlessly, and only an hour later, when she was lost in reminiscences, did he understand that the names she mentioned, the people she spoke of, were most of them long ago dead. The family spread not out and around, but back, back into time. At last, she looked at him and said, "I feel as if I can pour myself into you, everything I've learned, everything I know, and you will take it on into your life." Then she rose and withdrew from the room. The aunts – only they weren't aunts, Jeff remembered, but cousins from different branches of the family – remained where they were, staring into the television, chattering like birds to themselves. Jeff too went upstairs to bed.

In his room, he changed to pyjamas, folding his clothes neatly into the drawers, putting soiled socks and underwear away. He went down to the bathroom, peed, lowered the seat, brushed his teeth, then washed his face so that he could have the pleasure of drying it on the thick, soft towel. The night was too warm for even a sheet.

There was something about the house and the women in it that made him feel contented, as if to be contented was something you actually did. He thought lazily that he would figure out what it was and lay back on the softness of the bed, under the dark air. But he fell asleep.

After the first couple of days, Jeff didn't see so much of his mother, unless she took him with her to a meeting or to help with stuffing envelopes or distributing posters. But her presence marked the day for him. She knew, somehow, what he wanted her to do, or say, as if she could read his mind and know how he was feeling. It wasn't that Melody did exactly what he wanted to do, but that everything she did made him feel good, feel loved. It was as if she could see what he saw the way he saw it; as if they were close, even when they weren't actually together. Whenever they were together her eyes shone with affection and pride. He knew he was doing the right things for her, learning about discrimination and pollution, being no trouble to Miss Opal, who praised him for his personal neatness, good appetite, and gentlemanly manners. Gambo talked to him and talked to him, until Jeff had pieced together the names and events so that he could follow her conversation and ask her the questions she wanted to answer. The aunts seldom spoke, but he was conscious of their admiring and approving eyes. During the days he wandered around the historic parts of the city, or travelled by bus to scenic spots beyond its industrialized outer ring, to see plantations and gardens. He had, in the first days with Melody, spent all his money, even the four dollars left from Brother Thomas's ten dollars when she had bought the most expensive possible bottle of local wine for him. However, he found that Gambo was more than happy to finance an expedition. If he told her at breakfast how much he needed, she would take out her black change purse and give him the dollars he asked for.

Jeff learned the songs Melody liked, until he could sing with her, and in the late afternoons or on evenings when she was at home, they sang together. She started to teach him how to play the guitar, then didn't have time, so gave him the books she had used. He spent long hours with the instrument, conscious as he held it that she, too, had so held it. He placed his hands where she had placed hers and could almost feel the imprint her hands had left, warm beneath his own. His sense of contentment continued and became the tone of every day. He listened and learned.

Even Miss Opal had stories to tell him of growing up in the old city and the life of the black communities on the nearby islands. Miss Opal lived now in a public housing apartment with her grandson, Willum, whom she had raised since he was five, when his parents both moved up north to take better jobs. Willum was in high school and gave his grandmother a deal of trouble. Miss Opal didn't complain about Willum. This was the way men were, she seemed to say; you have to give a young man plenty of freedom. When the devil got into Willum, she prayed for him, and chuckled over the scrapes he got into and saw to it that he was punished too.

Miss Opal called him Jefferson, as did Gambo and the aunts. His mother called him Jeffie. He had asked her what he should call her, and she told him Melody, "because I'm your mother but I really want to be your friend." Her name, Melody, sang within him, like the music he could sometimes win out of her guitar. The slow days passed. Jeff passed through them, a Boudrault in his own country. Their general history with his own history, too, the story of his own family was part of the history. His ancestors, all the Boudrault men, had stepped in their long boots where he stepped now or riding tall horses.

Jeff knew, when July turned to August and the long August weeks went by, that he would soon be going back to Baltimore, but even as the day of his return grew closer he could not imagine it. In his final week, he took to travelling further out from the city. He rode the bus down around John's Island, then once all the way to the end of the southern line. The bus stopped at a crossroads, by a general store. Jeff got off and walked, heading away from the city, passing rickety houses up on cinder blocks, where clothes blew in a steady breeze, crossing between long fields of vegetables, walking under a tunnel of live oaks that arched over the road, where Spanish moss hung down like furry icicles. The trees were not tall and straight like the great northern oaks, but bent and convoluted. Their leaves grew small and thick. The hanging moss draped down from them, melancholy but not heavy.

Jeff walked on and on. He came at last to a broad marsh, through which a narrow creek cut.

Beyond it, a line of low trees, palms and pines, marked one of the sea islands.

If he had a boat, Jeff thought, he would like to go over and explore the island. It stretched as far as he could see beyond the marsh. It looked like a different world; it looked tropical.

It was late in the afternoon when he returned that day, but nobody questioned him, nobody criticized his dusty legs or long, unexplained absence. Melody had gone out to a cocktail party and would not be back until much later in the evening; he was in time for dinner, so Gambo and the aunts had not been disturbed. They did not even ask him where he had been, what he had been doing, as if whatever he had done, wherever, must – because he was himself – be as it should.

The next day Melody took him to the bus. She had exchanged his airline ticket for a bus ticket, saying that the Professor had no sense of money, that there were better uses for the extra dollars. Jeff's bus, which left Charleston at five in the evening, would take sixteen hours to make the journey to Baltimore. They stood beside the big Greyhound saying goodbye. With his eyes, Jeff drank in his mother's face. She held both of his hands in hers, and her beautiful grey eyes filled with tears. "You never met Max, and he wanted to meet you," she said. Jeff didn't know what to say. "I've been so proud of you, Jeffie. And you've been happy, haven't you?"

Jeff agreed, although happy wasn't the word he

would have chosen to express the wonder of the summer. The driver leaned down and urged Jeff into the bus. Melody wrapped her arms round him and kissed his hair. "You have money?" she asked him.

Jeff shook his head.

"And I don't have any with me," she wailed. "Oh, Jeffie, what a bad mother I've been."

Jeff smiled at her. "No, you aren't, Melody," he said. "It doesn't make any difference, I won't starve to death in a few hours."

He had to climb on to the bus, then, and find a seat. By the time he was settled by a window she was gone.

Jeff sat alone, towards the back of the bus, beside the window. Few other people rode on it. The bus went west on the highway out of Charleston. Once they had left the city, they were travelling through a scrub pine forest and then, as they turned to head north, over flat land – flat fields, flat marshes, little flat ponds up against the highway. Slowly, the late afternoon light faded into the golden shades of sunset.

Going from Charleston, which lay behind him, to Baltimore, which waited ahead, Jeff felt not so much that he was travelling as that he occupied one single place, which rested between the other two. He looked out of the window.

It was not simply going from a warm to a colder climate, or from his mother to his father. It was also going from one self to another. In Charleston, he was Jeffie, Jefferson, Melody's son, the last in a long line of Boudrault men. In Baltimore, he was Jeff Greene, self-sufficient and reticent, no trouble at all, occupying his corner of the world. But he knew now how it felt to be loved, to be happy.

The bus rumbled on.

One of the small ponds came up into view. A solitary blue heron stood at its edge, half hidden in the pale marsh grass. The heron's legs were like stilts under its clumsy body. Its dusky feathers hung shaggy, ungroomed. It was perfectly motionless. Its long beak pointed down from a head both unnoble and unbeautiful. Its beak aimed down into the still, dark water. The heron occupied its own insignficant corner of the landscape in a timeless, long-legged solitude.

The bus swept past the pond. After a while, the sun completed its setting and darkness came up beyond the windows, a darkness lit by the occasional farmhouse window, the occasional crossroads, the occasional sign, the occasional town.

Jeff sang Melody's songs to himself, under his breath, under the rumble of the motor. He thought that some day, maybe, he would have to choose between his parents, the two of them. At the thought, his heart beat painfully in anticipation: he knew who he would choose, he knew why, and he said her name.

3

Jeff climbed down the steps of the bus. He didn't
see the Professor. He had picked up his suitcase
and stood looking dazedly around – before he
caught the eye of a short, round man in a black
suit, who was waving to attract his attention. A
clerical collar shone white round the man's neck.
Brother Thomas. Jeff's suitcase felt heavy.

"Welcome back, welcome home," Brother
Thomas said. "Your father asked me to meet you.
You look taller than I remember; have you
grown? And brown too; did you have a good
time? The car's right outside, unless somebody's
slashed the tyres or removed the engine. Whatever made you take the bus back? How was the
trip?"

Jeff tried to put an answering expression on his
face. He followed the short figure through the
waiting room and out to the street. He walked
into a wall of heat, hesitated, then forced himself
on. Brother Thomas put Jeff's suitcase in the
boot; Jeff collapsed weakly into the front seat. He
had stopped being actively hungry some time in
the middle of the night, but ever since then he
had felt as if he was getting paler and paler. He
knew he only had to wait until they got to the

house to eat, but the closer that time came, the less he felt the strength to hold on that long. He leaned his head back against the car seat. He closed his eyes. He was thirsty, too, so thirsty his tongue felt twice as thick as usual.

"I can't sleep on buses either." Brother Thomas spoke beside him. Jeff opened his eyes, turned his head. "Planes, I can, and trains and cars. But not buses. I don't know what it is. Do you feel all right?"

"Just hungry," Jeff said.

"Didn't you get enough breakfast?"

Jeff smiled at that and shook his head.

"Did you get any breakfast?" Jeff shook his head. "Why not? But what about dinner last night, did you have dinner?" Jeff shook his head. "The bus must have stopped, they always do; why didn't you get out and eat something?"

"I didn't have any money."

Brother Thomas opened his mouth, then closed it. He pulled the little car out into traffic. Jeff closed his eyes again. The air steamed and smelled thick with exhaust fumes. The noise of traffic rang in his ears.

Brother Thomas pulled the car to a stop and Jeff opened his eyes. They were in the car park beside a small stucco building. Jeff wanted to protest that he really wanted to get home and eat, but he didn't have the strength. "Come on," Brother Thomas urged him. Jeff obeyed.

Brother Thomas led him into a restaurant,

where they sat at the counter to order eggs, sausages, fried potatoes, toast, juice and milk for Jeff, and a cup of coffee for Brother Thomas. Jeff gulped down a glass of water, then another. When the food came, he ate unhurriedly but with full attention. When he had finished, he could feel the energy being carried around his bloodstream. He turned to his host, whom he discovered staring at him. "Thanks," Jeff said. "Really. I was hungrier than I thought." He picked up his water glass and emptied it again.

"I wish I could eat like that and not put on weight," Brother Thomas said. "You do look better. Less like a cooked noodle. Did you have a good time?"

"Yes. I've got a bottle of wine for you. In my suitcase. My mother" – his heart lifted at the word and at the memory – "helped me pick it out."

"Ready to go?" Brother Thomas put a five dollar bill down on top of the counter.

"I'll ask the Professor to pay you back. I'm sorry," Jeff said.

"Nothing to be sorry about," Brother Thomas said. They went back to the car. "He really wanted to meet you, your father. In fact, we were going to have dinner at the airport tonight, when your plane came in, all of us. There's a pretty good restaurant out at the airport. But he had a faculty meeting this morning." Jeff shrugged. Brother Thomas, his face blotched by the heat, beads of moisture on the bald top of his head, didn't say anything else about it. "Was your mother as beautiful as ever?"

"She really is," Jeff said. His words were caught up in a terrific yawn.

"You can tell us all about it, tonight," Brother Thomas promised him. He made sure Jeff got into the unlocked house then drove off, waving aside Jeff's thanks.

In the narrow hall, then in his own small room, unpacking his bag, Jeff had a strange sense of disappointment. It wasn't because the Professor hadn't been there to meet him; maybe it was because summer was over, or because the house was so – dark and small. Jeff fell on to the bed in his underwear and fell asleep. Heat lay over him like a wet woollen blanket.

When he awoke, it was late afternoon and his body was bathed in sweat. For a long moment, he did not quite know where he was. Then he opened his eyes. The cracked and yellowed paint on the ceiling, the cramped room, the window framed by limp curtains and itself framing a view over rooftops to the flat surfaces of distant buildings, the sulphurous sky – he sat up in bed. Everything looked dingy, although it looked also as if it had been recently cleaned. Jeff felt the little house pressing close around him.

He went to take a shower. From downstairs, he heard noises. In the shower, which he ran cool, he concentrated on folding close in around himself the remembered contentment of the summer, like armour against – he couldn't name it, but it threatened him. He summoned up Melody's image, he summoned up her voice; to himself he sang her song about the calf being taken to market and the swallow soaring above.

Jeff dried off, stepped back into his underpants, and went to put on a shirt and a pair of shorts. He combed his hair in front of the mirror. Glancing into the glass, he caught his own eyes: grey, a smoky grey circle rimmed with darker grey at the outside, faint darker grey lines radiating out from the pupil; the eyes were circled by thick dark eyelashes; they were large eyes, a rounded almond shape. He stared at them, his glance going from one to the other mirrored eye, surprised.

These were his mother's eyes. His eyebrows did not arch over them, as his mother's did, but were straight. His hair lay flat on his head; his mouth was broader, thinner than Melody's. But the shape of the face – he almost traced it in the mirror with his finger – the straight, narrow nose, the chin, was very like hers. He looked back into his own eyes, a grey so deep that it did not ever change colour. They were like hers, they were hers. He felt almost as if he could convince himself that he was looking at Melody, that she was with him now. He hugged the idea to himself and went downstairs.

The Professor sat in the kitchen, and Brother

Thomas stood at the sink, peeling potatoes. The back door stood open. Both windows were open. They were trying to relieve some of the heat that poured out of the oven. Jeff smelled roasting beef.

The Professor studied him for a moment with mild blue eyes behind big glasses. Jeff studied his father. Finally Jeff said, "It's hot."

"That it is," the Professor agreed. His face was flushed and not tanned. "Did you enjoy your summer?"

"Yes," Jeff answered. "Did you?"

"Yes," the Professor said. Jeff sat down. Brother Thomas continued peeling potatoes, then he put them in a saucepan to parboil. He turned round to face the two at the table.

"Is that all you have to say?" he asked them. "Well, I've got questions. You two may be incurious by nature, but I'm not. Shall we open Jeff's wine?"

When they each had a tall glass of wine, Brother Thomas proposed a toast, "To Jeff on his return." He tasted the wine solemnly. "Your father had a quiet summer," he told Jeff. "Work, work, work. Drone, drone, drone. Buzz, buzz, buzz." He looked at the Professor as he said this, his expression friendly.

Jeff's father didn't seem to mind the teasing. "And Jack is a dull boy," he said.

Brother Thomas smiled. "Well, you didn't say anything. 'Did you have a nice time? Yes, how

85

about you? Yes.'" His voice as he mimicked them was flat, monotonous. "For all he knows you spent the summer in and out of jail."

"On what charges?" the Professor asked.

"I don't know, Horace, inciting to riot, being a public nuisance, you know, your everyday criminal charges. Murder and mayhem."

Jeff looked at the two men, surprised, amused. They had always talked like this but he had never heard the undercurrent of joking before. He had changed, he thought, Melody had changed him. His hearing the joking was because of her, his enjoyment of their conversation was because of her.

"Moral turpitude," the Professor suggested. "I always liked that, that and breach of fiduciary trust."

Jeff tasted his wine and remembered something. "I spent the change. But I'll pay you back," he told Brother Thomas.

"Don't worry. What did you spend it on? Or, how did you like the South?"

"I liked it fine," Jeff said. "Gambo's house is – old and big." He looked around his own kitchen, seeing the smallness of it, the black places – where white porcelain on the stove and sink had chipped away, the yellowed paint on the walls and cupboards, the musty brown linoleum floor. He thought, looking at the Formica table and the slightly rusted stainless steel tubing of the chairs they sat on, of Gambo's dining room, with its

86

long, polished table, its high windows, the china and silver set out on lacy mats.

"You look like sleeping beauty, waking up," Brother Thomas said.

Jeff flushed, and smiled. He didn't look at his father. "It's all so old and beautiful. Even though it's hot, it's not hot in the same way, because of the trees and grass and the bricks and the breezes off the harbour." He couldn't explain how the large airy rooms made him feel.

"And who is Gambo?" Brother Thomas asked. "No, first, why did you take it into your head to come back by bus? I gather" – he turned to look at the Professor, who nodded agreement – "that you refused to fly."

Jeff didn't know what to say. "It doesn't cost as much," he explained to his father. The pale blue eyes behind glasses showed no expression. "And we could walk to the bus station. She doesn't have any money, not very much, I think." The eyes flickered, then returned to expressionlessness.

An uncomfortable silence occupied them. Jeff looked at Brother Thomas, who was staring at the Professor, and the man's brown eyes looked surprised, but he didn't say anything. Jeff knew he had said something wrong; he'd forgotten the rules for this house. He couldn't be sure what was wrong about it, except that something was. But he wasn't going to tell on Melody.

"Gambo's my great-grandmother," he said, to

change the subject. "She's a Boudrault, that's an old family; she knows all about her ancestors. She told me about them. It's her house, down on the Battery – that's the old part of the city. I guess" – he decided to say the words boldly – "my mother lived there when she was growing up." He looked at his father.

"I never met Gambo," the Professor told Brother Thomas. "Melody" – he looked at Jeff as he said her name – "used to go down in the summers for a long visit, but I never went. I gathered that Gambo's always lived in Charleston, a rather wealthy family, something of a southern belle. She must be pretty old now, although I think she was married young – not that old really, if her husband died in 1918, not at all old for a great-grandmother. In her seventies? Jeff, do you know?" Jeff shook his head.

"She doesn't look as old as the aunts," he offered.

"The aunts? What aunts?" Brother Thomas asked.

Jeff tried to explain about the aunts who were really cousins, and then about the mornings and how the air was sweet and fresh. He talked about the shaded streets of the city and the outlying plantations, restored so you could see what life had been like. They ate roast beef and oven-roasted potatoes, and the two men finished the bottle of wine. Brother Thomas asked Jeff questions and Jeff answered them.

"What did you do all day?" Brother Thomas asked. Jeff told him. "What did you like best?" Brother Thomas asked.

"I liked it being so beautiful," Jeff answered. "I like playing the guitar." He didn't mention other things he had liked, the fluttering attentions of the aunts, his great-grandmother's way of telling him and telling him that he was a Boudrault of Charleston, Melody kissing him goodnight.

"Are you going back next summer?" Brother Thomas asked.

Yes, Jeff wanted to answer, wanted to be able to answer with confidence. But "I don't know," he said.

"You never can tell with Melody," the Professor told Brother Thomas, his eyes on Jeff.

Jeff didn't argue, but he knew what he knew.

Jeff wrote his thank-you note to Gambo right away, and after a week, when school had opened and he had something he could write about, he wrote a letter to Melody. He made it as interesting as he could – telling her about his classes and teachers, especially that there were no women teachers because he thought that would interest her. He thought he might get an answer after a week, and for the last two weeks of September he waited impatiently every day to get home and look at the mail. The Professor usually got home first, because he had scheduled all of his classes in the morning that year, to clear away the afternoon and evenings for work, he said. But in the pile of magazines and advertising on the kitchen table there was never a letter for Jeff.

Jeff thought maybe his letter had got lost. "Do letters get lost?" he asked his father.

"Sometimes," the Professor said. "Not usually."

So Jeff wrote again. He spent a long time planning what he would say, several days, to gather the most interesting topics. That way he could always be thinking about Melody. He sang to himself, sang the songs she had sung to him, and that also kept her close. "I wrote to you before," he wrote, "did you get the letter?"

While he waited for her answers, he started reading about the South. He found books in the library about the Civil War, first, about Lee and Beauregard, Manassas, the burning of Atlanta. He read *Gone with the Wind*. Then he found books about Colonial days and the South during the Revolutionary War, Marion the Swamp Fox, the Oglebys of Georgia. He hurried through his homework so that he could read. During the school day, he thought about the South and himself as a Boudrault, because that also was thinking about Melody. His grades went down further, and the teachers said he was daydreaming during class. The other boys formed themselves into friendships and ignored Jeff. He played soccer, if they needed someone, but always ate lunch alone.

But his mind was on Melody, remembering, holding her close. He knew that if he didn't hold the memories close they would drift away, and she would drift away. The Professor gave him five dollars a week for allowance, and Brother Thomas gave him ten dollars for his twelfth birthday present, so after a few weeks Jeff had enough money to go to a pawnshop and buy himself a guitar. It was a heavy old steel string guitar, a Stella. At first, when he played it for too long a time, his fingertips would throb with pain and sometimes the tips would bleed. Then he learned how to use a flat pick and developed callouses on the tips of his left hand. After a while he could play for as long as he wanted.

And still Melody did not write him a letter. Jeff didn't think about that. He thought instead about love, and if you loved someone – well, you just loved them, you didn't love them just if they did what you wanted, like write you letters. You either loved them or you didn't. He wrote her another letter at the beginning of November this time with news of his guitar. He told her that when he played it he thought about her and that was why he liked it so much: that was the truth. One rainy November day, during Civics, he had an idea. "What if you write letters and the person has moved or gone away?" he asked the Professor that evening.

"Then the letters are returned to you," the Professor said.

"So if they don't come back they've been delivered."

The Professor nodded. "Why are you asking? Are you considering a career in the postal service?"

Jeff didn't know what to say, so he didn't say anything. Melody had got his letters and she didn't want to answer, or she was too busy. Probably she was too busy, she did have a busy life, he'd been there and seen that. He felt his father's eyes on him and wondered if his father knew why he was asking; but he didn't say anything because he wouldn't criticize her. He would be Melody's knight, here in their scruffy little house, like old-fashioned knights who loved their ladies sometimes without seeing them for years. But the knights were always faithful, no matter what. Jeff liked that idea, and he felt a little smile form itself on his face. Knights wore tokens, scarves usually, that their ladies had given them; and he had a guitar. He would, he decided, write to Melody every month, at the beginning, so she would know about him, about how he was faithful. If he made his letters interesting enough, she might answer. If she didn't answer, that didn't mean she had forgotten him. If she forgot him that was just because he was easy to forget. So he didn't have any right to have hurt feelings.

"Jeff?" the Professor asked, breaking in on his thoughts. "What are you thinking about?"

"Melody," Jeff answered, looking him straight

in the eye, like throwing his metal gauntlet down on the table in challenge.

But the Professor just nodded his head, as if he understood, and went back to his hamburger. He changed the subject: "That guitar of yours – it isn't as pretty as some I've seen around campus. Does that mean anything about its quality?"

"It's not a very good one. But I'm not very good at playing it."

"Are there good ones?"

Jeff had spent a couple of Saturday afternoons hanging around instrument shops. But he didn't know his father was interested, so he hadn't said anything. "There are Gibsons, some of the old Gibsons are pretty good." His father still paid attention. "And the Martins, they're terrific, if you know how to play. I've never played on one, but I heard some people in a shop. The wood on those is beautiful."

The Professor's eyes grew vague, and Jeff dropped the subject. Then the Professor said, surprising Jeff, "There's a man named Bream. Brother Thomas has tickets to a concert he's giving over the Christmas holidays. He thought we'd like to go."

"OK," Jeff said. It didn't interest him very much, he'd never heard of the guy. His guitar was his link to Melody, his token; that was its value for him. "Is he a guitarist?" he asked, to be polite, because it was something his father seemed to want him to be interested in.

"He plays the guitar and the lute, I think. This is a lute concert. We thought you might like to hear him."

"OK," Jeff said again.

"We wondered if maybe you'd like to take lessons."

"I don't think so," Jeff answered quickly. He knew how the guitar worked for him, just like looking into his own eyes in the mirror worked, to bring her close. He didn't want to risk any change. "Thanks anyway," he added.

The concert surprised Jeff, caught him unawares. It was given at the Peabody Institute, in a narrow auditorium that was crowded with people. Julian Bream came on to the stage carrying his own chair to sit on, and the audience clapped for just a little bit, then stopped, rustling into an eager silence. Jeff couldn't see the musician clearly, just a figure on a chair on the stage, holding what looked like a misshapen guitar. But when he started to play and the music filled the air of the room, winding and weaving until it lay over Jeff like a net, Jeff almost forgot to breathe. It was like guitar music, the plucking on strings, the tones reverberated out from the belly of the instrument, the one hand on the neck, the other on the strings; but it rang like church bells, quiet church bells. Melodic lines, chords, harmonies – how the almost motionless figure could make such complicated music Jeff did not know. He felt the music enter his body and flow along with his blood.

Some of the pieces were slow, some in quicker rhythm, some were one simple clear line and others were dense progressions of chords. For a long time, Jeff gave himself over to the music.

Until he realized what he was doing and then he tried to stop. He resisted the notes as they called out to him, because he could hear how weak and thin Melody's songs were in comparison to this man's mastery. The concert was wonderful, but he wouldn't let it capture him. When he found himself sitting forward in his seat, he made himself lean back. He forced his eyes to wander over the rest of the audience rather than stay riveted to the figure on the stage. If he was Melody's knight, he could admit no imperfection in his service to her, no disloyalty.

"How'd you like it?" Brother Thomas asked him as they made their slow way out of the auditorium. "Isn't he something?"

Jeff nodded agreement and added, in honesty, "I've never heard anything like it. Thank you." Music with song was one of his links to Melody, and nothing would come before that; but he couldn't deny the truth, so he said, "It was wonderful."

4

Jeff had sent Melody a scarf for Christmas, a green silk scarf painted over with pinks and golds and oranges, like a garden. She would have to write him a thank-you note for that, he thought, but that wasn't why he'd sent it. He sent it so that he would be perfect in his love.

They didn't celebrate Christmas at their house, not with a tree or stockings or lots of presents. They never had, Jeff supposed, since he couldn't remember any Christmases, even from when he was young. Usually, the Professor got him a present, a book – he'd got a fire engine one year, he remembered, with a ladder that went up and down. Since they'd been alone together, Jeff always got a present for his father, too, a book about wines, or a new and fancy corkscrew, or a keycase. This year, he'd got his father a belt, because the Professor's old one was cracked and worn where the leather had been too often rubbed. Jeff couldn't remember what he'd given his father last year, or what he'd been given. But the present for Melody felt to him like no other he'd given, or got. He knew it was perfect, and perfectly beautiful. He thought about how much she would like it. When he thought like that, happiness swelled up warm within him.

On Christmas morning, Jeff brought down the box for his father when he came to make breakfast. Usually in the holidays they ate breakfast and lunch whenever they felt like it, because the Professor often worked late and slept late; but on Christmas Day they ate all three meals together. Jeff put his box, gift-wrapped by the shop, at his father's place. When he heard the Professor stir upstairs, going into the bathroom for his morning shower, Jeff started to cook sausage links and broke eggs into a bowl. When everything was ready, he called up.

The Professor, dressed, his white hair damp on his head, came to the table empty-handed. He unwrapped his present silently and thanked Jeff, then ate his breakfast slowly. Jeff didn't mind not getting a present, but he was worried that his father might mind having forgotten. He wondered if he should say something to the Professor, to reassure him; he wondered if he could remember next year that they weren't exchanging presents any more. He ate as slowly as the Professor and wondered if Melody had opened her scarf yet.

The Professor cleared their plates from the table and poured himself a second cup of coffee. "Well," he said. "Merry Christmas." He sounded uncomfortable, and he stood uncomfortably beside the stove, holding his coffee mug awkwardly. Jeff tried to think of how to say to the Professor that he didn't care about getting a present, when his father abruptly left the room. Before Jeff had time to figure out – listening to the footsteps in the hall going down to the study – if his father was angry, or what, the Professor returned, carrying a large, flat box across his arms. He had wrapped the box round with red tissue paper.

"Merry Christmas," he said again, still uncomfortable. He put the box on Jeff's lap. He took his mug and sat down to watch Jeff.

Jeff looked at the flat box and then at his father. His father's discomfort was catching. "Thank you," he said. "It's not a book," he observed.

The Professor leaned his elbows on the table. An uneasy smile moved at his mouth, just a little. "Open it."

Puzzled by his father's strange mood, Jeff did. He took the paper off carefully, then prised up one end of the cardboard box. As soon as he saw the smooth curved strip of wood, he knew it was a guitar. He pulled it gently out of the box.

A Martin.

And one of the old ones.

He put it across his lap and laid his hands on it, touching it. The six steel strings stretched taut up over the belly and along the fretted neck. The frets and tuners glowed, their metal worn to a deep shine by age and by use.

Jeff ran his fingers all around its outlines, its deep curves, its straight lines. He plucked at low E and heard the mellow, clear reverberation of a perfect note. He looked up at his father, across the table. "It's an old one," he said. Then his voice choked and he swallowed. "May I be excused?" he asked quickly. He didn't wait for an answer because he could feel tears swelling up behind his eyes. He left the kitchen hastily. Halfway up the stairs, he remembered and turned back. He put his face just through the doorway. His father had been staring into the mug of coffee, his face expressionless. "Thank you," Jeff said. "Thank you," he said again. His voice sounded steady, but emotions pushed up behind his eyes as he repeated his thanks, and he rushed down the hall. The Professor didn't like tears and emotions – and it would be a rotten way to show how much he liked the guitar to throw all that emotion at the Professor, to show how he was feeling.

And he was feeling – Jeff sat on his bed just hugging himself – he didn't know what he was feeling; it wasn't just happiness because it hurt him. It didn't hurt anywhere particular, but as if he wasn't large enough to hold the feeling and still he had to hold it. It was as if something he wanted so badly he didn't even dare to notice how he wanted it, because he couldn't ever have it, had come to him – just fallen out of the sky. He didn't deserve it. He couldn't understand how it happened now to be his. He couldn't even think, he could just feel.

Jeff got a pick and sat down again, holding the

Martin. He put his fingers on the strings and started to play. He played a simple progression, A-D-E, and the perfect sound brought tears to his eyes again. He waited, then played again, the song that reminded him most of Melody. "On a wagon, bound for market, sits a calf with a mournful eye." After a few minutes he found his voice to sing it.

He played and sang the few songs he knew over and over again. At last he realized how hungry he was and went downstairs, where he discovered it was well past lunchtime. The Professor emerged from his study to stand in the kitchen doorway while Jeff hurriedly ate a peanut butter sandwich and gulped a glass of milk, impatient to get back to the Martin. The Professor looked like he wanted to say something, so Jeff waited. Music rang inside his head.

"If you'd rather have a new one," the Professor said, "there's no trouble. I'd rather you have what you want."

Jeff felt laughter rising in him, and he let it ride through him. The last thing he wanted was a new Martin, not with this solid gold old one, made in better days by better craftsmen. His father's ignorance in suggesting that made him laugh; a clear bubble of happiness made him laugh.

The Professor's eyes flickered once, and his face didn't change. He nodded, once, briefly, and walked away. Jeff heard the study door close behind him. Shaking his head, smiling to himself, he swallowed down the rest of the milk. He rinsed out the glass, then washed it and set it upside down on the rack to dry. He capped the peanut butter jar and put it away. He washed the knife he had used. But the flicker in his father's eyes had looked like hurt feelings.

Jeff stopped smiling. But that was ridiculous, the Professor didn't fool around with feelings, they weren't a part of his life. But what if – ?

What if Jeff had got the greatest present anyone could have given him and the Professor thought he didn't like it? But he'd said thank you. Melody would have understood, he thought impatiently. But what if the Professor didn't?

Jeff moved thoughtfully down the hall and stood before the closed door. He shouldn't, he knew, interrupt his father at work. But he *really* didn't want the man to misunderstand; because, after all, the Professor knew nothing about guitars. Jeff knocked on the door.

"Yes?"

So Jeff opened it and went in.

The Professor sat at his desk, in the middle of the room facing the door, working on a pile of papers.

"I'm sorry," Jeff said. He stepped into the room, one step, then stopped.

"Don't worry about it, it doesn't make any difference. We can go back tomorrow so you can pick out the right one," the Professor said.

"You really don't understand. Because it's the best present anyone could give me." Jeff hurried the words out because his throat was choking up again. "The old Martins are – they're wonderful, the way they sound. Much better than the new ones. I didn't expect – anything like that." To his horror, tears were in his eyes.

"I'm sorry," he apologized again. "I don't mean to be – emotional at you – I just – I just like it so much."

His father looked at him. "Thank you for taking the trouble to make that clear."

Jeff heard the humour in that and a little laugh came up through his choked throat. "Yes sir," he said, smiling back, leaving the room, returning to his Martin.

By the end of the afternoon, calloused as they were, his fingertips throbbed. He had learned, among other things, that he was much more limited than his instrument. He wanted to learn more chords, more songs, more strums – he wished the shops were open so he could rush out and buy a couple of instructional books.

For Christmas dinner, Jeff roasted a chicken, made stuffing from a mix, cooked a packet of frozen peas. He poured out a glass of white wine from the carafe in the refrigerator and called his father to dinner. They sat down in silence, and Jeff carved. The Professor couldn't carve a chicken without hacking it into unrecognizable, unappetizing slabs; when the Professor carved, the chicken looked as if it had been torn apart by some inner explosion.

"Not much of a Christmas dinner, is it?" the Professor said.

Jeff was surprised. It had been years since he had thought about that. "We never do much for Christmas," he reminded his father. "We never did."

"That's true. But I wonder if we should have."

"I don't see why," Jeff told him. "It doesn't make any difference."

"You know," the Professor said, lifting a bit of breast meat to his mouth, "I don't think I ever realized that there's a lot of your mother in you."

Jeff didn't know what to say. "I'm sorry," he said, apologizing for the tears yet again.

"When she first loved me," the Professor said, thoughtfully, without expression, "when she loved me, I felt as if – I had swallowed sunlight. Like the sun was rising inside me."

Jeff just stared at his father.

"I've never felt so helpless, before or since. Happy, too."

"Then why did you get divorced?" Jeff asked.

"We're not divorced," the Professor told him. "But what I mean to communicate to you – however clumsily – is that you should not be sorry to be like her. She had a way of knowing how I was feeling; I don't know how she did that." He returned his attention to his plate. Jeff watched him for a minute before lifting his own fork again.

"You know, I never call you anything." He didn't look up.

The calm voice answered: "Thomas noticed that, years ago. I'm not the Daddy type, or Pop – I can understand your difficulty."

Jeff looked up.

"When you think of me, do you call me anything? More than just *he*?"

"Yeah. Professor," Jeff answered, with a grin.

His father chewed. "Yes. That would do."

Jeff thought it might. "Yes, sir," he said, then tried it out, "Yes, Professor." Yes, that would do fine. "And Professor," he said; his father lifted his eyes again, chewed without speaking, "the Martin is perfect. I can't ever thank you enough."

"Good," the Professor said. "That's what I hoped. That it would be perfect, that is. Not that you would feel bound by everlasting gratitude."

Brother Thomas never came to see them on Christmas Day, because it was a holy day; instead, they had a special dinner on the day after Christmas. This year, he made them veal·Marengo, "A ragout, *not* a stew," he told Jeff as he cut a veal joint up into chunks. "With mushrooms and tomatoes, a little wine and the peel of an orange. Why don't you bring down that famous guitar of yours and give me a little musical background while I labour here?"

104

Jeff hesitated. He'd never played for anybody. "I'm not very good," he said.

"I don't mind, do you?"

"Well," Jeff said.

"Do you want to be better? Do you plan to be?"

"Sure."

"Then what's the harm?"

So Jeff brought the Martin down and played on it. Brother Thomas seemed to be listening at most with only half his attention, so Jeff forgot he had an audience. When it was time to lay the table, Brother Thomas made his assessment: "You're not very good now, but I'll be surprised if you don't turn out to be quite good. Do you want to call the Professor?"

Jeff was pleasantly surprised. It turned out to be an evening of surprises, because Brother Thomas told them, as they sat full over empty plates, that he was going to England for a year to study at Oxford. He beamed at them, "Can you imagine it? The dreaming spires and me. Me and the dreaming spires."

"I'm very happy for you," the Professor said. "You must be pleased to have won the grant."

"Pleased – that's an understatement. This is Tommy Richardson from Peoria, whose father worked in an assembly line – the unsuccessful son, not the black sheep among the children, but certainly the maverick – you've been there, Horace, but I never thought I ever would."

Jeff looked up; his father had been to Oxford? Brother Thomas had been a kid named Tommy, whose brothers and sisters did better than he did?

"When do you leave?" the Professor asked.

"In a couple of weeks, which means I have to ask a favour."

"What's that?"

"Could you two give a home to my stereo while I'm away? The books and pictures I'll box, but the stereo – I'd like it to be used, it's better if it's in use."

"We could keep it in the living room."

"You could play it," Brother Thomas said. "There's room at the back of the kitchen, there, just as long as you keep the cover on when you're cooking – it's about the only room in the house with any space. Anyway, thanks. And then, if you'd come over during the summer . . .?"

Jeff looked at the Professor. He didn't want to make any plans for the summer. His father smiled, shaking his head. "We can't possibly afford it, you know that. We can barely afford to live the way we do."

"Don't be such a stick-in-the-mud, Horace," Brother Thomas insisted. "Your salary isn't that bad, your expenses can't be that much. What've you got, a mortgage at least ten years old so the rates aren't high – "

"But I had to borrow the down payment too, from the University. I'm still paying that off, as well. With interest. And then, there were bills

106

Melody had run up, and she'd borrowed some money so she could make donations big enough to do some good. She wanted to. I've pretty near cleared those away now, but there's the school, too, and living expenses. We don't have any savings, Thomas. I'm really sorry, we just don't have the money."

"I thought you didn't have to pay for me," Jeff asked.

"That went out when you were in fourth grade."

"I'm sorry," Jeff said.

"It didn't make any real difference," the Professor said.

It wasn't just the tuition, it was also uniforms, books, supplies, lab fees, Jeff knew. He felt bad, because his father's money was being wasted. He wasn't doing very well in school, Cs at the best; and somehow, over that first seventh grade term, he had become a real nobody. He had gone from being nobody much to somebody nobody liked. He wasn't disliked, exactly, he was just in the way. It used to be that he was sort of there, in the playground for a soccer game, or at his desk in the classroom. Nobody minded him being there, but nobody actually wanted him there. Now, they would just as soon not have him there; not because he was disliked, but because he was in the way. Like a fly in the room. You didn't really mind the fly, you just waved it away. You didn't notice when it had gone. Jeff didn't think about school, except to dislike the careless tone of voice in which he was told to change his seat or that he wasn't welcome in some game. "Move it, Greene," one of the boys would say. Jeff never even bothered looking to see what boy it was. In classes, except that he seldom spoke because he heard faint sighs whenever the teacher called on him, it didn't make any difference to him. It didn't make any difference to him away from school. He had the guitar and now the Martin, he had his memory of Melody, and nothing could touch him.

Jeff wrote to his mother on the first of the month, January, February, March, April, May and June. He gave up hoping for a response. He did get postcards from Brother Thomas occasionally, pictures of castles, or the pages of illustrated manuscripts, with an informative message and the signature scrawled at the bottom, *BroT*. But from Melody, nothing, not even after Christmas. Jeff didn't let himself think about that. The stereo sat at the back of their kitchen and often poured out music, because Brother Thomas had also left his records for them to take care of. Jeff became familiar with names like Mozart and Handel, Bach, Brahms and Beethoven, Shostakovitch, with their music, in which melody – song – was only part of it. Out of his allowance he bought himself a couple of records of people who played guitar and sang: Joan Baez who reminded him of

Melody; Pete Seeger, many of whose songs were familiar to him; Judy Collins. By listening, he learned to mimic some of what they did on the guitar; the Martin could do anything he asked of it. It could do, he knew, more than he asked of it, more than he could yet ask.

One day in May, Jeff finally asked his father whether he had any photographs of Melody.

"No, I don't," the Professor said. "I never needed them – I never had any trouble remembering her."

Jeff waited, but he didn't add anything to that. Jeff wondered why Melody had said so confidently that the Professor would have pictures, but he didn't ask.

Melody's name came up again at the end of the month, again over dinner, but this time because Gambo wrote a letter to the Professor saying, yes, of course they would have Jeff for the summer, asking when he would arrive. The Professor showed Jeff the letter, which was about two lines long and signed with an unfamiliar name, Mrs Boudrault Melville. The handwriting looked old, thin and wobbly. It looked much older than Gambo did, and weak – as if she didn't have the strength to close her Os or lift the pen cleanly off the page to start a new word.

"That can't be her name," Jeff said.

"Her husband's, she's a widow. I believe her name is Eulalie. Melody called her 'Gambo', and I never met her. Do you want to go?"

"Yes. If it's all right with you? Did you write and ask her?"

"Well, I thought you'd want to, and I thought I'd waited long enough for them to contact us. I'll get the plane tickets. Unless you want to take the bus?"

"No," Jeff said quickly. Then he thought. "Unless – it's a lot cheaper, isn't it?"

"Not enough money to make any difference. I think, this time, I'll ask the airline counter to hold the return ticket for you to pick up. Unless you mind that?"

"Why should I? But Professor, how come you never met Gambo?"

The Professor shrugged. Then decided to answer, but kept his eyes on the bits of rice he lifted on his fork, kept his face expressionless. "We had a quiet wedding, so she didn't come up for it. Then, Melody, when she visited her home, stayed for weeks and . . . somehow they were always inconvenient weeks. I taught summer courses in those days, we needed the money, and there was you to take care of. Gambo wasn't used to children, not little children. And then . . ." His voice drifted away, and he picked up his knife to cut meat off his piece of chicken.

"Professor, why did you two – separate? If it's any of my business," Jeff asked.

"I guess it is," the Professor said. Jeff knew he hadn't offended his father. "But I don't know

110

how to explain it. Do you know what Tolstoy says?"

Jeff just waited. The Professor knew perfectly well he had no idea what Tolstoy said.

"Happy families are all alike; every unhappy family is unhappy in its own way," the Professor told him.

"That's an answer?"

The Professor chuckled. "I must admit," he said.

It was all right, Jeff knew. He knew he shared a sense of humour with his father. He hadn't always known that, but he had learned it. And he was going to spend the summer with Melody.

"I think," the Professor said, arranging his utensils side by side on the plate, "that I was a continual disappointment to your mother. From the beginning. At the beginning, she wanted a particular engagement ring – something like what her grandmother has. I never saw it, but it sounds expensive."

"It is."

"I couldn't afford that, of course, not with the down payment on this house, and she wanted a house, of course – and she didn't want a small diamond. I explained it to her, and she said she understood. But she didn't understand. And she understood less as time went on; she minded it, she was always disappointed. That's the kind of disappointment I mean. And this house wasn't what she wanted either."

111

Jeff heard that the Professor didn't want to say any more about it, and since he didn't want to make his father uncomfortable he didn't ask any questions.

"When do you think I can go down there?" he asked instead.

"A couple of days after school finishes?"

"Can I take the Martin?"

And he was thinking *Melody*.

5

Jeff waited patiently at the Charleston airport. He didn't even mind the waiting, because it prolonged the pleasure of anticipation. He felt warm and eager, inside himself. He felt his own face smiling, and he couldn't have stopped it if he'd wanted to. He hadn't brought the Martin because it would have had to have its own seat and that was too expensive. But if that was all he had to give up for a summer with Melody, he didn't mind.

He couldn't sit still. He walked around the waiting room. This time he had arrived during the evening commuter rush and the big room thronged with people. Jeff stood by the windows overlooking the field, looking out to the hot sky, looking back across the crowded room to the doors. He wanted to hug himself.

It was almost two hours later and Jeff stood dreaming by the tall windows, half watching a jet taking off into a blood red sunset, the air shimmering behind the turbines, when he heard his name called. "Jeffie? Jeffie?" His heart beat fast. The sunlight within him seemed to explode. He turned round.

She stood back from him and had a camera

with which she took two quick pictures. Then she lowered it and smiled at him. "Oh Jeffie," she said softly, and she hugged him tight. The camera hurt his breastbone, but he didn't mind that. "Melody." He said her name, breathing in her perfume at the same time. She was smaller than he remembered, more delicate.

"You're growing." She smiled at him. Her eyes were just as he remembered, deep, steady grey, the dark eyelashes framing them, beautiful. But her hair –

"Your hair," he said.

"Do you like it?"

It was curled into a frizzy profusion, cut shorter so that it came just to her shoulders, and a curly fringe covered her forehead. She stepped away and pirouetted around, so that he could see it from all sides. It rested round her head like a dark cloud. "Do you?" she asked, smiling into his eyes.

"You're beautiful," he said. Her laugh flowed over him, in the remembered way.

"Are you glad to be back? But we have to hurry, Max is waiting and he hates to wait; you remember Max – it's his car, but you never got to meet him, did you? We're late – I guess you know by now I'm always late. Do you mind terribly? Where's your suitcase?"

Jeff followed her out of the door. She wore a sundress, blue this evening, gathered in at her slender waist, and she was tanned. But she wore

114

sandals with heels this time, and when she walked there was a delicate clicking noise to mark every step. She tucked one hand under his arm and led him to the car. He opened the back door and put in his suitcase, then followed it. He had barely closed the door when the car started off.

The man behind the wheel had mousy brown hair that hung around his collar. He had a long, skinny neck and his nose, in profile, bent sharply at the middle, as if it had changed its mind about which way it wanted to point. "Jeffie," Melody said, turning sideways so she could see both of them, "this is Max, the man in my life."

Intense blue eyes studied Jeff in the rearview mirror.

"How do you do?" Jeff said.

"Don't you see now, he *could* come with us," Melody said to Max. She explained to Jeff, "There's a party over on Mt Pleasant. Max? He's perfectly presentable."

"I told you, babe. We've had this all out; you aren't going to try it on me again, are you? You don't have to come with me, but I'll need your camera if you don't. It's no skin off my teeth."

"All right," Melody said, disappointed. "But we can stop and get Jeffie a hamburger, can't we? So I can at least have a little time with him?"

"I guess so."

"That's OK," Jeff said. "I didn't know you took pictures."

"I just started six months ago, or so. Max did

115

an article on industrial pollution, and we wanted some pictures – so I got a camera. And then, it was so successful that I kept on with it. I even have a darkroom, down in the cellar; you'll see. You'll be proud of your old mother." Melody smiled.

"You're not old," Jeff said. He wondered if she was in love with Max, and he thought from the expression on her face when she looked at him that she was.

They sat at a booth in a café, Melody beside Max, the camera placed carefully on the seat beside Jeff, who faced them. Max had a long, narrow face, out of which his blue eyes shone. His eyes were sky blue and intense, as if some fire burned behind them. Jeff could feel a kind of power coming at him out of those eyes. He wasn't comfortable.

Melody went to the loo. Jeff watched her walk away and then turned his eyes back to those blue ones – they were like the eyes of an Old Testament prophet, he thought, somebody who had lived in the desert and gone a little bit crazy from talking with God.

"How long you staying?" Max asked him.

"The summer, I guess."

"I was out of town most of last summer," Max said. It sounded like he was warning Jeff.

Jeff didn't know what he was supposed to say to that. "What business are you in?" he asked. He heard his voice cracking on the question.

"What business are you in?" Max's voice mocked him. "I'm a journalist, when anybody has the courage to print what I write. Freelance. When they won't, I'm a pretty good carpenter-handy-man, or I do PR for people, lawn work, just about anything. Tonight I'm a society photographer for some stupid chick's engagement party. And what's your business?"

Jeff felt the man's hostility. He shrugged his shoulders, kids didn't have business.

"No, seriously, what's your name, Jeffrey? Jeffie's no name for a kid of – what are you, thirteen?"

"Almost."

"I don't know why anybody has kids, in this world. But then I suppose she wasn't planning it, she just got pregnant so she had to get married. It wasn't as if she wanted to have a kid, or get married. But abortions were illegal then and she was such a straight chick – that's what she says anyway. I never believe half of what she tells me."

Jeff held the gaze of the probing blue eyes, but he couldn't speak. He didn't think his face was giving away what he was thinking.

"As chicks go she's not too bad. We've been together, off and on, for more than three years."

A waitress brought two cups of coffee and Jeff's supper. He didn't want to eat, but he made himself. Melody came back and slid in beside Max. "Are you two getting to know each other?"

she asked, but her eyes watched Max's face for his response.

"Don't be any more stupid than you can help," Max said. Melody looked across the table to Jeff and smiled apologetically.

"He's terrible, isn't he?" she asked. Jeff almost grinned in answer, but stopped himself by jamming hamburger into his mouth. "Jeffie, Gambo had a stroke in March, and she's weak. So it won't be quite the same. She stays in her room a lot of the time; they have a nurse on nights when Miss Opal isn't there. Her mind's all right, but her heart — I guess it was always weak. You'll be careful with her, won't you?"

"Of course. I didn't know."

"She was in the hospital for a long time — well, she's old and it's to be expected. Are you finished? We have to go. Max'll get two hundred dollars for this job, and we can't be late. We have to catch the guests arriving. Do you have any money to pay?"

Jeff did, his father had given him twenty dollars again.

"If I'd known it was the kid's treat I'd have ordered myself something," Max said.

"Don't be awful, Max," Melody said. She put her slender brown hand over his on the table, the hand with the silver and turquoise rings. Then they slid out of the booth. Max wore a shirt and tie and blue jeans that rode just at his hips. He moved smoothly, like an athlete. He put his arm

118

over Melody's shoulders; she smiled up into his eyes. Jeff passed her the camera and she slung it over her shoulder. "Let's get going. We have to drop Jeffie off, but that won't take long. I'm sorry, Max, his father just wrote to say when he was arriving, he didn't ask if it was convenient."

"What the hell," Max said. Jeff followed them out of the café.

They dropped him off on Broad, because ten minutes taken negotiating the one-way streets to get to Gambo's house and then back again would be ten minutes too many, Max said. Jeff watched the car drive away, its two bright red lights at the rear, the two heads inside moving close together, as Melody shifted over to sit next to Max. She had said she would be very late and she'd see him in the morning. She had said he should go in quietly, so as not to disturb Gambo. "Miss Opal is waiting for you. See you in the morning, Jeffie." She reached back to lay one of her soft hands against his cheek.

She did love him, Jeff believed that; she wanted him to go to the party with her. They had the whole summer, after all. He picked up his suitcase and walked to Gambo's house. The dark air smelled of flowers, and the houses showed lighted windows above the high fences. He passed people walking towards the busier streets, he overheard soft voices in conversations that floated down from the second-storey verandas. He entered Gambo's house by the kitchen door.

Miss Opal sat at the table, drinking a glass of iced tea, thumbing through a magazine. "You're late," she said, at the same time Jeff said, "I'm here." They greeted one another. He told her he wasn't hungry. He apologized for being late, keeping her late at the house.

"Oh, I sleep over here now, this is my home now," she said. "But you'll want to see Mrs Melville."

"Is she feeling all right?" Jeff asked. "I didn't know she'd had a stroke."

Miss Opal nodded her head slowly. "She's mending. It'll take more than a stroke to kill off your great-grandmother. Your mamma treats her like spun glass, but that's wishful thinking, if you ask me. Let's go and let her know you've arrived. She's not what she used to be, though. You'll see that."

Jeff followed her down the passage to the dining room. He set his suitcase by the staircase. The size, the symmetry, and the beauty of the rooms opened around him. He took deep breaths, to swallow it all at once.

Gambo sat with the aunts in front of the television. She held a cane in one hand and the remote control in the other. She looked older, about a hundred years older. She was dressed in silk and jewels, the diamond flashing on her left hand, the little jade adorning her right. Her hair was perfectly arranged. But her face looked bony, and her fingers moved nervously along the top of the cane, and her dress was loose, bunched in at the waist. Her skin was pale, and her eyes riveted to the TV screen. She lifted her cheek to his kiss, "You go on to bed now," she told Miss Opal. "There was no call for you to wait up for him, and you're tired. He's a Boudrault, we find our way home."

Her voice, too, had changed: it creaked, and she took deep breaths between sentences.

Jeff sat down beside her. "Hello, Gambo, you look fine," he said, even though she didn't. But the more closely he looked at her, the more she looked about the same, essentially the same. He felt as if he had never been away.

The aunts turned to him with twittering voices. "The boy's back," they said. Jeff got up and greeted them. They said hello, hello, and then their eyes flicked back to the television screen.

"Oh look, it's that new Japanese car."

"I saw one, last week, parked all afternoon, right out front."

"You didn't, you're making that up."

Jeff returned to Gambo. "They just get worse," she told him. "Some day, they'll have to go into a home, but not while I'm alive," she said. She read the expression on his face. "They'll live for ever, not that I envy them, and they'll be taken care of. How did your mother look to you?"

"The same," Jeff said.

"Even with that hairdo?"

"Well," Jeff admitted. "I liked it better long."

"At least your taste is sound," Gambo said. "I don't know why she can't resist fads and fashions. It's that man, of course – with Melody it's always some man – and that one just doesn't go away. I wanted to meet your father, but Melody never would bring him down here. She said he wouldn't be comfortable in this setting, she said it was too rich for him, as if we were a chocolate mousse. I always thought she was afraid I'd win him away from her, I always did have a way with men. And Melody has a jealous streak – I've always suspected that."

Jeff didn't know what to think. "She's always beautiful."

"Beautiful," Gambo said. "Since it all comes to the same end, I'm beginning to wonder myself what even that's worth. In another five years I'll be just as brainless as they are." She indicated the aunts with a gesture of her hand that made her diamond catch the light and glitter. But her fingers trembled, and she caught hold of the cane again. "I told him it was too big, flashy, but he would have it," she said. "And in another sixty or so you'll be just like us. I don't know why we bother."

Jeff didn't say anything.

"Go away, Jefferson. You make me tired," Gambo said. She leaned her head back against the sofa and closed her eyes.

Jeff went upstairs to his own room. He unpacked his suitcase into the drawers. He

122

changed into his pyjamas and folded back the bedsheets. Then he turned off his light and sat by the window, looking out over the back yard to the familiar lighted windows, savouring the remembered sounds and smells. But he'd thought Gambo liked him, he'd thought he was welcome, he'd thought this was his real home. The disappointment tasted bitter, but he swallowed it quickly, because what Gambo and the aunts thought didn't make any difference. It was Melody, only Melody who mattered.

After a long time, he went to bed. He hadn't heard her come in, and he thought he would wait up until she was home safe, keeping watch over her even though she'd never know. But he fell asleep.

When Jeff went down to breakfast, Melody was not yet awake. Gambo had eaten and was drinking a cup of coffee, taking pills that she selected out of a tiny gold box set by her place. He said good morning to everyone, first Gambo, then the aunts. Gambo rang for Miss Opal to come and ask what Jeff wanted for breakfast. "You're going to have to amuse yourself, I don't know what you're going to do with yourself," Gambo said to Jeff. Her eyes were not friendly.

"I don't mind," Jeff said.

"Very generous of you."

"I'm really grateful to be here. I'm very glad you asked me," Jeff said. He didn't understand what he had done wrong, so he didn't know how to undo it.

"I didn't ask you, you asked yourself."

Jeff didn't know what to say. "I'm sorry," he said.

"As long as you understand that."

"I'm sorry you're feeling tired."

"Not tired, old. Young people don't understand so I can't expect you to." She breathed raspingly twice before continuing, "I must admit I thought your father would know better."

Jeff thought she shouldn't talk, and he looked around him at the long windows with their folded curtains, at the smooth, creamy walls and the portraits hung on them. He smiled at the aunts, who chattered with their heads together, casting sidelong glances at him. He heard Melody's footsteps on the stairs and he looked to where she would appear.

She stood in the doorway for a minute, slim and smiling, her eyes seeking Jeff's before she went to kiss her grandmother good morning. Miss Opal set a plate down before Jeff and he picked up his fork. Melody wore a flowered sundress and sandals and she moved as gracefully as wind over a garden of flowers.

"I'll never understand why you did that to your hair," Gambo said.

"I like it," Melody said. "I like the way it looks."

"It looks common."

124

"If you want me to, I'll grow it out again," Melody offered, her hand on the back of Gambo's chair.

"I've given up trying," Gambo said. She reached for the little bell again.

"You know I'm going to eat in the kitchen," Melody said.

"Take the boy with you," Gambo said.

Jeff got up happily, carrying his plate and juice glass. He ate at the kitchen table, watching his mother ask Miss Opal for scrambled eggs, then sit down across from him while Miss Opal set the table with a fork and coffee cup, with a little bowl of jam and a glass of juice. Melody didn't think there should be servants, so she always ate breakfast out in the kitchen, because she didn't think Miss Opal or anyone else should have to wait on her; Gambo didn't approve but Melody stuck to her principles.

"She's crotchety this morning," Melody said.

"What can you expect?" Miss Opal asked, beating eggs in a little bowl. "She never likes it when you're out with that young man."

"He doesn't come here," Melody said, "and she can't ask anything more than that."

"Oh well," Miss Opal said, "once she faces up to things, she'll be herself again. Facing up is the hard part."

"Well, I wish she'd hurry up," Melody said. "I don't know what she's got to complain about."

Miss Opal poured the eggs into a pan and stood

with her back to them. "Just the usual things, and they're enough," she finally said.

"Jeffie, Jeffie. What would you like to do today?" Melody reached over to take his hand, which he reached out to have taken. "I've got to work in the darkroom for a couple of hours, developing, and then I'll have to run off prints this afternoon – how would you like to take your old mother out to lunch? Would you like that? It'll give me something to look forward to."

"Yes," Jeff said. "Yes, please."

"Can you amuse yourself this morning?"

"Sure. Can I borrow your guitar?"

"I sold it last autumn. But I thought you had one of your own."

"I didn't bring it. That's OK. How come you sold yours?"

"You know, I can't remember. Miss Opal, can you remember?"

Miss Opal set a plate of eggs down in front of Melody, flanked with strips of bacon and slices of buttered toast. "You said you needed the money, that's all I remember."

"Well – there must have been some reason," Melody said. She ate hurriedly.

"I could come down and help you out in the darkroom."

"Oh no. No. Not today anyway. Are you interested?"

"Sure."

"Then I'll teach you, I promise, first thing. It'll

be our project for the summer, OK? I'll meet you up there, about noon; that should give me enough time. I'd steer clear of Gambo if I were you. She's having a bad day. Why don't you take a walk?"

So Jeff did that, because he wanted to do what Melody wanted him to do. When he was doing what she wanted, they were connected – in a way – they were touching, even if they weren't really.

He wandered for a while, and then walked uptown, to one of the cemeteries beside one of the old churches, where he strolled along the stone paths, reading inscriptions. The high walls made it seem like an overgrown garden, and muffled the city noises just beyond. The air grew hotter so that even in the shade of live oaks and glossy magnolias it was uncomfortable. Jeff sat beneath one of the oaks and waited through the ringing of the church clock, which marked off the quarter hours as the morning passed on towards noon. The thick silence of the graveyard was broken only by the chiming of the clock, 9:30, 9:45, 10, as he waited; 11, 11:15.

He was a little early getting back to Gambo's. He could hear lunch being served in the dining room. He sat on the bottom step of the stairs and waited for Melody. By the time she finally appeared, the women had finished their meal and gone back into the living room, to watch the afternoon soap operas. Melody ran up the stairs past him, "I've got to wash my hands and get my

127

purse, I'll be about two seconds. Are you terribly hungry?" She stopped halfway up, came back down to where he stood and put her arms round him, then kissed his head, just above the ear. "It's so good to have you back," she said, then ran up the stairs.

When they had ordered their lunches, after conferring about how much money Jeff had, she leaned across the table to smile into his eyes. Happiness welled up in Jeff so that there was nothing left of him but the beating of his heart and the grey of his mother's eyes. "What did you do this morning?" she asked.

It took him a minute to collect his thoughts. She laughed as if she knew the effect she had on him. "I went up to see the cemetery," he said.

"I missed you terribly, all the time," she said.

"Me too."

"You've got taller."

"Not much, only an inch or so."

"Did you like Max? Isn't he wonderful? I'm so glad you two finally got to know each other. Gambo can't stand him – you probably figured that out. She won't have him in the house. Isn't that perfect? Just like somebody in Faulkner's books? Well, he's not one of her southern gentlemen, he doesn't bow over her hand and make pretty speeches. But Jeffie, I have to go out of town for a week, just a week, I wanted to tell you. You don't mind, do you?"

He minded terribly. "No," he said. "Where are you going?"

"There's a folk festival in the mountains, the first annual South Carolina folk festival and fiddling contest. All the proceeds, after expenses, are going to the environmental group that's sponsoring it. I don't know if you've seen some of the eroded areas, the rural poverty – little children, Jeffie, who never get enough to eat, or medicine or shoes. Max wants to write an article on the festival and I'll take pictures. We talked it over and he said there wouldn't be anything for you to do, so it's better if you stay here with Gambo. That's all right, isn't it?"

"Sure," Jeff said.

"And it's only for a week. And I have a picture I want to show you, I want to show you all my pictures."

"I'd like that," he said truthfully.

"Maybe this afternoon; we're leaving tonight. I'm really sorry, Jeffie," she said, watching his face.

"I'll be fine. Don't worry about me."

"I wouldn't go if I thought I needed to worry about you. I expect – living with your father – you're used to being left alone. That man left you alone even when he was with you."

"I'll be OK, I promise," Jeff said. He supposed he knew what she meant about the Professor; he knew he didn't want to argue with her. "Melody?" he asked, then waited until their

129

plates were set down in front of them. "Can I ask you a question?"

"You sound serious."

"It's OK, I'm not. I don't have to know."

"Go ahead, you silly goose, ask."

"Why did you marry the Professor? I mean – " Jeff couldn't think of how to finish the sentence, so he let it dangle. Max had said she was pregnant and had to. The Professor hadn't said that.

His mother nibbled at a potato chip, drank some of her iced tea. "He was so handsome," she said. "I was younger then – well, of course. Distinguished is the word I suppose, he was so distinguished looking. I was taking a course with him, and we used to laugh because he got so embarrassed if you tried to talk to him. He was so – good-looking, and shy and stand-offish. I thought about how lonely his life must be and the more I thought about it, I began to feel sorry for him. So I set out to be friends with him, just to see if I could, to see if I could make him like me. It was kind of like a challenge. And – well, when he talked with me he laughed and wasn't so dignified. He'd been so lonely and I made him happy. The poor old thing."

That had made sense. Jeff could see how that would make her feel and she might decide to marry him if she felt that way. "But – then you left – " he started to say.

"I was so unhappy, Jeffie. He didn't notice, he didn't care. That horrible little house and all

130

those stuffy professors and their horrible frumpy wives, and he didn't *do* anything to make things better. We never had any money – I always had to pinch pennies, everything, no matter how small. There wasn't ever enough. You don't know how that can wear a person down." Her eyes grew unhappy as she remembered.

Jeff felt so sorry for her he didn't know what to say. He wished he hadn't brought up the question at all. He was angry at himself for making her unhappy. "It's OK, really; I understand."

"I don't think you can," she said, her voice low and sad. "Sometimes, I don't think any man can."

"I don't mind," Jeff said. "But tell me about this festival; does it last all week? Who's going to appear, do you know?"

That cheered her up. "Max will, that's the important thing, for a whole week." She smiled at Jeff as if they shared a secret. "And Gambo would be livid if she knew." Then she mentioned a list of other names, some of which he had heard before, and the rest of the lunch went too quickly by.

Melody returned to her darkroom after lunch, telling Jeff to wait in the kitchen please. Then she took him by the arm and led him with her to the cellar stairs, to whisper in his ear: "Don't say anything about Willum to Miss Opal. He's in jail, for five years – he was selling marijuana. But if

131

he'd been white it would only be two years and – don't ask about him, OK? It breaks her heart."

But Miss Opal did want to talk about Willum, explaining how Willum couldn't help going bad, with the friends he had and his parents living so far away, with her having to work for their living, with the schools the way they were, and the job situation. "That boy – he never did have a chance," she said, stirring sugar into her cup of tea. "But I tell him, his old granny won't desert him, he always have a home with me. I ask the Lord to spare me for that time."

"How old are you?" Jeff asked.

"Why, seventy-eight."

Jeff stared at her. "But you're older than Gambo. I didn't know you were."

"Well, I always was," Miss Opal said.

Melody came back upstairs to show him a print so fresh she held it in tweezers and let it drip on to the table. "Look, Jeffie, what do you think?"

It was the happiest picture Jeff had ever seen. The boy in the picture had just seen something that he'd always wanted to see and never hoped to. Whatever it was, it made his eyes bright and his shoulders, all of his body that showed in the photograph, looked like he was about to run towards it.

"But that's me," Jeff said.

"A candid portrait. Now will you believe I'm good?"

"The boy never doubted it, Miss Melody."

"I'll make you a copy," Melody promised him, "and Gambo too – would you like that? You can keep this one."

Jeff didn't know he ever looked like that.

"But I'm going to have to work downstairs all afternoon, I'm afraid; you're going to have to find something to do. We took hundreds of pictures last night. You can find something to do, can't you?"

Finding something to do was what Jeff did – for a month, because Melody was away from the middle of June to the middle of July, as it turned out. The trip kept getting prolonged, for a few days, or a week. Jeff figured out in short order that Gambo's stroke had altered her interest in him, somehow. When he asked her questions, she answered impatiently and always concluded with something about "you young people". She wanted to talk, that summer, with the aunts, and their conversations began with the question, "Remember when?" Jeff didn't remember, but he would have liked to listen. The women, however, looked at him as if he were eavesdropping, moved closer together so that he couldn't hear, or simply ignored him. He didn't know what he'd done wrong, he didn't know how to do it right. Miss Opal, busy keeping the entire house, had no time for him and refused his offers to help her with her chores. "She'd be furious to see that. She'd fire me, and then what would I do? And then what would *she* do?"

After the first four phone calls, Jeff stopped hoping that Melody would be home soon. The disappointment of hearing her voice on the phone, after he had been expecting her to walk in the front door at any moment, of hearing her explain what had happened, asking if he could stand it if she was away for another few days, promising to really be back on Thursday, or next Saturday . . . It was better not to hope.

Instead, he kept himself out of the house, wandered around the city, did some sightseeing, and took to riding buses out as far as they went. Gambo asked him every morning where he'd be going, how much money he needed, whether it was raining or not. She wanted him to be away. "I'm too old to entertain children," she said, opening her black purse. "I don't know what your mother is thinking of."

Jeff had more money than he could spend that month, because his father sent him ten dollars every week, the bill wrapped around with the yellow lined paper the Professor wrote lectures on. The Professor also had something to say, some sentence. "Hope your weather is better than ours", or "Here's your allowance." Sometimes he included a postcard Brother Thomas had sent from England to Jeff. So Jeff could take Melody out for as many lunches as she liked, when she got back.

One day Melody did return and was there in the living room with Gambo and the aunts when

Jeff walked in the front door. He didn't remember where he'd been when he heard her voice and saw her face, her eyes shining at him, her hair damp and curly from a shower. "Where have you been?" she asked him.

Jeff just let the happiness grow inside him.

"Nobody knew where you were," Melody said. "You shouldn't just go wandering off like that."

She was angry. "I'm sorry," Jeff said. "I told Gambo this morning."

Melody stood up and took him out into the front hall to say, "You know she can't remember anything. Honestly, Jeffie, I thought I could trust you."

Jeff felt ashamed of himself, although he couldn't be quite sure why, and he hadn't noticed Gambo forgetting, just not being interested. "I'm sorry," he said, and then said it again. "I'm sorry."

She wasn't satisfied. "And I told Max I'd go with him out to Santa Fe, and now I don't know if I can," she told Jeff. "All you can say is, 'I'm sorry'. Just like your father."

Jeff just stared at her. He couldn't have spoken. He was confused, between guilt at failing her, dismay that she was going away again, and the desire that she not be angry with him.

"Well?" she asked.

He swallowed. "When?"

"We have to leave tonight and drive straight through, to get there in time. I had to wash and iron everything, and Miss Opal is so slow – it takes her ages to do anything these days."

"But Melody . . ." Jeff heard his own voice complaining and saw anger rise in her eyes again. He didn't protest any more. "For how long?" he asked.

"A month, maybe five weeks. It's a really important chance for Max. And you're here to keep an eye on Gambo for me so it's all right. If you weren't here I don't know how I'd get away."

Jeff made himself accept it, right then. He knew that if he waited even for a second, he would start complaining, and then she really wouldn't like him. "OK," he said.

"Oh Jeffie, I knew I could count on you," and she smiled into his eyes. But her smile was as painful to him as her anger. He didn't know what to do. But he thought, if he was careful, he could keep a grip on himself until after dinner, until he was alone in his room. He held his face expressionless. "Sometimes," Melody said, leaning forward to kiss him gently on the cheek, as if to take the sting out of her words, "you really do remind me of your father. That's silly, isn't it? Come and watch me pack? We can catch up with each other. Oh, I missed you, Jeffie," she said. She looked like she meant it. He felt like she was telling the truth, even though he knew she must be lying.

When Jeff was at last alone in his room that night, he lay across the bed and cried. He didn't even take off his clothes or turn on the lights. He felt so bad – sorry for himself, and angry at himself for losing her – and helpless. He didn't know what he should have done, what he could have done. He felt – rolling over on to his back and wrapping his arms across the pain in his chest and stomach, pain that wasn't even real – as if he had been broken into thousands of little pieces. Broken and then dropped into some dark place. Some dark place where he was always going to stay.

Because Melody was going away, again. Because she didn't want to stay where he was. And he wasn't sure he could stand that.

He had never suspected how easy he was to break.

He couldn't think of anything he wanted to do. Ever.

Jeff made it through several long days, trying not to think. He mostly stayed up in his room. He did not come down for meals, but ate sandwiches in the kitchen if he felt hungry. Nobody paid much attention to him. He paid no attention to anybody, just struggled with the sadness that always threatened to overwhelm him into crying again. He was ashamed of himself, but he couldn't help it. So he stayed upstairs. He watched out of his window, but what the weather was he didn't notice. After several days, he realized that with the exception of Miss Opal,

137

nobody in the house knew he was there. Not really knew. If you'd asked them, he supposed they would have looked vaguely around and said, "Jefferson? He's somewhere around, isn't he? Or has he gone away?"

Because he was easy to forget, easy to leave behind – Jeff understood that. He had interested them for the one summer, but that was more because of being a stranger and the last of the Boudraults than because of what he was like. He'd misunderstood that.

Everybody could leave him behind. But that was OK, he decided, waking before dawn one morning when he had fallen asleep fully dressed on top of the bedspread. If nobody owed him anything then he didn't owe anybody anthing. So at least he could do just what he wanted. If there was anything he wanted to do.

That morning he rode the bus along the same route he had followed on his last day last summer. Then he walked down along the same road, through the live oak tunnels. The island lay as he had remembered it. Jeff stood squinting at it over the broad field of marsh, over the narrow river. He wouldn't mind going out there, he thought. He was hot – he could feel sweat running down from his armpits, over his ribs. His hair stuck on his forehead. Bugs buzzed around him. If he had a boat.

Jeff walked slowly back up the road to the bus stop. There, he went into the ramshackle shop where the screen was ripped and the dim air inside uncooled even by a fan. He bought himself a Coke from the white-haired man behind the counter. A strip of fly-paper hung in coils down from the ceiling, covered with dead flies. A fly buzzed around Jeff's ear.

"If I wanted a boat," Jeff said.

"Suh?"

"Like a rowing boat," Jeff said.

"Whuffo?"

"Never mind," Jeff said. He drained the last of the Coke from the bottle. His sorrow was rising up in him again, and he needed to get outside.

"M'neighbour's boy – he got him a barque he be glad to get shot of," the old man said.

Jeff hesitated. He didn't know why he'd asked. He brushed at the fly that hovered near his ear.

"Come wi" me, suh. It's just a pace out around back."

Jeff followed him, going by oil drums that overflowed with rubbish, down a short dusty road to a line of five wooden cabins, built up on cinderblocks. Cars were parked all over the place, some rusting away on wheelless axles, some shiny new. A creek ran behind.

A younger man, who wore only denim overalls, led him on to a sagging dock. At the end, a flat-bottomed, unpainted rowing boat was tied up. Its oars had weathered splintery grey. The man's skin glistened with sweat, his dark eyes barely looked at Jeff. He yawned and scratched at his neck. Jeff looked down at the boat.

It had one seat, just a board nailed across at the centre. There wasn't any water in it, so he figured it didn't leak.

"She be fifteen," the man said.

"I don't know how to row," Jeff said. He didn't know what he was doing back here, anyway.

The man shrugged and walked back along the dock. Jeff walked with him.

"It's not hard to row, is it?"

"Nosuh."

"Fifteen dollars?"

"Yessuh."

"If I give you another five, can I have it tied up here? When I'm not using it?"

The man shrugged. He turned and faced Jeff, looking over Jeff's shoulder.

"I'll bring you the money tomorrow," Jeff said.

The dark eyes finally focused on him. "I be here," the man said.

It took Jeff three days to learn to handle the little boat well enough to dare an approach to the island. By that time he could row with confidence along the creek that ran behind the cabins. He had run aground on the shallow creek bottom often enough to know how little trouble that caused, had asked the nameless black man about currents and tides, had looked at a map of the area and found the island on it. He bought himself a hat to protect his head. Out on the water, the sunlight was reflected and it scorched his face and his eyes especially. He had also heard a couple of songs he'd never heard before. "They's gospel," the man answered his question. "She sings over to the church." Whoever she was. But the man was no more curious about Jeff than Jeff was about him.

One morning, Jeff pushed himself away from the dock, turned the boat round, and rowed down the back creek, heading towards the island. He had sandwiches in a paper bag and two quart jars of apple juice. He'd learned how thirsty you could get out on the water.

He rowed down between standing marsh grasses. It wasn't long before he was out of sight of human habitation, out of the sound of human voices. He could see only the low wall of grass and the bleached sky above it. An occasional bird burst out of cover when he came near. He could hear the silence made by the surf breaking on the other side of the barrier island, by the splashing sound of his oars in the water.

Although the map he had looked at was clear in Jeff's memory and he turned north when the back creek joined the deeper creek that separated the island from the mainland without hesitation, the strangeness of the scene affected him. The tide was up and made the water look deceptively deep. Over towards the island, across the grasses, he could see the line of trees and underbrush: it looked wild and dangerous. He was afraid.

He was always a little afraid in the boat. That was, in fact, why he liked it. That fear came from outside, from the unfamiliarity of the place, from his being so far from people that if he yelled for help nobody would hear him. He slipped into that fear like slipping into the water to go swimming. Because the fear that came from outside distracted him from the fear that was living inside him. The fear inside him threatened at any moment to take him over and sweep him away, and the only way he could manage it at all was by avoiding it. In the boat, alone on the water.

That first day he went only half a mile up the main creek. Then he tossed over the ten-pound anchor he had purchased and sat. The boat swayed gently on the water of the narrow creek. He sat and looked around him and listened and became easier in his spirit as the scene grew familiar. This had been the pattern of his days on the back creek, too: he would move the boat out until he felt more frightened than he had courage to match; then he would anchor and wait.

Jeff ate his sandwiches, drank juice, and watched the slimy underwater stalks of the grasses grow visible as the tide ran out. He sat on the floorboards, his back against the side, watching and listening. A rustle of wings announced the arrival of one of the great blue herons. The bird

142

landed a few yards up from the boat and proceeded to walk along the water's edge, its long beak pointing down. The bird's legs, more like pipes than legs, bent backwards at the knee, so it looked like the bird was going backwards or was trying to go backwards when it was actually moving or like it could only move forwards by going backwards. Every now and then it would halt and stand motionless, then plunge its beak into the shallow water, shake its head two or three times, and swallow its catch, whole.

The blues were always alone, Jeff had noticed. They came at low tide to fish along the edges of the marshes. They stalked the shallows, their flat, elongated, triangular heads facing down, to where their prey hid. This blue hunted up about a hundred yards, then backed up until he stood camouflaged against the grasses. The blues were big, awkward birds on land; in flight they spread long wings out, tucked their necks in against their chests, and trailed their legs out straight behind them, looping across the land or the water.

At the end of the afternoon, Jeff rowed back down the creek, then along up to the dock. The last bus to town left at sunset.

It was a week before he actually landed on the island, tying the boat up to the poles of an abandoned dock that sat beneath the overgrown lawn of a burned-out house. There, the steep mudbanks were inhabited by land crabs. Their holes, as large as fifty-cent pieces, made the steep

143

brown banks look like Swiss cheese. The crabs came out into the sun – to eat, Jeff supposed. When he had first seen them, from a distance, he had thought they were large beetles, and not until he had come so close that they scurried back into their holes had he recognized them. The first time he landed, Jeff watched the crabs for a cautious half hour before he brought the boat close enough to tie up to a piling. As he had deduced, they scrabbled quickly into holes when he set his foot on the mudbank and scrambled up its slippery surface to the weedy lawn.

For several days, Jeff stayed around the shell of the house, venturing up across what must once had been a well-kept lawn, where bush-like trees were overgrown with vines and the Spanish moss on the live oaks grew down to the earth like old men's beards.

Gradually, hampered by the occasional day of rain, Jeff explored inland, along a double rutted path he found leading away from the house. The tangled woods closed in over him, low myrtle bushes, palmettos at various stages of their life cycle, honeysuckle, pines. These days he wore jeans over his swimming trunks and a long-sleeved shirt, because the mosquitoes bit mercilessly in the dense woods. He left his hat at the boat – the sun couldn't penetrate much into the semi-tropical growth. He walked along cautiously, a dead branch in his hand, and his fear at the strangeness and solitude never entirely left him.

He discovered a pond, a long, narrow pond so large it might have been considered a lake. Sitting at its side to watch a chameleon, his hand waving away clusters of gnats, Jeff saw a log moving on the shallow bank opposite: an alligator, as brown as the mud beneath the grasses, slipped into the water.

Jeff leapt to his feet and ran, thundering along the now familiar path. Heedless of the noise he was making, he ran until he had climbed back into the safety of his boat. An alligator!

He sat on the wooden board, his head held in shaking hands. An *al*-ligator. He was sweating. His chest heaved. He'd never been so frightened in his life.

After a while, the sun made him so hot he stripped off his shirt and shoes, then his trousers. He lowered himself gently over the side of the boat, paddled for a minute, carefully keeping his feet from touching whatever might be on the bottom of the creek, and then hauled himself back up over the side, cooled.

An alligator. Jeez. He'd never thought – he'd thought of spiders and snakes and even snapping turtles, but never alligators.

One of the songs he'd heard the woman in the cabins singing had an alligator in it: "When a gator hollers, folks say it's gwina rain." Jeff ate lunch in the boat that day and then rowed to the

145

dock. He got back to the city in time to look up alligators at the library, to see how much the appearance of the creatures might curtail his exploration of the island.

He should have gone straight to Gambo's, as it turned out, because Melody was there. He didn't know that at first, entering the cool hall and picking up the Friday note from the Professor. He didn't hear her voice, just the television. He opened the note, read the postcard from Brother Thomas about brass rubbings, unfolded the sheet of yellow legal paper, and pocketed the ten dollar note. This note was longer, three lines of bold, slanted script. "I expect you in a couple of weeks. Let me know the day and time. Sold a book – imagine that – I'll tell you about it."

Only a couple of weeks. Jeff guessed he could manage that, and he thought he would feel easier once he got back to Baltimore. At that thought, the spacious indifference of Gambo's house to his presence started to swell out from his stomach and threatened to take him over. "Sold a book," he said loudly within his own brain, "I wonder what that means." The Professor sounded excited, for him. Jeff thought maybe he would write the Professor a postcard and ask. He thought maybe he would go out right then and get one to send. And a stamp, he reminded himself, feeling his tension abate as he planned out where he would go to get them.

But just then Melody came to the head of the stairs. "Jeffie?"

Jeff didn't have the power to just get out. When she stood there, so close, her voice unsure and asking him, her hair curled round her beautiful face, it took all his strength not to run up the stairs and throw his arms round her. "Hello," he said.

"Come on up, Jeffie. I want to talk to you. Privately."

She went into Jeffie's room, where only the brush and comb on the bureau and the picture of himself stuck into the edge of the mirror showed that anyone lived there. He had put the picture up to remind himself – of what, he did not know, but when he looked at it the cold, wet feeling inside him froze to ice and was easier to handle. Melody sat crosslegged on his bed. She spread her skirt over her knees and patted the space beside her. Hating himself for his inability to resist her and to resist an insistently happy feeling, Jeff sat down. But he wouldn't look at her.

"Oh Jeffie." She put her hand under his chin and turned his face towards hers. "It hasn't been the way you wanted it to be, has it?"

"It doesn't make any difference," Jeff said. All he had to do was remember how badly she had hurt him and he would be all right.

"And I'm going away again tomorrow, and you'll be gone before I get back," she said, her voice sad.

Jeff couldn't stop himself from asking. "Do you have to?"

"Yes, of course; would I go if I didn't have to? Max is going to do an article on an Appalachian community, on rural poverty – but don't tell Gambo that" – she smiled into his eyes, mischievously – "she thinks I'm the one doing it. What she doesn't know won't hurt her. But what have you been doing? Oh, I've missed you and thought about you all the time," she said.

Jeff knew he couldn't believe her, but he wanted to believe her so badly that he did. "I could take you out to dinner, just the two of us."

At that she laughed and hugged him, pleased. "You do love me, despite it all. But we can't. It would hurt Gambo's feelings. You don't want to do that, do you? She has only us, you know that."

Jeff nodded.

"So we have to stick around here tonight, even though it would be good to have just the two of us, just this once. But what have you been doing all this time? Miss Opal tells me you're out of the house and she doesn't set your place for dinner unless she's seen you. You're not getting into trouble, are you?"

"No," Jeff said. He opened his mouth to tell her about the island and the boat and the black families in their houses beside the back creek.

"You should have come with us." She didn't give him time to speak. "We were up in the mountains – well, the foothills – and it's a wonderful countryside. The pueblos are a disgrace, outhouses, rubbish. Whole families live in one room where the smoke isn't ventilated. When I think what we've done to the Indians." She went on and on about New Mexico and what to do about the Indians out there, how much help they needed; Jeff listened and did not let himself think. Because she didn't even mean her questions to him. At last, she wound down. "Are you awfully sad to be going back to Baltimore?" she asked. "I always was."

Jeff looked over at the picture on his mirror.

"No," he said.

"Jeffie, what a terrible thing to say – after all everybody's done for you. I hope you don't talk to Gambo like that, it would break her heart. It breaks my heart a little, truth be told."

Something burst inside Jeff. "Don't lie to me," he said to his mother. "I don't believe you. If you really cared you'd have stayed here, and you wouldn't be going away tomorrow and lying to Gambo about it, and – " He was making her angry, he could see that. But he couldn't stop. "And I don't like the way you lie. You make it sound like the Professor is so terrible, but you're terrible yourself. What you do to people," he said. "Lying to them so you'll get what you want."

Big tears rolled down Melody's cheeks. Jeff

didn't mind that. He got off the bed and went to stand by the window.

"I've made you unhappy," Melody said. "I'm so sorry, Jeffie."

"I'm not unhappy," Jeff lied. "I just don't care."

"Like your father."

"Don't say that. Don't say it that way just when you want to criticize me. He's not so bad."

"Well, what do you think of a man who lets you nearly die of pneumonia because he just doesn't notice?"

"Bronchial pneumonia."

"Bronchial pneumonia, plain pneumonia, what's the difference? I don't know how you can stick up for him. It just goes to show – "

"Show what?" Jeff asked, angry himself. He'd never had a fight with anybody, and it felt oddly good.

"Show how men always take their own side. I should have known better than to try to get you down here, but I felt so sorry for you – stuck with him and ill and nobody noticed, I cried myself to sleep when I first heard. I thought I could at least help you a little – but men always stick to their side."

"That's stupid," Jeff said. His voice was loud in his ears.

She jumped off the bed and stood with her hands on her hips. "Are you calling me stupid? You don't know anything, do you? You don't

150

know anything about the world; he hasn't taught you anything up there in his ivory tower, safe and secure, not about the dangers or what really goes on, not about the way some people have to live or what we're doing to the world – and you call *me* stupid. Well, maybe I am, I was surely stupid to marry him, that was about the stupidest thing I ever did. Unless having a boy wins the prize. I wanted a girl. You didn't know that, did you? But you should have figured it out, if you're so smart. If you'd been a girl I'd have taken you with me when I walked out on him. I thought you were a girl when I got pregnant, I was sure of it."

"Oh yeah?" Jeff answered right back. He didn't know what to say to show her that he knew she wanted to break him to pieces. And he could see that; she wanted to hurt him, as badly as she could. Then he thought of something. "Well, Max told me why you got married, because you had to. So don't go blaming me for anything. You probably lied to the Professor too, he probably isn't even my father."

Jeff wondered where that idea came from, where in the icy black spaces inside him that idea had been hiding.

Melody's hand went to her throat. Her eyes were huge and grey. "That he is," she said, her voice cold. She wasn't saying it to make Jeff feel better, he knew that. So he knew what she was saying was true. "I'd never have married him

151

otherwise, if I hadn't had to. You can bet your boots on that."

Jeff said the only thing he could. "Go away. Please, go away."

She went. Jeff stood at the window for a long time, so angry he felt he was shaking, all the little pieces of himself he had so carefully tried to put together broken again and rattling around inside him. Sorrow welled up in him again, and he was frightened. He had thought if he could just say what he thought, if he was just strong enough to do that, then he'd be all right. But he wasn't.

But he made himself go down to dinner, because Gambo might have her feelings hurt, and there was no reason for him to do that. He figured he could get through dinner with Melody, somehow. Nobody noticed much about him anyway; they'd probably miss noticing how upset he was.

But at the table Melody pretended nothing had happened. She sat next to him and kept trying to hold his hand as if nothing had changed between them. She was putting on an act for Gambo, about how much she loved Jeff and how much he loved her.

Jeff felt broken and bruised. When he looked at her, she smiled right into his eyes, so he tried not to look at her. He'd thought he wasn't really vulnerable any more and maybe not even angry now that he'd let some of his feelings steam out. But there was some feeling like anger in him. He hated her, he thought, and he knew it was true

152

when she left the table to answer the phone and came back to say she'd been invited to a party; nobody minded if she went, did they? She kissed Gambo's head when she asked permission and then kissed Jeff too, on the top of his head, with her perfume in the air all around him.

He thought: alligators stayed near water, if he kept well away from that inland pond he'd be able to continue exploring the island. And what did it matter if an alligator got him, anyway; at least it would hurt so much he wouldn't be able to think about Melody. Because he was beginning to hate himself for being so fragile, so easy for her to break.

6

The day before he was due to leave Charleston, Jeff crossed over the top of a low, sandy dune, overgrown with scrub bushes. He saw the beach stretching away to the south; the ocean stretching out to the endless east; the line of waves breaking on the shore; sandpipers in nervous bands fishing the waves' edge; three pelicans flying in a line over the surface of the water. He breathed in the salty air, the wind against his face. He saw a world in which he was the only human inhabitant.

It was mid-morning and hot. Jeff ran down the dune and across the water. To the north, he saw a narrow spit of land and a turbulence of waves where the tip of the island made currents, marking the entrance of the creek into the ocean. To the south lay an unbroken distance of beach, thirty feet wide, sandy white. Jeff ran south. He had to run, he didn't know what else to do to celebrate what he had come to find here. And found. Sandpipers and gulls fled from his approach, circled and landed again behind him. When he had run himself out, he walked, mile after empty mile. The waves broke beside him, and he succumbed to the temptation to walk among them. When he realized how hungry he was, he turned round and walked the long miles back to where he had dropped his brown paper bag full of food on the dune side.

The afternoon flowed over him. He sat at the water's edge, watching. Watching the birds, the waves, and once the gliding backs of porpoises cutting arcs through the ocean in front of him. He took off his clothes and waded out into the water to swim. He lay down to bake dry on the fine sand, first on his stomach, then on his back, soaking in the tireless whispering of the wind, the dry warmth of the sand, the heat of the sun, the spacious solitude all around him.

When the shadows grew longer and the temperature started to drop, he knew he ought to cross back, return to the boat. But he couldn't do that. He made no decision to stay the night, but he couldn't make himself leave the beach. Gradually, he understood that he would miss the last bus. That made no difference.

Jeff walked the beach again, this time picking up sand dollars, which lay flat and bleached white on the mudflats, and whorled conch shells. He made a pile of them by his empty paper bag and folded clothes. Then, sitting at the very edge of the waves, he discovered how the little pastel plaid cochinas tumbled down from the sides of pools his fingers dug. A shower of fragile molluscs poured down with the water that came to fill up the pools.

At his back the sun went down. The sky's

colours, reflected by the ocean, went from orange to pink to velvet blue to midnight blue and then black. Stars – millions of stars – came out. The moon rose, just past the full, and shone down with its sad face. The path the moon made on the water glowed silver.

Jeff slept on the beach hungry, but that made no difference. He awoke to a sky the colour of thick smoke. All the stars had faded but one: Venus, the morning star, low on the eastern horizon, large and white; it too shone bright enough here to make its own narrow silver path on the water. Jeff sat up and watched, watched light and sunrise. During the night the wind had shifted to the west and blew into his ears from behind, heated by the closer air of the inner island. He saw fishing boats hundreds of yards off shore, so distant they looked like toys. All morning long he walked, through puddles between sandflats left by the receding tide, until he came to the southern tip of the island. Then he turned to go back.

He felt – washed clean, healed. He felt if he could just live here he would be all right. He felt as if he had never been alive before. He felt at ease with himself and as if he had come home to a place where he could be himself, without hiding anything, without pretending even to himself. He felt, thinking his way back up the beach, as if his brain had just woken up from some long sleep,

156

and it wanted to run along beside the waves, to see how far and fast it could go.

When he turned to where he had left his clothes, he put them on. He picked out one perfect sand dollar from his collection of shells, then walked back to toss the rest gently into the waves, returning them. He jammed the paper bag into the back pocket of his jeans and carried the sand dollar tenderly in his hand.

At the top of the dunes, under a blazing noon sun, Jeff turned to take a last look. He drank in the scene with his eyes, to be able to carry it away with him. The empty beach, the line of breaking waves groping up on to the sand, the restless ocean.

He crossed the island as quickly as he dared, giving the alligator pond a wide berth. When he came to the drive leading to the burned-out house, he began to jog; his plane left at eight; he'd have to pack and get a cab. But when he sat in the rowing boat again, the oars ready but not yet dipped into the water to take him away from the island, Jeff looked back. He didn't see the busy land crabs nor the overgrown interior; he saw the beach, knowing it was there just beyond sight, keeping the sight of it clear in his inner eye. He splashed the oars into the water. Behind him, a great blue squawked – Jeff turned his head quickly.

The heron rose up from the marsh grass, croaking its displeasure at the disturbance, at

Jeff, at all the world. Its legs dragged briefly in the water before it rose free to swoop over Jeff's head with a whirring of powerful wings. It landed again on the far side of the ruined dock, to stand on stiltlike legs with its long beak pointed towards the water. Just leave me alone, the heron seemed to be saying. Jeff rowed away, down the quiet creek. The bird did not watch him go.

Part Two

7

The Professor stood waiting among the throng of people at Friendship Airport. He was taller than most of them, and the first thing Jeff saw was his glasses. Then the Professor raised one hand. Jeff made his way over to his father.

The Professor's brown seersucker suit was rumpled. He didn't wear a tie. He looked at Jeff as if he hadn't seen him for so long he needed to be reminded of what Jeff looked like. But Jeff had made himself a place, inside himself, a kind of tower room, round, without any windows. In that room, he had locked his memory of the beach on the island, all the memories from the day hours and from the night hours. He had discovered how to step inside that room and slide the curved door closed and bolt it across.

"You've only got a couple of days before school starts," the Professor said. "Is there anything you want to do? Go to Ocean City or anything?"

Jeff shook his head.

"Let's get your suitcase. Did you have a good time?"

"It was OK," Jeff said. They walked along with the throng, heading down the central aisle, then down the escalators to the baggage claim.

161

"I bet we're going to have to get you a whole set of new clothes," the Professor said. "You look like you've filled out a bit and have got taller."

"Ummm," Jeff said.

"So," the Professor said, "what's new?"

"Nothing."

The Professor waited a long time before asking, "How's your mother?"

Rage surged up against the outside of Jeff's tower room, a tall, black wave. "She's OK," he said, holding the door safe. Inside the room lay miles of solitary beaches, a spacious, peaceful place. As long as he could go there Jeff would be safe. If the room were not there – he was afraid of what he might do, what he might say. If the room were not there, he would fall apart, disintegrate like music broken into individual melody lines, the lines turning into notes, the notes exploding into unconnected sounds, the sounds dissipating into space itself.

If the room were not there in his mind, Jeff thought, there would be just a sharp-stoned wall, and he would stand in front of it and whack his head against it. Until his head burst open like a pumpkin.

Protecting the room became the thing he did, the only thing, all of his days. He couldn't play his guitar, and neither could he look too carefully at the Professor nor the house they lived in together, because all those things distracted him from his watch over the tower door. Luckily, the

Professor didn't say much to him anyway; he was busy with his own life. At school, the classes of boys didn't bother Jeff either. The teachers left him alone as long as he kept quiet in class, although when they called on him and discovered that he couldn't answer questions, they looked at him in anger or suspicion or even pity. None of that made any difference to Jeff. He handed in his homework if he had done any, whether it was complete or not. He didn't even notice the other boys in his classes.

The only thing Jeff could do, could really do outside his tower room, he discovered by accident. One Saturday afternoon in October he found that he'd wandered to the amusement park. He had money in his pocket so he took a couple of rides, the roller coaster and the Octopus. The sheer physical sensations of speed and swooping were exciting in the same way that the island beach had been exciting. He rode the roller coaster time after time, alone in the car, soaring out on thin rails over the edge of the city, rising slowly up, up, up a steep grade until the train finally made its way over the top of the hill. And fell down, dizzying and uncontrollable.

The Octopus was inside, within a huge warehouse-like building, which held also a merry-go-round, a few rides small children could take, bumper cars, food concessions, and a bingo hall. The Octopus turned in circles, the round covered motor section at the centre, eight metal arms spreading out from that, and at the end of each arm four round cars, like the suction cups on a starfish. The cars circled on their own axles within the large circling machine. They swung so close to each other it seemed they must collide, but they never did. While the arms turned and the cars turned, music played, and coloured lights flashed overhead, pouring down over Jeff like fragments of sunlight. He sat back alone in his car, facing three empty seats, wearing sunglasses to make it impossible for anyone to see him, his arms spread along the back of the seat. If he relaxed, as the car swung around building up speed, if he concentrated on the rain of colours over him and the wind rushing by his ears, he could feel – almost – as if he were back on the beach.

It was like trying to recapture a dream, and Jeff never could precisely feel as he had. But it was the nearest he could come. That first day he stayed at the park for hours. He went back every weekend and gradually, when he learned it didn't make any difference, during the weekdays too. As the weather got colder they closed down the outside rides; but Jeff only wanted to ride the Octopus anyway. The indoor rides stayed open all winter, so Jeff would be all right. The only times he could relax his vigilance at the door of his inner room was when his body swung with the movement of the Octopus, and calliope music drowned out human voices, and the shattered prism of colour poured over him.

Jeff knew that somewhere outside his tower room he was flunking courses; but the Professor didn't know because Jeff had forged the Professor's signature on his report card. He checked the mail before the Professor saw it, to throw out unopened any envelopes that came from the University School. Jeff didn't ever know for sure what day of the week it was, so it wasn't exactly as if he was cutting classes. Some days the park was more crowded, some days not. Autumn turned into cold weather, and on Christmas Day, it was closed. Then it opened, and Jeff had some place to go again.

It was on an afternoon in deep winter that Jeff sat in the round seat of the Octopus, alone, whirling under a waterfall of colour. Inside himself, he was within the tower room. He could almost really taste the salt in the air, he could almost feel that what was pouring down over his skin was the sun. It was only almost, but almost promised so much and was so much better than nothing that he concentrated on losing himself into it.

When the ride stopped he rose carefully from his seat. If he moved slowly, he would not shatter his inner concentration, even when he went to give the man another ticket. So that when he heard someone call his name, it was as shocking as if somebody had slugged him in the face. He whipped round, frightened.

The Professor stood just beyond the gate.

Brother Thomas, back from England, was with him. Jeff looked round for some place to run. They couldn't catch him. They were going to hurt him, he knew that, and he knew how easy he was to hurt. There was no way out, so he just stood still, inside the tower. He made them come to get him while he stayed safe.

Each man took one of his arms and led him out of the enclosure. Brother Thomas stood in front of him, staring into his eyes. Jeff lowered his eyelids. Brother Thomas pulled them up with gentle fingers. He looked worried, puzzled. "Are you on anything?" he asked.

Jeff shook his head.

The Professor's hand was on his shoulder. "I was so afraid," the Professor said.

"I'm sorry," Jeff said.

They all went out to the Professor's car. Jeff sat in the back, but they both turned round to stare at him. "You're supposed to be in a maths exam now," the Professor said. "You missed English and geography yesterday. Exams, Jeff. I don't understand. They called me, the principal did." He knew everything.

"I'm sorry."

The Professor looked at Brother Thomas. "Take him home, Horace," Brother Thomas advised. "Take him home and feed him and make him talk to you. Your father," he said to Jeff, "wanted to leave you be, since you wanted to be left alone. But you're going to have to tell him. Whatever it is."

Jeff didn't say anything at all. He had an hour, anyway, for the drive back into the city, he had an hour for the sun-bleached stretch of beach, where waves broke and spread.

When they sat across from one another at the little Formica kitchen table and Jeff had finished his peanut-butter and jam sandwiches and the Professor had brewed a mug of coffee, the Professor said, "I'm sorry, Jeff; you're going to have to tell me about it. You've been different, and I don't know what it is. I didn't think it was drugs – I didn't think you'd be that stupid – but people say it's so hard to tell . . . Look at me, Jeff," he said, making Jeff meet his eyes. "I don't care about the schoolwork. I'm not angry, I'm frightened. Tell me what's bothering you, and we'll figure out the best way to handle it."

"I'm OK," Jeff told him. "There isn't anything."

"No, you're not OK. I'm not much of a father, but I can see that. You're not even really here, are you? You act as if you're a hundred miles away. Where are you?"

"I'm sorry," Jeff said.

The Professor sat back in his chair. He looked at the coffee in his mug. He moved his glasses back up his nose. His voice, when he spoke, was expressionless. "I thought myself, the way you've been acting, that it was probably Melody. I thought it had to have something to do with her. Judging from my own experience, I've been assuming that she told you, somehow, the way only Melody can, that she didn't love you. And you thought she did."

Jeff saw his own hands clench up into fists. His stomach too, was clenched. He started to talk, fast. "I'll tell you where I was. The last day, I went over to a beach. The last full day. An island, one of the sea islands, uninhabited. I had a boat, I bought it. I'd never explored that far before, and I spent the night there. And – it was so beautiful. Nobody but me was there. I spent all day and all night and half the next day too. I have a sand dollar I found; it's upstairs, I can show you." He looked down at his fists. "I can remember it; I can go there, inside."

"It wasn't the worst time when Melody left me," the Professor said. "The worst time was the years before. Because I didn't know I could hate anybody that much, I didn't know I could be that angry, I didn't know what to do except concentrate on my work. I didn't know anybody could hurt anybody else that much; it was like she'd stuck a sword into me, one of those Japanese samurai swords, do you know the kind I mean? Heavy and razor sharp – and curved – and she'd stuck it in me and then she was . . . pushing it around." His hand rested on his stomach, remembering. "I couldn't get free from the feelings. I didn't know how frightened I could be, all the time. But whenever we had to go out together, she'd smile at me and talk to me and listen and look at me the way she did – and I wanted to hit her," he said, his voice low and ashamed.

Jeff let his head down to rest his face on his fists.

"When I found out how many lies she was telling me, I finally realized that she had always lied to me. About my lectures. About boyfriends; and even after she knew I knew, she'd still lie about it. I hated her. Or the bills she ran up, without asking, without telling; then she'd say she'd taken care of them but she just – ignored them. I know I looked all right to other people – maybe more of a dry old stick than usual, maybe even more boring than usual, but inside I was knotted up, all the time, because I hated her so much, and I hated myself, and I was scared."

Jeff looked up at his father.

"I didn't think she'd do that to you, Jeff," the Professor said. "But she did, didn't she?"

Jeff nodded. He knew he was crying, but he didn't know what to do about it. Neither did the Professor. He just sat and waited, until Jeff got up to blow his nose.

"It was the lies," the Professor said. "They were what really scared me. Even now, if I think about her – and the kinds of things she says . . . I don't know what she told you, but I never was sorry I'd married her or loved her because of you.

169

You always made a difference, made a real difference, from the very beginning. I always knew that, inside me, but I didn't bother to learn how to show you. I'm sorry, Jeff, I should have taken the trouble."

Jeff didn't know what to say, didn't even know what to think. He could see, as if it were familiar, his father during those early times. And see too what his father had seen: his son, unchanged by Melody's leaving, everything going on the same, although never the same because Melody had left, taking her own light with her. He could see what the Professor's days had looked like to him: long, empty, to be endured until he could get used to things, day after day of waiting to get accustomed. And he could see the Professor now, too; what the Professor was seeing now – his father was frightened and worried about Jeff. Jeff knew that; suddenly, he knew it as clearly as if the Professor had said it aloud. He could receive the feelings, like some musical instrument, whether he wanted to or not. He could see what the Professor saw as the Professor saw it.

"Jeff, please, say something," the Professor asked him.

"She told me she wanted a girl, she told me if I'd been a girl she would have taken me with her."

At that, the Professor laughed. It was shaky, but it was a laugh. "She's still a liar," he said. "Besides, I wouldn't have let her."

"Really?"

"Really. I may be a dry old stick, but I'm not a fool," the Professor told him. He got up from the table, spooned coffee from the can into the top of the coffee pot, and poured the boiling water through. Jeff washed his plate and poured a glass of milk.

"What was that about a boat? How could you get a boat?" the Professor asked in a normal voice.

"I had the money you were sending. It wasn't much of a boat, it only cost fifteen dollars. Plus five to tie it up at the dock. It was only a dinghy, not even painted." Jeff remembered how it felt, once he'd learned how to handle it. He remembered going a little further each day. "It took me time to get used to it, to be not as frightened. I explored the island the same way. There was a lot to see. And the day I left, I saw this great blue heron – have you seen one?" The Professor hadn't. "They're so beautiful and ugly – awkward – it flew over my head, right over. Because I'd disturbed it, but it landed not very far up at all, and it stayed there when I rowed away. It didn't mind me."

"Where is the boat now?"

Jeff looked at his father: "I sank it."

"You what?"

"I didn't want anyone else to – have it. I won't be going back there."

The Professor, calmer now, thought. "You

171

haven't played your guitar since you've been back, have you?" It wasn't easy for the Professor to think about how to say to Jeff what he wanted to say. Not like it was easy for Jeff to see. But the Professor was doing it, trying as hard as he could, making himself. Because Jeff mattered to him, and Jeff saw *that* now, too, and saw that he could count on that. He could feel himself relaxing.

A memory that had been blocked away somewhere with other things Jeff didn't want to remember at all struck him like an unexpected wave. "You told me you sold a book."

Now the Professor looked surprised.

"You did, in one of your notes, the last one. What happened to it?"

The Professor didn't know what to say. Jeff could see that. He didn't understand, now that he had remembered, why the Professor had had nothing further to say about the book since Jeff's return.

"Tell me," Jeff asked. "Unless you don't want to." Unless whatever the deal was had fallen through?

"No, I do want to; it's just – I thought you weren't interested, I thought – "

"I'm sorry. I just forgot. You mean. . . you wrote a book – to be published?"

The Professor nodded.

Why did he look embarrassed, Jeff wondered.

"What kind of book is it?"

"It's a sort of history book, biography; it's due

172

to come out next autumn. I'm finishing up revisions now."

"Is the university press going to publish it?"

"Actually" – the Professor looked even more uncomfortable – "it's not one of the academic presses, it's a regular publisher."

"Is that . . . does that make a difference?"

"Evidently. It will be . . . more available to the general public."

"It must be good," Jeff said. "What's it about?"

"It's a series of short biographies. Just some people who have – caught my attention."

"Can I read it?"

"I thought about that. I'd like you to wait until you're fifteen. I think – then you'll be old enough. Will you promise me that?"

"Sure. I promise. What's it called?"

"Earth's Honoured Guests. Not a very scholarly title. I don't know, I can't tell – the scholarship in the book is solid. I think they're afraid it'll be too scholarly. I don't know who would want to read it, but that's their business. I mean, they bought it – which means we have some extra money, and more when I get the revisions done and the second half of the advance. It gives us some leeway. Brother Thomas says."

"Leeway for what? Aren't you proud?"

"I am proud, yes. Well, sometimes I am. It's pretty foreign country for me, Jeff. Leeway about you. About school. About what we're going to do about school. You can't possibly pass the year, they told me that. So we have to decide what to do."

Jeff began to feel frightened again. "It doesn't make any difference," he said.

"And you sank the boat?" the Professor asked. "How do you sink a boat?"

"It was old. I pounded the oar on the floor-boards; it wasn't strong at all, really. Then I swam to the dock."

"I'll try to make it all right, Jeff," the Professor said. "Whatever we decide to do."

While January turned to February, and a week of warm weather was followed by sharp, sporadic storms of snow and sleet, the Professor didn't do anything about Jeff. Jeff stayed home and played on his guitar. Brother Thomas came round frequently, but if he had anything to say about Jeff, he kept it for the Professor. He brought Jeff a thick volume of songs, collected in England by a man named Childs. Jeff put the volume aside for later and went back to re-learning the songs he had once been able to play well.

In mid-February, the Professor took Jeff for an appointment with the Principal of the University School. Jeff sat silent while the two men talked – he had worn the grey flannels and blazer – and stared unseeing at the toes of his polished shoes. The Professor wanted to withdraw Jeff from the school, and the Principal agreed that that might be all for the best. He talked about academic pressures on a student of less than average ability, and he didn't look at Jeff. He suggested testing, to get a precise fix on just what the limits were, he suggested therapy because 'socialization was well below norm'. The Professor didn't disagree. When they finally walked out of the office, down the hall, and out on to the icy brick front steps, Jeff said, "I'm sorry."

"We'll see," the Professor said. He didn't seem to be listening to Jeff. "We'll give it some time and then we'll see. Don't *you* worry, Jeff." Jeff left his father alone to think it out. His father needed time to think things out.

They also went to visit Dr Baker, who did a complete physical; then listened as the Professor recounted what Jeff had done. Jeff listened too, as if they were talking about somebody else.

"It sounds as if some counselling is in order," Dr Baker said. He smiled at Jeff as he spoke. Jeff didn't say anything.

"I'd like to give it some time," the Professor said. "I'm not ruling the possibility out, but – I don't believe anyone can understand as well as I can what effect his mother could have had on him."

The doctor laced his fingers together and said to the Professor, "It's not only his mother. He hasn't been primarily in her care, has he?"

The Professor didn't answer that right away. "I understand," he said at last. "I see what you must think – and you're correct, I understand that. I suppose I'd like a little time, myself. Circumstances permit a little more freedom this year." He looked at Jeff. "I would like to keep him out of school and have him repeat eighth grade next year. Somewhere else."

"Jeff?" Dr Baker asked. Jeff looked up at him. He had been thinking about the beach again and how the pelicans swooped low over the water, scooping up their prey with buckety beaks. "What do you think?"

"It doesn't make any difference to me."

Dr Baker studied him for a long time. Jeff kept his face expressionless and looked right back.

"I don't know, Dr Greene. I can testify to his being run down, and it certainly doesn't sound as if he should go back to school especially not if the year is already shot. I have to say that I think counselling is strongly indicated. But not urgent. Not at this point. But I'd have to have your word to get in touch with me if . . . I don't know, if there was any smallest sign of trouble. Or even lack of improvement."

"You have my word. Thank you," the Professor said. "I hope I've learned; I think I'm learning. We have a family friend who's much quicker than I am – Brother Thomas," he said to Jeff's raised face. "You have my word," he said to Dr Baker.

The Professor didn't speak to Jeff again until they had arrived back home and Jeff was about to go up to his room to play the guitar. "I can't change, not really," the Professor said.

"That's OK," Jeff told him. He already knew that, and he liked that in his father.

"But even if we can't change me, I've been thinking, we might change this." The Professor waved his hand around, indicating the hall. Jeff didn't understand. "Would you mind moving?" the Professor asked him.

"No."

So they became acquainted with an estate agent, who carried a large zip case with her wherever she went, wrote everything down with a quick, nervous hand, and talked constantly, called the Professor, "Dr Greene". She drove them round to show them houses, in the city, in the suburbs. She advised them not to fix their house up. "I thought about that, Dr Greene, and while it would cost you thousands just to have it painted inside and out, you wouldn't ever realize what you'd spent in the sales price. I think we should sell it as a bargain." She drove them round in her big white car and walked them through other people's houses. She even showed them a mansion out in the western suburbs, built out of white stucco with a tall fence enclosing a garden and green hills rolling behind it.

"We can't afford it," he said to his father.

"Hardly. A pity, except if you think about trying to keep the lawns mowed," the Professor said.

"Yeah," Jeff agreed. What he really liked about the property was the garden and the hillsides around.

It was at that point, in April, that they started looking further afield. They drove out to the north, but that was being developed too rapidly; to the south, but Annapolis was too much like a city; and over the long Bay Bridge to the Eastern Shore. As soon as he saw the flat landscape, the sky stretched out flat like a blanket overhead, the water appearing at unexpected places, Jeff breathed easier. The Professor had no Friday classes, so they spent weekends driving round, going further south each time, to find something they could afford that still suited them. They spent nights in motels, where Jeff played his guitar and the Professor made notes on pages of books or wrote lecture notes. They spent days with estate agents or just driving round towns. They saw houses they liked on land they didn't; land they liked with a house neither of them wanted to live in. It seemed that if they liked a town they could find nothing for sale in it, and if there were a lot of houses available they didn't like the town.

Until, deep in the western corner, an agent drove them down a dirt road to a little cabin that sat on high land – high for that part of the country. A one-room, red-shingled cabin that faced across a broad creek to marshes, that sat right on a point where the creek emptied into the

Chesapeake Bay. The cabin was just one room, with a bathroom tacked on to the back; the whole front wall was plate glass doors that looked out over to where the creek flowed by, hurrying into the bay, and where the level tops of marsh grasses were all you could see, except for a line of low trees at the distance. Mice and roaches scurried away as they entered the room. Spiders had made complex webs at the places where bare roof beams came together at the peak. A bunk bed, a stove and refrigerator, a chipped sink, a table, three chairs, two rollaway beds, a woodburning stove made out of thin tin and rusting through in many places, stacks of newspapers – the room was crowded. The walls were bare plywood, the floor plywood laid down in sheets. The air was damp and musty.

Jeff stood by the window, looking out, not listening. He went outside, leaving the two men inside, looking around and talking. He made his way down to the creek, down a five-foot muddy bank to a band of sand too narrow to lie down on. He had to force his way through honeysuckle vines and the branches of low wild cherry trees, so his approach was clumsy, noisy. As he slid to his feet, a great blue heron croaked loudly just off to his left and at the same time rose out and flew away – complaining – to land on the far side of the creek. From there, the bird stared at Jeff. Jeff stared back, not moving, except for the smile on his mouth. The bird decided Jeff was harmless and paced slowly upstream, its attention on the shallow water where prey might be found. The long stilty legs, the long curved neck, the awkward perfect body moved inland, away from Jeff. He watched it. He watched it not find anything to eat, watched it come to a rest and blend into the stillness of a dead tree that had fallen out into the creek.

The two men were still inside when Jeff rejoined them. The Professor looked at his face and said, "You like it?"

Jeff nodded. "I saw a blue heron."

"They're common around here," the agent said. "You-all birdwatchers?"

But the Professor remembered and understood what Jeff meant. "You take that as a sign from the gods?" Jeff nodded. "Well, I like it myself. Let's take a walk around and see. If you'll excuse us?" he said to the agent. The agent dusted off a wooden chair and sat down, ready to be patient.

Behind the cabin grew loblollies, wild cherries, holly, swamp oaks. The small area of lawn that circled the cabin was sparse and untended. Jeff and the Professor walked to the bank and looked down the creek to the bay. "They'll be mosquitoes," the Professor said. "There are only these three high acres in the property, it'll never be worth anything for development."

"Good," Jeff said.

"It's awfully isolated; you'll be alone a lot."

"That's all right." Jeff waited for his father to

180

finish thinking out the major objections. That was the way the Professor did things.

"But I agree with you, it's like an island, isn't it?"

Jeff hadn't thought of that, he'd thought only of the quiet water noises, the sense of space and peace. "I guess it is. I really like it, Professor."

"Not at all what I imagine Charleston looks like."

"Not a bit," Jeff agreed. "Except – it's like that island, just like you said."

"You didn't see alligators?" The Professor sounded alarmed.

"No, Professor, I didn't. Alligators need a warmer climate. Just the heron."

"Then we'd better make a bid on it, don't you think? It doesn't do to disregard a sign from the gods. Back to the office. We'll have to add on some rooms – redo the bathroom entirely – finish off that room for year-round living – maybe gravel the drive so it won't wash away in bad weather. I guess the septic system's all right; he says it's only two years old. And a dock, we'll need a dock."

"What for?"

"For your boat. Let's go and get the business over."

"I thought so," the agent said with satisfaction, "I thought you were the right people for this, soon as I saw you."

"You appear to have been correct," the Professor said. "What's the nearest town, and how far are we from it?"

"Crisfield," the agent said. "You're about eight miles out, as the crow flies. Maybe ten or a little more by road."

"But what about you, Professor?" Jeff had a picture of the map of Maryland in his mind. He remembered where Crisfield was and where Baltimore was in relation to that. "How will you get to work?"

"I can arrange my schedule so that it's only a couple of nights a week I'd need to be away. I can stay at the Faculty Club or with Brother Thomas. As long as you can take the solitude, it shouldn't be hard to arrange."

"I can take it," Jeff said. "You know that." He thought his father might be teasing him.

The Professor bought the property, as he called it, and sold their little house in Baltimore. Before they moved, they had a lot of work done on the cabin. They added halls and two bedrooms going off opposite sides of the kitchen. They ripped out the old bathroom and had an entirely new one put in. They had the cabin insulated, its walls finished. New double-paned glass doors replaced the old ones in the kitchen. They both wanted to leave the ceiling unfinished, so they did. They had the long drive graded and covered with oyster shells. They put a short dock out into the creek and steps down the steep bank

182

leading to it. They drove down frequently to check on the progress and watched the swarming workmen; carpenters, glaziers, roofers, painters, and listened to the sounds of saws and the pile driver.

Brother Thomas seemed to find unflagging humour in everything about the new house. "How big is this piece of wilderness?" he asked, and "How's Jeff going to get to school – dog sledge?" and "You putting in any crops, Farmer Greene?"

The Professor answered him mildly. "When it's done, you'll come down to visit. On the property."

Jeff didn't call it that. To himself, he called it a safe place, and when they were finally settled in at the end of July, living in the three-room house where windows gave out over the water and woods and sky, he knew he had been right. When they had bought a little skiff, an eleven-foot wooden boat, painted white, with a seven and a half horsepower outboard engine and he took his father exploring up the creek, winding among the branches of fallen trees, staring up at the backs of little cabins or waterfront homes, or meandering across the marshes on one of the canals that ran into the creek – the water so shallow they had to raise the motor and pole the boat – he knew he had been righter than he'd thought. The Professor didn't seem to mind the inconveniences: the distance from the grocery store and libraries, the mosquitoes that rose up like mist on windless evenings, the necessity of keeping Coleman lanterns available for power failures when thunderstorms moved up the bay. Sometimes the Professor would even suggest himself that Jeff take him out in the boat. "I need to get away from myself for a while. Want to go up the bay shore a ways?" They didn't talk much on such trips, but looked about them. The Professor wore a floppy white spinnaker hat to protect his face from the sun and looked out over the water where a fish would often reward his vigil by leaping up out of the water. Jeff wore only shorts, or trunks, and studied the shoreline. He was learning the names of birds and trees, learning also how to scan the water's edge for where a great blue might be standing in camouflage, looking like a branch of one of the fallen trees or blending into the grass. The blues roosted, he had learned, on the high branches of trees. If he wandered outside at night and let the door slam behind him, he could hear them taking off – squawking – from their roosts. They never travelled together, they never shared fishing territory; he liked to think that they squawked their displeasure with one another and him and the state of the world. Great Cranky Birds, the Indians had named them.

He told the Professor this as they sat in the boat at the mouth of the creek, rocking gently as the tide carried them out into the bay. "I don't know why they're so jumpy," Jeff said. "There

184

isn't anything that preys on them, is there? What spooks them?"

"Women with big hats," the Professor said.

Jeff looked at the back of his father's head. His neck was getting tanned, Jeff noticed. Jeff always ran the boat because the Professor couldn't seem to learn how to handle it. He tried to figure out what his father meant. A fish jumped off to starboard. An egret, snowy white, fished along the muddy shallows, its path crossing with two of its fellows. Egrets shared their fishing territory with one another. "C'mon, Professor," Jeff said. "I was serious."

"Oh, so was I." The Professor turned round to look earnestly at Jeff. "When women wore those picture hats, with hat pins – one of the prized adornments was heron feathers."

Jeff thought about that and thought about his father's response to his question. He started to laugh, a small bubbling of humour in his stomach. "But that's funny, what you said."

"I have my moments," the Professor answered, and turned back to the water. But he was pleased, Jeff knew that.

In the evenings, the Professor studied or wrote or read a mystery. Jeff played his guitar. They had decided against a television, had bought a stereo, instead, and a radio, so they could hear the news and weather. Sometimes the Professor joined Jeff in the kitchen, which they had turned into what

185

magazines called a family kitchen, with sofa and chairs near the Franklin stove the Professor had insisted on having. Sometimes he worked in his room. "Are you writing another book?" Jeff asked his father, one night, watching him wander to the window to look out over the water, which ran red under the last light of the setting sun.

"Hmmm?" The Professor turned, but didn't focus his eyes on Jeff. "I think maybe," he said.

Jeff began playing on his guitar again, softly. The Professor didn't mind, he'd given Jeff only a fraction of his attention, Jeff knew, because he was thinking something out. Jeff worked out a background for one of the songs he'd heard in Charleston. It needed, he thought, a kind of jingle to it, almost like a tambourine, as if the guitar were one of those cigar box banjos. He thought the Martin could make that kind of sound, if he could figure out how to get it out of his fingers. "Oh Lord, you know, I have no friend like you," he sang. He almost had it, but not quite. "And I cain't feel at home in this world, any more."

The Professor drifted back to his room. "This world is not my home, I'm only passing through," Jeff sang. He was getting closer to the sound he wanted.

They registered Jeff in school and got him a ten-speed bicycle, for days when he didn't want to take the bus. The guidance counsellor didn't even ask him why he was repeating the eighth grade. The Professor didn't ask whether Jeff was strong enough to bike the miles to the school, but he did suggest that Jeff might want to build up his muscles. So Jeff packed sandwiches and took long rides on the empty roads, roads that went along for miles between intersections. He learned every turn of the flat road into Crisfield, became familiar with the farms set back behind fields, their barns bright tan or bright red, with the little houses set up close to the road, with the clusters of trailer homes, the rectangular fields framed by loblollies. He learned the names on the mailboxes along the road to school, most of them standing opposite trim drives, as erect as soldiers. Only one mailbox was neglected, tilted over, its door always hanging open, its paint chipped, its name faded away to *llerma*. He became familiar with the stores in the shopping centre a mile before the school – the large antiseptic supermarket that carried medicines as well as school supplies and even some clothing – and with the less modern stores down at the town centre, the hardware, the restaurant, the small grocery whose windows were streaked with grime.

On good days, Jeff took the boat out. He learned to dangle chicken necks at the end of pieces of string to catch crabs. He could, he knew, set pots out in a line, then run the boat along the line, pulling up the pots to see what he'd caught. That would have been more efficient. But he preferred the quiet of the boat anchored in the middle of the creek, he preferred the lazier pace. He'd bait five or six strings and dangle them over the side of the boat. He left them undisturbed until he saw, by the movement of a string on the gunwales, that a crab was feeding on the bait. Then he would take the string in his fingers and pull it gently in, feeling the crab at the other end, knowing it had one claw firmly fixed on the chicken neck while the other ripped off pieces of flesh to eat greedily. Gently, smoothly, so the crab wouldn't sense anything unnatural, Jeff pulled the string in, until he could see the crab, now a few inches beneath the water's surface. He held the bait steady by stepping on the string and picked up his net. He scooped the crab up in the net, dumped it into the bushel basket, and tossed out the string again, feeding out line until the bait came to rest on the creek bottom. They often had steamed crabs for dinner, eating them with cornbread made from a mix, or biscuits, and glasses of beer or wine or iced tea.

Jeff tried to teach the Professor how to catch crabs, but his father's hands were clumsy. Somehow, his crabs always swam off from the bait before the Professor could net them. Jeff, watching, admired the crab's sideways retreat. The crab slipped away, angling into darker, deeper water. "I don't know how you do it," the Professor said to Jeff.

"I don't know how you can't," Jeff answered.

"High natural ineptitude," the Professor said. "I'd rather read anyway." He sat and did just that most of the time, moving his legs out of Jeff's way when Jeff moved round the boat to check the lines.

Brother Thomas, who came to stay for a week in late August, took a more voluble interest in crabbing and in Crisfield, especially the workboats that moored up at the town dock, especially in the history, especially in everything. "Look at all the churches," he said, walking along the residential streets that ran back behind the town. "Look at those old Victorian houses, the gingerbreading. I'd think someone would fix them up. Who do you suppose built them?" Brother Thomas, in the bright Hawaiian shirts he wore on holiday, wandered happily through the shops, talking with anyone nearby. He met the local priest, he talked with the old men who sat in the shade of shacks by the dock, among miniature mountains of oyster shells. "This is a wonderful life. I don't know how you found this place," Brother Thomas said. "It must be your background as a geographer, Horace."

"Your what?" Jeff asked. They were all sitting outside on low chairs. The men drank a chilled white wine and Jeff watched the egrets feeding on the opposite side of the creek. A wind blew the mosquitoes away, so they sat in comfort.

"I started out specializing in geography," the Professor explained to him.

"Why?" Jeff asked.

"I was interested. It seemed like a good way to get grants to travel."

"Did you know your father won a Rhodes Scholarship?"

Jeff didn't know that.

"But that was in 1945, so he couldn't take it. Honestly, Horace, it's almost pathological, your secretiveness."

"It never came up," the Professor said.

"Besides," Jeff said, "it's not the kind of question you think of to ask – 'By the way, what academic prizes did you win?' It's not like 'What do you want for dinner?' or 'Can I take any library books back for you?' Is it?"

They were all stretched out in their chairs, and the quiet stretched out around them.

"My only question now is, how often can I come back?" Brother Thomas asked.

"As often as you like. The sofa bed is there for you," the Professor said.

Jeff heard in their voices their contentment. They were two of a kind, he saw, two quiet men, each able to respect what was central to the other's life, both intellectuals. Brother Thomas had a deep, stabilizing faith; although he didn't talk about it, it was always there in him. The Professor had his study of history, whether reading it, writing about it, or thinking it over; it was always there in him, always important. Jeff saw why they were friends.

"You going to get a dog to keep Jeff company?" Brother Thomas asked.

"And a red wagon too?" the Professor asked.

"Why would I need a red wagon?" Jeff asked.

"It's what every boy should have, a dog and a little red wagon," the Professor told him.

"No thanks. Not that I'm ungrateful. But a dog would chase away the birds and the raccoons."

"But," Brother Thomas said, "it could pull you to school in your little red wagon."

Jeff chuckled.

8

Jeff knew what the Professor wanted from him in school, although the Professor never said anything about it. He wanted the same thing Jeff wanted, just for it to be OK. He didn't expect top grades. He didn't expect Jeff to get popular or play varsity sports or join activities. The Professor's classes didn't start until two weeks after Jeff's so the Professor was there every day when Jeff came home. "Everything OK?" he'd ask.

"OK," Jeff would answer.

That was the truth. The school was pretty big, so a newcomer could be invisible among all the old friends. Everybody was new to the school, because in Crisfield grades eight to twelve were in one building, an old two-storey brick with tall oaks beside the path to the main entrance. Jeff took six classes, five academic courses and mechanical drawing. He hadn't wanted to take mechanical drawing, he'd wanted to take home economics – after all, the way they lived, that would have been really useful to him, cooking and sewing. But the guidance counsellor told him he couldn't recommend home economics, not to a boy and new to the area, there was an unwritten policy. The main sport was football, which Jeff didn't play and didn't want to, so he took the regular PE class where he ran laps, played soccer, and did exercises with the other unathletic boys. He sat quietly in classes, moved quietly through the halls, ate quietly at the lunch table, and nobody paid any attention to him. Not that he wanted attention. He paid attention himself during classes, did his homework without any trouble at all and made sure it was neat, answered questions when the teachers asked him, answered exactly what he knew they were asking to find out if he knew. The work wasn't hard. Jeff thought maybe that was because he'd done it the year before at the University School; but he couldn't remember much of anything about that.

The first night he spent alone in the house, Jeff expected to be uneasy. The Professor would stay up in Baltimore for two nights. Jeff rode his bike home and leaned it up against the wall by the back door. He entered the empty house, made himself a bologna sandwich, then wandered down to the dock, getting himself used to being alone. He'd promised the Professor not to go out in the boat when he was alone, which seemed fair enough. He sat on the end of the dock and looked around. Behind him, on the low rise of land that passed him, the creek ran slowly, the long field of marshes swayed like waves under a breeze not strong enough to do more than rustle the leaves on the trees. A great blue paced its territory down to the west, towards the bay, where little waves rippled. In the opposite direction, the creek twisted up off to the east, going inland. The boat floated beside him, the dock was sturdy beneath him.

Unable to sit still, Jeff went back to the house and brought his guitar down. He hesitated, trying to decide what song to sing. Far up in the sky an osprey circled. Jeff ran the pick down across the strings – and the heron rose, complaining. Jeff watched it, the great wings spread out smoky blue, the long neck tucked in until the bird seemed full of dignity, full of ridiculous dignity, looking pompously ahead, the long legs held stifffly out behind him.

Jeff sat and played, song after song, until the mosquitoes rose with the lowering sun to drive him inside. There he made a supper of steak and salad and baked potato. After he had washed up, he began on his homework, spreading the books and papers out over the kitchen table. The silence and solitude wrapped themselves around him.

As he was diagramming the last of a dozen sentences for English, the silence was shattered by a harsh, clanging sound: the telephone. Their telephone never rang, and Jeff knocked over his chair in his hurry to answer it. It was the Professor. "How is everything, OK?" he asked. "OK," Jeff said. "Really, Professor – except for the phone scaring me half to death. It's going to be OK."

"I thought so, and Brother Thomas thought so too, but we thought we'd just call and check in."

"Thanks," Jeff said. Then he asked, "Is everything OK up there?"

"Everything's fine. I'll see you the day after tomorrow."

"See you then. Thanks for calling."

As the first weeks of school went by, Jeff worked out how things went in Crisfield. He learned to wear jeans to school. Most people wore jeans. It didn't matter what you wore for a shirt. Some people, girls especially, dressed up more, some always looked ratty, but if you wore jeans you didn't stand out. His homework papers, then quizzes and tests, kept coming back perfect. It wasn't because the school was easier than his old school, because it wasn't; and it wasn't that the other kids weren't smart enough, because they seemed smart enough. Maybe not like some of the brains, the really brainy kids up in Baltimore who planned to finish high school in two years and go straight into college – but smart enough, and most of them did their work. They were just regular kids, each one different, everybody a lot alike.

They hung around in packs, the girls in one pack, the boys in another. They didn't know anything about Jeff and didn't seem very interested, but by listening he learned about them, what they thought of themselves, what their fathers did, when they had parties, how they got along with their families. They thought Crisfield was a dull and dumpy little town, the boonies, they called it. They liked to go up to the mall in Salisbury, where life was more exciting. They longed to have cars so they could get away. They liked the mechanical drawing teacher all right, they thought the science teacher was the best ever, they were awed by the elderly Latin teacher, a minister's wife who never raised her voice at a class but was so steely and strict nobody dared talk back or come unprepared. They thought the English teacher was a phoney, the PE teacher a hero because he rode a Harley to school and was rumoured to race it at the weekends. Jeff agreed with them, on the whole. If he hadn't, it wouldn't have made any difference.

A couple of the guys played in a band, a rock band they had formed; Jeff learned that. A couple of other guys, one from English, the other from science, struck him as more interesting than the rest. He couldn't have said why, precisely. Phil Milson, in English, was pretty funny, without being a clown about it. They were talking about stories by then, and Phil usually had some unusual angle on a story, which the teacher didn't appreciate. But Phil was funny in a subtle way, which Chappelle, the teacher, didn't always get, Jeff suspected, along with most of the rest of the class. Then Andy Barrows in science always had questions and questions and questions, why and how. Listening to his questions and the answers he got, Jeff learned a lot more than the book taught. He wondered how Andy figured out what questions to ask. He didn't talk to either of those two, they had their own friends, but they made his school day more interesting.

The girls giggled and whispered, passed notes, combed their hair, talked about being too fat or too skinny. In class they were more serious, and they were always willing to try talking about what the teacher wanted – but Jeff wasn't much interested in girls. He had the feeling that they were pretending, looking around to see who noticed them. And there was something else, something secret, that they were always trying to get.

Jeff's first report card surprised him by being all As. He brought it home for the Professor to sign. The Professor didn't seem surprised or particularly overwhelmed. "I suppose that's good enough," he said.

"It's OK," Jeff said. He thought he knew what his father might be thinking, so he told him. "Even if it had been all Fs I would have shown it to you."

"I hope so. Do you like the school?"

"Yeah, sure."

"Is it easier?"

"Not really. At least, I don't think so. I don't know why my grades are so good."

The Professor stared at him for a long time, making up his mind about something. They sat outside, on low chairs. Jeff ate an apple. "You've got a high IQ," the Professor said. "Not genius or anything, but high. Of course, the relevance of IQ tests is under question, and their accuracy. But you've always tested at the top percentages in any standardized test."

Jeff stopped chewing. "But – "

"But what?"

"But – I don't know. The Principal up at the University School said . . . and Melody told me . . ."

"The Principal hadn't read through your file, he just wanted you out because you were messing up his class averages. But what did Melody say?"

"She said I'd got her brains and you must be disappointed."

"I don't know why she said that – it's not true," the Professor said. "She's smart enough. I never thought she would have – I should have told you sooner. I'm sorry, Jeff."

"I'll forgive you," he told his father, who smiled back at him. "I don't mind. So I'm a classic under-achiever?"

"Not this year."

"How come I never did well in school before?"

"What do you think?" the Professor asked. Jeff didn't know the answer. "It might be worth thinking about," his father said.

Jeff tried, off and on. He couldn't remember much from school, or before that, kindergarten, and before that the day care centre. He remembered some of the teachers, some of the other kids, but not himself, Jeff Greene. It was almost as if he'd been a ghost in all those rooms, all those days, a ghost in his own life.

At the end of October, the Professor showed Jeff a copy of his book. He brought it out one night after dinner and put it on the table in front of Jeff. Jeff looked at it: a book, *Earth's Honoured Guests*, with a picture on the cover of the outline of a man's head and shoulders, with a medal hanging down from where his shirt pocket would have been if more than the outline had been drawn. By Horace Greene. Jeff just stared at it.

"That's what I said too," the Professor said.

Jeff sat there wishing he hadn't given his word to wait until he was fifteen to read the book. He turned it over and saw a photograph of the Professor. His hair shone white, his tie was slightly askew. "Horace Greene is a Professor of History at Baltimore University," he read. Jeff turned the book over in his hands, feeling the weight of it

"I'm really impressed," he said.

The Professor's face was expressionless.

"C'mon, Professor," Jeff insisted. He knew that that expressionless face was put on to hide something, and he was pretty sure he could guess what. "Aren't you proud of yourself? Just a little bit? You can tell me."

"Don't pick on me, please," the Professor said,

giving way and smiling. "Yes, I am – proud. I think it's an honest book. I'm just not very comfortable with having a book published. Maybe it will fade into immediate obscurity; I think I hope it will."

Jeff handed the book back to his father. He didn't want to do that, he wanted to read it, right away; but he had given his word. He knew he'd better give it back, because if he didn't, he wasn't sure he'd be able to keep his promise.

They were assigned an essay in English, to write about conflict in a real character. Jeff decided to write about John C. Calhoun of South Carolina. He'd often visited the park in Charleston that was dominated by a statue of Calhoun.

When Chappelle finally returned the paper Jeff wrote, Jeff's grade was a perplexing A/F. Chappelle talked a little about all the essays, then read a couple aloud that he thought were good, then hauled one girl over the coals for not writing it herself. Then he called on Jeff. "Greene," he said, his face serious under carroty hair, one hand on his narrow tie. "Do you have any questions about your grade?"

Jeff shook his head.

"You should. I rather suspected you hadn't taken the trouble to write down the assignment. Do you write down assignments?"

"Yes."

"Have you got this one written down?"

"Yes."

"Do you think you could trouble yourself to look it up?"

Jeff was suddenly nervous, even frightened. He didn't think he'd burst into tears and have to leave the room, but he remembered – he'd forgotten it for so long, he'd been stupid to forget it – that he was easy to break down. He read out the assignment nervously. "Write about conflict in someone real." He remembered, it had been written on the board; he didn't think he'd have forgotten to copy down an assignment written on the board. But what if he had? "At least one thousand words," he finished reading.

He could remember, as clearly as if it was still on the board, the assignment written out in Chappelle's irregular print. He could trust his memory, couldn't he?

"It was supposed to be somebody you knew, as well," Chappelle said. "I'm presuming you didn't ever meet John Calhoun."

His sarcasm was so clumsy it couldn't frighten Jeff. And Chappelle wasn't exactly angry, Jeff could tell, just superpatient and patronizing.

"You'd be right in that, sir," he agreed. He heard a rustling of attention in the class around him.

"So the grade is fair, even generous," Chappelle said.

Jeff breathed easy again. If that was all he'd

done wrong that was OK. "I didn't question it," he said.

"You'll have to work hard to get your average back up, if you want to stay on high honour roll," the teacher told him. "Do you want to do an extra credit assignment? Write another essay?"

Jeff thought about that, because he didn't want to. "No, I don't," he said. "Thank you anyway, sir."

Chappelle was staring at him, but the bell rang so that was an end of that. It was Friday, and Jeff hoped the whole thing would have blown over by the next Monday. A question waded along at the edge of his attention, like the blue heron fishing the creekside. But somebody nudged him in the ribs. He turned his head sharply.

It was Phil Milson. "Man, you are as cool as a cucumber," Phil said. "Old Chappelle couldn't get you nervous at all, could he?"

"Oh, yeah, he could," Jeff said, glad it hadn't shown.

"He could? I like that even better. See you around, OK?" Phil ran ahead to join his friends. But he came over to the table where Jeff sat in the cafeteria and said, "I don't know if you know this, I've got a brother and a sister who've been through it with Chappelle, but you're new this year, aren't you?"

Jeff nodded.

"He'll sulk, a week, maybe two – then he'll forget about it. He's a case of arrested emotional development. Just keep a low profile for a couple of weeks."

"Thanks," Jeff said. "I'll remember." He thought he ought to say something friendly, but he wasn't sure what that would be. "What do you mean arrested emotional development?"

"I mean, we're kids, so we're supposed to act like jerks; it's OK for us. But it's supposed to be a phase you pass through." The bell rang and Jeff didn't have to think of anything else to say.

He went out crabbing that evening, while the Professor did some shopping so they'd have something for Brother Thomas to cook when he came down the next day. Jeff didn't expect to catch anything, and he didn't. In the cooler weather most of the crabs moved on south or buried themselves in the deep mud at the bottom of the bay. The herons and egrets too were growing scarce; only gulls remained in any numbers.

Jeff sat back in the boat, which he hadn't even untied from the dock, and let it rock under him. He didn't even look at the strings hanging over the gunwales.

He didn't think Chappelle had said it had to be somebody you knew, but probably the man had and Jeff hadn't registered it. He hadn't registered it, even though he usually listened well and remembered accurately; so he hadn't let it get into his head. Sometimes he did that, he knew; and then he would remember suddenly and wonder why he had forgotten. That was the way he was.

Why hadn't he ever done well in school before, if he was clever, and the Professor said he tested clever. The Professor didn't actually say he was clever though, did he?

If he was a ghost in the life he remembered, Jeff thought, he was also a ghost in his present life, just the same way. Except, in all the fourteen years, just a couple of times. With Melody that first summer he had felt alive. On the beach on the island. And when he played the guitar.

Most of the time, he thought, he practised not being anybody. If you weren't anybody then nobody could – what? Hurt you or leave you behind? Make you unhappy? But then they couldn't make you happy either, could they? If you played it safe, then you kept safe. Jeff figured he was pretty good at keeping safe – he didn't even look in mirrors because he didn't want to see Melody's eyes. But one result of that was that Jeff didn't know anything about himself. And he thought, sitting in the little boat, alone on the creek, alone with the creek and the sky and the marshes, that he might want to know more.

But as soon as he thought that, he got scared that there wasn't any more to know. As soon as he got scared, he thought that being scared was one of his problems. As soon as he thought about one of his problems, he got impatient with himself, irritated – and that felt better. The Professor, after all, had loved Melody and lost her and been hurt by her too, Jeff suddenly realized. Probably at least as badly as Jeff had been; and now he'd written a book, and before that he'd made friends with Brother Thomas, so the Professor survived. Hadn't Melody said, meaning to criticize, that Jeff was like his father? Jeff hauled in the baited strings and climbed out of the boat. He hadn't stopped thinking. But he was going to take it slow and quiet, this thinking about himself.

Chappelle did act funny about Jeff for a couple of weeks, calling on him every day at the end of class to read off the exact assignment, paying exaggerated attention to whatever Jeff said in class. Then he seemed to forget about it. Thanksgiving came, and a short holiday from school, which Jeff and the Professor used to haul the boat out of the water and stock up on some food in case they got snowed in. "It's always good to be safe," the Professor said, placing tins of beans and soup in a row at the back of the shelf, lining up tins of ravioli, boxes of grits and oatmeal, as well as dry mixes for cornbread, biscuits, and milk.

"As a general rule?" Jeff asked. This was, of course something he had been thinking about.

"As a general rule, well – I'm not the one to ask about that," the Professor said. "If you mean, as I take it, a general rule for life. I'm awfully good at playing it safe and not good at all at taking risks."

"But you have," Jeff pointed out.

"Never by my own choice," the Professor told him. He turned around to look at Jeff, who passed him more tins and boxes. "Always somebody else pushed me. Even my book; Brother Thomas is the one who pushed me into submitting it – the man is implacable, once he gets his teeth into an idea. I'm very grateful to him."

"I like him too," Jeff said.

And he did. All the more when, after the Christmas holidays, on one of the days when the Professor stayed up in Baltimore, he picked up a brown manilla envelope from the mailbox. Brother Thomas had sent him some xeroxed copies of newspaper articles, he saw; also a note. The note read: "If I know the man you won't have seen these. I thought you'd enjoy them. BroT."

There was a review (from *Time* magazine, Jeff noticed, impressed; more impressed when he read it and saw words like *intelligent, readable, thought provoking*) and an interview from the Baltimore paper. It was the interview Jeff read three or four times. Because he didn't know any of this stuff about his father.

"Born in 1924," he read, collecting the facts, "graduated from University of Chicago in 1943". So the Professor had accelerated through school. "PhD, University of Chicago." The Professor had told the reporter that he had studied political geography, because he wanted to travel, but had

206

gone to work for Army Intelligence instead. He'd worked in Washington, analysing information from aerial photographs of central Europe, mostly, because he knew about the countries. After the War, he'd read Philosophy at Oxford for a year, then taken the job at Baltimore. He said it had taken him fifteen years to write his book. He'd finished it two years earlier and a friend had bullied him into submitting it to a publisher. The Professor told the reporter that he thought that was an awfully long time to spend on one book, but he'd enjoyed the work so much he had been almost sorry when he finished with it. Yes, he said, he might write another, he had filing cabinets filled with notes. At the end of the article, there was a paragraph of personal information: married in 1962, separated, lives with his teenaged son. "A handsome, ageless man," the reporter described the Professor, "whose eyes twinkle with dry humour . . . a thoroughly charming man, who weighs his words and is worth listening to." The article closed with a quote from the Professor: "Some of my best work is in that book, which is, I take it, what a book should contain." Jeff put down the papers. He didn't know what to think. He didn't really know his father, not this way, not as this kind of man. He supposed he was pretty proud of the Professor, and thought he was going to have even more trouble now keeping his promise to the Professor. He went to his room and got the Martin, sat strumming on

207

it, looking out over the winter brown marshes and winter clear creek water and winter grey skies. Good for the Professor, he thought.

Jeff felt a little embarrassed, greeting his father after school the next day. He didn't know why the Professor hadn't told him about the review or the interview. Or about his life. He didn't know why he himself hadn't asked the Professor more about his life. Riding his bike back from school, arguing with himself whether or not he'd been a fool to take the bike on such a cold day, Jeff didn't know what he was going to say to his father. What he finally said was, "Your eyes don't twinkle."

The blue eyes, of course, did look bright and amused at that. "I agree," the Professor said. "Am I to gather then that Brother Thomas has been in touch with you?"

"I'm really impressed," Jeff said.

"Thank you. It's probably as well he warned you, because I'm afraid the book is successful."

"That's OK, Professor, I won't hold it against you. How successful?"

"British sales and a contract for a paperback edition. Is there anything you need money for?"

"No," Jeff said. Then he thought. "Don't you want an electric typewriter?"

"Yes, but I've got one on order. What about you? Schools? I don't know, what do boys want these days?"

"Just a dog and a little red wagon," Jeff said.

"But you aren't serious, are you? You are, aren't you? I want a Martin, and I have it. I want to live in a place where it's beautiful, and we do. And a boat. I think getting rid of the money's going to be your problem, Professor, not mine."

"I meant, we could move back to Baltimore, to one of those houses we couldn't afford before." His father's face was expressionless.

Jeff made his face expressionless too. "Is that what you'd like?" After all, it was the Professor who supported them, who had the work. Jeff carefully didn't look out of the window.

"I asked you first."

"No, you didn't. You suggested, you didn't ask. I asked *you* first."

"But I want to hear what you want."

"Then you should have asked first," Jeff insisted. This was crazy, like two little kids quarrelling.

"But . . . all right. The truth of the matter is – no, I don't want to leave. But I always was a hermit. I don't know about you . . . if you're making friends, if there's enough for you to do, if the school is good enough."

Jeff did get up from the table then. He walked to the glass door and looked out, across the marsh then down to the sweep of bay, larger now that the deciduous trees had shed their leaves. "I love it here," he said, trying to say it as clear and true as he could.

"You really do," the Professor said. After a pause, "I don't mind it myself," he added.

As spring approached, Jeff began preparing the boat. He scraped and repainted the bottom and had the engine overhauled. In late March he began to see ospreys. By mid April, the trees started to produce new leaves. The egrets returned and, during May, the herons. Jeff saw his first heron of the season one sunny afternoon after school. The blue stood on the trunk of a tree that had fallen over into the creek, stood motionless and unaware. For a long time, Jeff watched it from the dock. The sun-warmed air smelled of moist earth, and somehow green, of growing things. Without moving, Jeff watched. The heron stood on stiff thin legs, its long neck tucked in, its flattened head still. Finally, Jeff couldn't contain himself: "Hello," he called down the creek. "Welcome back."

The bird didn't even look towards him. It took off, raising itself awkwardly from the tree, and flew up the creek, squawking its resentment as it disappeared into treetops. Jeff laughed aloud.

At school, he often joined Phil for lunch. Phil's father was a farmer, so they didn't get together outside school – Phil had chores and had to help plough up the land, then plant it. He didn't seem too curious about Jeff, but he seemed to like him all right. They talked about classes, mostly, although sometimes Phil made cracks about girls, and he asked Jeff what his father did, and if he had brothers and sisters, and how his mother liked living in the boonies. Jeff just said his mother lived in Charleston. "I wish my mother lived in Charleston," Phil answered.

Jeff liked Phil; he liked his sense of humour and the practical turn of his mind. Phil's life was so normal, so practical – and Phil couldn't see that. Phil figured, Jeff thought, that everyone was pretty much like him; he didn't have the imagination or experience to see what differences there could be. He was a four-square, solid person, and Jeff liked that. They weren't friends, exactly, but he wouldn't mind being friends.

Everything was going smoothly and Jeff slipped through the days, until Mr Chappelle asked one day in class if Jeff's father was the one who wrote the book. After that, people seemed to look at Jeff with more interest and give him a wider berth. Except Phil, who tackled the subject head on. "He wrote a book? What are you doing down here?"

"We like it here."

"Does that mean he's an egghead? Or you?"

"I don't know."

"You *are* high honour roll, every time."

"I'm sorry." Luckily, Phil thought that was funny, so Jeff, hearing how stupid it sounded, had a chance to say, "I'm repeating eighth grade – I don't know how I'll do next year."

"You don't *mind* being high honour roll, do you?" Phil looked surprised.

"You know, I don't know."

"Greene, you're unbelievable. I can't tell if you're a total fink or a really unusual guy."

"Probably something in between," Jeff said.

Jeff did have the chance to ask Phil if he'd like to go out in the boat, crabbing or something, once school let out. Phil knew where they lived, "on the old Mitchell place; they used it for hunting." He said he'd call if his father took the chains off for a day. The Milsons sold some of their vegetables and all their eggs in Salisbury during the summer, as well as having a roadside produce stand, so he was pretty busy. "I wouldn't mind a day off, I'll tell you," Phil said. This was as they left school on the last day, when everybody burst out of the doors, and some of them yelled aloud their joy. Jeff took his bike from the rack and rode home alone. He was satisfied, he thought, with the way he'd spent the year. He hadn't made any enemies and he might have made a friend. That made it a terrific year for him.

Brother Thomas spent two weeks with them that summer. He and Jeff learned how to bait and set out a trotline, then how to run it, the engine at its slowest speed, one of them steering while the other netted the crabs that clung to the pieces of bait as they rose to the surface. It took them most of the two weeks to get good enough at it, and it wasn't until the last week that they made the kind of haul Jeff read about, three bushels in two hours. They couldn't, of course, eat all those crabs. They culled out the very largest to cook and turned the rest loose, dumping the crabs overboard, like a living landslide. They were out in the bay that day, wearing just shorts. When the sun got too hot they slipped over the side to cool off, avoiding the translucent jellyfish who had arrived in mid-July to make swimming unpleasant. The jellies clustered near the surface of the dark water and clung with stringy formless tentacles to anything that caught them, the net, the line, a shoulder. Jeff had been stung often enough to learn that, while it hurt a bit, it only lasted for about half an hour.

That day was, he thought, just about perfect. Brother Thomas liked to sing, so they sang as they waited between runs down the trotline, and Brother Thomas taught Jeff the elements of harmony singing. They watched workboats run by single men or crews. They saw sailboats and motor yachts trailing fishing lines and a little red motor boat run by a solitary woman whose hair was a tangled mass of grey curls. She went up along the coast then turned into a dock that seemed unattached to any house. They went back home so baked by sunlight that Jeff felt as crusted with salt as a pretzel and was surprised not to see large salt flakes on his arms and legs.

One day, when they were downtown so Brother Thomas could soak up local colour, Jeff was killing time wandering up and down the street by the town harbour, waiting to meet Brother Thomas for a Coke before driving home. Brother Thomas had gone into the fish market to get them some lobsters, "for a present, to go with that champagne I brought". A woman came out of the little grocery store, carrying two huge bags. Jeff looked at her and thought he should offer to help her carry them. She looked old, but she didn't move as if she was old. He hesitated, inching towards her. She had leathery, tanned skin and wore a long skirt with a baggy blouse over it. Her hair was iron grey, and her eyes looked at him as if she was angry with him. Over her shoulder he saw Brother Thomas approaching, so he stepped aside without offering to take the bags. She walked on past him, but as she passed she said something that sounded like "manners of a chicken".

Jeff felt her anger towards him, and he felt unaccountably shaky. Why should he be afraid, he asked himself. He didn't even know her. She couldn't possibly do anything to him. But he felt – inside himself, and he didn't lie to himself about it – as if she could, even though he knew she couldn't.

"Who's that?" Brother Thomas asked. "What did you say to her? I'm trying hard to imagine – I mean *you*, I've known you for years – what could you have said? Tell, Jeff, I'm going crazy with curiosity." His humour masked genuine concern for Jeff, Jeff saw that.

"Not a word." Jeff still felt quivery from the odd encounter. "Honest, I didn't do anything. I was even thinking about offering to carry her bags."

They watched the woman go out on the dock, then climb down into a motor boat and rush off.

"That's the same red boat, isn't it?" Brother Thomas said. "Wait here." He went into the grocery store and came out in a few minutes, carrying a bag of potato crisps. "Well" – he justified the purchase – "I couldn't just go in and pump her for information. Her name's Abigail Tillerman, she's a widow, had three children, all of whom left home years ago. The youngest died in Vietnam – she might be a little crazy with solitude, at least that's what people say. That shop is withering from neglect."

"How'd you find out all that?"

But Brother Thomas was watching the now empty water of the harbour. "When you think of all the lost souls in this world. What life does to people. Do you know what I mean?"

Jeff did, because he was one of them. "I suppose so," he said.

"And that shop – the woman in there was another one. But this Tillerman woman – at least her spirit wasn't broken, wouldn't you say?"

"I wouldn't like to meet her again," Jeff said, "and not in a dark alley." He'd need to be tougher

215

than he ever could be, and it wasn't just this one old lady, it was most people in the world. Jeff felt as if he'd been keeping a secret from himself and had come round a dark inner corner to rediscover it. He felt shaky, but as if he'd learned something. Probably it was good for him. He thought it was. It wasn't good for him to get confident; just like he'd been confident about Melody. It was when you got confident you got taken by surprise and really banged around.

It was strange, he thought to himself a couple of weeks later, that he'd thought of Melody. It had been such a long time, since they lived in Baltimore that strange autumn, that he'd even mentioned her name to himself. He had put her away and shut the drawer on her. The coincidence struck him because the Professor sat him down in the long summer twilight to talk about her. "Your mother has written to me – about you."

"I don't want to go there. Professor? I don't have to, do I? Can she make me? I *can't*."

The Professor's eyes studied him. Jeff looked away, to the scrubby grass of the lawn. He didn't want to hear what the Professor would say. For a long time, the Professor didn't say anything. When he did speak, it took Jeff a minute to figure out that he hadn't changed the subject. "Right after she left, I was miserable and ashamed. I just wanted her to come back. It was like that for a long time. But then, when I got used to it, I began to be afraid she *would* come back; just thinking of it scared me. Really scared me – it took courage just to answer the phone if it rang. In case it was her. I think I understand how you feel, Jeff."

Jeff appreciated that, but it didn't answer his question. "Can she make me go to see her?"

The Professor sighed. "Let me tell you what she wants; it's much easier and much harder than what you think. She wants a divorce; she doesn't say why. She wants custody of you."

"No!" Jeff couldn't sit any more. But he couldn't go too far away because then he couldn't hear his father. "No, I won't," he said. He walked away, to where the lawn sloped down. "You can't make me."

"I don't want to make you, you know that." His father's voice spoke from behind him, patient, trustworthy. "Come back, sit down. I've talked to a lawyer, and they never guarantee, but at your age a court will listen to what you want. A judge will. The lawyer says he's pretty sure of that. But she wants to divorce me, she wants it uncontested, for incompatibility."

Jeff was back, seated again. "That's OK."

"Well," the Professor said, "the lawyer doesn't think so. He says that if it goes through uncontested she could make a strong appeal for custody, at least half the year."

"What can we do?" Jeff asked. He heard how small his voice was. He looked up at the sky, above the smooth line of marsh grass and the ragged line of trees. The sky was streaked with pastel clouds, yellow and orange and pink.

"I can divorce her for desertion, or adultery if she contests that."

"You mean with Max?"

"Only you'd have to be willing to testify against her, if she contested it. In court. And that seems like an awful lot to ask of you. She is your mother, after all."

Jeff looked at his feet. They were bare and brown. The soles had thick callouses. "But it's true; why would she contest it?"

"I don't know." The Professor sounded tired, really tired, and discouraged.

Jeff's attention focused on his father. "Professor, how long has this been going on?"

"She wrote to me in March, the first time."

"That's five months ago, you should have told me."

"I didn't want to worry you. I was hoping not to have to. Maybe you'd better read her letters."

The Professor had kept Melody's letters in a manila folder. Jeff opened it. The first one – he had to read it twice, because on first reading he was thinking about Melody's handwriting, the shapes of the letters and the way her sentences sounded, eager and happy, just the way her voice sounded.

The first letter talked about how she had been surprised to read about his book and asked wouldn't it be a good thing if they formalized the

218

separation by getting divorced. She couldn't possibly give up Jeff, she said, so she would ask for custody. "Unless you've changed radically, Horace, he'll be better off with me. He needs affection and attention, and I know you don't want to deprive him. Do you?"

The second letter sounded like her feelings had been hurt. She said she didn't think the Professor would go to a lawyer; but if he wanted to be that way he was lucky to be able to afford it; she said she missed Jeff and had become suspicious at not hearing from him. Was the Professor allowing her son to communicate with her?

The third had a photograph clipped to it, the picture she had taken in the Charleston airport. "Did you ever see him look like that?" she asked. "Was he ever so happy when he was with you? Have you thought at all about Jeff in this or only about your own convenience?"

Jeff looked at the photograph. The boy was so young, and his smile so broad it made even Jeff smile to look at him, and he knew better. "I'm sorry," he said, not looking at his father. Everything Melody wrote, every word she used, showed how well she could guess what the Professor was like, how he would react – as if she could see him. That was her real talent, Jeff thought, for feeling what people were like; and he had, he could see, that same talent. But she was using it to get what she wanted from the Professor.

219

"Oh, well," the Professor said, accepting the facts as he had been told them by Melody.

"But – but she's lying, I know she's lying. She lies. She doesn't mean it. She didn't take any other pictures of me. You know you can't trust her, Professor. Don't let her get to you."

"What I want to know is, if you're absolutely sure," the Professor asked.

"I am. Honest. I'm sure."

His father didn't speak.

"Don't you believe me? You have to believe me. If you don't believe me, then who will?"

"It's all right, I do. So – we'll fight her. She says she knows I'll be a gentleman, which really means she's counting on that. As a weakness."

"Can we win?"

"The lawyer thinks so, with your testimony. About Max. About – I told him I thought she'd never answered your letters that first year when you came back. I was correct in that, wasn't I?"

Jeff nodded. "Does she know where we live? I mean, these letters all came to the university."

"I didn't tell her."

"Good." Jeff picked up the photograph.

"What are you doing? Don't rip it up. I'd like to keep it, if you don't want it."

"Is the lawyer sure?" Jeff gave the photograph to his father.

"Pretty sure. I wouldn't even have told you about it except – I never knew what Melody would do. When there's something she wants, she's unpredictable. It'll take a long time, of course. The law always does. Don't brood over it."

"I'll try not to," Jeff said. Even the Professor was scared of Melody. And what if she could make Jeff live with her?

"You wouldn't like to serenade me for a while, would you? I feel like – a glass of wine and some music to soothe the savage breast."

So Jeff brought out his guitar, and they ignored the mosquitoes while the sun set. After a while, Jeff felt better, and he thought his father did too.

But Jeff couldn't shake the vague, unsettled feeling. He didn't think about Melody, he didn't want to; but he was aware of her, without thinking about her, like clouds rising up at the horizon or footsteps behind you on a dark and solitary street. He didn't mention her to the Professor. Carefully, he didn't think about her. Carefully, he kept on with his usual life.

A couple of days before school opened, when Jeff was sitting on the dock, playing the guitar and singing while he watched the little waves at high tide bouncing against the sides of the creek, Phil Milson came to join him. Phil's hair was bleached white blond, and his skin tanned to coppery brown. "Would you believe this is the first day off my father's given me? How've you been? I'm about ready for a holiday, aren't you?"

Jeff stood up awkwardly. He didn't know what to say.

"Keep playing, you sound good. Are you good?"

Jeff shrugged, he didn't know. "How'd you find us?"

"This is a small town, I keep telling you. I told you I knew the place you'd bought. You've done a lot with it, and it's not half bad now. What do you play, not rock, I can hear that. Country? Blue-grass?"

"I don't know," Jeff said. They settled themselves on the dock. A mid-morning sun shone down hot.

"Play me something. I already heard you so there's nothing left to be modest about."

Jeff was glad to be able to look at the guitar, rather than at the boy he didn't know how to entertain. He strummed a few chords, thinking, then decided to play a song about the Springhill Mine Disaster. "Through all their lives they dug a grave, two miles of earth for a marking stone, two miles of earth for a marking stone."

"That's folk," Phil said, happy to have labelled it.

"Now I know what I play," Jeff joked.

Phil grinned at him. "You been playing long? You look good too, you look like you know what you're doing, but – I hate that kind of song. It's depressing. I mean we all know we spend our lives digging our graves, but I'm not interested in writing songs about it." They talked about that for a while, then about their courses, then Jeff asked about Phil's summer, which had been consumed by back-breaking labour, Phil said. They decided to take the boat out. "Did you see my father?" Jeff asked.

"No, I just followed the sound of music."

They went back to the house, had some juice and a couple of sandwiches, and introduced Phil to the Professor. In the boat, Phil asked, "Your mother's still in Charleston?"

"They're getting divorced."

"How come you're with him not her? I thought women always got the kids." There was nothing subtle about Phil.

"She left home when I was in second grade," Jeff told him. He didn't look at Phil when he said that. He didn't really want to talk about it, but he didn't want to sound unfriendly.

"She walked out on you? Women are something else, aren't they? They don't play by the same rules. You ever think about that?"

"No."

"Yeah, I agree; it's too depressing to think about."

In ninth grade, he discovered, people began to pair off, to talk about dates and steadies. Jeff wasn't interested in girls, but decided that since he'd had good luck with Phil he'd try to be friendly with Andy Burrows as well. Pretty soon the three of them were hanging around together a lot. They suited one another. Phil refused to be serious, and Andy was always serious, so no matter what they did things were pretty lively.

Sometimes they went out fishing or crabbing, and once they tried tonging for oysters. Sometimes they just hung around at Andy's house in town, up in his room where his mother and sisters couldn't get at them, Jeff playing his guitar and listening to the other two quarrelling about the tax advantages given to farmers or the relative importance of theoretical and practical physics. "What do you think, Jeff?" one or the other would ask him, and he'd tell them.

Phil went to parties and on dates and decided he was in love with someone for a couple of weeks before he decided he was in love with someone else.

Andy had a crush on one of his older sister's classmates, which they teased him about. "Well, she might get to like me, when I'm older; age difference doesn't matter so much when you've grown up," he told them.

Jeff suspected that Andy didn't really care, except he didn't want to be freaky. What Andy was really interested in was science. He read science books and science magazines, he often skipped other assignments to work on science and was surprised when the teachers of his other courses yelled at him about that. He was clever enough to see how odd that made him, and he was frightened of being too odd, Jeff saw, because

224

he was afraid of being laughed at. Jeff could sympathize with that.

A girl named Carol Sutter put notes on Jeff's desk in maths class and tried to get him to talk to her in the library and cafeteria and stared at him in the halls. But he didn't talk about that. He felt sorry for her and embarrassed for her. She was pretty, he supposed; she had long blonde hair that she wore loose down her back and big, violet-blue eyes. A lot of the boys liked her, and Jeff wished she would like one of them back. Phil found one of the notes before Jeff did. "You're the cutest boy in the whole school." It wasn't signed, they never were, but Phil recognized the handwriting.

"Greene, you're wasting opportunities," he said. "Do you know how many guys would kill for this?"

"Oh, well," Jeff said.

"You ought to take her out, or something. Why not?"

"I don't like her."

"So what? She likes you."

Jeff shrugged.

"That's weird, really weird, Greene. But I forgive you. I'm glad you decided you wanted to be friends with me, whatever weird things you say," Phil told him. "You'll outgrow this phase."

Jeff was stopped in his tracks by that. Was that what had happened? Had he, in fact, chosen his friends? And not the other way round?

* * *

225

For Christmas that year his father gave him a book, his book. They also had a tree they'd decorated, and Jeff sat beside it in his pyjamas, with the book on his lap. "It's OK for me to read it now, isn't it?"

"I didn't know you wanted to," the Professor said.

"Professor – you made me promise not to until I was fifteen. And then you didn't give me one for my birthday. What do you mean I didn't want to read it?"

"I'm sorry," his father said.

"No, that's OK," Jeff tried to reassure him, tried to keep his eyes off the book, which by then he wanted to read so badly he wanted to end the conversation and get started.

"I never know how to communicate," the Professor said.

The Professor looked half asleep. Jeff had no idea from his face what he was thinking. "Hey," he said, "that's not true. That sounds like the kind of thing Melody would say, the way she does. Has she been – ?"

The Professor looked up. "Now I think of it, yes. You'd think I'd learn."

Jeff opened the cover of the book and turned the blank first page. He read the title, turned the page, read the copyright information – he had no idea of what he'd find in this book, how it would read, what its subject was. He saw the dedication: for my son.

He put his fingers on the page. He stared and stared at the words, especially at the one word, son. "Professor," he said, "I'm honoured."

The Professor didn't answer. "She knows we don't live in Baltimore, she knows we moved."

"It's OK, it's going to be OK. Trust me; I'm your son, it says so right here." He pointed his finger at the word. "She can't make me live with her. She doesn't even want me to, I bet. There's something, and if she thinks I won't tell the truth she's making a big mistake about me."

"But – she's your mother."

"So what?"

He wouldn't choose Melody, not now. He knew that, but he tried to think about why: he'd liked her being beautiful and the sound of her voice, but he didn't trust her and he didn't like the way she talked about need. He suspected that it made her feel good to feel sorry for people. She was dangerous, the way she pulled at your emotions. No, he wouldn't choose her now.

Jeff continued to be satisfied with his two chosen friends at school. They even, at the end of the year and a couple of times over the summer, went to a few parties, where Jeff would play his guitar and sing, or jam with some other people who played. Jeff and Andy got along all right at parties, but it was Phil who really fitted in, dragging the other two along with him. Jeff even learned how to dance and put his arm round a girl and how to kiss one, although he never took a date and always arranged it so he didn't have to take anyone home. He figured he was still learning how to have friends, and he wasn't interested in having a girl friend. So he kept his distance clear. There was no sense in hurting anyone's feelings. There were enough hurt feelings in the world without him adding to that.

By the time tenth grade began, the Professor was well into another book. "Like the first," he told Jeff. He wouldn't let Jeff read it in manuscript. "What if you don't like it?"

Jeff didn't pester his father. He was taking driver's ed and would get his licence by the middle of October. He didn't mind school, he liked the way he'd got along so far, and he kept his eye out for anybody else he might choose for a friend. One girl, an eighth grader, kept catching his eye in the hall – a mature-looking black girl with a ringing laugh and lively, intelligent eyes. Wilhemina Smiths; he found out her name. Everybody knew her already, even though she was just an eighth grader. "A real fireball," they said. Jeff thought she looked strong, inside and out, and he thought to himself that he wouldn't call her a real fireball, but a real person.

Except for the permanent uneasiness of what Melody might do, he felt pretty good. She had sent him a note. Why would she do that? How stupid did she think he was? And she'd enclosed it in a letter to the Professor. He knew why she'd sent it that way, instead of sending it separately. The letter accused his father of being unnaturally cruel to her and trying to get back at her by using Jeff and being selfish and having no sympathy for what she'd been through. The note to Jeff was short. It said she missed him, he knew that, and if he was allowed to see the note, which she doubted, she'd know that if he answered it.

Jeff didn't believe a word of it and didn't answer. It didn't make any difference what Melody got up to now, because she didn't matter to him any more. He had locked her out of his mind and out of his life. She could no longer get through to him, to make him feel the way she used to. He just wanted to forget about her and the way she played on his feelings – the same way she used to play on the guitar, he thought, remembering for a minute. He knew now just how badly she had played the guitar.

9

Sophomores on high honour roll didn't have to go to the study hall for their free periods, so Jeff had the last period of the day entirely free. He liked to spend it outside, sitting on a low wall by the bicycle racks, playing his guitar and working out songs. When the bell rang to end school, he would watch the kids emerge from the double doors, hurrying out and talking. Then he would either join up with Phil or Andy for the afternoon or just say, "See you", before getting on his bike and going home. Some days the Professor came and picked him up. On those days, Jeff drove the car and the Professor rode beside him, because Jeff had his learner's permit. The afternoons were slow, easy hours, and Jeff savoured them, whatever happened in them.

Early in October, he was working out a song he'd heard on a record, trying to figure out how to keep the rhythm in his back-up without losing the sense of flowing melody. It was a matter of balancing, of keeping things in proportion. He kept trying to get it right. "When first unto this country, a stranger I came, and I courted a fair maid and Nancy was her name."

About one second after the final bell rang, a

kid came out through the doors. A kid with somewhere to go, Jeff thought, continuing to play. The kid wasn't anyone he knew, a narrow head with ragged, dark hair, cut-offs, T-shirt, and long, skinny legs. What held his eye, as he sat playing his guitar in mild October sunlight, was the lift of the kid's chin. That chin raised – not high, not angry. Brave maybe. Purposeful. He looked at the kid's face. Even features and a straight nose, eyes dark and the mouth large. His hands played as his mind wandered.

The kid turned in Jeff's direction, as if the music were some kind of string winding round the long legs. Jeff kept his eyes down, watching at the periphery of his vision the awkward and reluctant approach, as if the long legs were trying to move away from him but moved instead towards him. He'd never seen more tired-looking trainers in his life, he thought, and looked up into a pair of dark hazel eyes, brown shot with greens and golds – a girl? What did she want? An eighth grader, probably; she had no figure – especially in those clothes.

"I've never heard that song," she said. She didn't want to say that, she didn't want to be drawn over to him, but she couldn't do anything to stop herself. She couldn't stop herself from coming over or from asking, even though she wanted to.

Jeff sang the song, all the way through. Her presence affected his voice, which had settled down over the summer: she listened so intently he was confused; she stood so still he barely dared look at her. Or maybe it was her eyes he didn't want to look at, because he had seen the way the music coiled around her and drew her to him, in her eyes, seen something helpless in her against music and melody. She stared at his hands playing and soaked in his song in a way that made him think – for the first time in a long time – of the island, of solitude and space and the waves tumbling up onto the broad white beaches. He finished the song and looked up at her. She had her hands jammed awkwardly into her pockets; the melody of the song still played behind her eyes, he was sure of it. He played a couple of chords so the thread of music wouldn't be broken between them. "Have a sit, kid," he said, himself awkward, and that broke the spell, and she was free because he'd said it wrong.

She shook her head and turned abruptly away. He watched her back, her straight shoulders, the long-legged way she walked.

About a week later, she marched back up to him, wearing a boy's shirt this time, chin high, and demanded: "What are the words for that song?"

Jeff didn't know how to take it, and why she came up cross to ask a favour. He felt like smiling at her, but kept his face expressionless, because he didn't know how she'd react. He recited the verses, without playing any music. He had all her

232

attention and he was willing to bet she'd remember the words. Her face and expression looked intelligent, alert. She didn't thank him, just went to get on her bike and ride off.

He saw her a couple of times in the halls, always alone. He watched for her after school. He would cast out his song like a fisherman his line, and she'd get drawn in because she couldn't help it. Finally he introduced himself. "My name's Jeff Greene." She nodded her head, her eyes wary. "What's yours?" he asked. He kept on playing, not even a melody, just any music so she wouldn't take off.

"Dicey Tillerman," she told him.

He knew the name and remembered the old lady with the red boat. "You related to that old lady with the farm?" he asked. That was the wrong thing to say, he could see it in her eyes, in her chin. He held her with music. "What are you, a grandchild?" She nodded again. She wasn't going to say anything: stubborn. Jeff kept himself from grinning: stubborn and prickly.

"Listen, can you sing the melody for 'The Coat of Many Colours'?" he asked on impulse. "I want to try a harmony."

She didn't want to, she didn't sit down, but she started to sing. He kept the guitar soft, listening to her voice and trying to harmonize with half of his attention. She didn't have a great voice, but it sang true notes. She sang the song plainly, her voice round and strong; he could hear in her singing how much she liked the song. He had her now, and he thought he'd say something she wanted to hear. "You sing pretty well."

"Not particularly. Just better than you." Jeff didn't know how to take that. He didn't know what to say next. "My sister is the one who can really sing," she continued. "You should hear her sing this song." She liked her sister. And she wasn't fishing for compliments – that was for sure – and she sure wasn't trying to flatter him. He couldn't imagine her telling a lie.

He put a friendly expression on his face, "I'd like to." He waited for her to ask him out to her house.

"I gotta go now," she said.

Jeff was surprised. He felt things shift on him, like a shift in the tide. She was about to run away on him. "Why?" he asked. "I've got another song you might like."

All she answered was, "I gotta go."

Well, he probably couldn't stop her, he supposed. He bet nobody could stop her when she wanted something or had something she had to do. Probably that was what appealed to him, her determination; opposites attracted, they said. That, and the way he could hold her helpless with music. That and the way she didn't act like most girls, saying one thing and hinting at another with her eyes. She just went her own way, in her own way – she didn't ask or even want anything from him. She was as distant as an ocean, even when

234

you're up close to it. Independent, but he could pull her in with music.

He saw her in the downtown grocer's shop, working there. So they must need money, her parents, because eighth grade was young for a job. She didn't expect to see him, and her chin went up when she did, so he spent his time talking with the owner while Dicey stubbornly swabbed down the floors.

One day, just before Thanksgiving, there was a story Phil told him, about how this squirty eighth grader had flattened Chappelle, something about whether or not she'd cheated on the character sketch essay. The kid, Phil said, delighted to be telling such a good story, had stood up to the teacher, and then Wilhemina Smiths had joined up with her and between them they'd reduced Chappelle to nothing. To a puddle of nothing on the floor. "You've got to feel sorry for the guy," Phil said. Jeff heard the same story, with several variations, over the day and wasn't surprised to see Dicey walking out of school that afternoon with the black girl. It was too cold to play the guitar outside, so he had to keep it in a case, but he tried greeting her anyway. "Hey, Dicey. I hear you put Chappelle into his place." He waited to see how she'd react to the greeting, to the compliment.

"That wasn't me, that was Mina," Dicey told him. "Do you know Mina?"

Jeff looked into a pair of laughing eyes. She was as tall as he was. "Everybody knows Mina."

"Yeah," the girl answered. "Everybody knows you too, friend."

"That's what they think," Jeff told her, thinking how nobody knew at all what he was really like, inside. She chuckled, amused, friendly. He relaxed.

"So, was this essay as good as everybody says?" he asked Dicey. He watched her eyes, wondering how she'd react to a question not about music.

She didn't know what to say, and her eyes looked back into his, brown, green, gold, distant and close, both. "No, of course not," she said, and he grinned at her. He knew she'd tell the truth. "But it was pretty good," she said, to be exact. The two girls walked away from him, and he felt his face, smiling goofily, watching them.

That afternoon he risked going back to the little shop on purpose, because he had the car for their Thanksgiving shopping, which the Professor didn't want to do. A little kid was with Dicey, a little blond kid with the same hazel eyes, only rounder and not as dark, and the same prickly attitude, her brother. Jeff made his purchases and offered her a ride home. It turned out she was taking her brother with her on her bike, so she was glad of the offer. Sammy, she called him. Jeff didn't mind waiting. He tried some music on Sammy, who wasn't glad to meet him, but who obeyed Dicey.

236

"Does she always ride you home?" he asked the boy, after he'd played the longest song he knew and the kid had settled down.

"Nope."

"How come today?"

The kid shrugged. He didn't want to answer the question. Jeff saw marks on his face and decided he'd been in a fight. He looked tough enough to be able to do well in a fight. Jeff tried another question. "You live with your grandmother?" He thought he'd say next how he lived further out along the same road.

"So what?" Sammy asked, a wave of anger coming at Jeff. But it was kid's anger and he knew how to answer it.

"So nothing," Jeff said. "I'm innocent, officer; I didn't do nothing," he teased.

Sammy giggled. He wiped his hand across his cheek, still smiling; He sat cross-legged on the floor, a sturdy little kid in trainers.

"You and your sister have the worst-looking trainers I've ever seen," Jeff said.

"Oh, yeah?" The kid was ready to fight again. Jeff changed the subject, puzzled:

"What're you in, third grade?"

"Naw, second. I've got a sister in third."

"The one who sings?" At that his face changed again; he liked his sister a lot.

"Yeah."

"Boy, do you remind me of Dicey," Jeff said.

237

Sammy looked at him for a long time, then nodded his head. "Good-o."

Dicey told Jeff it was all right, so he went to their house the next Saturday. He rode his bike over through unseasonally warm weather. He walked it up the drive, trying to avoid puddles where Thanksgiving snow flurries had melted. He walked it up because he was nervous about getting there.

The drive went between two neglected fields and then under a stand of pines. At the front of the house, which looked like nobody ever went in that way, a big tree stretched out bare branches, held firm by thick twisted wires. The path went round the side, past a screen porch. Jeff didn't see anybody around. He had his guitar slung across his back and he stood for a minute, looking around him, feeling awkward, thinking maybe he'd go home, noticing that they had a big garden out behind the house and a path through it that led down to the marshes. He considered just turning round and riding home, but he was curious about this singing sister. The door of the barn, its bottom rotted away in large pieces, had been braced open. He looked inside.

Dicey had her back to him. She wore cutoffs and a T-shirt. She didn't know he was there. She was scraping paint off the hull of a little boat, a sailboat he guessed from the deep curved keel, and he could see a mast laid on the ground over by some stalls. She moved like she was dancing, leaning into each stroke, her legs long, her shoulder blades outlined under the T-shirt. Her short raggedy hair shone dark in the warm sunlight. Except for the noise of the scraper it was absolutely quiet. "Dicey?" he said.

She wheeled round and she was angry at him. He could feel it.

"Watcha doing?" he asked. He felt like saying I'm sorry.

"I'm the one to ask that," she said, anger in her eyes and in her face. She held the scraper like a weapon, up against him.

Jeff looked over her shoulder to the stalls, then over her other shoulder to the work table. Back and forth. Her feelings washed over him, like waves, and he didn't know how he'd let this happen. He had been in this scene before, with Melody, with the anger and dislike attacking him and breaking him down. He could feel himself cracking, inside. He didn't know why he kept forgetting what he was really like. He didn't know it mattered so much to him. If he'd known that, he never would have come out here, he never would have wound her around with music. He'd been fooling himself. Again.

Dicey stared at him and he could see in her face that she didn't think much of him. He agreed with her, he wasn't much. But she didn't have to get angry. He didn't understand women, girls, he never would; he didn't even much want to. Except he hadn't thought Dicey was like that.

Kidding himself that he understood her. Thinking he had cast out his line of music, baited with glittering song, cast it out into the water and slowly reeled her in, so gently that she didn't even know what was happening.

"Look," he said, keeping his voice expressionless, hiding everything about himself. "I thought I'd come out and see you, and I want to meet this sister of yours. If you're busy, I'll go. If you don't like the idea" – he thought for the right, unemotional words – "of me being here – you just have to say so."

"No," she answered quickly, her face relaxing, her hostility flowing away and out, like a wave, washing past and gone. "It's not that. Come on in, I've only got a little more to do here. I was just surprised to see someone."

Jeff was surprised himself at how relieved he was to hear her say that. But if this was what she was like when she was only surprised, she would be a terror if she was angry. He leaned his bike against a post and came closer, cautiously. He took the guitar off his back. "If that's the way you react to surprises, I'll be careful not to surprise you again," he promised her. It was, now that he thought about it, pretty funny, the whole scene.

For a long time she kept looking at his eyes, and then she smiled at him, just briefly, because her smile disappeared as fast as it came, even though it stayed, somehow, bright behind her eyes. He was glad he'd stayed out her anger. Glad because of the smile and glad because he'd had the courage. Her smile told him she liked him for fighting back.

When she asked him to play a song while she finished, he had to strum chords for a while and pretend to be tuning up until he settled down. He didn't want her to see how unsettled he'd been by the whole thing. How unsettled he still was. He had thought he was the fisherman, but he saw now –

She had pronged him, with a single stroke, pronged him through the heart and he was caught. Just like with Melody, caught. But this wasn't Melody, Dicey wasn't. And besides, he didn't feel pronged, he felt – overwhelmed, out of breath, breathless.

Dicey watched him, but he did not look up to meet her eyes: he had things to settle inside himself first, he thought, recognizing that he felt easy, at ease, and also alert, eager, as if he had just fought his way through some thick overgrown jungle to the ocean beaches beyond.

10

Jeff's life that tenth grade year became suddenly crowded, with people he liked, with things he wanted to do. Sometimes he caught himself protesting to himself: life is too rich. Like one of the French meals Brother Thomas cooked for them, where when you concentrated on the taste of chicken you knew you were missing out on the sharp, winey sauce and the sweetness of onions or mushrooms sautéed so briskly that their musty flavour got locked inside each slice. Life is so rich, Jeff said to himself, gratefully.

Much of this had to do with the Tillermans; especially Dicey, but – since you couldn't separate her from her family, and Jeff didn't even want to – the whole crew of them, individually and together. He spent a lot of time at the farmhouse after that first day. One way and another he did a lot of work with them. That first day it was Maybeth who knocked him out. She was almost ten and so lovely Jeff had to be careful not to stare at her. Staring at her, he knew, would make her more shy. He could feel how frightened she was of anyone strange.

Her eyes were large and round, clear hazel, and looked right at him once she got her courage up.

They were the kind of eyes that you could look all the way into and know there was nothing ungentle in her. At first she was shy and silent but, like Dicey, she could be looped in with music. He watched the way the songs and the singing won her over slowly. He watched how quietly she moved and how quietly she sat, her hands still. He watched how her skin shone as if from within, like fine porcelain. All her reactions were slow. When he asked her how she liked a song, or if she wanted to choose one, he had to wait for her answer while she looked at him out of clear eyes. You couldn't hurry Maybeth, and he didn't want to because he felt how that might hurt her. Once he caught on to her particular rhythm, the slowness didn't bother him.

Walking their bicycles down the drive at the end of the afternoon, he asked Mina Smiths the question he didn't dare ask Dicey. "Where are their parents?"

Mina was tall enough to look him straight in the eye, a measuring glance, wondering if she could trust him. "Do you gossip?"

"No."

"That kid can sing, can't she?"

"Yeah," Jeff agreed wholeheartedly.

Mina kept looking at him until she finally said, "I'll tell you what I know. Their father's been gone since before Sammy was born and never married their mother anyhow. Then, last summer, their mother went nuts. She's in a mental hospital somewhere."

"So their grandmother took them in," Jeff finished. "Poor kids." He could see them, just the four of them standing alone in a hostile world.

"You stupid, friend?" Mina asked. She was laughing at him. "You know how they got here? They walked. Dicey brought them, just the kids, just the four of them. There was some cousin in Connecticut, and that's where they started if you want to look at a map. Dicey didn't like it at the cousin's, so they ran away and came down here. Mrs Tillerman wasn't going to let them stay – "

"Why not? She seems to like them."

"I think Dicey convinced her. I guess when Dicey wants something she gets it."

"They're alike, Dicey and her grandmother, don't you think?" Jeff asked.

Mina hadn't thought of that. "Maybe they are. That would be funny, because Dicey said their grandmother didn't even know they were alive. They hadn't even heard about her until Connecticut."

"You mean they came down here without knowing anything?"

"That's it."

It would be like jumping off a cliff and hoping the water was deep enough, Jeff thought. Only Dicey had to jump with the three little children holding on to her. And travelling all that way, too.

It would be like whistling in the dark and following the sound of your own melody. He couldn't have done that, he knew; he hadn't had to, but he could see the kind of courage it took, and the kind of hopelessness. He just shook his head. "I guess they're not exactly pitiful," he told Mina.

"Not exactly," she agreed.

"And they really feel like a family, all of them," he said.

"More than mine, and mine hasn't ever been disrupted," she said. He looked across at her and began to see why she liked Dicey.

"I'm an only child," he said.

"And you're not stupid, are you, friend?" she said, her eyes still laughing, but friendly.

"Not a bit of it, friend." He was sure of that.

What he liked about the Tillermans, he decided – after knowing them for winter and spring, after taking care of the little kids when Mrs Tillerman took Dicey out sailing, after working with the stubbornly energetic Sammy on the spring planting, after arguing ideas with James, after learning how to play the Martin behind Maybeth's voice and how to sing harmony with all of them . . . What he liked was the person he became around them. He liked the complicated interactions, trying to keep aware of what each person was feeling. He liked being able to move comfortably among them.

With Mrs Tillerman, you had to stand up to her and not let her bully you and also let her be

245

herself, let her wander around in bare feet, let her
say what she thought even though half the time
Jeff couldn't tell how she made the connections
between one idea and the next. With Sammy you
had to wrestle and play catch and be ready to
tease him into laughter or let him clown at you
until you laughed. With Maybeth you had to go
slowly, gently, let her open up like a flower. With
James you had to be smart like the Professor and
Brother Thomas, carry on the argument, but not
tell James what to think. You had to understand
that some of his wrong thinking was right for a
clever kid in fifth grade and trust him to grow out
of it at the proper time. Jeff could do all these
things, he discovered, and do them pretty well.

With Dicey – he didn't know, he could never
be sure. Sometimes she wanted to be left alone,
and sometimes she wanted to chase down crabs
with everybody running around in circles. Always
she liked music, of any kind, and she was cleverer
than she'd figured out yet, he thought. He'd
watched her turn quiet and inward after her
mother died. That had happened just before
Christmas – the mother had never got well and
Dicey was as private as the Professor in her
sorrow, as solitary. He had known she needed to
be left alone, just as he had known that Sammy
needed to be wrestled with, hard, during that
long time of grieving, that James's absorbed
interest in entomology came from the same
source, and that Maybeth was all right, stronger,

somehow, for this than any of the others. Stronger even than Mrs Tillerman, whose temper flared, whose eyes watched Jeff warily.

If he stayed too long she would come into the room. "Go home, boy, we can't feed an extra mouth."

"Yes ma'am." He would leave quickly, knowing that her greeting when he returned would be as direct.

"It's a good thing you came by, James keeps talking about bugs at me."

Jeff kept up with his friends, with Phil and Andy, partly because they were his friends and partly because he couldn't crowd the Tillermans. Phil asked him, that spring, what was going on with Dicey. "What is it, you have a thing for that Tillerman kid?"

"She's not a kid. She's a girl."

"Yeah, but Greene – OK, OK, none of my business, right? Don't bother telling me to stuff it, I know what that kind of stiff-faced look means. We'll drop it. I mean, for all I know, she's as sweet as honey and a real hot number, for all I know."

Seeing Dicey as Phil saw her, Jeff just laughed. Phil joined in and Jeff didn't say what he might have because Phil wouldn't have understood. Honey, Dicey wasn't. She was tart, bitter – alive; and she made him feel alive too, awake. They all did. And he thought she liked him too, anyway more than she liked most people – and that was pretty good.

Jeff kept up his own friendships, pestering Andy with the questions James asked about insects, until he finally introduced the two of them and left them to their discussions. He kept up with his schoolwork. He kept up with his guitar and his hours appreciating the water, marshes, sky, birds, trees – sometimes just the whole world. He kept up with the Professor, too, especially; listening and talking, living together.

That summer, because Andy was going up to Baltimore for some advanced classes at Johns Hopkins and Phil worked at the business of farming, Jeff set up in a crabbing business with the Tillermans. They had to learn how to lay and run a trotline, but between Mrs Tillerman's experience and James's research, it didn't take them long. Dicey had a couple of regular baby-sitting jobs as well as her grocer's shop job, so it was Sammy or James who waited at the dock for Jeff, a shadowy figure in pre-dawn light. Sammy had more endurance for the work. He had the energy to pick up a badly set line and reset it, never complaining about the sheer hard work. James had the kind of mind that never rested quiet. Either way, Jeff enjoyed the long hours.

It was James, sitting in the back of the little boat while Jeff did the job of hauling in the trotline, who asked him about his parents. "Is your father really the one who wrote that book?"

Jeff stood up straight, relaxing tired back muscles. He looked back to where the younger boy leaned against the silent engine. "Yeah, why?"

"I read it, it was good," James said. He rested his feet on top of one of the bushels of crabs they'd deliver downtown.

"He told me, asked me anyway, not to read it until I was fifteen," Jeff said. He had to wipe sweat from his forehead and the smell of ripe salted eel asaulted his nostrils. "Ugh," he said.

"What about your mother?" James asked. But then he changed the subject. "So I shouldn't have read it? I could re-read it later; it was a good book, I don't mind. It was dedicated to you."

"I know," Jeff said, making himself bend to the task again.

"Why not your mother?"

"She walked out on us, when I was in second grade."

"I didn't know that. So did my father, but I wasn't that old. I suppose it's not so uncommon. So did my mother, but that was different. I used to think it was me, or us."

Jeff didn't turn round, but he thought hard. "I suppose everybody thinks that. Kids. Maybe adults too."

"I don't know why people have kids if they're just going to walk out. Did you ever ask your mother? Did you ever see her after?"

249

"A couple of times," Jeff said. "I asked her, but she lied."

James didn't answer right away, then he spoke quickly, the way he did when a new idea had just occurred to him. "Maybe it's women; maybe women are liars, maybe that's one of the differences. Dicey knows how to lie, you should have heard her. When we came down here, and it was just us? She would spin stories – sometimes I thought I'd burst out laughing. Every time different, every time perfect. Cripes – now I think of it – she was really something."

"Dicey doesn't lie," Jeff said. His stomach felt cold, even with the heat and sweat out on the water.

"Sure she does."

Jeff heaved the cinderblock that anchored down the line's end, heaved it up and into the boat.

"No, she doesn't."

"Why shouldn't she? Cripes, Jeff, you don't know what we were up against, even I didn't and I'm glad I didn't. Sometimes when I think about it . . ." He stared at Jeff. "Never mind," he said, closing Jeff out. "I shouldn't have told you. I know what you're thinking, but you're wrong." Jeff just shook his head. He couldn't answer.

The whole day had gone black and cold around him. James couldn't know what he was thinking, and Jeff didn't want to be thinking what he was thinking, about Melody. He knew James was closing him out, but he didn't care.

He felt as if he'd just learned that Dicey was dying of some incurable disease. He felt the fragile inside part of himself cracking. He could hide it, he felt pretty sure about that; he knew he was strong enough to hide it. From everybody but himself.

So that when Dicey finally did what he'd been wanting her to do for a long time and asked him if he'd like to go for a sail, he almost said no. It wasn't that he liked her any less or expected her to be perfect. He knew she wasn't perfect – she was often bossy, and she always knew what she wanted, so she was impatient with anyone less decisive. She was harsh, sometimes; too quick to judge, especially people who didn't work the same way she did. He knew that. But he didn't want her to be imperfect in that one particular way. And if she was (and James would know) Jeff didn't feel necessarily safe with her alone. He looked over her shoulder, thinking up excuses.

"Hey. You don't have to," she said, puzzled, irritated. Well, he'd certainly hinted, so he could see why she was puzzled. Her eyes studied his face, trying to figure out what he was thinking; but he kept his face expressionless. "I mean, if you're scared because I'm not very good yet, that's OK."

How did she know he was scared, Jeff wondered. The same way he knew she was more puzzled than angry, however she sounded. "It's just that I promised the Professor," he said, seizing the half-truth.

"You don't need to make excuses," she told him.

Jeff didn't know what to say. He had let himself get tied up in his feelings with Dicey and through her with them all; and this was what happened, it was probably bound to happen.

"I've got life preservers. Gram made me plunk three weeks' earnings into them," she told him impatiently, "and I don't care if you don't want to."

That was true, Jeff knew, she didn't care if he didn't want to, even though it meant a lot to her. He was confused and kept looking at her. She waited impatiently for a couple of minutes, chewing on her lower lip, then turned her back on him and started walking down the path to the dock. He watched her walk, her long legs and bare feet, the cutoffs and T-shirt, and he followed her. He hadn't made up his mind, either to go or not to go. He felt that he'd disappointed her and he should apologize; he didn't want her to be angry with him. He got into the boat.

She hoisted the sails and cast off from the dock without saying anything. They moved out into the bay, and still she didn't say anything. When Jeff finally turned to look at her, he realized she didn't even know he was there. She paid attention only to the boat, to the tiller and to the wind in

252

the sails. She looked the way she sometimes did when they were all singing. She caught Jeff's eyes and grinned at him.

"You really like this." He was surprised at the intensity of her happiness.

"Yeah."

"But you said you only sailed once before you came here," he reminded her, checking up on the truth.

She brought the boat about, heading to the southwest on a reach, and instructed him to sit on the gunwales so that it would ride level. Waves slapped up against the side. Dicey sat back, her legs stretched out, her hand brown on the tiller.

"Across the bay, on a yacht. Boy, that was a time. Because we had to get across, to see what Crisfield was like, if we could live here. And Gram. We got to Annapolis, and we were sleeping out on this lawn – that was pretty easy because they were renovating the house so there was nobody there to know about us. We had to convince these two guys to sail us across. They wouldn't have done it to help out, they weren't that kind. So I told them we were going to visit relatives, an aunt who worked full time, in Easton, whose children were in day camp so it didn't matter what time we got there, and I told them we were staying with an old lady who knew our parents, but was too old to keep close tabs on us." She stopped speaking, thought. "The hardest thing, all the time, was trying to remember all the different ends you had to cover and let it slip out in conversation, not as if you were making it up. And trying to look casual, too, because if these guys had figured out that we really needed help they wouldn't have offered it. James kept asking them if the boat could sail all the way across the bay – and I kept thinking to myself what a stupid question. Until I figured out what he was up to. Then it had to be some kind of a dare, because – it was a funny kind of friendship, no friendship at all. I couldn't have pulled it off without James that time."

"That time?"

"Other times – I just kind of knew what to tell people so they'd leave us alone."

"How come you wanted them to leave you alone?"

She ignored the question.

Jeff remembered that they had come down alone from Connecticut, and he saw a picture of the four of them, and those trainers. He didn't feel sorry for them at all, any more, just impressed. "But you could have got help from someone, the police, or welfare. Couldn't you?"

"Once we tried. Once. They wanted to put Maybeth into retarded classes, or something, and Sammy kept getting into trouble. My cousin dressed Maybeth up, and they all fluttered around her, because she was pretty, and talked about her marrying a rich man. My cousin didn't want to keep Sammy, she wanted him to go and live

254

somewhere else. There was this priest, he meant well but . . ." Her voice trailed off. She didn't want to talk about it.

Listening to her, imagining it, knowing them all, Jeff knew he couldn't understand; but he understood the important thing. James had tried to tell him, saying, "what we were up against". Jeff hadn't understood before he heard Dicey's voice, telling it. He saw now what they had had to fight through to get to Crisfield. He felt his insides ease up, relax – and he felt tears behind his eyes. And he understood himself a little more, too. He changed the subject. "I know a priest, he's OK. Actually, he's a monk, a brother, but a priest too. He's – a really good man. Where'd you live, before?"

"In Provincetown, out on Cape Cod. Right on the ocean. Not right on, back behind the dunes, but it really was right on it."

"I was at the ocean once. Not Ocean City, that doesn't count, but – " Because he felt suddenly like talking, Jeff told her about the island, about the beach there. Then, when she asked him, he told her about how he'd bought a boat and gradually worked up the courage to explore because of being frightened.

"What were you doing there anyway?" she asked him, not interested in his fears.

"Visiting my mother. But she took off with her boyfriend. There was just my great-grandmother and a couple of elderly cousins we called aunts;

they weren't interested in what I did. So I did what I liked." He could hear in his voice some of the feelings of that time, and he made a business out of adjusting the jib. Because he didn't want Dicey thinking he wanted her to feel sorry for him, because he knew he'd been lucky after all. In the long run. And the long run counted more than the short run.

"Where's the boat?" Dicey asked.

He told her about the last night in Charleston, on the island, and how he'd sunk the boat. That made her smile. Then he told her something he had only just remembered, wondering why the memory had sunk so far back into his mind that he hadn't ever recalled it. "The man who sold me the boat and rented me docking space, he was waiting when I swam back to the dock. I'd thought that nobody knew or cared where I was, what happened to me, as long as I was out of the way. Well, I was right. But he came out on to the dock with a towel. He'd known where I was, it turned out. When I hadn't come back by sunset, the way I usually did, he'd gone out looking and seen the boat tied up. Listen, Dicey, I can't say it the way he did, but he said he figured *if she gator gotchuh you's already a goner*. He called me *suh*. He said – I wish I could imitate it the way it was – *Suh, you come down here looking like she hounds of hell be chewing at your heart and no gator bites so bad. So I be watching this morning*. I suppose, if I hadn't turned up, he'd have found my bones. Or something. I guess."

Dicey didn't say anything. He thought she might ask about his mother and was glad she didn't. Then she said, "I wouldn't have sunk the boat. I wouldn't ever."

"I wasn't in your kind of trouble," Jeff pointed out.

"I suppose you were in your own kind," she said. "It's time to bring her about. Will you please get your weight back into the boat so I can do it?" she asked impatiently.

Brother Thomas came down for a week at the end of July, and the week stretched out to two, then three. He seemed tired, Jeff thought, subdued, and he didn't seem rested. He talked late with the Professor, night after night. Jeff fell asleep to the sound of their voices. Jeff went to bed early because he got up so early, before dawn. One dark morning, Brother Thomas sat drinking a mug of tea and watching the silky grey sky when Jeff came into the kitchen. He didn't greet Jeff, didn't even seem to know he was there.

Jeff went to the bathroom, took a quick shower, brushed his teeth, and was awake by the time he came back. Brother Thomas sat in the same position, his hands in his lap, not leaning back against the chair. The level of tea in his mug hadn't changed. "Good morning," Jeff said. "It's early."

Brother Thomas greeted him then, his face pale above the black suit and white collar he had never, on that visit, gone without. "Couldn't you sleep?" Jeff asked. "Can I get you a bowl of cereal?"

"No, thank you; I'm not hungry."

Jeff sat down to eat. "You look like you didn't sleep."

"I suppose I didn't. Do you always go off at this hour?"

"I have to pick up whoever is coming with me, then get the line set. Sunrise is about six," Jeff explained. Then he had an idea. "Do you want to come?"

But Brother Thomas wasn't interested.

"You might like it," Jeff said. He couldn't understand Brother Thomas's lack of energy; it wasn't like him, not like him at all. Something was wrong, he knew that, and he realized that this same barren feeling he was getting from Brother Thomas now was the only kind of feeling he'd got from the man this visit. Something was very wrong.

Jeff chewed and thought. Whatever it was, even talking with the Professor wasn't doing any good. But what was it? OK, Jeff said to himself, surprising himself, if you're supposed to have a talent for knowing how people feel, what's Brother Thomas feeling?

He glanced at the man sitting hunched, staring out at the sky but not seeing it. Bleak, Jeff felt, bleak and hopeless, some inner landscape as barren as the moon's surface, cold and lifeless.

What can I do? Jeff asked, inside himself. He figured, if the Professor's intelligence couldn't help, then that wasn't the way. He wondered if he should do anything, even if he could think of what. But he thought he would try. Something was wrong, he didn't know what, but he wondered what he could give to Brother Thomas – who had given so much to him one way and another. "You ought to come," he urged him. "You ought to try it, you used to be good at netting crabs off the line. Besides, you'd like my friends. I don't know who it'll be today."

"Are these the Tillermans?"

"Yes. It would tire you out, too; we'll let you do all the work. You remember how much work it is, don't you? So you'll sleep well tonight." Jeff worked to persuade him. "But it gets hot."

"I don't mind," Brother Thomas said. Although he didn't say he wanted to go along, he went. They needed a flashlight to get to the boat and check the supplies, but once they were away from the dock, Jeff told Brother Thomas to turn it off. The engine worked noisily as Jeff took the boat out to the deep centre of the creek, then along into the bay. In pre-dawn darkness, black waves made the boat buck slightly. Brother Thomas's shape was black at the bow of the boat. The last stars faded from the sky, but Brother Thomas didn't notice them.

It was James who waited at the end of the Tillermans' dock, in sleepy untalkativeness, two apples in his hand. But after the dawn had begun, a pool of light on the eastern horizon spreading out to illuminate the whole sky, and after he had eaten the apples and tossed the cores into the water, he began questioning Brother Thomas, as Jeff had known he would .

"Apple cores are biodegradable, so it's not like throwing rubbish. Do you worry about rubbish, are you an ecologist?"

"Isn't it because they're rubbish that they're biodegradable?" Brother Thomas asked.

"Yeah, maybe. No, wait, that's not true, rubbish means everything even tin cans and plastic. Who are you, anyway?"

"He teaches at the university with the Professor," Jeff told James when Brother Thomas didn't answer. James was off, what did he teach, what did that mean, what kinds of books did he teach out of, what did they say, how did you get interested in teaching stuff like that, how did you learn about it, were his students smart? Brother Thomas answered all the questions, and at last his eyes met Jeff's – humorously – over James's head. Jeff just smiled back.

In between, they ran the line, culled through the haul, waited a few minutes then ran it again. Jeff drove the motor, because James got impatient at the slow, careful speed you needed to maintain. Brother Thomas and James took turns netting the

260

crabs. Brother Thomas tried to pick up an escaped crab with his fingers and got bitten for his trouble. That seemed to please him.

"You'll have to wash that out with antiseptic," James told him. "Crab bites tend to get infected. We think they have some kind of mild natural poison on their shells for protection. Either that or it's because they're scavengers – they'll eat anything, you know."

"Apparently," Brother Thomas answered, sucking on his bleeding finger. James grinned. "What grade are you in, James?"

"Going into sixth. Why don't you take off your jacket, or is it one of the rules of your order that you can't? Aren't you hot?"

By then they had three bushels, more than enough to sell, as well as feed both families dinner. Jeff tried to ignore the stiffness in his back muscles, tightened by hours of sitting on the hard seat, leaning forwards to watch where the trotline rose up out of the water, and now straining against the weight of anchor, boat, and line as he hauled the trotline in. He hoisted up the final cinderblock and set it gently down on the bottom of the boat. He stretched his arms out trying to relieve his back. "You wouldn't like to run us in, would you?" he asked Brother Thomas.

In the round face, the brown eyes were awake again. "And I shall make you fishers of men," he joked to Jeff. "It would have been, in those days, more like crabbing than the fishing industry is now. That's something I don't think I understood before."

"You mean, with the nets they used?" James asked. Then he yelled – "I'm so hungry!"

"You're always hungry," Jeff reminded him. "The line needs rebaiting – "

"Let Sammy do that. Maybeth's busy helping Gram tin beans, Sammy won't mind, and besides, he got to sleep late."

"Usually," Jeff explained to Brother Thomas, "we unload at their dock, then I go home to get the car to take the catch down to the restaurant. You can stay there and help cull – "

Brother Thomas held up his finger in mute protest.

"We've got tongs," James told him. "Gram used them when she was a little girl. Her uncle made them. They're wooden. He was a bootlegger."

Brother Thomas's face shone red with heat, and beads of sweat speckled the top of his head. He decided to stay at the Tillermans' to clean his hand, maybe to cull, at least to set eyes on these historic tongs.

Jeff drove the car back to the farmhouse. He parked by the barn. Dicey, he knew, worked downtown all day Saturday. Mrs Tillerman was in the big vegetable garden, her hair wild and her loose shirt flapping in the breeze as she crouched over bushy green-bean plants. At the other end, Brother Thomas in his black suit worked with a hoe around the staked tomato plants, bending to pull out clumps of weeds and toss them into a heap, chopping at the dirt, to loosen it. His face was even redder, and sweat ran down his cheeks.

"Do you want to come downtown with us?" Jeff asked him.

He stood up straight and leaned his weight on the hoe. He was breathing heavily. "I'll finish here. She doesn't talk much, does she?"

"No. But when she does you better look out," Jeff said.

"Hostile?"

"Just sharp. She's pretty terrific. Why don't you take off your jacket and waistcoat and all?"

The brown eyes moved from Jeff's face down to the far opposite end of the garden, where Mrs Tillerman hunched over the beans. They moved to the green marsh grasses beyond. "If I do I might never get it on again," Brother Thomas said. "So I think I'd better not."

"Ummm," Jeff said, wondering how he should respond.

"There's a Botticelli angel inside, snapping beans," Brother Thomas said.

"Maybeth."

"Yes. She didn't say a word, looked frightened of me. She applied antiseptic, bandaged my finger, stared at me. Then back to the beans. She doesn't look a bit like James. Why was she frightened? Who *are* these people?"

Jeff didn't know what to say. He went on down

263

to the dock, said hello to Sammy, who was rebaiting the long trotline at a steady pace, then lifted one of the bushels while James carried the other. They delivered the crabs and split the money – putting aside enough for a five gallon tank of petrol and ten pounds of salted eel. Jeff had tried not to split the money, because he certainly didn't need it; but the Tillermans didn't work that way, although as far as he could tell they did need it.

Brother Thomas yawned all through dinner that night, and when they sat afterwards over the bright-coloured glasses of wine he was, he said, so tired he couldn't talk in complete sentences. "You could sleep in Jeff's room, you could go to bed now if you want," the Professor said. "You don't have to entertain us."

Brother Thomas shook his head, sunburned above the white collar. "You know? I'm enjoying the fatigue. But Horace, what's Melody up to? We've been talking about nothing but me, and I'm too tired to agonize tonight. You agonize."

The Professor smiled at Jeff, who was playing softly on the guitar. Outside, the sun slid down the western sky, and the creek ran beside the marshes, blue shot with ripples of gold. "We had the hearing, uncontested. I should get the decree next week, then there's a thirty-day period during which she can appeal. If she doesn't, the thing is finished. So it's been easy, in the end."

"The machinery of the law," Brother Thomas

said. His eyelids drooped and he lifted them, sipped at his glass, held it up to turn it around in the light, then asked, "How do you feel about it, Jeff?"

"It doesn't make any difference to me," Jeff said. "I mean, I wouldn't have gone to live with her. I'm almost seventeen, they couldn't have made me."

"You never can tell what people can make you do," Brother Thomas told him. "You can't even tell what you'll want to do. My brother's daughter just got married, and his son is starting college in the autumn. It's all the future with them. And they're right. It was in California, Horace, I was out among the beautiful people. They think I'm an anachronism. Something of a lost soul. A funny old man."

"And what do you think?"

"Me, I don't know. I don't know what I think. Except I'm tired, bone tired." He yawned.

"I've never met these friends of Jeff's," the Professor said. "I know Phil and Andy, but not the Tillermans."

"Why not?"

"No reason," Jeff said.

"There are even a couple more I didn't see, one of them a girl, about Jeff's age, I take it." One eyelid raised and one curious brown eye looked at Jeff.

"She's much younger," Jeff said. He put down the guitar. "Her name's Dicey," he said, looking at his father's face. "She's a lot like her grandmother."

"That is one strong old lady," Brother Thomas said. "She could work me into a stupor without even straining her own resources." He yawned again and admitted that he had to get to bed, if it was OK with Jeff if he used Jeff's room.

After he'd left, Jeff picked up the guitar again and played what he called to himself Dicey's song. He didn't sing it, just played the melody against a strum, the words inside his head: "With my hands all in my pockets and my hat slung back so bold, and my coat of many colours like Jacob of old."

"How'd you come to take him with you today?" the Professor asked.

"He was awake and I asked him. Why?" He wondered if his father felt left out. "You don't want to, do you? Do you mind not meeting them? If it ever works out, you will. It's just that I go there, not them coming here."

"No, no and no." The Professor smiled at him. "It's clear that it was good for him, that's why I asked. He's at a bad time – "

"I thought, this morning. He hadn't slept, he said. He seems better, tonight."

"Sometimes, I think, it's hard to accept exactly who you are. And there can't be much harder to get through than a genuine spiritual crisis."

"A spiritual crisis? But . . . I don't understand." Yes, that would make sense, Jeff thought,

266

that would explain the barren feeling Brother Thomas seemed to have – if you lived your life in faith, with faith, and then something made you question how you'd lived your whole life.

"I don't know and neither does he," the Professor said. "But he seems to have had a good day, and that's the first in a long time for him. I'm grateful to you."

"I didn't do anything. It was mostly the Tillermans. But they didn't really do anything, either."

"We never do. But sometimes, things get done. Don't they? And I wouldn't mind meeting these Tillermans, if it ever works out."

Jeff nodded his head.

"Are you courting this girl?" the Professor asked.

Jeff felt his face grow hot. "You don't court Dicey," he told his father. "That's not what she's like."

"What's she like?"

Jeff didn't know what to say. "She's – I guess – she's straight. You know? She likes to sail. She works hard. Clever, I think, very."

"I can't picture her," the Professor said, thoughtfully. "No, that's OK, I'm not prying. I'm only trying to behave like a responsible father and be familiar with my son's social life."

"I appreciate the effort," Jeff teased him. "If there's anything to report, I'll tell you, maybe. Is there such a thing as a one-woman man, do you think?"

The Professor's face went expressionless. Then he met Jeff's eyes and answered Jeff's real question: "I wouldn't be surprised if you were; it seems to be in your character. And what's in your character is what you've got to deal with."

The next time Dicey asked Jeff to go sailing with her, he waited until they were heading out before he asked if she'd come by his house.

"Why?" Dicey asked.

"Well, you've never met the Professor and when Brother Thomas was here he met your family – "

"Gram said – do you know what she said? I *don't dislike the man*, as if – as if that was a big compliment." Dicey grinned.

"He said she was one strong old lady," Jeff told her.

"He sure was a help."

"The Professor said he hadn't met you, you Tillermans. And if he wanted to, I thought – he doesn't ask for things, and he didn't ask but he said he'd like to, and for him that's asking. Would you mind?"

"We should get somebody else. James is home; he'd love to meet someone who wrote a book. Ready to come about?"

"No. Just one at a time, he's – "Jeff didn't know how to say what he was thinking, because it was so complicated. Something to do with treating the Professor gently, or maybe letting him meet them the way Jeff had, sort of one at a time, or naturally and not as if it was arranged. He didn't want to explain, he just wanted Dicey to go along with what he wanted.

She shrugged and gave her attention back to the sail. He pointed out the entrance to the creek. "We'll have to tack up it," she said, and that pleased her, because it was harder. "When we get past the point, haul up on the centreboard. Your creek is broad."

"It's not my creek."

Jeff pulled up the centreboard and set it down on the floorboards. They negotiated the entrance. "Is that your house?" She looked up at the windowed front of the low building. Jeff nodded.

They had to tack six times. Dicey decided to sail up above the dock so they could approach it with the wind behind them. As they turned around to head down – and Jeff crawled on to the deck to pull down the jib – he saw a blue heron standing on a little muddy point of land across the creek. He pointed and Dicey followed his eyes.

The blue raised its flat head to look at them. Its feet were in the water, its feathers slightly rufffled as if by a recent annoyance. Jeff watched the bird, waiting for it to take off, anticipating the squawk with which it would trumpet its disapprovals.

But the blue seemed not to find them threatening. It stared across the creek at them, then turned its back on them in a stately gesture of dismissal. Jeff knew the bird knew they were there. But, from all you could tell, the bird had never noticed them. It raised its head to look out across the marsh, unconcerned, solitary, ignoring them with great determination.

Dicey's low voice told him to pull down the mainsail, and he did. When he had it gathered around the boom, he looked back to the bird. The great blue still stood there, its back still to them. It wasn't going to let the suspicion that they were there chase it off its fishing territory.

Jeff wrapped the sheet around the loosely furled mainsail and went up to the bow to fend off. Dicey concentrated on manoeuvering the boat, propelled now only by its own weight. Her hand rested on the tiller as she waited patiently for the sluggish hull to respond to her directions. The landing was perfect.

Jeff held on to a piling with one hand while he looped a clove hitch round it. Then he looked back at Dicey. "You know who that bird reminds me of? You."

Her expression changed, and he didn't know what he'd said wrong. Then he saw that the change was caused by Dicey trying to hold back laughter. "I was thinking how much it was like you," she told him.

He didn't know what to say. "Come on up to the house." He didn't offer her a hand. Dicey liked to do things for herself.

270

"Are you sure you shouldn't have James here?" she asked him. "James would really like it."

Jeff was sure. He turned for a last look at the heron, now glancing over its shoulder to be certain they were leaving. "Who's that?" Dicey asked.

A woman stood at the top of the steps leading down to the dock. Her skirt blew around her slim legs, her dark hair blew back from her face. She raised an arm to wave, although she was close enough to have called out. She looked like a photograph of a dancer. She looked eager and happy. She ran lightly down the steps.

"Melody," he told Dicey.

"Who's she?"

They stood side by side, watching.

"My mother," he told her, wishing she would stop asking questions.

Dicey stood away as Melody wrapped her arms round him saying, "Jeffie, Jeffie, it's so good to see you, I've missed you so terribly." Melody was shorter than he was now, and she had grown her hair out straight, but shorter than she used to wear it. Her perfume was the same. In the sunlight, the sounds of the little creek behind him, Jeff didn't know what to do.

"And who is this?" Melody asked, looking at Dicey. Jeff didn't answer, so she went over to Dicey and held out her hand. Dicey shook it briefly, looked at Jeff, looked back to Melody. "I'm Jeffie's wicked old mother," Melody said, laughing. "He didn't know I was coming – did you, darling?" Her face turned like a flower briefly back to Jeff, who shook his head. "I hope I haven't interrupted your plans for the day. Your father – I might have guessed – had no idea of what you were up to, where you were, when you'd be back – "

"Yes, he did," Jeff said, his face expressionless.

"Well, maybe he did, and I just wanted you to be right here, right then, so I could see you right away. You don't have any plans that can't be postponed, do you?"

"No," Dicey said when Jeff didn't answer. "I'll go along then."

"Maybe tomorrow?" Jeff asked her.

Her eyes, trying to read his expression, were bright with their secondary colours, green, gold. She shook her head. "We've got some friends – they have a circus and we're all going over to Ocean City. I was going to tell you, there won't be anybody to crab with you for a couple of days."

"OK," Jeff said.

"Oh dear, it *is* just the wrong time, isn't it?" Melody said. "I'm so sorry – what did you say your name was?"

"Dicey." She wanted to go, and fast, Jeff could see.

"A good, old southern name," Melody said. She tried to get Dicey to like her, to smile at her. "And I am sorry to ruin your day, truly I am. But

272

you know how demanding mothers can be."
Melody smiled as if she and Dicey shared an
amusing secret.

Dicey's chin went up and her eyes snapped.
"No," she said, "no, I don't." She turned
abruptly and got back into the boat. Without
looking at either of them, she raised the jib and
unfurled the main.

Jeff looked at Melody, who had said about the
wrongest thing to Dicey anybody could say.

"Well, I am sorry, Jeffie; whatever your little
friend thinks."

Dicey had the main up and cleated. The sails
flapped in the wind, snapping with a sound like
whips. As she waited by the tiller for the boat to
swing round and catch the wind, Dicey stood to
sudden attention. Jeff looked where she was
looking. He saw the great blue, alarmed now by
the sound of the sails, draw itself clumsily up out
of the water. It spread out its great wings and
looped out towards the bay. Dicey turned to grin
at Jeff and raise her hand in farewell. He had his
face under too careful control to grin back, but
he waved.

"Let's go where we can talk, really talk,"
Melody said to him. She tucked her hand under
his arm and he looked down at her face. She wore
make-up on her eyes now, and her hair shone like
the night sky. "I'm sorry I drove your little friend
away, Jeffie."

"It doesn't make any difference," Jeff told her.

He said it just to say something, but he realized when he heard himself that it really didn't, not to his friendship with the Tillermans. He wondered who these circus friends were, but James would tell him if Dicey wouldn't, because James liked to talk. If they were all going, then their grandmother must know them too.

"It doesn't make a difference to you, of course," his mother corrected him as they climbed the wooden steps then stood staring at the windows along the front of the house. "But you ought to think of her, what it might mean to her. She looked like such a bedraggled, lonely little thing. I felt really sorry for her. The poor girl probably has a crush on you."

Jeff bit at his lip to keep from smiling.

"But I can't feel too sorry for her, not while you're here. I was so impatient."

"Have you been here long?" Jeff asked. Where was his father?

"It felt long to me. Your father said you're getting As in school. I'm so proud of you. I always knew you were clever; I was always on your side. I'd love to sit out here. See? I've been sitting and waiting. He even gave me a glass of iced tea. Really, sometimes he seems perfectly civilized, just like a real human being. Then he went inside to work. What work does he have during the summer?"

Jeff sat down in the chair, and she sat on the grass close beside him, her body turned eagerly to him, her eyes fixed on his face, all her attention on him. "I think he's writing another book," Jeff said.

"Well," she said. "He is clever after all, isn't he? I haven't had a chance to read it yet, but I saw it in a bookshop. 'That's my husband,' I told a perfect stranger next to me. A perfect stranger, I was so proud. Of course, I can't say that any more, can I?"

Jeff just shook his head.

"Poor Jeffie, I was so worried about you in all this. It's the children who really suffer during a divorce. It must have been so hard for you. But I just knew, somehow, we haven't been communicating properly, you and I. That's really why I'm here. If he wants a divorce, that's all right with me, and goodness knows I wouldn't say I've been much of a wife to him. But really, this selfishness with you – I just couldn't believe it. So I thought it over and decided to come right up here and get the question settled openly. Your room is all ready for you. Gambo – she's failing so badly she even made a will and she never would do that before – she needs to see you again. The schools are at least as good as the schools here, I'm sure of that. So I just came right up here to collect you."

"But – "

Melody waited, her eyes smiling into his, light grey rimmed with dark, lovely. She didn't look any older, she never did, she probably never would, somehow. She was always beautiful.

"But I thought that was all settled," Jeff mumbled. What was he supposed to say and *where* was his father? He looked over his shoulder to the house. A shadowy figure by the kitchen window.

An expression of great sadness washed over Melody's features, and she turned to hide her face from Jeff. Her voice changed, to a hesitating, little-girl voice. "He said that. Your father. He said you were sixteen and knew what you wanted. But I suppose I have to hear that for myself. I couldn't just believe what someone else told me about my own son. Could I?"

"No," Jeff agreed. He felt how sad this made her and how brave she was being, how hard it was for her to be reasonable when she was so sad.

She stood up slowly, dusted the back of her skirt, subdued now. She walked back to the house. They slid back the big door to enter the kitchen. The Professor stood with his back against the stove, like a man facing a firing squad. Jeff took Melody's glass to refill it with iced tea, and she smiled sadly at him, sitting down. He glanced out of the window of the kitchen door and saw Max's car.

Melody leaned her elbows on the table and said, "Well, you win, Horace."

"Oh, Melody, it's not that way at all, you know that."

276

The Professor sounded terrible. Jeff looked at his father, whose face was absolutely expressionless, but whose eyes behind the glasses stared at Melody.

"I don't know *what* way it is. I only know – when lawyers get into it the human beings go out. I even hired a male lawyer – me! I thought it was practical; you don't go up against men with women; I thought I'd have at least an even chance. You're going to make me beg, aren't you?"

"Oh, Melody," the Professor said.

"I can talk to him, can't I? I don't need permission to do that, do I? Sit down, Jeffie, and just listen. Just hear my side of it. You know your limits, Horace; you know the kind of man you are."

The Professor lifted his mug and swallowed helplessly, nodding his head.

Jeff looked from his mother to his father. His father's expressionless face masked something, he couldn't see what.

"Although this book – you must be very pleased. And the dedication – moved me. Jeffie tells me you're working on another."

The Professor nodded again.

"I wouldn't mind a dedication." Melody smiled across the room into the Professor's eyes, warm and amused at herself, confident again. "A girl would like a little immortality. Isn't that right,

Jeffie?" She reached across the table and put her hand over Jeff's. He studied the turquoise rings.

"After your last visit" – she switched topics abruptly – "I did some serious thinking. About myself – I wasn't any too pleased with myself, I have to admit it. Or with Max – and I finally figured out that he was jealous, jealous of you, Jeffie. I broke it off with him." She was lying again, Jeff knew. "He was a bad influence, on me," she went on, "and on everyone he came in contact with. I don't know how he managed to fool me for so long. Some real soul-searching went on that winter, I can tell you. I had neglected – so many things. Even Gambo – it's Gambo I'm thinking of too, Jeffie; she needs to have you around, especially now, because . . . you let her know that the family goes on. She's dying and she knows it, and she'd like to have her family around her. Did you think of Gambo? Did you?"

Jeff shook his head, no. But the decision had been made, it was settled. She couldn't do anything now.

"It's a secure life for him, Horace; it's safe for him. And civilized, too, and not just because it's lovely there, gracious and – " She laughed, stood up, and walked to the window. She turned around to face both of them, where they were frozen into place. "I must admit, with all the money you must have made, I don't know why you moved down here. It's not much of a house, nothing like

278

Gambo's, is it, Jeffie? And the bay – you could have done so much better than that, the bay is a dying body of water, between pleasure boaters and those factories up north dumping who knows what into it, it can't flush itself clean, you know that, Horace, in ten years . . ." Her voice trailed off on the threat. "John Smith wrote about the bay and how fertile it was. You could stick a sword into it and fish would jump on to the blade. It's not like that any more, is it?"

The Professor cleared his throat. "John Smith was a terrible liar," he said, but there was no humour at all in his voice.

"He's my son," she said. Her voice was low and sad. "He's my only child. I don't know how you can be so uncaring and selfish. You didn't used to be so uncaring and selfish. You didn't used to be unreasonable, Horace; I always admired you for that, and that's probably the reason I've never been serious about another man. Can you honestly say it's right to grudge me my only child? The only child I'll ever have?"

The Professor didn't answer. He held on to the handle of a mug as if it were a lifeline. He looked at Jeff.

"I'm not asking for everything, not for all the time, just for the summers, just for a month, or a week, just for a little bit I can count on."

Jeff didn't think he could stand it. It hurt him to feel so sorry for her.

Melody kept looking at the Professor, talking

to him, with the sun behind her making her hair shine gold around her head. "What can you offer him, Horace? Be honest, you always were honest. Don't you think he needs what I can give him? What you can't give him and never could?"

Jeff had to break the tension, somehow. He couldn't think, not even about what he wanted. He only knew that the longer she talked, the worse he felt, and the Professor too, if his face was any indication. The Professor was looking from one to the other of them, back and forth, his head moving in a helpless and bewildered gesture. His father was frightened, miserable and frightened; Jeff saw through the mask to that. Because the Professor still loved her, even though he didn't want to, even though he didn't like her or respect her. How could he still love her? The Professor was helpless, and he knew it. And she knew it too, Jeff saw; she was taking advantage of the Professor's weakness. Somebody had to protect the Professor, or she would really get to him again.

"How'd you find us?" Jeff demanded. He sounded angry; but then he was angry. Somebody had to stand up for the Professor; somebody had to defend him against what she was doing to him – and doing on purpose too. Jeff knew that intuitively.

Melody looked as if she had forgotten Jeff was there. "I called the publisher – it's a wonderful book, Horace, I loved it. I explained who I was, and your editor gave me the address. I thought I might telephone first, but – well, I knew I had to be brave and face you two head on. I was right, wasn't I, Horace?"

"But how'd you get here?" Jeff interrupted again. He could figure out what she was up to, and he tried to keep her attention on himself.

"I rented a car and drove. It's quicker than flying, with the bridge-tunnel highway. My goodness, Jeffie, why are you grilling me? Then I asked directions. You're quite a famous man down here, Horace."

She hadn't changed a bit, Jeff thought to himself. And he hated her as much as ever. He thought he had put her behind him, put himself beyond her. He hadn't changed either, after all. He made himself say it, she made him; well, it was her own fault:

"It's my choice." He heard how cold his voice was. "It was up to me, the Professor said; he always let me choose. I don't want to live with you. Not all the time, not for the summer, not for a week. Not ever. It's my decision, not his. It's what I want."

All her attention turned on to him; and he already felt like he'd been battering himself. He didn't need her to add to that. He looked briefly at his father, to remind himself what was at stake.

Her beautiful eyes looked into his, hurt, surprised. "How can you say that? To me. I'm your mother; doesn't that mean anything to you? I carried you inside me, under my heart. I'm the one who endured giving birth to you. I nursed you, took care of you. He doesn't love you the way I do. He can't, he doesn't have it in him."

"I mean it, Melody. I don't love you. I really mean it." Jeff kept his voice level.

Her eyes were wide and beautiful, drawing him in. "You're killing me," she said. "Here," and she drew one fist up under her heart and pressed the other hand against it.

"I'm sorry," Jeff said.

"You owe me more than that. I'm your mother," she said, angry now.

"I'm sorry," Jeff said again.

She stared at him. He stared back at her. His shoulders hurt from holding them stiff. After a long time, tears poured out of her eyes. "You've made me very unhappy – you, Jeffie." He nodded, expressionless. "I hope you're pleased, Horace," she said.

"It's nothing to do with him," Jeff reminded her, and she just walked out of the door. He heard a motor start.

Jeff didn't look at his father, who hadn't moved. "I'm sorry," he said, yet again, but meaning something entirely different.

"Me too," the Professor said. His eyes were now on the door, and he didn't really hear Jeff at all, Jeff guessed.

"I was bringing Dicey over too."

The Professor did look at him then, like a man

waking up, and asked, "Were you? Well," and a little humour was back in his eyes, Jeff thought, or hoped. "The best laid schemes gang aft agley. Don't they? Another time, maybe."

"I couldn't have picked a worse one. Anyway, she won't be back again."

His father understood who he was talking about. "You can't predict what Melody will do," he told Jeff. "I wonder what made her do this," he said thoughtfully. "Are you OK, Jeff?"

"I'm fine," Jeff lied. "I'm just glad it's over. How about you, are you OK?"

"I think so," the Professor said, without confidence.

11

Jeff wasn't fine, and he knew it. But the Professor didn't know it, which was the important thing.

Five days after Melody's visit, school started. During those days the subject of Melody didn't come up. In fact, both the Professor and Jeff avoided it. Jeff didn't see that there was anything left to say. What he was thinking – about himself and how he'd acted, about the Professor and what Jeff had guessed – he didn't see any reason to burden the Professor with that. Jeff knew he'd done what he really wanted to do, and he knew why, and he even thought it was the right thing. But he wasn't too pleased with himself, all the same.

On the first day of school, Phil came up to him smirking, his face so brown his grin looked like a TV advertisement for toothpaste. "I met your mum. I'm still recovering. I mean, Jeff – "

"How'd you do that?" Jeff asked. It was the end of lunch break and they sat outside, while people with new school clothes and deep summer tans made themselves re-acquainted. Jeff figured Phil had made some mistake.

"I was covering for my sister at the stand, last Wednesday afternoon and to think I almost didn't do it. This dusty old car pulled up, the kind you expect fusty middle-aged people to ride around in, you know? And look at every tomato before they decide which to buy then try to argue down the price. And then buy exactly three ears of corn because she only eats one, and more than two is bad for his digestion. This car pulled up. I didn't pay any attention, except to notice that it had South Carolina plates, because we don't often see those. Then the legs emerged – and the rest of her. By then I was riveted to attention. And that voice. And those eyes – they're like yours only . . . not the same. I mean, she looks right into your eyes with hers. Wow."

Jeff didn't want to talk about Melody.

"When she asked for *you*, I almost asked if she was your mother. She asked if I knew your address, as a matter of fact. I said you were in my class. She said I looked older than you. She couldn't remember the directions, which makes sense, I guess; we're so rural and she said she lives in the city – so I drew her a map. Is she still there? I'd sure like to see her again. She knows about pesticides and herbicides – she liked our tomatoes."

Jeff just shook his head.

"I mean, what a great mother for anybody to have," Phil went on. "Did she say she'd met me?"

Jeff shrugged. He guessed, in her way, Melody was something special.

"With women like that in the world, it makes you glad to be a man, doesn't it?"

That too, Jeff couldn't answer, because he judged himself to have acted like not much of a man in relation to Melody. He had acted the way he felt: scared, and cruel because he was scared. As far as he was concerned, nobody should ever be as cruel to anyone as he had been to Melody. There was no excuse. Phil drifted away from his unresponsive company, and Jeff continued his own thoughts. He'd do the same thing again and the same way if he couldn't do better, but he'd never kid himself about liking what he'd done.

It wasn't that he regretted it, it was just that he couldn't forget. The knowledge was always with him, wherever he happened to be. Nobody else knew. Nobody else could know. Jeff felt as if there was an invisible wall around him that separated him from everybody else. Because he had done to Melody just what she had done to him: she had thought he loved her and he had told her he didn't. It was the truth, but that didn't make it any better or make him any better.

Except occasionally, when he saw Dicey in the hall, he didn't see the Tillermans, now that school was in session and their crabbing business closed for the season. He was still friendly with her and with Mina and with Phil and Andy. He still played the guitar and got straight As. He even went to football games and to parties. But he didn't tell anybody, not even the Professor, what he was thinking. It wouldn't do any good, and it would be like asking for comfort. He didn't deserve comfort, or even sympathy.

He was responsible for what he had done, and that responsibility buzzed around his head like birds – like seagulls in a flock, squabbling in mid-flight about some morsel of food, trying to grab it from whichever bird had it, attacking each other so greedily that the food fell into the water. He and only he had done that – that knowledge flapped inside his head. He couldn't undo it. He didn't even want to.

So he kept himself aloof, inside himself. When he remembered – waking up in the middle of the night – what he had said, how she had looked, what he had answered, shame washed over him like waves, and he buried his head under the pillow. He woke frequently at night that autumn and would wander out from his bedroom to the kitchen. Hang on, he told himself, just hang on and it'll get easier.

He drank a glass of milk, looked out into the blankness of the night, and reminded himself that it was just what he deserved; it was fair enough. He had known what he was doing and he had done it. He thought, he hoped, that the vivid memory would eventually fade. He was young and in good shape: he didn't need eight hours of sleep every night. He would endure, like the Professor had, until his feelings faded a little.

He was sorry the Professor hadn't got to meet

Dicey, and the Professor even mentioned that once, but not again. He also missed seeing the Tillermans, but that was just something he'd have to put up with. A part of some punishment, a part of the gulls quarrelling and reminding him he wasn't to be trusted – like Melody. Not exactly like her, but enough. Phil and Andy were all wrapped up in talking about colleges that autumn, and Jeff listened to their conversations, adding in his opinion when he was asked. Jeff didn't think about colleges for himself.

One November day, when an icy rain sleeted down from the sky, making it chilly even inside the heated car, Jeff passed Sammy Tillerman riding on his bike, a sack of newspapers over his shoulder. The kid's yellow hair was pounded down over his ears by the rain. Jeff pulled the car over and waited for Sammy to ride up. He made Sammy put his bike into the back, and the two of them drove the rest of Sammy's paper round. Sammy was starting to grow. His legs, in soaked jeans, were getting longer and his feet looked big. He was going to be a big, muscular man, Jeff thought. He looked pretty strong, even shivering beside Jeff in the car.

Instead of taking Sammy straight home, Jeff took him to his own house and told him to take a hot shower while he put Sammy's clothes in the drier. He couldn't stand looking at Sammy so cold, even for the ten minutes extra it would have taken to drive him to his grandmother's house.

Jeff made cocoa while Sammy called up to explain where he was. It was Maybeth he talked to, saying Jeff would bring him home in a little while. Jeff knew it was Maybeth without asking, because the pace of Sammy's conversation was slower than usual.

"She says hello to you," Sammy reported. He wore one of Jeff's long-sleeved T-shirts while his clothes dried. "She's funny. She asked me if you were all right, because we haven't seen you, I suppose. She didn't ask about me."

"Well," Jeff said. "That's interesting."

Sammy stared at him, as if he'd said something pretty stupid. "But she's right, isn't she? I mean, she knows I'm all right, so she doesn't have to ask. They used to say she was stupid – retarded. Dicey never believed it, but I did. And she is, in some ways, anyway she acts it sometimes – sometimes it drives me crazy she's so slow."

"Not me," Jeff said.

"I used to think," Sammy continued, sitting at the table, drinking cocoa slowly, "that she was going to end up like Mamma. I used to think that was bad. Because of how Mamma was. But Mamma wasn't just one thing or another, she was more than one, all at the same time. And now I'm older, when I think about it I can understand her better. She's dead. She died."

Jeff could see that Sammy was making himself say that. "I never knew her," he said, because he

289

thought he ought to say – something, and the Tillermans didn't like sympathy.

"She was a lot like Maybeth, I think," Sammy said. "I was too little to really know."

"If she was like Maybeth, I would have liked her," Jeff said.

"Yeah."

"Liked who?" the Professor asked. He had come out from his study. "I heard voices. Is there enough cocoa for me? This is miserable weather." He sat down with them, and Jeff introduced Sammy, then explained why Sammy's clothes were in the drier. Sammy told the Professor about his paper round, and how much money it brought in. He boasted a little. Then he said, his hazel eyes mischievous, "James'll be jealous I met you. Won't he?" he asked Jeff.

"Why should he?" the Professor wondered.

"Because of your book."

"How old is James?"

"Eleven."

"That's too young to read my book."

"He's clever," Sammy explained.

"But it doesn't have anything to do with being clever," the Professor said, a little surprised.

Sammy sat back and grinned. "Good-o. Wait'll I tell James you said that. It'll serve him right."

"Serve him right for what? Being clever?"

Sammy squirmed in his seat. He didn't want to answer that question.

"But I didn't even let Jeff read it until he was fifteen, and he's clever too."

"Is that true?" Sammy asked Jeff. Jeff nodded. "Why?" Sammy asked the Professor.

"Because there's more to it than just brains, or just being able to read the words. You have to be able to read the ideas, too."

Sammy studied the Professor. "Could James meet you? He'd like that."

"I might like it too," the Professor said. His eyes, full of humour, met Jeff's.

As Jeff drove Sammy home, the boy asked him, "Is that what fathers are like?"

"I suppose so. What do you mean?"

"I never had one," Sammy said. "Mine left before I was even born. I never wanted one, but yours has thought about things. He's really steady, isn't he? Mine wasn't – he couldn't have been, and Gram met him and she said so too. Maybe they're all just different. Do you think?"

"I think," Jeff said. He didn't go inside to say hello to anyone, just dropped Sammy off in the yard and waited while he unloaded his bike.

"Thanks a lot," Sammy said.

"Any time," Jeff told him. He ought to bring James over, he thought, because the Professor would like talking to him. He wondered what the Tillermans' father had been like. He supposed a man could walk out as easily as a woman. He supposed he was sorry he'd met up with Sammy, because he knew now how different remembering was from being there, being with them.

Melody didn't try to get in touch with Jeff or, he thought, the Professor. He couldn't be positive about his father, who was perfectly capable of keeping a secret. But he thought, watching him, that the Professor kept on in his usual way. He thought also that the Professor would tell him this time, rather than try to keep it secret. Sometimes Jeff worried over Melody and almost wished she would get in touch just so he would know if he'd really hurt her. Most of the time, he was just relieved not to have to deal with her, or think about her – he had enough trouble living with his own sense of guilt. He had bad days, when he despised himself and guilt gnawed at his heart; he had not-so-bad days, when he felt responsibility buzzing around his head like flies. He was managing, he reassured himself, getting through the bad days all right, trying to measure if they were growing easier.

All that winter, Phil and Andy were preoccupied with the future: where they were going to apply to college, what they were going to study, what jobs they wanted to have when they had finished school. Even the Professor started to talk colleges. Jeff, feeling that he couldn't make any decisions, tried to put the whole subject off. "Have you thought about it at all?" the Professor asked him.

"No."

"Why not?"

"I don't know what I want to do or study, I don't have any plans or ambitions. It seems like a waste of time."

"What, college?"

"Thinking about it. Thinking ahead, maybe."

"Why?"

Jeff shrugged. He didn't want to answer. His father couldn't guess, and Jeff didn't want to tell him about how much energy, and work, it took to make it through every day. His father would worry and feel responsible, if he ever did guess.

"Jeff, you know I don't like to pester you or nag at you."

Jeff waited.

"But I'm afraid I'm losing touch with you."

"No, you aren't," Jeff said, "I'm not. I wouldn't let you."

"Maybe not, but I'm getting the feeling – the way I got it that autumn before we moved. I'm trying to learn from experience – what kind of an historian would I be if I didn't? I get the feeling something is worrying you, and I thought maybe it was college."

"I'm not worried about college," Jeff told his father. His father wouldn't ever guess what it was, because his mind didn't work that way. "Honest. If you really want to talk about it, I will." There was just the one thing he wasn't going to talk to his father about. In a way, it was for the Professor's sake he had done it. The

293

Professor had needed him to do it. If the Professor could forget about Melody then that was the best thing for him.

"I've been sort of thinking about it. For example, I sort of think I'd like to go into ecology." The Professor's face went expressionless. "No, not saving the world or getting back to the good old prehistoric days, not that. But responsible management of it, somehow. I'm thinking about marine biology – with some chemistry and – some economics, because it's never going to be a simple problem – and computers too, because that's the only efficient way to collate material, so you have to know programming, I think. Don't you?" The Professor nodded, watched, waited. "Nobody understands the bay, nobody really knows how it works. It's an incredibly complex system, but . . . I want to preserve it, I'd like to do that for a job. Maybe even enrich it." The Professor nodded. "Or be a waterman, that would be OK too; it's hard work, but I can do it."

"You are thinking about it then."

"Of course. What did you think?"

But the Professor didn't answer. Anyway, Jeff knew what his father had been thinking, and he hoped he had reassured him.

"And you haven't seen your friends the Tillermans, have you?"

Jeff shrugged. He hadn't, and he really missed them – missed the singing and the way they were

294

always working at some project, and the way when they laughed together they egged one another on. The first time that had happened, he'd got so choked up he'd had to pretend he had to go home. "I know," he said, and heard the sadness in his voice.

"I don't understand," the Professor asked.

Jeff could see that, and he was glad, because it wasn't the Professor's responsibility, it was his own. If the Professor couldn't understand, that meant Jeff had done something right, at least in that one respect. "I'm going to be OK, I think, Professor."

"I've never heard you say that before."

"Anyhow, I think it's the truth," Jeff said. Keeping an eye on the truth was one of the hardest parts; accepting what he'd done to Melody. No matter what anyone would say she'd done to him, he had still done what he had done to her.

That year, Brother Thomas didn't come down for Thanksgiving or for the days after Christmas or for any weekends. He sent Jeff a postcard at Christmas-time: "*Adeste fideles*. Did you know that the preferred meaning of *fideles* is trustworthy? Seasons greetings to the Tillermans. Thinking of you. BroT." During the Christmas holiday, Jeff saw a couple of movies with Phil and Andy, went to a couple of parties, but didn't go to the Tillermans". The reason he didn't go was simple: he didn't go because he really wanted to.

Dicey never said anything about it, but she didn't seem angry with him or anything. When they ran into each other at school she'd talk to him in the ordinary way. She didn't say anything much except she'd answer his questions carefully. They were usually "How are you?" or "What's new?"

There was no snow that winter, only a long spell of cold weather that froze the muddy fields into ruts, as if they had been fossilized, that sharpened the edge of the winds so that Jeff rode the bus to and from school every day.

The weather broke in February, near the end of the month, into a long thaw. March was warm and gentle, without any lion to it at all. In the middle of March, the Professor told Jeff that Brother Thomas wanted to come down after Easter for the remaining week of the spring holiday.

"That's great," Jeff said. "But how come?"

"I don't ask him questions," the Professor answered. "What he said was, he thought we should do some planting. He wants to put in a vegetable garden. I think he's inspired by your Mrs Tillerman."

That was a curious word, inspired. "He said she was strong," Jeff said. "He's pretty strong too, isn't he? I mean, you have to be, to be a brother."

"I think so," the Professor said. "Maybe it's like love; it's so easy to fall in love – the way you fall into the water when the weather is hot – but living in love is different."

"I wouldn't know," Jeff pointed out.

"Um," the Professor said.

One afternoon in early April when the Professor's holiday had begun but Jeff's hadn't, he got home to find the Professor vacuuming the kitchen. He shut off the vacuum when Jeff came in. He wore flannels and a regular white shirt, with a sweater waistcoat. His hair shone from a recent washing. He had tidied up the room and even washed the big glass doors. "Professor, what's going on?" Jeff asked. He took his books into his room and hurried back. "What do you want me to do now?"

"Make a pot of coffee," the Professor said. He finished the floor and coiled the vacuum cord round the machine. "It's not warm enough to sit outside, is it?"

"Too damp still," Jeff said. "Who's coming?" Brother Thomas wasn't due for another ten days, and besides, they didn't clean like this for Brother Thomas. He put water on to boil, then emptied the dishwasher. The Professor's nervousness was catching.

"A gentleman named Beauregard Jacobs," the Professor said. "Jeff, Gambo died last week. It was a peaceful death, he told me."

Jeff didn't know what to say. "I'm sorry," he said at last.

"This Beauregard Jacobs is her lawyer. He said he had to see us, me because I'm your guardian."

"You're not my guardian, you're my father."

"He called this morning, he'll be here in about half an hour. I don't know, Jeff; does it look all right?"

"She can't do anything," Jeff told his father. "She won't. Don't worry." He knew that, for sure. He had finished Melody last summer, finished her for good and all. She couldn't get at the Professor again, not any more; and Jeff could only hurt himself.

"I just want to look as if I'm doing a good job," the Professor said, his eyes going round the room, to find anything he'd neglected. "Just in case."

But it turned out that Beauregard Jacobs wasn't interested in the Professor or the housekeeping at all. He had come to see Jeff. He came wearing a white suit and carrying a straw hat in his hand. His shoes narrowed to polished points. He was a big man, as tall as the Professor, but broad and heavy as well. He had dark hair with silver streaks in it and small brown eyes under shaggy eyebrows. He carried an attaché case.

They sat at the table, Jeff and the Professor at the ends, Mr Jacobs in the middle so he could spread out papers, with a view out of the windows. He had shaken their hands and presented his condolences as soon as he came in. He had been grateful for a cup of coffee. It had been, he said, a long drive down from the Baltimore airport. This was surely, he said, the most secluded spot he'd ever seen, but then he guessed writers naturally hankered after seclusion.

"Is that right, Dr Greene?"

"I'm not a writer." The Professor too had a mug of coffee to fiddle with.

"But surely Miss Melody told me – "

"Just a history book," the Professor said. "But you said you wanted to talk to Jeff?"

"Yes. Yes, indeed, I do."

Jeff waited attentively. He thought about getting a glass of water, so he too would have something to turn in his hands, but decided not to. The lawyer looked straight at him. He waited, listening.

"Your great-grandmother was a fine lady, very old-fashioned in many ways, which I for one find a rare virtue these days. A rare virtue."

Jeff nodded.

"My father was the man she originally consulted. I inherited her, as you might say."

Jeff nodded.

"I've administered her property for a number of years. I think you might say I'm more intimately aware of the structure of the estate than anybody else. She trusted me, I'm glad to say, absolutely. Yes, absolutely."

Jeff nodded again and saw the Professor's head going up and down at the opposite end of the table.

"That's by way of introduction. Preamble you might say. Because you see, young man, you are her heir."

"Her heir?" Jeff echoed, and the Professor at the same time sighed, "Oh no."

Mr Jacobs chuckled at their reactions. "She did tell me you were an unusual pair, Miss Melody – I think I'll believe her."

"But what about Melody?" Jeff asked. "I thought she was going to inherit."

"Mrs Melville has left her an heirloom ring, jade, and a portrait – not a valuable portrait, but it had sentimental value to Mrs Melville. She decided, however, that the male descendant should inherit the estate."

Jeff didn't know what to say. "But Melody thought – "

"She has had a hard time of it, you might say," Mr Jacobs agreed. "Mrs Melville had a hard decision to make. But she decided that it was better for the family if the property went through the male line. That was Mrs Melville's choice. Miss Melody knew about it. She's had time to get used to the idea. Mrs Melville told her after she'd drawn up the will."

But it wasn't fair. Even Gambo didn't like it.

"We ought to get the facts straight first," the Professor said. "Don't you think so, Jeff?"

"The facts, I must say, Dr Greene, are going to be difficult to keep straight. Which is why I came up here myself, rather than trying to communicate to you by letter."

"But I didn't even go to the funeral," Jeff said.

"Miss Melody particularly asked that you not be told," Mr Jacobs answered, but he looked at the Professor as he spoke. "You had, shall we say, protested for so long, Dr Greene, all these years and so hard, she felt that it would be more of an emotional strain than she had strength for. She did say that since you finally agreed to a divorce and it has gone through, she hoped your bitterness has faded."

The Professor didn't say anything.

"He's not bitter," Jeff told the lawyer.

"Yes, well," Mr Jacobs said. He cleared his throat, drained his mug of coffee, leaned down to open his attaché case and remove papers. He spread the papers around in front of him. "The estate consists of personal property (jewellery and household effects), the one piece of property, as well as some stocks. Much of the personal property can be sold at auction and the appraisers have given me an estimate of what they think it will bring. The property is, of course, the house, which is quite valuable in today's market. The investments represent only about fifty thousand dollars in capital. The difficulty is that much of the estate has outstanding loans against it. After taxes, depending on the markets, you should realize from twenty to thirty thousand dollars."

"I thought Gambo was rich."

"She had expenses."

Jeff thought about the big house down in Charleston and the proud woman with her black change purse and her rings and the sun-filled dining room in which they ate breakfast. "What about the aunts?" he asked.

"Fortunately, she had purchased annuities for them, several years ago, so they will move into a nursing home together. She has specified to each the furniture from her own room in the house. Miss Aurelia and Miss Belle will be able to end their lives peacefully."

"Had she mortgaged the house?" the Professor said.

"I'm afraid so, mortgaged it heavily. She also borrowed against the investments. Whatever real legacy there is will come from the personal possessions. She did make one specific bequest to you, which is the best single piece. I brought it with me. I've had it appraised so there should be no difficulty about giving it over to you now." He reached down and brought out a small black box, which he passed to Jeff. Jeff knew what it would be: Gambo's diamond ring.

He passed the open box to his father.

"Is that the one?" the Professor asked him.

"That's it."

The Professor stared at the diamond, glittering white in its black velvet setting. "It certainly is big," he said finally.

"It's worth – oh – you could probably get

302

twenty thousand dollars for it. Her silver also is worth a fair amount, some of the china pieces, some of the furniture."

The Professor passed the ring back to Jeff. Jeff looked at it. Twenty thousand dollars, two or three years of college, Jeff thought; and it was his own. He couldn't imagine a hand that the ring would suit, but he could imagine the difference that much money would make to some people. The Tillermans, for example; if it was a question of paying for college. "Thank you," he said to Mr Jacobs.

"Thank your great-grandmother. I was only glad to have some good news to bring, so to speak. Now, you'll have to instruct me. Unless you prefer your own lawyer to handle your interests? No? It's just as well. I think I really do understand just what needs to be done, to realize as much as possible from the estate. I'm not, Dr Greene, the lawyer who handled the divorce. So we can work together without being hindered by whatever has gone on in the past."

"Fine," the Professor said.

Mr Jacobs studied him for a long time. Then he put his pencil neatly across the top of his yellow pad and said, "I've known Miss Melody for years, of course. And I consider myself in a sense her lawyer now. But you aren't at all what I'd been led to expect."

"I can only hope the surprise is not unpleasant," the Professor answered.

"No, sir, it isn't."

Jeff liked this lawyer, the way he wanted everything set out clearly.

"But what about Miss Opal?" Jeff interrupted.

"Mrs Opal Carter, yes. She wasn't specifically mentioned in the will. Miss Melody tells me that she can remain in the house until it is sold, but after that – she herself is in no position to pay Mrs Carter's salary, much less support her. It is legally your house, so to speak; do you object to Mrs Carter living there free?" Jeff shook his head. "There were only the four specific bequests, that ring to you, the items to your mother, the furniture to the two elderly women. The rest comes to you as single heir."

"Why didn't Gambo leave Miss Opal anything?"

"Perhaps she felt it would be possible for Mrs Carter to find work. I would expect that is what she had in mind. Mrs Carter will have social security."

Jeff got up from the table. The whole thing was wrong. He shouldn't inherit. It wasn't because Gambo liked him or anything. It was just because he was a boy. Miss Opal shouldn't be left with no pension, not after all those years of work. It should have been Melody's estate, or even her mother's, and there were other grandchildren as well, weren't there? He walked to the window and looked out, thinking.

"Jeff?" his father asked, after a while.

"If there are mortgages against the house, and she borrowed against the investments, where did all the money go?"

"As I said, she purchased annuities for her cousins. For that she sold a great deal of stock. Then, Miss Melody had an allowance of ten thousand dollars a year. There were taxes. Old loans came due and she would borrow again to pay them off. The maintenance on the house is costly."

"If," Jeff asked, watching the Professor's face, "if she borrowed against stocks, the bank wouldn't have given her their full value, would it? I mean, you have to put a deposit down when you buy a house even with a mortgage, so isn't there some money left on the stocks?"

"That's true, but it's only a small part of the value."

"But if the auction went well, would it be possible to pay off what's owing just against the stocks?"

"I think so. Once the house itself is sold."

"Then the stocks could be given to Miss Opal. Even if it wouldn't give her enough income to live on, it would give her some security, wouldn't it?"

The Professor agreed with Jeff, Jeff could see that. He turned his attention to the lawyer. He came back to the table.

"You're declining the legacy?" Mr Jacobs asked.

305

"No. I don't mean to. I mean, I'll keep the ring, I'd like to."

"Have you considered what Mrs Melville wanted?" the lawyer asked. "It is her will, her intention, that you receive it."

"But she did leave it to me, didn't she?" Jeff argued. "So it's mine to do as I want with, isn't it? I don't see really why she left it to me, but she did. Didn't she? I mean I see *why*, but I don't agree. But it is mine, isn't it?"

They argued for two hours, first over what Jeff wanted to do, then about how to do it. At the end, they invited Mr Jacobs to stay for dinner, but he declined. They all shook hands. Mr Jacobs said he would be in touch, would be sending all kinds of papers for Jeff to sign. Jeff thanked him, the Professor thanked him, and he left.

They had sandwiches for dinner. Neither of them felt like cooking or talking. Finally Jeff said, "It's hard on Melody."

"She won't be pleased," the Professor agreed.

"Boy, won't she," Jeff said.

"I think we may know now why she came by last summer," the Professor said.

"Yeah." Then Jeff grinned. "You said once you never knew what she'd do. Boy."

"What will she do now, I wonder," the Professor said.

"It's not right," Jeff said. "I mean, she really did think Gambo would leave her everything; she must have had some reason for thinking that; and she is the one who lived there, who stayed with Gambo. How could Gambo have done that to her? Except she did leave Melody the ring she really loved. She told me so, the first summer, she told me about that ring. It was jade, Professor, milky green, set around with little diamonds, like stars. It had the initials of the woman it was first made for worked into the setting. The jeweller had been in love with her. She died young in childbirth. Gambo was left the ring by her mother. This one" – he indicated the closed box on the table – "was her engagement ring. It didn't mean that much to her. So she must have loved Melody."

"Oh, I think so. But you are the male descendant."

"Gambo couldn't have thought that Melody wanted the ring more than the inheritance, could she?"

"It depends on what Melody led her to think. She must have thought that Melody would cherish it."

"It was passed from mother to daughter, so she must have thought of Melody as a daughter."

"Yes, probably. I'm sure Melody tried to be what her grandmother wanted her to be. Or at least tried to appear to be. Don't you think?"

"Oh, yeah," Jeff agreed. "So it serves her right, I guess. But it's funny, Professor. Gambo loved Melody, so she gave her what Melody didn't want. She didn't love me, but – "

"It strikes me that love is just the beginning. If you think about it, Jeff. I think we can't help loving, but what matters is what we do about it. What we do with love. Do for it. What love does with us."

Jeff knew what his father was talking about. He could see what his father was looking at: the Professor was looking at his own love for Melody and for Jeff; the Professor was sitting up and away from them, studying them and trying to understand how they worked. The Professor was doing what he always did, using his knowledge and experience to try to understand things as they really were.

Jeff could do that too. He could look at what he'd done. In his imagination, he sat himself down in the Professor's seat and laid the facts out in front of him. He had been deliberately cruel to Melody, but – he saw – she had forced that on him, by her cruelty to the Professor. By the way she had taken advantage of Jeff's love for her and destroyed it. She had set him free from her, and as a free agent he had decided to hurt her so that she wouldn't be able to do damage to the Professor. Also, Jeff admitted to himself, because he wanted to get even for what she had done to him, Jeff. That wasn't all of his reason, but it was part of it, and it wasn't a pretty part.

Still sitting in the Professor's chair, Jeff looked around him, at himself: he had to make the choice he had, it was right for him and right for the

Professor. It was just too bad that what he gave up, or gave away, in that choosing was hard on Melody. Not like Gambo's estate, which Miss Opal would be glad to have; that was an equally right decision, and one that hurt nobody.

The real problem with choosing the Professor over Melody came from Melody. She said she loved him, and he knew better; but maybe she believed herself. But that was her problem, not Jeff's. Jeff's problem was to accept what he'd done, and why. He could do that, he found: he could sit in the Professor's chair and see how he had to do it, and how he had to not like himself for doing it. He liked himself for not liking himself, he thought – swivelling up and around out of the Professor's chair. He looked at his father and had to stop himself from singing the song that was rising up inside him.

"I'm proud of you, Jeff," the Professor said.

Jeff didn't disagree, although he didn't think he'd done anything much. It was pleasant to make the right decision, just simply doing the right thing.

"Does this ring have sentimental value to you?" the Professor asked him.

Jeff laughed, partly from a sense of release, partly because it was over, really over. This inheritance, Gambo's will, was like bringing the whole question before the law. Like Gambo he had – under a different kind of law than Mr Jacobs knew – decided against Melody. "No,

309

none. I just thought – you asked me once if there was anything I wanted to buy and there isn't – but there are some years for college in here."

"You don't need to worry about that. You aren't worrying about paying for college, are you?"

"Not for me, I was thinking of the Tillermans. And Dicey. Just in case. I don't know if I could convince them, only for college, but – "

"I think, after this afternoon, you'd probably find a way. I didn't know that about you."

"I'm full of surprises," Jeff said.

"I think you are. There's a lot of your mother in you."

Jeff looked at his father.

"That's a compliment," the Professor said.

Jeff knew what his father meant. "And a lot of my father," he said. "And that's a compliment, too."

Dicey worked from nine to twelve on Saturday mornings, Jeff knew. The Saturday after Mr Jacobs's visit, he stopped by the grocer's shop a little before twelve. Dicey's bike leaned up against the front window. Inside, he queued to buy a half gallon of milk and a packet of English muffins. They were out of both, and Jeff had decided to drive past the supermarket and on into town, to kill two birds with one stone. When Dicey came out, wearing jeans and a boy's shirt, she was

310

surprised to see him waiting. "I thought you might like a lift home," Jeff said.

She studied him for a minute before agreeing. She looked as if she was curious about him, as if he was unusually interesting. "OK," she said. They loaded her bike into the back of the car. They pulled silently away from the kerb.

"I wondered," Jeff said, keeping his eyes on the road, "if it would be OK for me to come over this afternoon."

"No," Dicey said quickly. "Gram's got some stuff she wants us to do."

"Oh, well," Jeff said.

"But after supper. We'd like it," Dicey said. "If you wanted to."

"I want to," Jeff said. They left the town streets, turning on to the long, winding road. He cleared his throat. "Actually, I really wanted you to come and meet the Professor now. I thought we'd get a sandwich and pick up the guitar and you could meet him."

Dicey didn't answer right away. He looked over at her. She was turned so she could look at his face. She was getting ready to say no, he could see it behind her eyes.

"Look, he wants to meet you. I mean, does your grandmother plan to get you to work before lunch? I'll take you right home after, honest."

"I don't think so, Jeff."

"He won't complicate your life. He's not that kind of person, not at all."

Dicey laughed. "Then you are all right again," she said.

"What do you mean?"

"You know what I mean."

"Yeah, I guess I do. Yeah, I think I am."

"Maybeth will be glad. Are you going to tell me about it?" It wasn't like Dicey to ask questions, so Jeff told her the exact truth.

"Sometime, maybe."

She didn't crowd him, either. "Why do I need to meet your father?" she asked.

Jeff thought about this. "If I want to know you, I have to know your family too. I think families are like that, when they're real families. It doesn't have anything to do with being happy. I've been thinking about it."

The thing about Dicey, one of the things about her, was that she really listened. Jeff could hear her listening to him.

"You're right about me, if there's someone I'm going to know I always want them to meet my family."

"The Professor's my family."

After a while, Dicey asked, "What about your mother?"

"You've met my mother," Jeff reminded her. "Besides, she's not my family. I know that sounds strange." Although it didn't sound so strange to him, now he thought of it.

"Nothing much sounds strange to me," Dicey pointed out. She turned round again to look forward. "And I'd like to meet your father, I think."

She sounded so doubtful that Jeff grinned.

"And Gram would tell me to do it. She likes you."

"Really?" That did surprise him.

"Really. She says you've got staying power and a gentle spirit. She says you're a rare bird."

Jeff didn't bother to try to hide his pleasure. "Wow," he said. Then, "She could be wrong." Then he didn't ask what he wanted to – what Dicey thought of him. If she thought anything, he supposed she'd tell him, sooner or later. He supposed she was telling him right now. He felt, turning off the road on to the shelled drive that ran up to his house, as if he'd just got a letter, out of the blue, from somebody wise enough to know the truth, from everybody, or at least everybody who mattered.

"Hello," the letter said. "Hello, Jeff Greene, I've been watching you and I like you and I want to know you better. This is just to say I'm glad you're alive in the world." The list of signatures, he thought, would include his own.

12

It was the first week in June, ten days before school got out. Jeff, his guitar on his back, walked the bike up the drive. The air shone bright with sunlight, the shadows shone cool. May and June were his favourite months, before the summer heat began. And September and October. He didn't mind the rest too much, either. He sang as he walked, "Oh Lord, you know, I have no friend like you, if heaven's not my home, O Lord, what shall I do?"

He sang the song happy because that was how he felt. Not for any particular reason, unless the shells sharp under his feet were a reason, or the patches of sunlight warm on his shoulders, or the idea for a slightly different riff to play between the verses of the song. He might, he thought, try to catch a few crabs for supper. He wouldn't succeed, not at this time of the year, but he'd like to get out on the water. That evening, he and as many of the Tillermans who wanted to, and Mina Smiths and a couple of her brothers, and the Professor, too, if he could talk his father into it, were going to see *Star Wars*.

He saw the car, Max's car, first. When he went into the house, he saw Melody, sitting cross-legged on the lawn. He stood for a minute, looking at her back. The sun shone around her, and her hair had grown long again. She wore it in one braid down her back. He slid the glass door open and walked out to find out what she wanted: he couldn't just ride away. He thought for a second he might, but the Professor would be home in an hour or so, and she was Jeff's responsibility.

She turned when she heard him, but didn't get up. "Jeffie? Are you angry at me? I wanted to see you."

He sat down in a chair. "Hi, Melody. Have you been here long?"

"A while. A while. It's poky, but it's quiet, isn't it?"

"Yeah." He cleared his throat. "What can I do for you?"

She shifted, to look directly into his eyes. She clasped her hands together in her lap, like a little girl. "Can't we put all that behind us?"

"All what?"

"Everything."

Everything. Starting when, Jeff wondered, and including how much? "I've already done that," he told her.

The beautiful eyes filmed with tears. "Oh, Jeffie, I don't know how to talk to you, you've changed so much. Grown up, I guess they call it, you're so tall, and handsome – and your voice – and I bet you've started to shave, too."

315

"Just once a week." She was flattering him, and he wondered why.

"But you used to love me. You'll deny it now, but you did. Men have convenient memories. But I remember, I remember that. What happened to us, Jeffie?"

Jeff couldn't take his eyes from hers and he felt – rising up within him – feelings so complicated he didn't know if he could stay cool, stay quiet. Anger, again, and guilt – he had been horrible to her. She looked so small and sad, he felt sorry for her. He thought he ought to apologize to her for what Gambo had done. And he had to get rid of her before his father came home. "What is it you want, Melody?" he asked.

"Oh, Jeffie, the way you say that. Nothing, I don't want anything. I just wanted to see you before I went away."

"You're going away? Where?" She'd let him know what she wanted, in her own time, in her own way. He could wait.

"Columbia. That's in South America."

"Why?"

Her hands separated, waved helplessly, then clasped together again. "You wouldn't understand, about the way people have to live in some places, about how ignorant they are. There's a village, in the mountains, and seventy-five percent of the children die before they're five. Diphtheria, typhoid, fever. Little children. And those that live – the girls marry at twelve and die

316

in childbirth or are old women by twenty-five. In this day and age, Jeffie. They can't read and write, they just work, just to get enough to eat that day, they don't know anything about farming methods, or sanitation. There's so much that needs to be done. Nobody cares about them, and the young men go off to the cities and get ruined and the old are left alone. Brief, miserable, unhappy lives – and it doesn't have to be that way. We sit here like fat cats and don't do anything about it."

She was right, in her way. Jeff could think whatever he liked about her, personally, but she really wanted to help people who needed it. She really did feel for them, she really tried. "Where's Max?" he asked her.

Her eyes slipped away from his. "He's there already. He wants to buy a farm – land is really cheap. We're going to – to live with them and teach them."

Jeff was beginning to see. His lack of feeling about it surprised him, pleased him. He looked out over the creek and marsh. He guessed Max would be putting in a crop of marijuana, or poppies – that was his guess. But he guessed Melody really might love the guy.

Her voice went on behind him. "I can't ever be happy, knowing about them and not doing anything."

Happy, unhappy – Jeff was beginning to think that wasn't the question at all. The Tillermans

never worried about that, they worried about . . .
living right for each one of them, together. He
guessed you might call that happy, but he didn't
think that was it, he didn't think that was the half
of it.

"You used to love me, I know you did." Jeff
kept his eyes on the spacious horizon. "But you
chose your father because he's the rich and
famous one. Well, I don't blame you. I want you
to know that I don't."

Jeff turned his face back to her at that. Because
he did love her, or at least he felt tied to her, in a
way; in a way as close as love would tie them.
Poor Melody – she didn't know the first thing
about love. "Why did you come?" he asked her
gently.

He saw her face light up with hope. Poor
Melody, he thought again, because she saw love
as something that gets you what you want. She
didn't understand at all.

"I need money. To get me there. And start
work, for supplies and some books. So we can
make a difference there."

"I don't have money, not that kind," Jeff told
her. "I'm sorry, Melody, I gave what there was
to Miss Opal, all I have is an allowance."

"You have Gambo's ring," she told him, angry.

He looked at her hand, then, and saw the green
jade. She followed his eyes. "This one's not worth
anything."

"Oh, OK," Jeff said, hiding his smile. Oh,

Melody, he thought. He went into the house to get the box out of the bookcase where he kept it hidden. He returned to find Melody standing up, watching for him. He passed her the little box, and she opened it. She slipped off the jade ring so that she could put the big diamond on.

"You keep that one," she said. "Really, I'd like you to." Jeff took the ring. Gambo wanted Melody to have it, but Melody didn't want it.

Melody had the diamond on her hand and held it out to catch the sunlight. "It's a pity to sell it," she sighed.

"Maybe you don't have to."

This was the ring she'd wanted when she married the Professor and was pregnant with Jeff. She'd finally got what she wanted; he didn't see why she should sell it – unless it was the money all along. Not the thing but its money value all along, in everything. Except Max, he remembered. There were always exceptions. The pieces of Melody didn't fit neatly together any more than the pieces of the Professor did, or of Jeff – or of anybody, for that matter, or anything. Even the blue herons nested in colonies, all of them together.

"Maybe you can keep it." He knew she didn't want to.

She laughed up into his eyes. "You are a goose, aren't you? But now I know you love me, whether you'll admit it or not, I don't need anything else to make me happy. And I better run, before your

319

father catches me here. He'll be angry with you, if you tell him."

"No, he won't," Jeff said.

She wasn't listening to him, she was slipping her sandals on to her feet, bending gracefully over to pull the straps tight, her long braid falling over her shoulder. Jeff held Gambo's ring in his palm. You couldn't send anyone to college with it, he knew. But all the same it was the one he wanted. He hadn't known that and was surprised at his impulse to wrap his fingers tightly round it.

This was the ring that connected to what had been, to whatever it might mean to be a Boudrault of Charleston, where the tombstones stood in silent rows along crumbling brick walls, where tall houses looked over enclosed gardens, where so many lives had been lived out. Where the silent white beaches of the sea islands were washed by ocean waves, washed up, washed away. Poor Melody, he thought for the last time, watching her walk around the house and away; she never knew what the real treasures were.